THE Songs THAT Beckon

M.A.Brown

Midnight Tide
PUBLISHING

Paperback, dust jacket and map art By Magdalene Jeanne @magdalene.jeanne

Undercover by Kaja Averil McDonald @bookishaveril

Full page interior illustrations by @asheskart

Developmentally edited by Beth Stedman @bethstedman

Copy/Line edited by EFC Services LLC

Content Warning

The Songs That Beckon contains descriptions of grief, suicidal ideation, drug use, withdrawal, and fantasy violence. Readers who are sensitive to these subjects please take note before proceeding.

"THE SONGS THAT BECKON is an ethereal tale of loss, the struggle to heal, and hold onto hope while forging new connections, discovering magic and the adventures that show you who you are."

-H. Reynolds

"The Songs That Beckon is a dark yet whimsical tale that will transport readers to new worlds. With elegant prose that evokes visceral reactions, M.A. Brown has crafted a hauntingly beautiful story of love and loss."

– Stephanie Combs, co-author of The Stars Would Curse Us @stephdevourerofbooks

"A story of grief, grit, and adventure, told in a vivid and unique style that will pull you into a world unlike any you've known before."

-Beth Steadman @bethstedman

For Kevin
I'll miss you always.

For anyone haunted by loss.

North Shore

of the Isle Thorne

W

S — N

E

Greenhouse

Reliquary

Church

This way to
Thorne Ferry

Galinna's
Grocer's & Teas

Beryl Sea

Faerlyn

This way to
Briar Lark

Part One

The Darkness stirred, coming alive in the blackness. It whispered through the cracks in the walls. It sharpened It's teeth, patiently waiting to be free, to feast, to swallow the light whole.

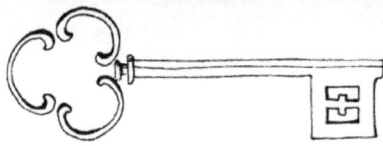

Chapter 1

A CRACKLE OF BLUE lightning unfurled through the billowing clouds of an impending snow squall and set Bianca's teeth on edge. Lightning on the winter solstice seemed like a bad omen from the gods, she thought, then silently chastised herself. There were no such things as bad omens.

"Could you help me with my hair, please, dear? I can't reach the pins in the back."

Bianca turned from the window, inhaling deeply. Her parents' bedchamber smelled of lilacs and unconditional love. It always made her feel like a little girl again.

The sound of her mother's charm bracelet chimed like miniature bells as she applied rouge and eyeshadow, the perfect accompaniment to her absent-minded humming. Bianca stepped up behind her and took the pins she passed back to her over her shoulder. She watched her mother in the mirror as she pulled and pinned locks of her honey-gold hair. "Are you sure you won't come to the celebration, dear?" their eyes locked on one another through the vanity's reflection.

Bianca shook her thick mane of curls, dark and disorderly to her mother's light and silken. "I want to study. The Academy entrance exams are only a few months away, and I still have to pack for our journey to the dig site in the Drowned Marshes." She smoothed the last strand of hair into place and set it with a pearl-tipped pin. "Besides, this year's guest list is full of stuffy dignitaries all trussed up like peacocks."

The corner of her mother's mouth curled into a smile. "Come now, they aren't that bad, and you haven't been to a function since the beginning of the Season. You're nearly nineteen, dear, you should come dance with at least one eligible bachelor."

Bianca sighed and refrained from rolling her eyes. She'd managed to turn down nearly every social event and male suitor of the Season, which wasn't difficult. The scandal sheets weren't particularly kind in regard to their opinions of her despite her family's wealth. "I'm not interested in eligible bachelors; I'm interested in passing my entrance exams." What she refrained from saying was that, much like the cook's solstice ginger-man cookies, every single eligible suitor was exactly the same; though unlike the cookies, they all lacked flavor. "After I'm done at the Academy, we can revisit the idea of dancing and bachelors."

Her mother's eyes softened. "Of course, dear, whatever you wish."

"Happy Solstice, my loves!" Her father burst into the room, dressed in his best suit of rich navy velvet to match the night sky. He kissed both her mother and her on the tops of their heads before producing two crisply wrapped packages, one for each of them, from behind his back.

They both tore into them. In her mother's lay a small silk box. She flipped it open, revealing a pair of carved sapphire earrings crafted to look like her favorite flowers in full bloom. "Oh, Eli"—her mother's hand fluttered to her throat, her voice choked—"they're stunning. Thank you, my love."

He smiled down at her, his eyes shining, and he took her hand in his and kissed it tenderly. "Anything for you, Beatrice."

Bianca smiled and turned away to give her parents privacy as her father leaned in to kiss her mother. Theirs was the sort of marriage she wished for. She peeled away the last layer of paper on her gift to reveal a book bound in soft red leather. She turned it over to read the title, *The Advanced Arts of Locksmithing and Picking* by Willard Dunn. Her heart soared. He'd remembered that rainy day in the bookshop months prior when she spent nearly the whole visit ogling the book's foiled lettering and detailed diagrams. Her father's recollection of the most simple and mundane moments they spent together always amazed her. It made her feel treasured, like every moment they spent as a family was worth remembering even if it was small and fleeting. Perhaps especially because it was small and fleeting.

She turned back around and leaned in to embrace her father. "Thank you, Papa, I love it."

He ran a hand over her hair. "For you, my star, anything. And I expect a full report on it by morning." He winked as he pulled out of their hug. He took her mother's arm and led her out of the room. They both called one last "I love you" over their shoulders, which Bianca echoed, already half distracted flipping through crisp new pages.

Bianca padded her way back down the carpeted hall to her bedroom, her nose in her book, the music from the party already threading its way to the upper floor. She pulled her favorite careworn quilt from the end of her unmade bed, wrapped it around her shoulders, and went to perch on the window seat overlooking the drive. Through the frost on the window, the bobbing of the carriage lanterns in the dark looked just like the flicker bugs that she knew waited for her in the Drowned Marshes.

For a moment, she startled and pressed her fingers to the glass, squinting into the darkness of the tree-lined drive. For one heartbeat, she could have sworn a face peered out from the tangled bare branches illuminated by a flash of lightning. But another strike swiftly came, and there was nothing there. She let out a relieved breath, fogging the glass, and settled back with her book propped on her knees, satisfied that what she'd seen had been nothing more than a fanciful illusion.

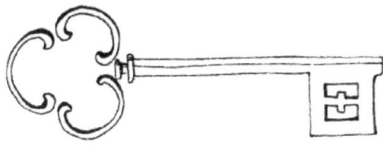

Chapter 2

THE TEACUP IN BIANCA Hastings's hand trembled with her shudder so sudden it was as though someone had walked over her grave. She looked around her room, the hair on the back of her neck standing up as the grandmother clock on the mantle struck the witching-hour's chime. Something in the old Hastings manor house was amiss; there was a shift in the air that made her fingers itch.

Bianca set the cup of bitter herbed tea down on her bedside—a daily tonic brewed by her mother—and padded softly on bare feet to the door. She eased it open, wary not to make a sound, although of what she was wary she could not say. At this hour, even the most debauched of her parents' party guests would have gone home to rest.

The silence of the house was unnatural; it curled around her as she took her first step into the hall, pressing in on her like a constrictor upon its prey. It seemed to hiss in her ear, "Not right, not right, something is not right." Her heart quickened along with her steps as she dashed toward the top of the main stairs.

Her mother lay sprawled like a broken doll across the marble entryway. The red train of her dress flung out behind her, caught in an invisible wind. Except, hadn't her mother's dress been an ethereal forget-me-not blue? And it didn't have a train.

Bianca blinked slowly, trying to make sense of the scene before her, even as her stomach dropped out from under her. Something deep inside her cracked, blood—it had to be blood, and the cogs of her thoughts seized. How had her infallible mother become so wounded? It could not be real; she must be in a waking nightmare. The bite of her fingernails into her fisted palms told her otherwise.

Floundering, she gasped for enough breath to shout for help, for her father, but then *it* emerged from the doorway to the sitting room. It was human enough in shape, but it was all wrong angles, scales, and talon-tipped too-long fingers. Bianca stuffed a fist into her mouth to smother a scream as the thing leaned down, its lank hair licking its razor-sharp jaw, and snatched her mother by a limp ankle. She dropped to the floor so hard the carpet burned her knees to hide behind the balusters from the hideous thing.

She had to get away, she had to find her father or someone, anyone who could help. The cook perhaps; she almost always stayed far later in the main house than was strictly necessary. If Bianca could slip down the hall to the back stairs without making any noise, she might be able to save her mother.

Steeling herself, she spun and rose to a crouch, ready to dash down the hall when her heart stopped. Three of the creatures somehow stood circled behind her barring her way. How had she not heard them coming? How had she not smelled their breath that had the fetid reek of old bones and soured blood?

The lips of the middle one peeled back in a smile, or a snarl, maybe both, revealing uneven rows of serrated teeth. The tallest one in the middle sprang for her, its slotted eyes narrowing, a predator confident in its kill. Bianca threw up her hands, feebly trying to fend it off. Its claws sank into her shoulders like ten spears of ice. A blinding white light erupted between them, and then Bianca was soaring, soaring, soaring, and the ground rushed up to meet her and cradle her in its crushing embrace.

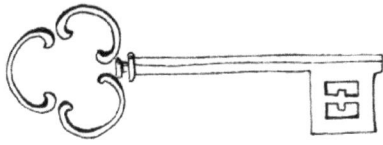

Chapter 3

H E PACED ALONG THE wall of the mine shaft. Their voices scratched at the inside of his skull, burrowing. Thousands of voices, thousands upon thousands of voices, talking as one. They were growing impatient. He couldn't blame them, he was growing impatient too. Hundreds of years would do that to you.

He crouched down, pressing his ear against the roughly hewn black stone walls as if it could help him hear them better like it used to.

He had to dig just a little bit deeper.

He snapped his head around at the sound of echoing footfalls in the tunnel behind him. His creatures were back. Hopefully, they brought live ones for the sacrifice. His supply of prisoners was dwindling, and you could never have too much fresh blood on hand.

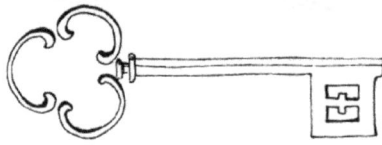

Chapter 4

BIANCA HASTINGS LAY SWATHED in cottony gauze, buried in a bevy of warm blankets in too much pain to move. The shadows dancing across her room were the only indication that time had passed. Doctors and healers of all kinds came poking and prodding and dosing. A bouquet of flowers grew wrinkled on her bedside table; a small spider made its home in the aged blooms, its silken web spun from one to the other like washing lines.

The scandal sheets were brought in daily but never cleared. A small mound of them taunted her from next to the vase of flowers, growing ever larger. She wanted to knock them to the floor, but anytime she moved, she could feel phantom claws burrowing into her skin all over again. The headlines of the papers speculated on her sanity and boasted over her father's contributions to the Academy; in particular, they noted the ancient relics he'd recovered from the Drowned Marshes. She'd gone along on that first expedition when she was only knee-high; it was once one of her fondest memories. Now the thought of it hurt more than her barely healed wounds.

On one particular morning after days or maybe weeks of infirmity as Bianca watched the gossamer streams of light billow through her open window, she caught the headline of a gilded-edged gossip rag, "Socialite Slain at Solstice Celebration: Who will take up her mantle next year and host the city's most anticipated event of the spring season?" A fire ignited in her stomach. How dare they? Those vapid, sycophantic leeches. In one monumental swipe, she shoved the pile of leaflets from their perch. She flopped back down onto her pillow and smiled for the first time in what felt like forever as she watched the papers flutter through the air like pigeons' wings caught in a breeze.

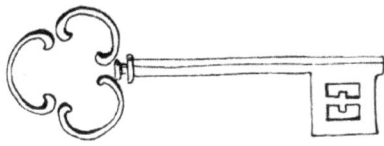

Chapter 5

PERDITA RUE WAS A governess. Her personality was well suited for it as if she'd been born a governess, and so she would always remain a governess. She embodied all that was sensible and stuffy. Every stitch and pin on her person was in neat order, not even a single graying hair dared to be out of place.

She was once the governess to the Hastings girl, a position she had loathed with every moral fiber of her being because the Hastings family, especially the girl, were peculiar, and peculiar things, in Perdita's experience, were always bad.

Try as she might, she could never get the girl to wear shoes, to sit primly or properly, or to play the piano forte. She did everything she could to turn that mongrel of a girl into a lady. Bianca was her grandest failure. The day she was dismissed after years of service was the happiest day of her life.

So, when a detective arrived on the modest stoop of her unpretentious home and asked her to escort the Hastings girl to some distant aunt's home, Perdita Rue balked, to say the least. The journey sounded like a nightmare given form—a day-long carriage ride, a ferry trip, and then yet another half day in the carriage, there and back again. But the detective was persuasive. He offered her a more than satisfactory sum in exchange for the service along with the promise that he would never darken her doorstep on behalf of the Hastings ever again.

Which was how the stiff old spinster found herself sitting across from Bianca Hastings and a bit green in the face from days of travel. Fortunately, according to the watch that hung from the pin on her brooch, they were mere hours from reaching their destination.

Perdita narrowed her eyes and studied the girl who had blossomed into a young woman during their time apart. She was quite beautiful with her heart-shaped face and pouty lips that always looked as though they'd just been bitten. It would have been easy to find a good match for her considering her sizable dowry if she wasn't so blessedly odd. Her hair was black but not the black of night or the black of print ink but the black of a raven's feather. When she turned this way or that, it shimmered in hues of deep blue and periwinkle. It was unruly as well, its coiled curls as elusive to pin down as smoke. Her mane had been the bane of Perdita's existence second only to the generous spatter of freckles on the entirety of her face and neck. It was impossible to get her ready for a function.

Then there was her innate ability to find her way into ink pots at the most inconvenient of times. There were always tiny splotches of ink along her hands and arms that seemed resistant to even the most aggressive of scrubbings. At least those could be hidden under kid gloves and long sleeves or among her many other freckles that dusted her entire body. Bianca never fessed up to drawing on herself just to irk her, but Perdita was sure of it. In fact, she would protest quite loudly that she had no clue where the ink came from, which only served to irritate Perdita more.

And her eyes. Perdita suppressed a shudder. The girl's eyes were so vividly bottle-glass green, which wasn't exactly strange, but—and Perdita was not a superstitious person or a believer in the supernatural—she swore something strange shifted behind Bianca's eyes. As though Bianca's eyes didn't entirely belong to her, which was, of course, impossible. Thoughts like those were exactly why Perdita despised working for the Hastings; peculiarity of that kind had a tendency to rub off on others and turn into madness. It didn't surprise her one bit that something tragic befell the family. To her line of thought, it was only a matter of time before it became even worse.

All of this added up to one thing: Perdita Rue was more than eager to unload her charge on this distant Hastings relation and wash her hands of the bizarre child once and for all. She planned to travel very far away where no one had ever heard of the Hastings family.

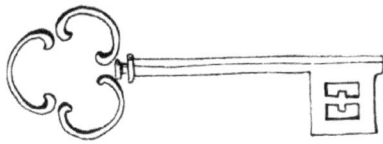

Chapter 6

BIANCA HASTINGS FELT AS though she had walked into a room and couldn't remember why she was there over and over and over again. Nothing felt right, like it wasn't real, and she didn't know what her reason for being there was in the first place.

The carriage lurched to a halt so swiftly Bianca had to dig her nails into the crushed velvet bench so she didn't fly into the lap of Ms. Rue, her old governess. The woman probably would have flung her off her lap as though she were a bug rather than a young woman anyhow.

Ms. Rue flicked back the curtains covering the window as the driver gave three quick raps against the roof to signal their arrival. Her lips pursed as tightly as a tart lemon as she turned her beady black eyes on Bianca. "Well, girl, can you manage your own affairs, or do you need me to hold your hand up to the front door?" The woman's words cracked like a whip and stung just as badly.

Stiffening, Bianca smoothed a hand over her unmanageable hair and quickly tried to knot it at the nape of her neck with a long silver pin. A sharp and sudden ache pulsed down her arms where her scars lay covered, still slightly tender. She winced, and her hand strayed to where the amber bottle of numbing medicine was tucked in her pocket. She withdrew it and took a dropper full quickly. Her former governess sniffed her distaste, her opinion on the numbing draft long since and many times over expressed. "I'll manage myself, thank you, Ms. Rue."

Slipping her shoes back onto her feet, Bianca gathered her shawl around her, clutched her worn travel bag, and plunged into the unknown. "It's been a displeasure as always,

Ms. Rue, please don't write," Bianca cast back at her chaperone, before she slammed the carriage door in the hag's flabbergasted face.

Her long held-back rudeness bolstered her nerves for mere moments only. The satisfaction quickly leached from her as the carriage rattled away along the snow-covered drive, and she turned to face her new home well and truly alone.

The house was imposingly haunting in the gloom of dusk with frozen snowy specters whirling through the air. They chased one another over the stony, vine-covered façade, up spires, and across darkened windowpanes. The house was more gothic castle in miniature than home. Snow-dipped trees silhouetted in the distance gave her pause as their skeletal arms reached for her. She shuddered, the wind cutting through her woolen travel clothes as though they weren't even there, and she trudged through the ankle-deep snow to the front door, each step punctuated by a loud crunch as though she walked on bones. Double doors stood ahead on a covered porch like sentinels guarding the keep. After repeated unanswered knocking, until her knuckles were raw, she jiggled a knob. It was blessedly unlocked, so she unceremoniously shoved the door inward, its hinges groaning in chorus with the wind's howls. She stumbled over the threshold and shut the doors behind her. No one waited with open arms to greet her. Not that she'd expected it, not really.

The inside was dark, and it had a strange smell that tickled her nose. It smelled of forgotten dreams, cobwebs, and dust. She blinked rapidly to adjust her eyes. A massive gaudy staircase loomed in front of her to the left of a narrow hall, the kind debutantes dream of. She squinted closely at the darkness on the stairs; it seemed to be moving. Bianca took a cautious step forward to get a closer look. Something moved, she was sure of it, and the beginning tinges of panic scratched at the back of her throat.

Orange flickering light flared from an arched door to the right, its glare reflecting off two almond eyes from the small black mass on the stair.

"Don't mind the cat, dearie, he's a love once you get to know him."

Bianca gasped at the hunched woman who appeared soundlessly in the doorway. Though perhaps she'd just been too distracted by the creature—the cat—on the stairs to notice her arrival. The medication in the amber bottle had a way of slowing her mind sometimes, making the world seem hazy around the edges.

"Come this way, Beatrice, and let your old auntie Imogen get a better look at you!" The woman, Imogen, crooked a finger motioning for Bianca to follow and shuffled back through the doorway.

The aforementioned cat slunk down the rest of the stairs, wound its way around her skirts with a purr, and then followed its mistress with one glance back at Bianca over its shoulder as though it bid her to follow as well.

The parlor she entered was in dire need of a maid's attention. Cobwebs hung like jungle vines from an unlit chandelier, and teacups and saucers teetered precariously on several surfaces plastered with discarded scandal sheets so old their print bled. Imogen sat down in a tattered wingback chair, half-moon spectacles perched on her nose like an old bird on a branch, and bent over an over-large embroidery hoop, the needle she picked up brandished in one hand like a sword, its tip glinting maliciously in the candlelight.

Her face was a roadmap of all the things she'd seen. The color of her braided hair, just as mangled looking as Bianca's, had been stolen by age. She squinted and plunged her needle into her work, seemingly oblivious of Bianca's hesitation to come much closer than the doorway. The cat pounced on the back of the chair, its long bottlebrush tail snaking down to wrap protectively across Imogen's shoulder.

"I'm Bianca; Beatrice is my mother," she corrected, her words coming out little better than a mutter. She always found talking rather difficult when meeting new people, especially without the buffer of her parents' easy charm.

"What's that, dearie? You're muttering. I can't abide mutterers, you know." The woman looked up, or at least Bianca thought she looked up, it was hard to tell with the way the candlelight flickered against her spectacles.

"I said my name is Bianca." She did her best to enunciate clearly, her hands wringing around the handles of her carpetbag.

Imogen waved a hand dismissively before voraciously stabbing her embroidery again. "Whatever you say, dear." Her voice creaked, full of dust, as though it were as worn out as her aged joints must be.

"Do I have a room?" Bianca asked as clearly as she could, feeling flustered by her aunt's obvious disinterest with her, though she was not entirely surprised. For if Imogen had had any interest in the Hastings family, it had not been recent.

"A room? Ah . . . yes, whichever one you like, dear. There are dozens of them upstairs. And I do believe the maid drew you a bath before she left for the night. Help yourself, dear. Now what did I do with those blasted scissors?"

Feeling as though she'd been dismissed, Bianca wandered back out into the foyer. The cat followed her out. She bent to scratch him, and he darted off down the narrow hall toward a shadowy cracked door. She followed rather than standing awkwardly in the entry.

The cat snaked through the open gap in the door, and Bianca trailed behind. Inside was a vast yet cozy-looking kitchen dimly lit by embers glowing in the hearth and by a guttering stub of a candle that oozed its wax across a rough wooden table.

A chipped plate, mounded with what appeared to be shortbread cookies, sat next to the candle. Bianca's grumbling stomach urged her to grab one. The tops were dusted lightly with powdered sugar and decorated with candied violets like an early spring garden. The first bite was blissful, the second divine, and before she knew it, she'd dropped her bag and eaten two, then three, and then the plate was bare save for a few crumbs and a sweet residue.

A low yowl echoed behind her, and she spun to find the cat staring at her from a discreet narrow servants' stair tucked next to a hutch. "Please don't judge me, cat." She sighed.

"I've been traveling for two days, and my former governess is a shrew who believes women shouldn't eat so as to fit their corsets."

The cat meowed what Bianca decided sounded like conspiratorial indignation. "Good, I'm glad you understand." She picked up her carpetbag and the dwindling candle. "Now, do you know if I can find a bedroom up that way?" She nodded toward the passage behind the cat who stood, stretched its paws, and bounded off in the direction she'd indicated.

"I'll take that as a yes." She hiked her skirts and followed, trying not to fumble on unfamiliar, uneven steps.

The stairwell let out on the second floor behind a painting of a stalwart-looking man along a coast. There was something distinctly strange about the painting that gave her pause. She could have sworn the image changed and that rather than sturdy trousers and boots for a blink he'd had nothing but scales and fins instead. Though no matter how she squinted or shifted, she could make neither appear again.

To her right, a shaft of buttery-yellow light cut through the gloom of the hall. Bianca crept toward it and peered through the doorway to find a kerosene lamp lit, bathing chamber. Bianca's shoulders slumped in relief; a bath would be so welcome to wash the travel and the hospital out of her hair and from under her nails and in between her toes.

Dropping her carpetbag, she quickly shut the door and shucked off her shoes, stockings, and travel clothes. She bit her lip to keep from crying out as she dipped her foot into the copper clawfoot tub. The water was frigid, the maid must have left hours before, but it was better than nothing.

She grabbed a pat of soap from a dish on a shelf next to the tub; it smelled of lavender and lemons like her mother. Her fingers quaked as she lathered the soap to scrub through her hair. She took a deep breath and submerged herself in the water. Her hair floated up around her like sea grass, and the water above her shimmered like liquid gold in the light of the lamp. She let the air out of her lungs and watched the little globes glitter and dance as they drifted away until her lungs screamed at her to resurface.

The air was filled with the tangy floral scent of the soap suds when she finally came up for air, her arms snaking around her tucked-up knees. The water was cold, so very cold. She had the odd notion that her skin would freeze like the frost on a windowpane. And she would feel none of it just as she felt nothing when the scent of her mother should bring burning tears. But that was the way of things now, long stretches of nothing, as though she were no longer human. As though she were a void in which feelings were lost. And then out of nowhere, every feeling she should have felt would swell and try to drown her in its undertow, and she would cry until she couldn't breathe, until she wanted to die. Then she would sleep and wake to start the whole dreary cycle all over again.

A muffled meow and pawing at the door jerked Bianca out of her reverie.

Careless of leaving puddles on the floor, she sloshed out of the tub, rummaged for a rumpled nightdress in her bag, and slipped it over her sodden head. She tucked her dirty clothes into a woven hamper by the door, then grabbing her bag and leaving her shoes behind, she crept back into the hall with the lamp in hand.

The glimmer of light against cat eyes at the end of the bleak hall drew her attention. "What are you up to, cat? Is there a room down there for me?" Her voice sounded too loud in the smothering darkness, and she fought the urge to look for monsters that she'd been told were the figment of her traumatized imagination. She hastened her steps to meet the cat where it sat, tail twitching in the same methodical, annoyed way one taps a foot while being forced to wait against one's will.

The bubble of light from her lantern leaked over the walls and floor, enveloping the cat and illuminating two large doors with heavy brass knobs. "Anything interesting in there?" she asked. The cat cocked its head up at her, eyes narrowed as if to ask why it would waste her time with anything that wasn't.

She pushed her way through and for a moment stood stunned on the threshold of a sleeping library. The smell of old pages, faded ink, and wisdom wafted toward her, greeting her like an old friend and sparking the memory of many nights in her parents' library. Bookshelves stood like tombstones in stoic rows covered in gray dust cloths. Dour curtains framed arched windows across the way. A cold hearth was tucked into a wall surrounded by a lonely looking set of wingback chairs, in front of which stood a mass of familiar-looking travel trunks.

The cat, whose shaggy coat was gilded copper in the lamp light strutted over to the chests and scratched his arching back along the corner with an audible purr. "Are those what I think they are?" Bianca wondered aloud as she walked over and set the lamp on the shrouded table next to where the trunks sat waiting.

She dusted off a thin layer of dirt from the top trunk to reveal the inked customs mark of the Drowned Marshes. "Mom and Dad's travel trunks," she whispered. There was no lock on the brass latches of the first steamer trunk, and with an echoing clack, she flipped them open and lifted the lid. Entombed inside was a hodgepodge of relics from her other life. She had yet to think of it as her old life, feeling as though acknowledging it as old meant she could never get it back.

The icy shell around her emotions didn't so much as splinter as she began to shuffle through the items. She tugged open her carpetbag and started stuffing things methodically into it, a white dress of her mother's embroidered with metallic green beetles and tangled thorny vines. A small stuffed owl with real feathered wings and glass eyes that had been a childhood favorite, her father's silver flask embossed with an old oak tree, a lock-picking set and practice locks that had been a long-ago winter's solstice gift. Her parents had always indulged her every curiosity and afforded her any learning opportunity they could, even if the skills she'd wished to acquire were of a more nefarious kind.

A few more possessions later, with the carpetbag's seams straining, she grabbed the lantern and trudged back into the deserted hall, the cat chasing her skirts. She tried the first door she came to but found it soundly locked. It was the same with the second and the third and the fourth until she came to a narrow linen closet door. The cat rushed forward, tangling her feet in the process, nearly causing her to topple over, and pawed at the door with a loud yowl.

Bianca scowled. "All right, all right, I'll open that one, but do you think you could have a bit more manners next time, please?"

The cat cocked his head to the side and blinked expectantly.

Bianca sighed, knowing better than to expect any sort of remorse from a cat, and pulled the closet door open, but it was unlike any other linen closet she'd ever seen before. It held no linens at all; in fact, it only had a scuffed set of steep ladder-like stairs, which the cat bounded up without hesitation.

"So not a closet, then," Bianca muttered to herself. She held up her lamp, her neck straining as she tried to peer up into the utter darkness, suddenly curious to see where it led. She could make out nothing but the faintest glint of light off the cat's eyes. It mewled at her, waiting.

"You might be the most impatient cat I've ever met." Bianca grunted as she bungled her way up the ladder like stairs, one hand clutching the lamp and her bulging bag and the other supporting herself on the dust-coated rungs. As she ascended, she scuffed her elbows and banged her knees and swore like a stable hand when her head finally hit a cobweb-crusted trapdoor. She glowered at the cat who was now at eye level. "Whatever is up there better be worth this trouble."

Awkwardly, she gave the hinged door a shove, it gave way far more easily than she expected with only a slight groan in protest as if admonishing her for waking it after being left alone to rest for so long. Coughing the dust from her lungs and dusting cobwebs from her skirts, Bianca stumbled into a large circular room that reminded her immediately of the woebegone lighthouse that she spotted through the mist while crossing on the ferry. On all sides, the room was outfitted with single-pane plumbiferous windows, the roof above her steepled into a spire. Shifting the lantern to the other hand, she dropped her bag in awe, its contents regurgitated by the overfilled bag all over the mosaicked wood floor.

"All right, cat, you're forgiven. This room is perfect." He jumped up onto a full-sized quilt-covered bed opposite her with a self-satisfied purr. "Don't let it go to your head." She half giggled as she spun to look at the rest of the room. There was a small potbellied stove with a kettle on top and a modest pile of wood next to it, as well as a vanity with a washbasin, a small bedside table with a violet glass lamp, a studious bookshelf, a trunk for clothes at the end of the bed, and a vibrant if somewhat worn rug on the floor.

Behind her, she noticed one of the large windows had hinges and a clever latch set discreetly in the scrolling on the frame. She kicked the trapdoor shut and went to open the glass door, setting the lamp down on the vanity as she did. Its panes covered in spidery frost nipped at her fingers. She stepped out onto a wrought-iron balcony that wrapped like a crow's nest around the tower.

Sometime earlier, the storm broke into a serenely calm night. A full moon shone upon the vastness of the grounds and illuminated the crystalline branches of the trees. Bianca's lungs stung, and her breath froze as she breathed the night air deeply. She looked around, no part of the house sat higher except for an icicle-encrusted weathervane perched atop the spire.

Shivering, she went back and left the starlit view for another night. She crossed the room and sat down next to the cat, stroking his bronze-furred head, and looked around. It was nothing like her room back home, with velvety plum-colored walls and mountains of soft white ruffle-trimmed blankets that made her bed look like a wedding cake, but that was perfect. It made this whole situation seem less permanent; she could only imagine her parents might come for her any day.

The cat purred as she picked him up and held him up in front of her as floppy as a rag doll. "Aren't you a clever cat, finding me just what I needed?" She noticed an old scar that ran down his face next to his left eye. "Scrappy, too, by the looks of it. Do you want to keep me company tonight?"

The cat mewled in what she decided was consent and not irritation at her manhandling him. "Well, that's settled, then." She sighed and set him down.

Her lids grew heavy with the day's burdens, so Bianca sluggishly set to work kindling a fire in the small stove to warm her tower room before tucking herself in between the frigid sheets for the night.

As her eyelids fluttered closed and the cat curled by her side, she thought she heard her mother humming an absent-minded tune to lull her to sleep.

That night she dreamed as she did every night—of beasts and blood. It was a welcome relief from her waking hours. In those moments of sleep, those precious seconds of recollection buried beneath all the aching pain and the fear, there was a seed of hope. Hope that her parents were still alive and hope that she could somehow save them.

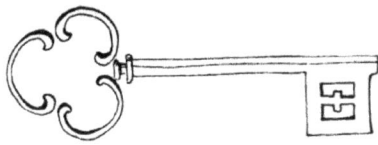

Chapter 7

THE CAT WATCHED THE girl sleep fitfully through the night. She was an odd one to be sure with hair more blue than black and a freckle in the shape of a star that kissed her face right under her eye. Though she was no more odd than any other that he'd seen come and go in the house, he supposed after a moment of preening himself.

She smelled pleasant, too, like lavender and unshed tears, like a garden right before the rain, the scent of petrichor thick in the air. It was a smell he recognized. It was the smell of magic.

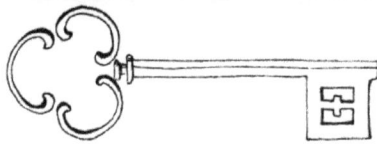

Chapter 8

THE MORNING SUN BURST into her room as though it had something to prove. From the moment the first rays tickled Bianca awake, she knew the thaw had arrived, if not outside, then inside of her. She felt all wrong, her joints too loose, her body too heavy all at the same time as though she were a fly trapped in fresh amber. Pressure built in her chest until it cracked a chasm in her that yawned wide open.

Her wail rent the air, startling the cat where he slept at the foot of her bed, but that was only the beginning. The sorrow possessed her like a daemon racking her body with bone-breaking, lung-shattering sobs until it wrung every possible tear out of her.

The rest of the day she drifted in and out of a restless sleep. Through fluttering eyelids, she dreamed that her room had changed and that little sprites made of flower petals danced across sunny window panes. The bookshelf flickered—sometimes it was a door, sometimes it was a bookshelf—but always she could hear a muffled hum. The sound was as familiar and distant as a fading dream.

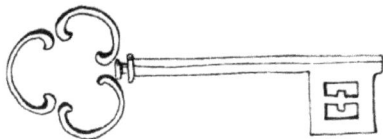

Chapter 9

S HE WOKE AGAIN IN the gray early light the following dawn. The cat watched her through narrow wary eyes as she swung her legs over the edge of her bed and stretched. She rubbed her sleep-crusted puffy eyes, and the bookcase flickered again at the edge of her vision, the ghost of her dreams. The cat mewled.

"I'm all right, cat." She reached out and scratched his ears, and he purred affectionately. "I'm all right."

The floor still clung to the chill of night, and she shivered as she shuffled over to her bag and withdrew her mother's white dress, fresh undergarments, and corset. She struggled with her laces, leaving the corset more loosely done than usual before shimmying into the dress. The cat politely kept his head turned as she tediously did up her buttons.

The dress fit well, if a bit snug; she and her mother were both small in stature but Bianca's curves were much more voluminous. She ran her fingers over the beetle's bright embroidery and the sharp points of the tread thorns until she found the seam of the pockets. Slipping her hand into one, she was surprised to find a cool coil of metal that she'd not noticed when she'd stepped into the gown. Her heart skipped a beat as she withdrew a long chain covered in tiny key charms. It was her mother's prized possession, a bracelet so long it wound around her wrist several times before latching. Bianca had grown up with the tinkling of the charms, like a cascade of miniature angel bells, signaling her mother's presence. The melody pulled at her heartstrings, still raw from the day before, and tears welled, happy tears. Holding the bracelet and putting it on her wrist kindled a small fire as warm as her mother's embrace inside her. Struck with a sudden and fierce sense of determination, she knew, as clearly as if the keys had spoken words, her parents were still alive.

She didn't know what to do with this revelation, but her stomach's grumbling reminded her that her last full meal, served on the ferry over to the isle, had been a pittance of stale bread, churned butter, and dry, stringy beef. Not to mention that had been over a day ago.

Taking the stairs barefoot and two at a time, her hair rough-and-tumble down her back, she made her way by servants' stairs to the kitchens. She was brought up short at the foot when she realized it was curiously empty for the hour of the day, nary a cook or a scullery maid scurried about. And now that she thought about it, there wasn't a maid or housekeeper bustling along the stairs to make sure beds were made and hearths swept. Peculiar considering the size of the house for there to be no one about.

Bianca ducked into the larder prepared to raid it for any sort of nourishment and came up empty-handed save for a wrinkled apple that didn't even have the decency to crunch as she bit into it.

She flung herself down at the kitchen table to devour the apple. Once down to the core, it seemed to have the opposite of the intended effect, serving only to make her stomach gnaw more aggressively, driving her into action.

Standing, she tossed the core into a scrap pail and went in search of Imogen. The silence when she reached the foyer skirted down her spine, prickling the back of her neck, recalling the night her parents were taken. Automatically, she slipped a hand to her pocket to retrieve the amber bottle that she didn't even recall putting there, an instinctual habit now so ingrained it was done unconsciously.

Three drops on her tongue chased away the creeping sense of dread. Swiveling her head toward the grand staircase, she found the cat watching her with narrowed eyes much in the same manner he had upon her arrival.

"You are a curious thing, aren't you?" she mused. "Clever too. Tell me, cat, have you seen the mistress of the house this morning?"

She laughed a dry mirthless laugh. "Ah, if only the dear doctors could see me now, talking to a cat. I know precisely what they would say, what they would think anyhow."

She tapped her temple. "Touched, they called me, cat, touched." She laughed again. "But I was touched, cat. Trouble is, no one believed me when I said by what."

With a flounce and flutter of skirts, she tossed herself down onto the stair. She was far too old to sulk, at least that is what her father would say if he could see her now, but at the moment, she didn't really care, not when a fathomless hollow was playing stand-in for her heart.

The cat plodded down the stairs and landed in her lap. It raised itself up to eye level, its gray eyes wide with what she decided was sympathy. He purred and nuzzled her cheek before settling in her lap to bat at the keys where they jangled at her wrist.

"Oh, cat, no, stop that. That isn't a toy; it's far too special to be meddled with." She snatched his paw back, unhooking claws from where they latched into the fabric of her sleeve. He grumbled in protest as she peered curiously at his paws. It flickered in her hand—one moment there were inklike splotches on his fur, and the next they were gone. She blinked and rubbed her eyes with her free hand, taking a closer look until the cat let out a yowl, yanking himself free and bounding from her lap with an indignant hiss.

"Sorry, cat," she muttered absently, withdrawing the amber bottle again and administering another drop of medicine, and another for good measure. "Maybe I am touched after all."

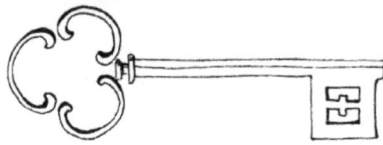

Chapter 10

THE CAT FOLLOWED HER as she wandered the halls like a wraith going from door to door, each one as locked as the next. Occasionally, she would startle at seemingly nothing. The cat wished he had the words to tell her that she wasn't touched, that she was in fact seeing the truth behind the veil, but alas, he could not, just as he could not follow when she left the house through the front door hours later, her feet as bare as the day she was born.

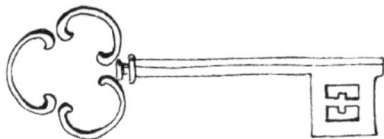

Chapter 11

BIANCA PICKED HER WAY through a labyrinth of snow-melt streams running down the dirt road to the town. The mud squishing between her toes and the sky above her head cleared her mind and brought her a sense of peace that she didn't feel inside the house with the light playing tricks on her. Things constantly flickering and shifting nonsensically. The spring breeze, still sharp around the edges, whipped her hair into a frenzy and teased the hem of her skirts.

The sleepy hamlet curled along the coastline below, picturesque, the slate-gray waters beyond bleeding into the horizon. Bianca pirouetted to see the snowcapped mountains behind her peaking above the thick band of forest from which she'd just emerged. This little sliver of island was gorgeous, almost magical, and Bianca found herself wondering if her mother had ever visited her aunt here. There was precious little she knew about Imogen and even less that she knew about the Isle Thorne, having never even seen it on a map until the day before journeying to it. Odd considering the amount of time she'd spent poring over maps with her father.

Quintessential stone walls rose up from dried rushes of grass on either side of the road, welcoming her into the town called Faerlyn. At least that's what the peeling painted sign that leaned as if exhausted against a crumbling section of wall suggested.

Bianca ambled until she found the main thoroughfare; on either side were squat stone shops, and chipped plaster-fronted homes were snuggly spaced with brown gardens, decayed by winter's touch, hugging their fronts. A quay jutted into the harbor, dotted along either side with a clustering of moored small boats. The bell at the top of a timber mast rang with each lap of water against the boat's hull and echoed down through the town. The tallest building in Faerlyn was the three-story Fisherman's Woe inn and tavern, whose front shuttered window flapped and clattered against the cracked plaster siding.

Given the hour, Bianca expected to see women out hanging wash or menfolk out on the wharf swapping tall tales of fish that got away, perhaps even a small child or two bold enough to run off from their mother's apron strings to play. But there was no one; it was as empty as the house had been.

A sick feeling churned in her stomach. What was wrong with this place? Movement in a shop window, Galinna's Grocers and Tea, caught her eye, and she hastened her footsteps, eager to investigate further.

Taking care to scrape her feet free of most of the mud coating them and thanking the gods for long skirts to hide her shoeless feet, Bianca pushed the door to Galinna's open. Bells tinkled in her wake, startling a wide-eyed shopgirl behind the counter who appeared to have been engrossed in a book.

"Oh, hello!" she said, surprised, and then gasped. Bianca froze as the young woman flung her book down, darted out from behind the counter, and flung her arms around her. "Welcome!"

The girl took a step back but still held her by the shoulders firmly and looked Bianca over as if examining a shiny new toy. Bianca did the same, if perhaps with a bit less enthusiasm. The startlingly forward girl's copper-bright hair was piled high in a messy wispy bun fixed with all sorts of odd pins and baubles that glittered and reflected light. She wore a deep-green shirt that brought out the flecks of emerald in her bespeckled hazel eyes and a rich woolen brown skirt with a ring of shopkeeper's keys dangling from a belt. So close Bianca could smell the warm summer sun radiating off her tan skin, which seemed impossible when spring was still in its infancy.

"You must be Beatrice!" she squealed, giving Bianca's shoulders a squeeze before letting her go. She pushed her spectacles farther up the bridge of her long nose. "Oh, it is so good to meet you! My dad is a gardener at Imogen's, and he said you were coming into town soon, and I just knew I had to meet you, Trixi! Oh, can I call you Trixi? I would just love to call you Trixi. It's so . . . so spunky, don't you think? It sounds like the name of a heroine in a novel to me."

Bianca blinked, she'd never met anyone who could speak quite so fast except maybe an auctioneer. "I, um, well, I wouldn't mind except that Beatrice is my mother's name. I'm Bianca."

"Oh dear, well, that is too bad." The girl wrinkled her nose prettily. "Oh well, we can't choose our names, can we? My name is Will, short for Wilhelmina, after my great-great-grandmother on my father's side. But everyone calls me Will. I'm pleased to meet you." She stuck out her hand with a sun-bright grin, and Bianca took it. An odd warm feeling spread across her chest, and she wondered if this is what it was like to make a friend. She liked Will, despite the fact, and maybe a bit because she was strange.

"So are you here to pick up Imogen's grocery order? I was planning on delivering it myself later. But oh! I was just thinking of making a pot of tea before you came in. Would you like a cup? It would be so wonderful to sit and chat and get to know you! I can read the tea leaves, too, you know. It's all for fun. My mother taught me. She's really much better at it than I am, but I still try!"

"I, well, I guess I could stay for some tea," Bianca replied.

Will clapped her hands as eagerly as a child. "Oh fantastic, come come, through here." She grabbed Bianca's hand and tugged her around the register counter and through a slightly moth-eaten brocade curtain into the back of the store.

It was like stepping into a carnival fortune teller's tent. Bianca's father took her one year when she was ten or so despite her mother's protests. The many layered carpets were as thickly layered as the heady haze of incense smoke. A low table surrounded by plush cushions sat at the center of the room, illuminated by a single dangling gas lamp. The edges of the room were shadowy and indistinguishable.

"Have a seat, I'll be just a minute with the kettle," Will called, her voice faint and feathery. She'd slipped through another shadowy doorway into what Bianca assumed was a kitchenette.

She settled herself on a tasseled cushion, her mother's skirts arrayed around her. The tea service was already set, minus the pot, the tulip-shaped cups printed with bluebirds and foxes in a repeating pattern, so the fox leapt after the bird in flight over and over again in the eternal dance of predator and prey.

"Here we are, I hope you like a strong brew. I'm partial to the potent spiced teas of the southern continent." Will strolled back in with a heavy enameled cast iron kettle in a cloth wrapped hand.

"I've never had southern tea," Bianca admitted. "My parents preferred floral herbs for their brews."

"Well, you're in for a treat! It's divine! And excellent for readings, it's imbued with all that southern mysticism." Will giggled as she poured the cups without straining any of the debris.

Not understanding what she meant about mysticism, Bianca smiled politely and accepted her cup, adding to it a healthy dose of honey and cream. For a moment, the only sound made between them was the clink of spoons on their cups.

The steam from the cup wafted, smelling of far-off places, adventure and daring. The first sip was bold and sweet with a hint of spice and smoky vanilla; the second sip warmed her belly and filled her with a cozy sense of nostalgia like a half remembered sunny day.

Will beamed at her from over the rim of her cup. "Good, isn't it?"

Bianca nodded. "I've never tasted anything like it. What's in it?"

"Oh, you know, this and that, I could give you a jar to take back with you if you would like."

"I don't have anything to give you in return." Bianca's gaze dipped shyly.

"Yes, you do, you're letting me read your leaves, and I sorely need the practice. I mean, it's all for fun and games, you know. But Ms. Tilly who lives in the next town over said that she really did meet the man of her dreams after I told her she would! How sweet is that? They are getting married next fall. I think. According to her last reading, either that or her fiancé is going to suffer a nasty fall."

Bianca choked on her tea, strangling a startled laugh. "Well, I look forward to hearing how it turns out for Ms. Tilly and her suitor."

"Oh, me too! It sure would be something for her to get married at her age. Ah, are you done? Oh good! Now swirl what's left counterclockwise three times and turn the cup upside down on your saucer. When you're ready, slide it over."

Bianca did as she was told. The pin prickle of raised hairs along the back of her neck as she turned the dregs three times made her stomach flutter. She sloshed the contents out onto her saucer and pushed it across the table. Her hand trembled as she pulled it away, tucking it in her lap, twisting it with the other to hold it still.

Will adjusted her glasses, picked up the saucer, and squinted at the scattered soggy leaves. She turned it this way and that, clicking her long nails against its bottom and muttering to herself.

"Well, there is an eye here, which means you have someone watching you, or watching out for you, or that you will solve a problem. There is an altar—that usually signifies distress."

Will pulled her glasses off, screwed up her face, and peered at the saucer with her head cocked to one side for a long moment before replacing her glasses. She set the saucer down on the middle of the table, pointing out lumpy bits to Bianca. "But this lump over top of it is clearly a book which symbolizes knowledge learned, so I suppose you could learn something distressing. Or you have to learn, which is distressing. Over here is a gate, which means new possibilities or travel."

Will pointed to a long stringy leaf. "It's this part here that has me concerned. It's the horned serpent with wings, which is a bad omen. I haven't seen one before."

Bianca blinked skeptically at the leaf, the serpent with wings? How did she see all of that in a sodden leaf? "May I have a closer look?" She reached for the saucer as Will nodded.

"Try and look past the leaves, let your eyes lose focus when you look so they can see through the mask of the mundane and the ordinary, through to what is really there beneath it all."

"Right. I'll, uh, try that." The lines of her forehead uncreased, her brow smoothed, and after a few deep breaths, her eyes drifted out of focus. Like shooting stars across the sky, silver light streaked across the saucer connecting to one another around forming abstract shapes like the markings on a constellation map.

She gasped as the outline of a horned and winged snake blazed to life around the scraggly leaf. She shoved the saucer back, its edge fracturing against the cup with a loud, haggard bell-like sound. The sight of the broken and chipped tea ware grounded Bianca. "My apologies, Will, I don't know what came over me." Her voice came out far breathier than it should have.

Seeing things, she was just seeing things again. Her heart pounded a retreat against her ribs at the notion again and yet faster again. She fumbled in her pocket, her fingers all pins and needles, for the amber bottle while Will's polite and soothing voice blurred into a ringing in her ears. The rancid liquid hit her tongue in a too-sweet explosion of anesthetizing oblivion. Instantly, the edges of the world softened, and her heart slowed and curled back up in its usual place.

"Oh my, what is that concoction you have there?" Will asked, her brows buckled in what was that, emotion? Concern? But that didn't make any sense.

"I have a prescription," Bianca muttered, her cheeks flushed as she tucked the bottle away as though it were a dirty little secret, and who knows, maybe in polite society it was. Perhaps it wasn't just Perdita's who would scorn such measures.

"I'm sure you do. It's perfectly all right. You've been through quite the ordeal from what I've heard. If you ever want to talk, just"—Will reached for her hand, but Bianca slid it out of reach— "just let me know." She smiled, but it didn't reach her worry-filled eyes.

Bianca's palms itched with the urge to withdraw the bottle again, to use it to unbury herself from the weight of this girl's sympathy. She could hardly bear the burden of her own consciousness. "Er, yes, well, thank you Will, for the tea, but I probably ought to get back with the groceries before Imogen worries." Not that Imogen seemed the worrying type, but that spurred Will into action.

"Yes, yes of course, let me just grab the basket for you. And I'll add a jar of tea too."

After an awkward goodbye with an empty promise from Bianca to get together for tea again soon, she trudged from the shop, a basket laden with supplies hanging from the crook of one arm.

The quicksilver glint of the sun across the rippling waters called to her. Taking a dive off the main road between two buildings, she found herself on a sliver of beach just down from the docks where the water playfully slapped at the hulls of boats. She sighed, setting the basket down and letting her legs buckle from under her. The pebbly sand bit into her thighs, and she plunged her hands in, relishing the wet tingling sting of the cold below the sun-warmed surface. The briny breeze off the water buffeted against her cheeks, flushing them with pink and blowing the thoughts right from her mind. She sat watching the gentle lapping of waves until the sun dipped and began painting the sky with streaks of gold and pink.

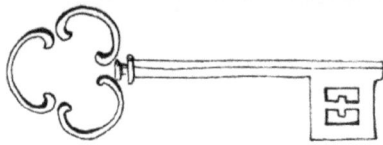

Chapter 12

THE KITCHEN WAS STILL vacant upon her return. Bianca set the basket on the table and went to the sink to wash. She was covered to the elbows in the sandy musk of the beach. The hand pump took only a moment to draw the water into the basin. Bianca lathered with a thick lump of lard dish soap, careful to scrub under her nails and rinse the sand off her mother's bracelet. She groaned when the final layer of grim washed away and fresh swirling black stains remained. She didn't even bother to try and scrub them away; many years of coping with the bizarre skin affliction had taught her to just let them fade on their own. Oftentimes the splotches would shift or change shape, forming whorls or blotches that half looked like some kind of ancient runes. The tea helped, that bitter tonic brewed by her mother. Just the thought of it and she could recall its taste, so often she drank it. A slight pang of sadness had her musing if she could acquire the herbs here, not to rid herself of the dermatitis, but to see if it could fill her with the warmth of her mother's love and care.

She dried herself on a clean dish towel, and flutters of pain ghosted across the scars on her forearms. She winced, tossed the towel aside, and went to investigate the contents of the basket. A crusty loaf of bread, a jar of butter, potatoes, celery, carrots, a wax paper–wrapped beef roast, and a few other assorted odds and ends littered the table.

A meow startled her, followed by the thump of a cane that ricocheted down the darkened hall. "Girl? Where are you?"

Bianca sighed. "Girl" wasn't much better than being called by her mother's name, but she followed the summons into the foyer nonetheless. "I'm here, Aunt."

Imogen was dressed much the same as she was when they were first introduced; the halo of smoke from the pipe clutched between her teeth was new. Bianca smothered a cough as the thick green smoke spun nebulously through the room.

"Ah, good, there you are. I was beginning to wonder where you'd gone off to. Come, let's eat supper." She went through the sitting room and through a pocket door into an informal dining room, each step punctuated with her walking stick.

Bianca followed discreetly, attempting to wave away the choking fog of potent herb smoke, her eyes watering.

The dining room was lit by a dusty gasolier wrapped in spider silk, its flames guttering. The walls were papered in velvety scenes of peeling trees, or perhaps the paper was just old. The plates on the table were chipped, and the silverware was set out of the order deemed appropriate in polite society.

They sat in near silence, each serving themselves lukewarm fish pie with a tarnished silver spoon. Imogen set her smoldering pipe aside and thanked the gods for their bounty before digging in. Bianca followed suit, if less voraciously. The pie was good, though she wished it was hotter, as the sauce was a touch congealed.

A few moments of scraping cutlery passed when Bianca noticed Imogen faintly humming. The tune was familiar, like the one she'd heard in her fitful dreams, but she couldn't quite place it. "Begging your pardon, Aunt, but what is that tune? I have the strangest feeling I've heard it before, but I can't quite place it."

Imogen's eyebrows crawled together in an expression that Bianca thought might be a mingling of curiosity and surprise. "Humming, you say? Well, it wasn't me. You must be hearing things."

Bianca frowned, and her hand slipped from the table, unconsciously thumbing the amber bottle through her skirts. "I, I don't think so." But then again, how could she be sure?

"Perhaps you're tired, dear," her aunt suggested, setting down her fork and leaning back in her chair.

Dear. Bianca almost snorted; well, at least it was a far cry from being called Girl. She pulled her hand away from the bottle and folded it neatly with the other in her lap. "Yes, perhaps you're right, Aunt. I think I'll head on up to bed then if you don't have any objections."

Imogen nodded as she picked up her pipe, puffing life back into the embers. "For the best, I think. See you on the morrow."

Bianca nodded as she pushed her chair back in. "Tomorrow, yes, see you then." She left as quickly as she could before the pipe smoke could permeate the air any further without a single glance back over her shoulder.

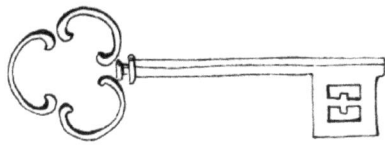

Chapter 13

THE LIGHT IN THE tower was wrapped in a sunset glow when Bianca ascended. The cat lay sprawled across her tousled bed soaking up every last ray before the sun inevitably slipped behind the mountains. Bianca flopped onto the bed next to him with a potentially melodramatic sigh.

She hummed the tune that seemed this evening to be an ever-present buzz in the background like a distant fly. Where had she heard it before, and where did it come from now? The cat curled close, kneading his paws into her arm.

Restlessness crawled all over her skin, biting at her until she gave in and stood up to pace the room. She pulled the amber bottle from her pocket, tempted to take yet another dose, the healer's warnings about not overdoing it long forgotten.

The cat yowled angrily, his eyes narrowed on her hand, giving her his opinion on the matter.

"Oh, like you know anything about it?" Bianca griped, but it was halfhearted.

She sighed and set the bottle on the shelf. Or she thought she did, but she must have been mistaken because a moment later, there was a gut-wrenching crash as the bottle shattered into a dozen fragments, its numbing draft seeping into the floorboards.

A vile string of curses spewed from Bianca as she fell to her knees, prodding the glass halfheartedly as if hoping she could momentarily reverse time. Oh, there were so many moments she wished she could do over.

The bookshelf flickered in the corner of her eye, there and then gone again. She stared directly at it, touched it, and it was there made of solid wood. Had she been looking at it directly when she set the medicine down? No, no, she was distracted. She'd barely glanced at the shelf.

She angled herself away from the shelf and looked at it askance. There it was again, the flicker. One moment it was a bookshelf; the next it was a door.

The cat sat up, watching her intently. "Please tell me you see this too?" she whispered.

With a stretch and a purr, he flounced from the bed. He crossed the room, stood on his hind legs, and pawed at the edge of the winking illusion before coming back to twist around the hem of her skirts.

Her feet, it seemed, succumbed to a paralysis born of her indecision. Was she going mad, or was the door behind the illusion real? On one hand, she'd eaten little and admittedly had much more medicine than was strictly prescribed. On the other hand, the cat, it seemed, could see it too.

"Right, because basing my decisions on a cat is a reasonably sane thing to do," she mumbled sarcastically.

She sucked in a breath. "Oh damn it all," she said, and flung her hand back toward the bookcase, through it, careful not to look at it directly, and fumbled for a knob. A jolt shot up her arm as though struck with static. The itch in her fingers became next to unbearable. The scars on her arm burned. The cat yowled. Bianca squeezed her eyes shut at a sharp flash of pure white light and turned the knob, wrenching the door open.

Blinking black spots from her eyes, Bianca turned slowly toward the open door. Something akin to panic slithered down her spine and nestled in her rib cage, making its home in her stomach. Insanity, this whole thing, it had to be insanity. She looked down at her hand, the one she'd used to turn the knob. The ink stains on it had darkened and crept farther up her palm forming a series of small runes that were all pins and needles. She shook it out and, still blinking spots, peered over the threshold.

A spiral staircase wound impossibly in either direction farther than the eye could see. A manic laugh burst from her unrestrained. She laughed until her ribs felt cracked. Until her knees gave way. She leaned against the doorjamb with hysterical tears rolling down her face, caught in the tumult somewhere between laughter and sobbing.

The cat drew itself up onto her shoulder to lick away the evidence of her fit. The affection was immediately sobering, and she was left hiccuping in the wake of her miniature breakdown. Again, she reached for the bottle in her pocket that was no longer there. She sighed, reached up, and scratched the cat's ears. "Thank you, cat."

His purr was soothing, almost melodic, akin to the hum that seemed to be dogging her steps since her arrival.

Her eyes snapped open, and she fell on hands and knees through the doorway, her head canting to one side to hear better, the wrought iron of the stairs biting into her palms. The song was not made by the cat; it burbled up like a phantom echo from the stairwell.

Cat, who'd sprung clear when she'd lurched, sauntered into the stairwell, his tail flicking back and forth. He trotted down a few steps before turning around and mewling softly as if to say, "Well, what are you waiting for?"

So, she stood and followed him.

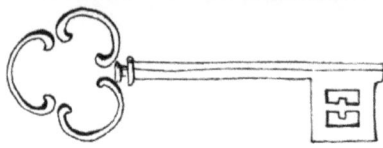

Chapter 14

THE AIR IN THE stairwell was light and breezy, despite the fact that it was narrow and seemingly windowless. It smelled of sunny spring days, the kind where you just lie in the grass and listen to the bees buzzing around dandelions. But there was also a bone-chilling undercurrent of wrongness, like the moments when the sky turns green before a tornado when all the birds cease singing. It was only a whisper, so subtle Bianca was almost unsure if it was really there.

The stairs were intricately designed in the shape of interlocking flowers made of twisted black metal bolted seamlessly into walls of stacked stone that glowed like twilight.

A few steps down, she came across a door, then another, and another, everyone different than the last. At each, she tried the knobs only to find them locked like all the other doors in the manor.

The indistinct melody thrummed through the stairwell, hooking her behind her navel and pulling her farther down. She pressed her ear to each locked door, lips parted, hardly daring to breathe, straining to hear. The tune seemed to come from none of them and all of them at the same time.

She scooped the cat up and allowed him to perch on her shoulder after a few meows that sounded awfully similar to protests. "Just a bit farther and then we'll go back. I just want to know where it's coming from."

A wordless dirge, a song in name only, a wailing of tormented souls. It swelled the farther she went. It was piercing, thunderous. Tears streamed down her face. The pain, oh gods, she could feel their pain as if it were her own. She stumbled on the stairs, flinging an arm out to steady herself. The cat yowled, digging his claws into her shoulder to keep himself aloft.

She pressed her palm to the wood of a door. The tune dulled to a whispering of anxious voices. Perplexed, she removed it, and the song resumed. Suppressing a shudder, she pressed her palm flat against the door, the keys of her bracelet clinking against one another like a cascade of bells.

The cat disengaged himself from her shoulder to stretch and press his paws to the door. Bianca looked the door over. It was exquisitely carved and painted in ornate detail. The image was of a precipitous mountainscape with a serene night sky overhead. Each of the tallest three peaks was crowned with its own rising moon. Its knob was seamlessly part of the carved design, as was the keyhole under it.

She crouched to examine the lock, brushing a finger over its opening as softly as if she stroked a baby blossom. Her fingers itched to pick the lock and find out who was behind the door. To discover whose pain called to her own. She wanted to help; she needed to help.

She groaned as the itch in her hands grew, a burrowing under her flesh. She dragged her attention from the lock to where her hand pressed against the door and gaped at the inky stains on her fingers shimmering like liquid night. The stains grew along the backs of her hands and bloomed into little diamond-shaped stars. Her mother's bracelet began to vibrate along her arm, one of the keys began to glow, and then it impossibly began to grow.

The cat beside her howled in her ear, butting his head against hers, nuzzling her cheek as if to reassure her. Like the tide called out, the light dimmed, the black on her hands dulled back to matte, but the key remained full sized. Her breaths rattled around her rib cage, frayed at the edges with panic. Her fingers fluttered toward her pocket, but she pulled the back and unlatched the key from its link instead, holding it up for closer inspection.

The key's bow was shaped like three peaks, each with its own moon, a twin to the image on the door in miniature. The cat purred, slinking around to brush his whiskers against it.

"Should we unlock it?" Bianca asked the cat in a breathy whisper.

He turned and gave her a flat, gray-eyed stare, blinking slowly as if to say, "Of course, we should. We've come this far, haven't we?"

Bianca choked back a laugh. "Insane, this is absolutely insane." But a small voice whispered from the darkest reaches of her mind, Is it?

She shook away the voice and stood up, her legs slightly cramped from being bent so long in a crouch.

With bated breath, she slipped the bit of the key into the lock. The whispers of the anguished behind the door paused, then let out a collective sigh of relief as she turned the key. Her heart stuttered at the audible click of the lock. She withdrew the key and reattached it to her mother's bracelet; it began to shrink back to its normal size immediately.

"Here goes nothing," she muttered as she placed her hand on the doorknob and pulled.

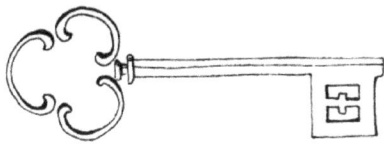

Chapter 15

A CURTAIN OF CLEAR water thundered down on the other side of the door. She blinked, eyes wide, in momentary disbelief, but she could feel the spray and smell the damp. It had to be real. Didn't it?

Water trickled over her bare feet and down the stairwell below, diverted over the threshold. She stuck out a hand and touched it. It wasn't as cold as she had thought it would be.

The fishhook behind her navel gave another tug, reeling her toward the doorway. Her breath hitched, catching itself in the web of panic quickly spun inside her. Her hand fluttered to the pocket of her skirt now damp from the spray of water. She clenched the fabric in a frustrated fist. She didn't have the crutch of her medication to soothe the wrinkled worries of her mind, to weigh what she saw against reality and determine what was true and real. This feeling in her gut, insisting, demanding she move forward felt real; the water felt real. But after so long of being told you're insane, it becomes difficult to judge.

The cat batted a paw into the flow, inspecting it, his head cocked to the side. Then with a startling yowl and a blur of fur, he dove through the doorway.

"Cat!" Bianca screamed. Frantically, she stuck her arm through the veil of water as if she could snatch him back.

She thought she could feel a light breeze against her wet fingers on the other side. She pulled her arm back and braced herself. Real or not, she didn't have a choice now. She took a deep breath and dove in after him.

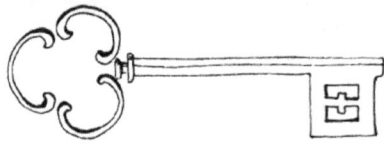

Chapter 16

BIANCA GASPED FOR BREATH as she struggled to get her footing on the silty bed beneath her feet. When she was finally able to stand, she was in a pool of waist-deep water. All around the pool were towering pines silhouetted against an ethereal orange sky swaying in an eventide breeze. She waded her way to the edge, slipping on the rocks and grabbing hold of shoots of plants along the muddy bank to pull herself out.

"Cat!" she sputtered as water dripped from her hair across her face. She scrambled to her feet and began to wring out her hair and her clothes. "Cat!" Her eyes darted around, but she couldn't see him, and he didn't come when called, of course, because what cat would ever be so reasonable.

She muttered a few choice expletives learned from eavesdropping on stable boys, handymen, and her mother while she attempted to darn stockings. She spun in a muddy circle to take in her mysterious surroundings. She seemed to be on a large natural terrace, and behind her towered a sheer cliff dotted with trees. A waterfall and streams draped over and around the ledge like ribbons and laces spilled from a haberdashery chest.

Her feet carried her along a narrow path as it wended through knee-high grasses and around moss-covered boulders. The air was heavy with the musk of impending rain.

She called for the cat, her eyes chasing the breeze around wherever it rustled hoping to see a flash of fur or a twitch of tail. Where had the blasted creature gone? And for that matter, where was she? She shoved that line of thinking into the deepest recesses of her subconscious and locked it away. If she examined any of this situation too closely, she might end up a muttering mess on the forest floor, and that would do no one any good at all. Besides, she had to find the cat. She suspected that though her aunt's attitude trended toward disliking her, it would turn sour or even volatile if she lost her pet. And though she had no way of knowing for certain, she still didn't want to find out.

The path curved around the terrace's outer ledge. Through the trees, Bianca could make out the dusky purple forms of precipitous peaks spanning as far as the eye could see. Along the horizon three peaks rose above the rest. Above one, the silver needle point of a slivered moon stabbed at the sky as it rose. She had a strong suspicion that if given enough time, two more moons would rise from behind the other peaks to mirror the image on the door. She shuddered, shoved that thought even farther down, and continued along the path.

There was no discernible way off the ledge, at least not that she could see in the half-light, which was slightly reassuring. It meant the cat couldn't have gone too far. If only she'd brought an oil lamp along, but then again, this was not what she had planned when she left her room. She hadn't planned at all.

The path cut past a strange little shack with a mossy roof made of wood slats and walls of rough stacked stone. Its round windows were shutterless. A faded blue symbol was etched into the arched doorways' keystone vaguely reminiscent of a teardrop. She peered inside quickly. "Hello?"

A gust of wind whipping through the trees was her only reply. Her teeth chattered as her wet skirts twisted around her legs, tangling with the gale that seemed to be growing in strength. Blast that cat, where had he gone? She picked her way along the trail, her eyes no longer scanning around her but fixed on the trail wary of gnarled roots and toe-stubbing rocks. In the growing dark, everything appeared to stretch and flatten out, making obstacles harder to see. She cursed the cat again as the trail deposited her back at the lip of the pool she'd crawled out of.

Squinting around, she called again for the cat. Perhaps he'd doubled back along the same trail ahead of her and gone back through the door. He did seem peculiarly unfazed by water in a very noncatlike way. Bianca slid gracelessly back into the pond and wadded over to the waterfall. She pressed her hand through the thundering veil of water and hit solid rock.

Blinking in surprise, she gripped the stone with both hands and gave a shove. Nothing. She must have the wrong spot. Sliding her palms over the slick and jagged stone, she made her way from one edge of the pond to the other, feeling for any lips or keyhole-shaped openings. She felt an angry sob burning at the back of her throat. She beat a fist against the rock, a jagged edge bit into her, and she gasped, the pain sobering her. She wasn't going home tonight. She needed to get dry.

Darkness blew through the trees on the back of an icy gale. She tipped her chin to the sky, and through the trembling limbs of trees, she spotted a thunderhead threaded with a pulsing web of ruby lightning. It would be upon her soon. She scrambled from the pool, her feet stuttering beneath her, and backtracked to the squat shack.

She tumbled through its arched door, a shivering wreck. She felt her way across a stone floor until she found what felt like a small fireplace. There seemed to be kindling in the hearth already, so she grappled clumsily in the pitch black until she found what she hoped was a piece of flint. She struck it, and sparks flew, but it failed to catch. She struck again and again and again; the only thing set ablaze in her attempts was her own desperate frustration. She'd started hundreds of fires before, why not this one when she so desperately needed to be warm? She struck again, her fingers tingling with cold, then a bitter cry of frustration sawed loose, and she struck the flint yet again. A blazing white ball of sparks, the likes of which she'd never seen, shot from the flint, finally catching the tinder.

She blinked spots out of her eyes and quickly grabbed for a bundle of small branches that came into sharp relief, stacked neatly next to the fireplace. She threw a handful onto the tinder, anxious to feed the flame enough to keep it from dying. Then as those caught, she slowly fed it larger and larger morsels until it grew enough that she could put on full meal-sized logs for it to devour. She leaned back, slumping onto the palms of her hands to bask in the warmth of her fledgling fire.

Outside of her small sanctuary, the wind became a pack of baying wolves ravenous at her door, the peal of thunder close at their heels. Only to be drowned a moment later by the drumfire of rain upon the roof, which, to her dismay, dripped in a handful of places.

She sighed and stood to survey the room, hoping to find something useful to help keep her warm and dry through the night. The single-room hut was small. A wide stone bench built into the wall along the far side could serve as a bed for the night; she'd slept on far worse on excursions with her parents. An altar of some sort took up the space across from her. Glittering stones, dried flower garlands, and half-melted candles were strewn around a central statue of a nude woman with wings, her hair arrayed around her head like the rays of the sun. She held a pitcher downturned in either hand as if she was pouring something out of them. The stone that made up her feet was worn smooth from people's reverent touch as they prayed.

She was beautiful, and Bianca felt momentarily pulled to touch the tips of her feet to follow in the footsteps of former supplicants, but she quickly pulled her hand back. Praying to an unknown god wouldn't do her any good.

Next to the fireplace, roughly hewn shelves were built into the wall arrayed with clusters of mismatched clay jars and utensils. At the base, a sturdy wooden chest, carved with sigils and ornate illustrations, was tucked behind a threadbare curtain. Bianca stooped and wrenched it from its place. Its hinges protested shrilly when she bent the lid back to examine its contents.

Bulky blankets made of roughly woven brown fibers came out first. They smelled a bit dusty, but better to smell than to catch her death in wet clothing. She draped one across her shoulders right away and set the others aside for later. Beneath those in neat bundles were clothes. She sorted through them, all in natural tones of bark browns and mossy greens until she found a peculiar dress. It looked more like a dressing gown than any dress she was familiar with, with a fitted top half and sleeves and a belt holding it together around the waist.

She stood and began the tedious process of unbuttoning and unlacing herself from her mother's dress and her undergarments until they sat in a pile like a snake's molted skin near the fire. She shimmied into the new dress, the fabric warm and comforting, wrapped it around herself, and belted it at the waist, wrapping the belt around her middle twice and tying it at the front like a kitchen apron. The flowing skirt fell indecently short, just below her knees, and she blushed, though no one could see her. Though she had to admit after a swish or two that the shorter length allowed for much more freedom of movement.

Bianca gathered the blankets in a heap and arranged them along the stone bench into a cozy enough bed for the night. She fed the fire one last time, piling it as high as she dared, before curling under the blankets. The moment she was at ease, dark thoughts began to swirl on the edges of her mind, but she shut her eyes and let her exhaustion do the work of fending them off for the time being.

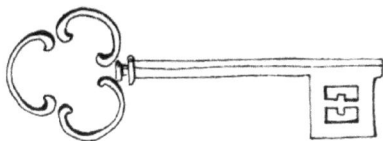

Chapter 17

THE CAT TROTTED INTO the shelter hours later as Bianca slept. He stayed by the still-crackling fire for a time to dry off. Once he felt satisfied his fur was dry enough, he wiggled his way under her blankets to curl up by the warmth of her belly. Asleep and unaware, Bianca put her arm around him and pulled him close.

He felt a little guilty at having run off, but the scent of anguish and impending doom was so heady in the air, it made his whiskers twitch. Even after hours of searching, he couldn't pinpoint it. He just hoped he hadn't pulled the girl into immediate danger. He'd just wanted her to see the stairs, to see if she could hear the song that beckoned. He'd never meant for her to go through a door, let alone to go through one himself. It wasn't technically allowed but he'd been overwhelmed by the pull. He shuddered at the thought of Imogen's fury when she discovered her new ward missing. She would blame him, of course, and rightly so. He sighed, stretching his paws out. Those were problems for the morning, now he needed to rest.

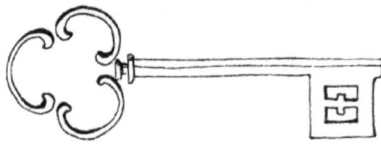

Chapter 18

H E LICKED HIS LIPS as blood dripped from the suspended corpse onto the glittering veins in twisted fractals across the black cavern wall and onto the floor. With each drop, a shuddering pulse ran through the opalescent stone, the echo of a heartbeat.

He watched the eyes of his latest sacrifice hollow out as life left it. The acrid combination of blood and dust coated his nostrils until he wanted to gag on the taste of it dripping down his throat. But then the air shifted, and the blood turned a deeper shade until it was a liquid as black as night with the shimmer of the cosmos spiraling within it. Its magic smelled of unsung songs, of dust storms beating across the desert, of a painful longing deep and raw. The magic was always the last to go, clinging to the bones of a body until there wasn't a single drop of life left in it. He suffered watching the blood drain just to see this moment.

Where the magic hit the stone, it sizzled and cracked, sloughing off in great chunks that disintegrated at a whisper of a touch into shimmering piles of dust.

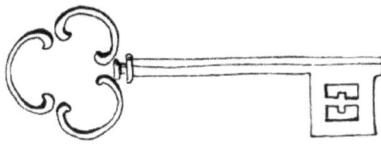

Chapter 19

*T*HE DECK OF CARDS, *wrapped neatly in a plum velvet bow, had crisp foiled edges that caught the lamp light, making them appear luminescent. Bianca had the strangest sensation when she saw them, as if she were looking upon something as ephemeral as a shooting star upon which she could make a wish.*

The ribbon slid smoothly from its place. She fanned the cards along the table, her fingers trailing along their embossed backs. She chose one and flipped it over. The Prophetess was inscribed below an image of a woman who looked eerily like her mother, with windswept golden hair and eyes the same shade as her own. The woman gazed down at a full moon held between her palms in wonder, her cheeks flushed.

Bianca ran a finger over the edge of the card in fascination. Where had it come from? She hissed as the gilt edge of the card drew blood as quick as a knife. Droplets of crimson sprayed onto the image as it spiraled out of her hand, dropped in her surprise.

It landed inversely, and as Bianca bent to pick it up, the image flickered and changed. The woman's look of wonder turned deranged her nails elongated into talons, and within them, she gripped a skull rather than a burgeoning moon. The lettering slithered and rearranged itself until it read, The Beldam.

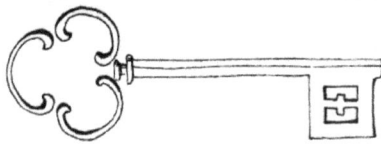

Chapter 20

T HE FEELING OF EYES on her and the hiss of a cat startled her from her unpleasant dreams. Thin threads of incense wafted through the room. A man sat back on his heels, watching her, or more accurately, watching Cat, his hands raised in what Bianca assumed was an attempt to show him that he came peacefully.

"Easy, easy," the man said. "I didn't mean to startle you both. I beg forgiveness by you and the Goddess, please." He touched a middle finger to a blue mark on his forehead, an upside-down teardrop with some sort of symbols on the inside, that stood out starkly against the deep brown of his skin. "I'm happy to see you, Travelers."

Bianca looked him up and down as best she could in the ribbons of morning light that wove their way through the small windows of the shrine. He was a burly tree of a man, dressed impeccably in a green coat with a flat collar that matched the make of the dress she wore and brown leather pants over which were belted an array of wickedly curved knives. The blue knots embroidered along his shoulder marked him as some kind of military inductee. Though he did not have the faraway look that Bianca had come to associate with the military men that often visited with her father, he still retained a soft innocence in his azure eyes. Though there was also panic, and a pain that seemed to reflect her own. So even though she had a hundred questions racing through her mind, the first one that slipped out was "What's wrong?" Her voice cracked like a desert morning as she rubbed the crust of sleep from the corners of her eyes.

"My parents and younger sister are missing." He ran a hand absently over his short-cropped dark hair and sighed. "For twelve sun cycles now. They were only meant to be gone one, two at the most."

Bianca opened her mouth to apologize for his loss as so many did for her, but she snapped it shut before the words could flee her mouth. She knew they were useless, and no matter how sincerely expressed, they often felt like a punch to the gut.

The cat hopped up next to her, his shoulders perfectly straight. He looked up at her and then back at the boy as if to say whatever they did next was up to her.

She cleared her throat and hesitated. "I, uh ... my parents are gone too. I used my mother's keys and followed the song and ended up here ... ," she managed to stammer, unsure of how to explain the whole story without sounding like a raving lunatic, or if she even should to a total stranger. Her hand twitched on the edge of the blanket as she fought the urge to reach for the bottle that wasn't there.

His face darkened as he looked up at her. "So, I was right, there are other Travelers missing." He growled.

Bianca cocked her head curiously, her hair tumbling down over her shoulder, wondering what he meant by Travelers. "They were taken, yes. I saw what took them, or at least I believe I did." She rolled up the sleeves of her dress and exposed her forearms, showing off the thick purple lines of scars. "Whatever they were, gave me these."

The man rocked forward onto his knees, his eyes wide as he took in her old wounds. "May I?" He lifted his hands and nodded toward her arms.

Bianca swallowed her nerves and nodded her consent. He was gentle, cupping one hand behind her elbow and softly tracing the scars down to her wrists. "Can you describe what did this? What took them?"

The cat leaned in, his ears twitching as though he too waited for her response. She pulled her arm out of the man's grasp, tucked her knees up under her chin, and wrapped her arms around them. With a shudder, she began to tell him about the night of her parents' disappearance. Partway through, when the words lodged in her throat, Cat leaned against her as if to lend her his strength. She scratched behind his ears appreciatively.

"You have to come with me and tell the Elder Council, "He said, his words sharply edged with a touch of eagerness and hysteria.

"My father received reports that others have gone missing, but the council refused to aid him in any action. Your account could change that. Your account could be the proof needed to make them see that something befell my parents rather than them simply being delayed."

Bianca looked at him for a long moment, refusing to let her mind acknowledge just how insane all of this sounded. "Just to be clear," she said, "you think whatever happened to my parents happened to yours?"

"Yes, your parents, my parents, and from the missives my father received, at least a handful of other Travelers have gone missing as well. Your account could help urge the council into action. They have the authority to contact the Circle directly to get their help to search for my parents and probably yours." His every word was punctuated with frantic, barely contained enthusiasm.

Bianca looked down at Cat. Her head was spinning, there was so much this boy said that she didn't understand. What did he mean by Travelers? What or who was the Circle? All of this seemed far madder than talking to a cat, which just yesterday had seemed very mad indeed. But none of those things mattered. The only thing that did was that someone here might be able to help her find her parents, and even if she was delusional, she was far happier believing she could do something to help other than just sitting twiddling her thumbs in an empty manor house. She took a deep breath and looked back up into those desperate blue eyes. A spark of hope burned there that was almost intoxicating. "What's your name?" she asked.

"Apologies, Goddess forgive me for my rudeness." He bowed his head slightly, his middle finger once again touching the symbol inked onto his forehead. "I am Alder, son of Cedre."

A jolt went through her as she realized Alder's fingers were stained, as though dipped in dark-blue ink. She stood mesmerized, pulled along as though on puppet strings, and took his hand to shake in hers. "Nice to meet you, Alder. I'm Bianca, Bianca Hastings."

As they stepped out into the light, Cat grumbling as he followed behind, Bianca wondered if perhaps there were more answers here than she could have fathomed possible.

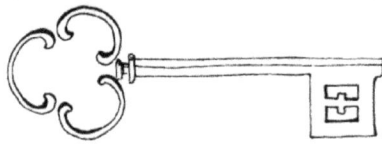

Chapter 21

THE WOODEN SLAT WALKWAY was wide enough for two horses to walk abreast, though she imagined that they, like her, wouldn't be comfortable being suspended along a cliffside. Bianca hadn't noticed the pathway the night before as she stood on the cliffside and looked at the sunset, but that was because it hung about three feet down from the cliff's edge. The drop down onto it caused her heart to jump into her throat, and it stayed lodged there while she clung to the solid stone of the cliff as she, Cat, and Alder steadily made their way down the path. Alder walked with the even grace of someone who lacked the sense to be wary of a several-thousand-foot drop with a carved quarterstaff in one hand.

"Don't fear," Alder called over his shoulder, "it is quite safe!"

Bianca stared at her feet and the planks just in front of her as they walked, and though she was quite sure he was right, she couldn't help feeling as though her ribs tightened around her lungs with every breath. "I'm sure it is," she said, a lot more breathily than she'd intended.

"You know Alatus is known for its peaks. You will miss the view if you stare at your feet the whole time."

The name sounded foreign to her, which was odd considering the many hours she'd pored over maps with her father, plotting his next archeological exploits, she thought she knew all the names of the mountain ranges by now. That niggling fear and worry over her sanity and where she was came pecking at the back of her mind again, but she quickly shut it down. She had to focus on her parents; she had to get them back. She paused her fingertips still brushing the jagged stone of the mountainside as she turned to look at the view. Sawtooth mountains that had looked beautiful in the dusky light the night before looked absolutely stunning by day. They were blanketed in trees of the most luminescent emerald greens embroidered here and there with splashes of color from trees of different flowering varieties. And as if the mountain range alone wasn't regal enough, the three tallest peaks were crowned in purple clouds with their barren snow-tinged summits spearing into the crystalline sky.

Her breath caught, stolen by the staggering beauty, Alder silently came to stand next to her. "It's my favorite view," he confided after a moment. Even the cat was sitting as if in awe of it.

She looked up at him and strangled a surprised gasp as she noticed his ears; they were bizarrely pointed at the tips. He turned to smile down at her, his brow furrowing. "You look a bit pale, are you quite alright?"

She swallowed her surprise, not wanting to offend him by bringing them up or embarrass herself if they were normal here in Alatus. She nodded. "Fine, I'm just fine. The height is making me a bit queasy is all, but the view, you were right, the view is lovely. More than lovely, it might be one of the most spectacular things I've ever seen. It's almost like a fairy tale."

He smiled, though it didn't reach his eyes, not entirely. "Don't worry, we're nearly in the trees. We'll have your feet on solid ground again in no time. Come"—he held out a hand— "let me steady you."

She hesitated a moment. It's not proper to let a young man touch you, even to escort you without gloves in polite society, but she supposed since they weren't in polite society, she could take his hand. His grip was warm and firm, his hand nearly swallowing hers whole, but it was reassuring, and he positioned himself between her and the edge, for which she was incredibly grateful. Cat leaped onto her back and draped himself over her shoulders, his paws dangling down in a fair imitation of the garish fur shawls she'd seen worn by some of society's finest. But his weight, like Alder's hand, was grounding.

The wooden path eventually gave way to a winding dirt trail, lichen-crusted trees stood on either side with wildflowers tucked into their roots. The old her, the girl she was before her parents were taken, would have veered off the trail immediately to take samples, to press petals between pages, and would have asked a thousand and one questions about each plant and its properties. The new her, the broken and put-back-together-again version of her, felt tongue-tied at the prospect. She knew she should want to ask, she wanted to want to, but she couldn't make her mouth form the words.

Instead, she asked, "What does the symbol mean, the blue one on your forehead?"

He looked down at her with a quizzical arch to his brow. "It's a symbol of my devotion to my Goddess. Long may she fly." His last words were intoned as if by rote.

"So, you're a monk?"

He frowned. "I don't know precisely what you mean by a monk. But I don't think so—all who follow the Goddess have these markings."

"But why blue?"

Alder glanced at her perplexed. "Do you know nothing of Alatus? Did they not teach you any of this? Don't you know how unsafe it is to travel without foreknowledge of where you're going?"

He pulled them to a stop and looked down at her, his goddess symbol wrinkled in consternation. Crimson embarrassment crept up her neck and face, she felt very much like a chastised young child when he looked down at her with the expression he had on now. "I . . . I . . . no one knows I'm here. I didn't even know I was going to come, but the song, my mother used to hum it, and I heard it everywhere I went. Like it was pulling me toward something. It pulled me here. I had to follow it . . ." She trailed off as Alder's brow smoothed, and he nodded understandingly.

"I see. I contemplated going in search of my family as well. I, however, do not have any keys." He drew her hand closer and brushed his thumb across the lower links that intersected across her wrist. Something flashed in his eyes briefly, and then it was gone as he cleared his throat and let go of her arm.

She pulled it close, placing her hand over her heart and her other protectively over the keys. "They were my mother's. She wore them almost everywhere, and I've been wearing them since I came across them in her belongings. I feel less alone when I wear them, as if they carry an echo of her in them."

Alder nodded knowingly and pulled a pouch from beneath his coat that hung from his neck on a leather cord. He gripped it tightly in his fist. "I understand. I too carry tokens of my family."

They walked on in somber silence for a few long moments before Alder finally spoke again, injecting artificial brightness in his words. "Well, we can't have you walking into the meeting of elders without at least some knowledge of Alatus." The trees around them grew denser, the trail leveled into a smooth, wide path free of stones. "So to answer your earlier question, the blue is a holy representation of the sacred waters with which the Goddess has blessed us. The moon and the star in the insignia represent her home, she flies with the wings of a great bird in the skies, and from her pitcher, she pours forth life-giving waterfalls and streams. Her tears bring the rain, and her breaths bring the winds. Every bird in the sky and on the ground are her sacred messengers. We mark ourselves once annually as a symbol of our gratitude, our devotion, our love, and our prayer that she will continue to bless us."

"Wow," Bianca whispered. "That's beautiful."

Alder smiled tightly, pain like shooting stars in his eyes. "The ceremony comes in two sun cycles. There will be a great feast and celebration. It is always my mother's favorite. Perhaps she will be back by then."

Bianca nodded silently, and her heart became a stone settling in a pond of grief. She remembered thinking something quite similar as her birthday approached not a few months ago. Melancholy rippled through her, threatening to pour out, but she damned it up quickly behind a shred of hope. They were heading toward help.

"I—" she began, but Alder cut her off with a finger to his lips. He grabbed her by the arm gently, Cat hiss-protesting the abrupt movement, and dragged her over to a nearby tree. He stood behind her with one hand on her shoulder. With him so close, she could feel his warmth radiating across her back. He smelled like a wood fire in the rain and staunch leather.

He leaned in closer to her and whispered, his breath hot against the shell of her ear, sending the stray wisps of her hair into a tizzy across her cheek, "Look, just there through the trees." Bianca followed his outstretched arm to peer through the trees.

The creature was so still she almost missed where it blended into the endless woods. It was a monolith of an animal on four lanky legs, its thick matted hair the exact color of the mossy trees around it hung like matted skeins of yarn in thick ropes from its body. Proud antlers spindled and sprouted from behind the floppy ears of the largest one. It tipped its head back and bellowed like a pipe organ. The melody was so low and guttural it almost sounded as if it were wrenched from its throat. Another called back from a distance, and she felt a tremor through the ground as a smaller one galloped through the trees. She stood as rooted to the ground as the tree upon which she leaned, unable to tear her gaze from the eerie and stunning creatures. The larger nuzzled the smaller creature as it approached, and they began to low together, their songs tangling together coalescing into a melody that made her soul ache.

"They're beautiful," Bianca whispered reverently. But the word seemed to fall flat. Beautiful was a pitiful excuse for a word when held up next to these beings. The cat nuzzled into her cheek with a purr as if to tell her he agreed or to remind her that he, too, was deserving of her attention. She reached up and scratched his ears.

Alder deftly crept back toward the path, motioning for her to do the same. When they had put plenty of distance between themselves and the creatures, Bianca finally asked, "What are they?"

"Loths. They are one of the only beasts you will find in these mountains, besides birds and jackalope, though there are plenty of them. Their hair is what we use to weave cloth. Some of the southern clans have domesticated them even."

"I've never seen anything like them," she said as she reverently ran a hand over the soft cloth of her dress.

"My sister loves to watch them. My mother brings her into the valley now and again to hear them sing."

"Where did they go—your family, I mean," Bianca asked. She immediately regretted it when she saw the small smile on his face twist into torment. "I'm sorry. I didn't mean to pry."

"It is all right," he said. "My sister, Iris, was sick and not getting any better. My mother—she's a particularly adept healer—was at a loss. She was convinced it was not a natural sickness, so her and father decided it would be best to seek help from the nearest Reliquary. My mother knows a healer there who she thought might be able to see whatever it was she was missing. They were only supposed to be gone for a couple of sun cycles. If they were going to be longer, I know they would have had someone send word. The council doesn't see it that way, they keep telling me not to worry, but I have a feeling they are doing nothing more for politics' sake."

Bianca nodded as if she understood, when in truth, the only thing that made sense to her was the underlying hurt in his words that was twin to her own. "I understand wanting to do something and being helpless to do it. Wanting to fix it but not knowing where to start. It's a slow and brutal kind of agony."

He peered down, his blue eyes bright. "It is. It is a pain I wouldn't wish on anyone."

Cat yowled as if he agreed, lightening the mood and eliciting a meager laugh from Bianca and Alder.

Bianca tugged his tail teasingly. "And what would you know about it, hmm?"

Pulling his tail free, he flicked her with it on the nose. This time when she laughed, it was full and genuine.

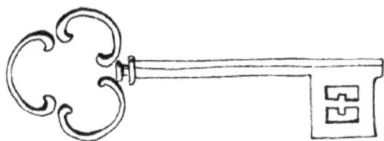

Chapter 22

MIDDAY SNUCK UP ON them as the walls of the valley narrowed into a gorge. A brook wended its way through the trees to keep pace alongside them until it grew and became a wide river. A warm breeze teased through the air, hinting that the day's heat was only just beginning.

Alder removed his coat and tucked it into the back of his belt, exposing his sleeveless under shirt and thickly corded arms. Along his left arm, dark markings spiderwebbed nearly from wrist to shoulder in a strange interlocking design. It took Bianca several moments of gawking to realize they were patterned to look like the leaves that littered the forest floor along their current path, shed from peculiar white-barked trees.

She wanted to ask more about the trees and why he'd marked himself with their leaves at all, but when she opened her mouth, the only thing that came out was "Dear gods, did that hurt?"

The cat snorted from his perch on her shoulder as if laughing at her. Alder chuckled softly too. "What this?" He gestured to his arm, and Bianca nodded. "I don't remember much of getting it to give you the goddess-blessed truth. My comrades did it when I was first inducted into our clan's guard. It tells the other clans who I belong to. But my commander slipped something into my drink before I ever even saw the needle."

Alder's voice suddenly pitched lower and darker. "And speaking of my comrades."

Bianca was startled as two figures seemed to materialize out of the trees. A man and a woman, both dressed in the same uniform as Alder, though they held menacing-looking spears rather than quarterstaves, and the woman carried twice as many knives as either of the men, as if she had something to prove. Both of them kept their hair short; though while the woman favored the same swarthy complexion as Alder, the man was a bit more fair, his hair leaning more pale brown than black.

The woman looked Bianca over from head to toe, her face pinched tight in a sneer before she looked away, as if deciding Bianca wasn't worth any more attention than an insect in her path. The man's face was as impassive as stone.

"Alder"—the woman's voice was as taut as her muscular physique— "the prime elder is looking for you."

Alder kept his face smooth as his eyes darkened. "As it so happens, Gaianna, I have guests with me who I am escorting. They have urgent business with the council. I'm sure the prime elder will want to attend of course. Perhaps you could send Oaklee here ahead to give notice and tell them to send word to me when they are assembled? I'm sure the prime elder will want to prepare."

Gaianna wrinkled her petite, angular nose in annoyance but jerked her head at Oaklee in a silent order to go. He took off in a quick, loping jog without so much as a glance back.

"You will not get out of trouble so easily this time, Alder son of Cedre. You walk a knife's edge," Gaianna spat.

Alder merely smiled. "A pleasure as always, Gai," he said, before he sidestepped her and continued along the path, motioning Bianca to do the same.

She followed with a muttered pardon to the woman. Unease squirmed in her belly. What sort of mess was she getting herself into? Her hand strayed to her skirt, and she plucked at the soft fabric uneasily where the pocket on her dresses was usually placed. This one, however, had none.

"What was that all about?" She reached up to stroke Cat's fur to give her twitchy hand something else to do and tried to keep her voice from wavering.

Alder just shook his head. "Nothing you need to worry over."

He smiled down at her in what she assumed was meant to be a reassuring way, but she found it did just the opposite. She had the oddest feeling. As though a trap had just been sprung, and the farther she walked toward their destination, the tighter the feeling cinched around her neck.

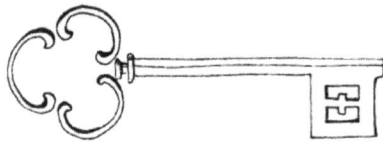

Chapter 23

BIANCA DID HER LEVEL best to shove her disquieted notions to the rear of her mind, locked behind a solid door. Some thoughts howled from behind it like bedlamites, though even they were silenced by the view.

The gorge abruptly opened into a large bowl with a pristine lake as clear as glass at its center. Water tumbled giddily over the edges of the walls, with jolly sprigs of vines growing here and there, strung over the rocks like a holiday banner. The water was so pristine that Bianca could see every rock and log on the lake bottom and strange blue crustaceans peeking out of the dark cracks to pinch at wafting green water weeds. A school of fish with gilded scales pirouetted through the water in a glinting swarm.

It was only when she noticed Alder smiling at her that she realized she'd drawn up short, her hand hovering over her stuttering heart that didn't quite know how to contend with her captivating surroundings.

"What do you say, Traveler? Have you ever seen anything like it?" Alder asked, an unknowable emotion heavy in his eyes.

"I can't say that I have. It's absolutely stunning!"

He smiled. "It is a blessing from the Goddess to live in such a place of plenty. Come, we are nearly there."

As they walked, nerves eddied through Bianca in a brackish blend of excitement and anxiety. Would anyone here believe her, or would they just believe her mad as everyone else had? Would this council help as Alder suggested? But then she caught her first sight of the village, tucked into and seemingly a part of a gargantuan cavern cut out of the back wall on the far side of the lake. Docks jutted into the water along the shoreline brimming with small crafts and fishermen going about their tasks bare-chested and barefooted, men and women alike. Some hauled ropes, others baskets or nets full of the catch of the day, their woven hats atop their shorn heads to keep the sun from beating their eyes.

A few men and women called greetings or gave a passing wave to Alder, giving the impression he was both well-known and well liked in the village.

At the open mouth of the cave, they walked along through rows of stalls in an open-air market. In the distance, she could see stone cottages and buildings carved into the cavern wall as far as the eye could see. People hawked their wares, calling over one another, their voices blending together like the lyrics of a strange song.

"Crustaceans caught today—fresh as you can get 'em."

"Scrolls! Scrolls for sale! We have everything from histories to romances! Best literature of our age!"

"Dishes! Stoneware dishes for sale! Teacups and saucers to match your wife's eyes!"

"Oy! Pretty lady! Would you like a new dress? How's about a blue one for the festivities?"

"Sharps here! Getcha sharps here! Sharpest knives, swords 'n spears"

A knobby man with tufty white eyebrows hollered at Alder by name from where he sat hunched over a fire next to a modest stall brandishing a ladle over a pot. "Your parents back yet, boy?" the old man asked as he pulled two wooden mugs from the counter of his stall and handed one apiece to Alder and Bianca.

"No, sir, not yet," he replied as he held out his mug for the vendor to fill with steaming liquid.

"And ye, young mistress, yer eyes are near as sad as my boy's here. Ye have someone yer missing, too, I'd wager." Bianca gawked at him as she held out her cup. "Oh, no need to look at me all fish-faced. In case ye didn't notice, I'm 'bout as old as dirt; I've seen just 'bout every look a person can have. I know the look of heartache better than most. But this'll fix ye both right up, 'n I'll be sending kindnesses to the Goddess on yer behalf."

He and Alder both touched their middle fingers to their goddess marks at the mention of her. Alder tried to pay the man with a black metal coin, but his payment was waved off with a scoff.

They wandered over and sat on a pair of hard wooden stools at the vendor's counter. The cat unwound from her shoulders to perch on a stool of his own, his eyes narrowed on passersby.

The drink was sweet with a rich, wild flavor. They sipped in silence, and Bianca tried to take in every sight, smell, and sound all at once. Mentally, she cataloged everything she wished she could tell her parents. The strange smell of the food cooking two stalls over, the color of the beads arranged in bowls like small pluckable fruits in another.

A boy, small enough Bianca could have pulled him into her lap and tucked him under her chin, dashed over, startling her and Alder as he skidded into an awkward bow. "I beg the Goddess's pardon for intruding"—he panted—"but the council sent me to find you. They're waiting for you now."

Alder slid off his stool, crouching so he was eye level with the messenger boy. He pulled another black coin from his pocket and slipped it into the boy's chubby-fingered hand. "Tell me, the prime elder, how did she look?"

The boy's eyes went wide above his flushed-red cheeks. "Not good, she looked fit to boil."

Alder righted himself and patted the boy on the shoulder. "Thank you, Yew, now run along home."

"Sure will, Goddess's luck be with you," Yew called over his shoulder in all manner of seriousness as he scampered off as quickly as he'd come.

Alder pulled his coat from his belt and quickly began to redress. "We had better hurry."

"Are we in some sort of trouble?" Bianca's brows pinched with worry as she scooped up Cat and let him settle back across her shoulders.

Alder took her by the elbow, hurrying her along the path through the market. She winced as pain shot up her scars, and she bit her lip to button in any cries as she struggled to keep up with Alder's long strides.

He paused only long enough to smile down at her in a not-so-reassuring way, his hand skimming anxiously over his shorn hair as he waited for a group of basket-carrying women to pass by before taking off again. "There is a good likelihood I may be."

He failed to mention whether or not she would be, too, a fact she was about to comment on when they came to an abrupt halt in front of a large, chiseled stone dome carved with swooping vines and soaring birds so realistic Bianca half expected them to fly off the wall in a flurry of feathers. On either side of an arched and curtained entrance stood two guards in uniformed coats just like Alder's, though with what appeared to be a lower rank denoted on the shoulders. Both men gestured with a salute as Alder strode confidently past with Bianca and the cat in tow.

As they crossed the threshold, thousands of tiny cocoons of worry hatched in Bianca's rib cage, each tiny flutter of winged anxiety quivering along her bones.

Alder leaned in close, his words rushed and whispered burned in her ear. "Trust me." What in the gods' names was that supposed to mean? Bianca's breath hitched.

Ten pairs of eyes from a raised dais that encircled the room scratched at her skin leaving her raw and exposed. The most offensive pair belonged to a slight older woman, elevated above the rest on a chair with a back of mosaicked wings that spanned across the walls.

With her punishing glare, her hooked nose, and her shorn head, she was a bird of prey ready to swoop down and gobble Bianca up.

"Alder," the bird crowed, and Alder bowed. "You have guests I see."

Her gaze narrowed on where Bianca stood trying not to cower, her eyes pinching. "Did I not expressly forbid you from leaving?"

Alder opened his mouth to answer but was swiftly cut off. "I did." Her voice cracked like a whip. "So explain, grandson, how it is you came to find these trespassers."

Bianca's stomach roiled at the words, trespassers. This was not how she hoped this exchange would go.

Alder shrugged nonchalantly. "Yarrow needed his patrol covered. He's taken ill with the sweating sickness, and as you know, our Healer is not in residence. I was simply obliged to cover for him."

"Lies! He lies!" A young man on the old woman's right leaned forward, and Bianca was struck by how similar his features were to Alder's.

Alder's shoulders stiffened, and something akin to hurt flashed across his eyes, but it was so quickly replaced with a look of utter aloof disinterest that Bianca thought it may have been her imagination. "Oleander, I didn't see you there. How funny you look in our mother's council chair, so small like you're playing at being her." Oleander spat on the ground at Alder's feet.

"I'm shocked to see you in it so soon after her disappearance." Alder continued as if his own brother had done nothing to insult him despite the gasps from the other council members in the room. "Perhaps it is that you finally believe me when I say something wicked has befallen her and our father?"

"No more of your folly, Alder," the birdlike woman hissed.

"But it is not folly, Grandmother."

"You will not address me so informally in council chambers, boy!" Her voice snapped around the room like a strike of lightning, but Alder didn't even flinch, though the cat on Bianca's shoulder hissed.

Alder bowed again, just slightly. "Forgive me, Prime Elder Ulrica. As I said, it is not folly. I have with me here Travelers like ourselves who also have family members missing. Who are witness to their taking. I implore you, Elders, to listen to the account and to take heed."

The prime elder's lips curled. "What the council will and will not do is not for you to decide, boy."

Alder's knuckles flashed white as he worked his fists behind his back. Cat jumped down from her shoulder and put himself between her and the volatile woman, the tension radiating from her palpable as it swept through the room like a poison gas.

Someone coughed. "Ahem, ahem. I, for one, would like to hear what the Travelers have to say." The breathy voice of the bargelike woman on the left side of the room cut the strained silence, and a low murmur of agreement swirled around the chamber.

Ulrica flushed an apoplectic shade of red as she ground out her next words. "If it is the will of the council, come forth and proceed with your account, Traveler."

Alder turned to look at her for the first time since entering the council chambers, his blue gaze as piercing as an icy spring as he gestured her forward to the middle of the room.

Cold sweat dripped down the nape of her neck, raising pinpricks of dread. Her lungs burned as she spun her story for the council of elders. She kept her eyes fixed on a point above the prime elder's head, refusing to meet her critical gaze. To punctuate the end of her story, she rolled up the soft green sleeves of her dress, exposing the long angry red and purple scars that marred her skin.

A few of the elders gasped, their hands darting to hide astonished and horrified expressions. Then the room flared to life, her story the apparent fuel needed to light a spark under them. Their uneasy words knitted together into an endless string Bianca heard but didn't quite understand. "Fury? It can't be . . . The Darkness could be rising . . . The implications . . . Lying . . . but was it one Fury or a horde?"

"Silence." The prime elder's demand squashed the frenzied whispers. Bianca pulled her sleeves back down and resisted wringing her fingers.

Ulrica narrowed her eyes and pointed a long-nailed finger at the cat. "And you, what do you have to say for yourself?"

Bianca turned a snorted laugh into a rather conspicuous cough when it dawned on her that the elder was serious. She chanced a glance over at Alder who seemed not at all surprised by the elder's demands; in fact, he too watched the cat with an expectant air.

Then she felt it; the air in the room seemed to pull toward the cat. His fur rippled like wind across water, his limbs impossibly growing and stretching. Clumps of fur disintegrated, his tail shrunk, his ears shifted, their points rounding until in place of a cat crouched a naked man.

Alder swept over to the man with a brown woven blanket like the one she had slept with the night before and draped it modestly over his shoulders. The man turned to look at Bianca, his face split in a half grin that was part apology, part wince. His hair was the same shade of coppery brown that the cat's had been. The same scar ran around the left side of his eye. The same ink stained the tips of his fingers that clenched the blanket around himself.

Bianca floundered, her lip quivering as it refused to let words tumble out of it. She pressed the heels of her palms into her eyes as if she could rub away the insanity of what she'd just seen.

"I'm growing impatient, changeling." Ulrica hissed the last word harshly as if the taste of them on her tongue were despicable. "How did you both come to be here?"

The man stood, squaring his shoulders as best he could while still keeping himself covered. "The song beckoned us into the void. Your Fragment along with many others were singing in anguish. We simply answered."

"Lies, more lies on top of lies," Oleander cried. Bianca began to think it was the only thing he knew how to say, though she had to admit what the cat, man, said sent her mind reeling even deeper into the dark depths of confusion. The words made sense individually, but strung together, it sounded nonsensical. Even more perplexing, everyone else seemed to understand it, leaving her deserted on the outskirts of the conversation.

Ulrica silenced her grandson with a gesture before narrowing her beady eyes on the man. "You lie," she parroted. "No one has sung the summoning song here." Her eyes jerked to where Alder stood. "Unless . . ."

She swooped down from her perch, landing right in front of Alder. "Show me your hands, boy."

Alder stiffly acquiesced, shoving them out in front of her for inspection. She grabbed each one, turning it this way and that, pushing up his sleeves to examine his forearms before pushing them back at him. The man watched the whole exchange between the elder and her grandson with feigned indifference, but Bianca could see the echoes of tension gleaming in his gray eyes, and she wondered if she, too, should be concerned.

The elder swept back up to her place, then she whispered to the occupants of the chairs to her left and right. The whisper traveled up and down the circle of men and women until it slithered back to her, and Bianca had the distinct and horrible impression that whatever was to be said next would not be good. "The elders and I have conferred, and we have decided that this tale of Darkness creatures is nothing more than a delinquent prank. And though juvenile may the intent have been, trespassing in another Fragment is an illegal offense, and we will be sending a missive to the Circle to alert them to your unsanctioned presence here as well. You will be placed under the custody of Oleander and confined to the city until the Circle is able to send someone to deal with you accordingly. You will be stripped of your keys to prevent any ill-conceived notions of escape."

Tears began to well in Bianca's eyes. The man who had been a cat began to shout, but his words were drowned by a loud ringing in her ears. The room tilted, and she fell to her knees, her palms slapping the floor to anchor herself.

"Forgive me, Prime Elder"—Alder's voice cracked through the ringing, his tone as stiff as his squarely set shoulders— "but I feel duty bound to remind you that as eldest in my family, in my parents' absence, my mother's council duties fall to me, not to my brother."

Oleander looked between his grandmother and brother, his face twisted in petulant fury, his jaw gritting as though he struggled not to cut in as Alder seized the advantage and pressed on, "I allowed myself in a moment of weakness to be swayed by the girl's tale. The council's swift ruling has allowed me to see the error of my ways. I brought them here; they ought to be my responsibility."

His words struck a knife blow in Bianca's gut; of course, he didn't believe her anymore. No one ever believed her. Why should he be any different?

"You haven't been particularly loyal as of late, grandson." An unaired question hung at the end of her statement as she shifted forward in her seat, leaning imposingly over them.

"Then let me prove to you I still am. This is my mess, allow me to"—he cast a blue, steely-eyed glance at Bianca, twisting the knife just a little deeper— "clean it up."

A silent conversation passed in a single glance between the prime elder and Oleander before she turned her attention back to Alder. "A final chance then, Alder. But if you betray me this time, well, I'm sure you are well aware what the consequences will be."

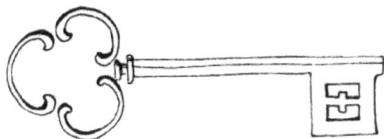

Chapter 24

THE MAN WHO HAD been a cat shifted worriedly from foot to foot as he watched the uncomfortable exchange between grandmother and grandson. When it was finally over, Alder bowed and pivoted to leave, his hand half raised to motion for the man and Bianca to follow.

"Aren't you forgetting something, grandson?" Ulrica's words halted his own steps, the hairs at the nape of his neck prickling at the cadence of her voice. "Her keys, Alder."

The man turned to Bianca, her eyes wide with fear and pleading as Alder strode over to her. "No, Alder, please, they're all I have, please don't!"

Before he could think about it, the man lunged, trying to put himself between Bianca and Alder, but his reflexes were too slow so soon after changing, and he made it there just as Alder hauled Bianca to her feet.

In a clash of arms and thrashing bodies, the three of them struggled until Alder growled at them both under his breath. "Trust me."

Bianca's eyes glazed over, and she stopped flailing against Alder's attempts. Tears rolled down her speckled cheeks as the clasp of her mother's bracelet was undone. Her shoulders shook, and her face drained of color as the chain was pulled free of her arm. He just barely managed to get an arm awkwardly around her waist as her eyes rolled back and her knees gave out. She sagged against him, her head lolling to one side, her blue-black curls unfurling across his shoulder.

Alder tossed the keys at the dais; Oleander rose with a look of dark triumph on his face as he caught them in his greedy palm. His fingers danced along the length of the chain like a pale-brown spider, and the man wondered just what sort of heinous things he and his grandmother intended.

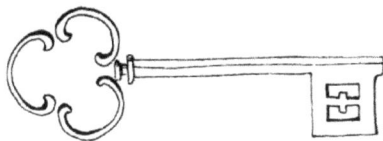

Chapter 25

THE THICK SCENT OF salted tears was more poignant than a funeral in a spring squall. It took Bianca a moment to remember what had happened; the absence of the familiar comfort at her wrist and the damp tracks down her cheeks brought it all tumbling back. The weight of it all cascaded into frustration. She threw off the blankets that covered her and stormed from the dark, cozy room someone had tucked her in and followed the drone of familiar voices out the door and down the hall.

The two men lounged against plush pillows opposite each other, conversing over a low table. The man who had been the cat spied her first and promptly choked on his cup of tea. Alder turned around; his dark cheeks flushed a deep shade of shame as they both scrambled to their feet. Their sputtered apologies tripped over one another in a tangled mess of words.

Bianca shook her head, her frustration suddenly sapped out of her at the sight of their frantic and genuine-sounding apologies. Her snarled tresses framing her face swayed wildly as she held up her hands for silence. "Just stop. Please, I don't know if I forgive either of you for your deceptions, but I do know you both owe me an explanation. For starters, my gods blessed keys, Alder."

Alder cleared his throat sheepishly, one hand running anxiously over his close-cropped hair. "I have a plan to get them back. I swear it, by my mother's life. I had to give them to her, or she never would have trusted me enough to give you both into my care."

As much as she hated it and wanted to argue, it made enough sense, so she sighed, pushing an errant strand of hair away from her face. "All right, I understand. I don't like it, but I suppose I don't have to. I will hold you to your word, though, Alder. I expect my keys back, and soon."

He inclined his head in a slight bow. "On my honor, I will see it done. Now, would you care to sit and have some supper or tea?"

Bianca nodded and sat on the offered cushion as Alder poured her a steaming mug of tea in a beautifully crafted stoneware mug, and the cat-man dished up a plate of food.

She murmured thanks to both before taking a long sip of warm tea, sultry and sweet with a heavy bouquet of floral flavors. She set the mug down before turning all her attention slowly and deliberately on the cat-man. He was tragically handsome despite the scar that marred the left side of his face. That slight smirking smile that turned the corner of his lips teased that he was trouble. She could see lightning crackling behind his eyes, his gaze as intense as a storm trapped in a bell jar. She strained to keep a blush from staining her cheeks under that smoldering, simmering look that felt somehow indecent. She summoned her most aloof tone to put distance between her and the strange sensation his gaze stirred in her belly. "You, what is your name, sir?"

"Felix Grayson and I would like to humbly beg your forgiveness for deceiving you." He brushed an errant curled strand of hair from his face; it almost immediately fell back again.

Bianca picked up her mug of tea and blew away the tempest of steam. "Well, all right then, let's hear it."

Felix canted his head to one side, his brows pinched. "Hear? Hear what?"

Bianca leaned forward ever so slightly, mimicking a move she'd seen her mother do a thousand times to make herself seem more imposing than her slight frame typically allowed. "Your begging, Mr. Grayson."

His lip curled, tugging up in the corner, and then he started laughing. Bianca tried not to squirm; instead, she leaned back, the picture of patience, and took another sip of her tea. She caught the briefest twinkle of amusement in Alder's eye and wondered just what about this ludicrous situation he found so amusing. She shot him a swift and cutting glare that dimmed the cerulean glint in his gaze.

"All right. Point well made." This time it was Felix who leaned forward, invading her space. He brazenly took her hand in his and effected a preposterously theatrical tone. "Ms. Hastings, I implore you to please grant me your forgiveness. I woefully regret my part in deceiving you. It was not my wish to do so. I, in fact, argued voraciously and exhaustively against it."

Bianca pulled her hand free. "Mr. Grayson, really. I know you think me a fool, having played me for one, but there is no need to be so deriding."

Felix's feline smile slipped. "I don't mean to come off that way, please. I was just trying to lighten the mood a bit. I am truly repentant. And I must insist you call me Felix; I think we are well beyond the societal bounds of propriety at this point, don't you?"

Bianca's face mottled with mortification as she recollected the several occasions he had curled himself intimately in her bed. Even though he had been in tabby form, it could still besmirch her reputation. Not that she had much of a reputation at the moment beyond crazed orphan girl, a far cry from her dreams of being a noted archeologist and academic like her father. She sighed and resigned herself. She needed answers, and this Felix Grayson could give them. She was stuck betwixt a rock and a rabid Marrat to be sure. "All right, Felix. I suppose I will have to accept your apology for the time being." She set her empty mug down with a hollow *thunk*.

Alder leaned across the table with the kettle ready to refill it. "Now that that's settled, I think we need to address the areas where you are woefully lacking in knowledge. Are Felix and I correct in understanding you don't know what you are?"

Bianca scooped up the refilled mug, finding comfort in its warmth. "I know I'm a Traveler; I've gathered that much."

Her hand drifted to her side, her fingers knotted in her skirt, and she loathed how Felix's gaze knowingly tracked the motion with pity in his eyes. It felt far too intimate. She swallowed a bitter lump in her throat.

Alder reclined on his cushions, his fingers steepled thoughtfully. "But do you know what that means, what that entails?"

Felix popped a plump piece of fruit into his mouth, plucked from a bowl at the center of the table. They resembled strawberries in shape, but they were a rich blue color instead of a sinful red. "Doubtful," he answered around his mouthful.

Bianca scowled. She was beginning to think she liked Felix better as a cat. "Why don't you both just explain, then?"

Felix cleared his throat. "Sure. Easy enough. Travelers are people with, let's call it, a unique set of abilities."

"Like turning into cats?" Bianca's stomach grumbled, protesting her tea-only diet, so she helped herself to a crumbly looking moon-shaped pastry.

"No, no, that's different. I can turn into a cat because I'm a changeling."

"A what?"

"A changeling. In my natural form, I'm human like you, but I can change my form into any creature I want," Felix said with a rather smug grin on his face.

"So you're like the Moon Wolves in children's stories. The ones who shift into feral dogs at the turn of the moon?" Bianca had loved those stories. When she was small, her dad had told them to her at bedtimes for years.

Felix scowled. "No, not at all, those are just tales to frighten children into eating their vegetables."

"Perhaps, "Alder interjected, "you should start with the histories? It's usually best to start stories at the beginning rather than in the middle, don't you think?"

Felix's scowl only deepened. "No, I've got this, trust me."

"I'm still confused," Bianca cut in, partly because she enjoyed the way Felix's brow furrowed as he grew more flustered and partly because she still wanted the answer. "What abilities is it that Travelers have then?"

"Magic, we all have magic. Well, for the most part."

Bianca's eyes widened. She mouthed the word *magic* silently as if trying to reconcile what she knew the word to mean with Felix's application here.

Then her brain caught up to the rest of the statement. "Wait, what do you mean for the most part? Did my parents have magic? Do I?"

Felix snorted, then grabbed her hand again, holding her stained fingers up in between them. "Of course, you do, see? The evidence of it is right here."

"I still don't understand."

He let her hand drop. "The discoloration is the cost, so to speak, of using magic." He rolled up the too-big sleeves of his borrowed shirt, he waggled his blackened fingers at her, and her breath hitched.

The dark splotches on his fingers shimmered, a smoky luminescence pooled in his palm, wavering like a flame. The stain of his magic dripped like candle wax, breaking off into individual teardrops, then they morphed into the same strange markings that she often found on her own skin. The markings danced up his arm, whirling around one another. One of the new black beads twisted, forming a jagged spiral as it drifted to join a moon and a whole constellation of stars. Bianca blinked rapidly and rubbed her eyes as if she could rub away what she saw.

"The marks indicate what sort of magic you've worked recently. My stars for instance"—he pointed to the stars, drawing a finger up his muscle-corded forearm to the crook of his elbow where the symbols began to fade—"reveal that I've been doing quite a bit of illusion work. From what I've seen of yours, you've been doing a lot of divination."

Things began shifting around in Bianca's mind like the tumblers of a lock clicking into place, then she turned her attention to Alder and his blue-marked fingers. "The prime elder, she was checking for markings when she asked to see your arms, to see if you had sung a song? The song that pulled me here, right?"

He nodded with a hint of a smirk. "She was, but I hid the mark with a glamor. She and my brother are both Inepts; they have no way of seeing through illusions."

Felix paused with food midway to his mouth, his eyebrows rising. "An Inept, really? That's fascinating. I've never met one before. Well, I guess I can't say that anymore, now, can I?"

"What's an Inept?" Bianca asked.

"A Traveler without magic," Alder answered. "They're usually fairly rare, so it's odd to have more than one in a family line. My grandmother has some peculiar notions on the subject. She seems to think my mother stole all her magic somehow since my mother is particularly gifted. It's completely impossible, but she made my mother's life difficult growing up."

"What about my parents? Why don't they have markings like yours? Were they Inept or just hiding them?"

"Oh, they were definitely hiding them with a very strong glamor. Imogen told me they are quite powerful," Felix answered as he shoveled a third helping of food onto his plate.

"I can only speculate of course," Alder cut in, "but from what I understand, a lot of Travelers are shunning the old ways and apparently refusing outright to tell their children about their heritage. But I think we're getting ahead of ourselves here." He shot a somewhat withering look at Felix who was still shoveling food into his mouth at an alarming rate. "Let us start again at the beginning, with the histories."

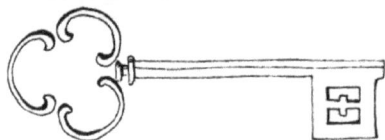

Chapter 26

THE AZURE FLAMES CRACKLED in the hearth setting the perfect storytelling ambiance. Bianca tucked her knees up and cozied deeper into the blanket on Alder's settee. Felix sprawled next to her, his legs outstretched, fingers laced behind his head, and an indolent grin plastered on his face.

Alder stood, his broad shoulders straight, in front of the fire, blocking most of the light from it, casting his megalithic shadow across the room. He'd taken his green military coat off and draped it over a nearby chair. In the muted light, Bianca could just make out the rippling blue glow of his magic along his fingers and arms, like moonlight along water.

He cleared his throat. "If you're both ready." His voice was low and husky in a way that sent shivers tiptoeing down Bianca's spine.

With a flick of his wrists, navy and white light flamed from his palms. He brought the twin flickers together until they merged into a cosmic sphere, spiraling together. He molded his hands in the air around it much like a ceramist worked clay until it became a wide spinning disk. Miniature land formations, flora, fauna, rivers, and beings sprang into existence on his crafted plain. "In the beginning, there was one. One existence for all of creation. Every beast and being walked together on the same land coexisting in relative peace, all except the Darkness. A group of parasitic beings whose origins are unknown. They were discontent with their place, craving power."

As he spun his tale, so too did the image he created, showing flashes of peaceful peoples and the race of Darkness in flashes like drifting memories. Bianca had never seen anything like it before, so she sat straighter in her seat, leaning in, pulled into the story he was bringing to life right before her eyes. Even Felix's attention seemed to stretch taut, drawn in.

"The Darkness began to spawn new creatures, such as the Fury, through despicable acts of twisted magic. They started to prey on innocents, taking and slaying whatever and whomever they desired. The rest of creation had no choice but to take up arms against the Darkness to defend themselves. But Darkness was winning, sweeping across the land in a terrifying tide. Until one male, Prayllus the wise, discovered a spark, a light that burned in himself and others. Magic. He gathered those like him and formed a mighty counteroffensive, but the more magic they mastered and gained, so too did the Darkness. For an age the war waged, with catastrophic losses on both sides."

Images of burning homes, bloodied faces, and savage monsters shuddered across Alder's illusion, so tangible Bianca could almost hear the screams and smell the metallic tang of blood.

"Prayllus miraculously discovered that mated pairs of magically gifted were stronger than those casting on their own. Something in the bond between their souls magnified the magics. He formed the Circle, a group of fourteen of the most powerful mated pairs. Together, they devised a plan. They knew that the forces of light couldn't last much longer. They were in a stalemate, but they were weakening. If the fighting went on much longer, they would all be dust. They eventually concluded that if they couldn't beat the Darkness, they would trap it. So in an event that is now known as the Breaking or the Schism, the Circle shattered the world in order to save it."

Bianca gasped as the image of the world Alder so carefully spun fragmented into thousands of shards like a glass dropped.

"The fragments hung like stars in the sky, spinning in the ether. But around each the Circle built walls of pure magic. The Darkness was cast out, banished to the Fade in between the Fragments to waste away, trapped for all eternity. In the fragile time that came after, the Circle wove into existence the Void, a passage knitting all the broken pieces of the world together. They crafted doors with locks only they could open, and in the centuries since, they and their descendants have patrolled the Fragments, rooting out remnants of

Darkness, answering any call for aid by their inhabitants, and ensuring that all with magic are trained to take up the mantle should the need arise."

When the image disappeared and darkness swallowed the room, it took Bianca a moment to realize the history lesson was over.

Alder used his magic to illuminate the wall sconces, flooding the room with lights and casting spots in Bianca's vision that she had to blink away.

Felix applauded slowly. "Wow. I must admit that was the most interesting retelling of the Breaking I have ever heard. I usually doze off in history. You are quite adept with illusions."

Alder bowed his head, graciously accepting Felix's exaltations as he sat in a chair opposite the couch. "Thank you, that is high praise indeed. And you, Bianca. What do you think?"

"It was stunning. I've never seen anything like it. To be honest, I'm a bit overwhelmed, and I have questions. A lot of questions, but I suppose they should wait." Her lids felt unusually heavy, and there was the beginning of a sickly throbbing in the backs of them. "I'm getting quite tired, the stress of the day catching up to me."

"Of course, my apologies. Come"—he offered her a hand— "I'll show you to the guest quarters."

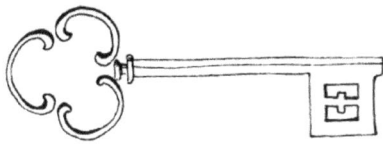

Chapter 27

F ELIX STARED AT ALDER over the rim of his tea mug. "Got anything stronger than this?" he asked, waggling the teacup.

Alder smirked. "Of course." He ducked back into the kitchen and returned with a corked clay jug. He poured Felix and himself a full cup each before sitting back in his chair. Felix thought he looked stiff, even now, too wound tight, though he supposed he couldn't blame the guy. He knew what loss like that felt like. Felix had just had a lot longer to get used to it.

He took a deep swill of the liqueur and winced as it lit a fire in his throat. "By all the gods, that burns all the way to my toes."

Alder chuckled, grimacing at his own cup. "Well, you did ask for stronger."

"I did, I did. It felt like the occasion called for it."

His companion nodded darkly. "Darkness creatures and missing Travelers. Just one of those things is reason enough to drink."

Felix's slouch deepened, his fingers and toes tingling in a warm pleasant sort of way. "How many do you reckon are missing?"

Alder leaned forward, his elbows resting on his knees. He rolled his cup absently between his hands. "I can't be sure. My father was receiving reports, but they were all stolen by Oleander, the bastard, when he scampered off to live with our grandmother."

"He seems like a real charming fellow." Felix gestured with his teacup. "Has he always been such a ray of light?"

Alder shrugged, taking a deep draw from his cup before refilling it and topping off Felix's. "I suppose he wasn't always that way. When we were little, he didn't mind that I had magic and he didn't. I'd cast whatever he wanted for him; all he had to do was ask. But the closer he grew to our grandmother, the more bitter and resentful he got. Then the second our parents left with Iris, he packed up and moved. It was almost as if he knew they wouldn't be back. I'd still like to get my hands on those reports, though, just to see what's what. See if anyone else has spotted Darkness creatures."

"I don't think they have." Felix's tongue felt thicker now that he was getting deeper in his cups. "Imogen, she's Bianca's great aunt, she was getting reports too. It was all very vague. Someone missing here, someone concerned about so-and-so there. Folk with odd feelings. Bianca's parents were the first real account she'd heard, and she couldn't even ask the girl outright about it. She didn't want to spook her. She suspected her parents hadn't told her much of anything. She's never even met the girl before, just had a few letters from her niece over the years or something like that. Most beings in Areth are Obliviots; they don't know about Travelers and magic or the true histories. It would be a pretty cushy place to retire if you ask me."

"Tell you what, though," Felix said after a long pause. "If all the songs being sung from the Void are any indication, there are a lot more than just a few Travelers missing."

Alder touched the Goddess sigil on his forehead absently. "I've heard them beckoning too. They're only getting louder."

Felix swilled his cup. "So. You know we can't sit around here waiting for the Circle to come for us."

It wasn't really a question, but Alder nodded anyway.

"Good, so what's your plan for getting us out? I'm assuming you have a plan."

Alder threw back the last of the hooch in his cup, slamming it down against the low wooden table in front of them with a hiss. "I do."

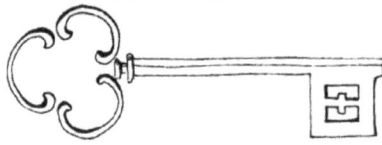

Chapter 28

The shudders flapped against the window as indecently as a painted whore's skirt. Perdita huffed from where she sat perched in her night shift and cap on the edge of the inn's bed, feeling aggrieved. She'd told that good-for-nothing innkeeper just that morning to get it fixed. She couldn't stand the man and the way he plodded about with those glassy eyes and that peculiar-colored greenish tinge to his hair.

She needed off this god's forsaken island. It had been days since she'd finally rid herself of that ungrateful whelp of a girl on her aunt's doorstep. The return journey was supposed to be smooth, but she'd arrived at the ferry dock only to find it out of commission. Some nonsense about a broken rudder. If all the folk in this town weren't so blessedly lazy, she could have been home by now, tidily packing her things so she could move far, far away. Perhaps even as far away as another continent.

A scratch at the door made her jump. "Who goes there?"

The sound came again, longer and more shrill. Perdita bolted indignantly to her feet, snatching her dressing robe from the hook on the bedstead. It must be that slovenly little innkeeper finally coming around to fix the shudders. Leave it to a man like him to wait for such an unseemly hour, he probably hoped to catch her unawares in her shift. Louts of his ilk always liked to leer.

Just as the silk of her robe belt slid into a firm knot, the soft snick of the lock being turned, and the door opening made her whip her head around. Her mouth froze midway, the admonishment that had been about to fall from her lips fell flat instead, fizzling into a small squeal of pure terror.

The thing that crowded the doorframe was decidedly not the innkeeper, nor was it human. Its clawed fingers were far too spiderlike, its sallow skin seemed to sweat shadows.

It moved toward her, sniffing the air with slitted nostrils. More filed in behind the first, swelling to fill the space between, floor to ceiling, until their ghastly faces were all she could see.

She struggled to breathe, to summon an ounce of will, to scream, to run, to do anything.

She raised a trembling finger as if to scold the creatures for intruding when the first one snapped forward, its talons twisting around her throat.

It leaned close, running its nose along her cheek like a lover's caress. Her skin erupted with gooseflesh where its clammy flesh lay slick against hers.

It sniffed.

Sucking in a rattling breath.

Its mouth opened, its heinous breath surrounded her with the smell of maggot-riddled corpses, then it spoke, "It lies. It smells like one, but it isn't."

Its voice was made of rattling death, scraping against her ears.

The rasping replies of the others were drowned out by a reverberating rip. A sucking, then dripping that Perdita could feel in her marrow.

Her eyes rolled to the creature's hand, which was blood coated. She tried to make sense of it, but the edges of her vision warped, growing sharper in spots and duller in others. Then the world tilted, falling and twisting, canting to the side.

Perdita's lungs burned; her heart flailed.

The last thought of Perdita Rue as she watched the reapers of her death drift on silent feet back out her door was that she knew, she knew that the Hastings girl was trouble.

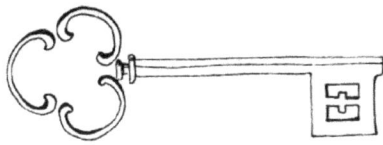

Chapter 29

A RAP AT THE *door drew Bianca from her chair by the fire. She opened it only to find herself in a strange hall, lit only by a glow, like flickering firelight, from the farthest end.*

Thousands upon thousands of pocket watches hung, suspended by their chains, from the ceiling. The light bounced off their backs, getting tossed from one to the other. They glittered like a storm of flicker bugs.

Unsure what to do or who had knocked, she cautiously made her way toward the light. She caught a glimpse of a forget-me-not skirt whip around the corner. Her mother. She had to get to her. She started to run, but the hall impossibly stretched the faster she went. The faint ticking of the clocks grew ever louder until it pressed into her ears, burrowing its way into her skull. Their chains quaked against one another like the chains of the damned. They swung at her, snatching and snaring until they held her more tightly than a mouse in a snap trap.

She called out for her mother, but the ticking, the horrendous, smothering ticking drowned out her words. It clawed at her throat and her eyes. It swarmed, suffocating her from the inside out.

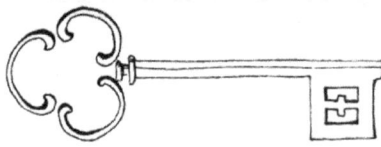

Chapter 30

B IANCA WRETCHED OVER THE side of the bed. Her head throbbed in time with her thundering heart. Her scars burned, and her fingers itched.

Sweat poured down her back in thick queasy-making drops, which didn't make sense because she was cold. So cold her teeth chattered between heaves.

Then came the light that burned her eyes. She clawed at them, trying to get them to stop hurting. She just needed one thing to stop hurting because, oh gods, it felt as if her bones were splintering.

There were hands on her, warm, gentle, calloused hands. There were curses and words muttered that she couldn't make out, but they sounded as though they were meant to be soothing.

Darkness swept in like a black knight, sweeping her off her feet. It wrapped her in its arms and pulled her down into a dreamless sleep.

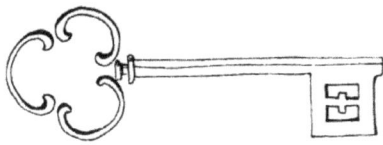

Chapter 31

THE SOUNDS OF SOMEONE sicking up drew Felix out of his slumber. As soon as he heard it, he knew. He cursed himself for not thinking of it earlier. He'd seen the way Bianca's hand strayed to her skirts more times than he was even sure she was consciously aware of.

He and Alder made it to the bedroom at the same time, and the acidic smell of vomit singed his senses as they flung the door open.

"Goddess bless, what's wrong with her?" Alder snapped, darting forward.

Felix swore, dashing in on his heels, both of them reaching for her, pulling her back into the bed. Her aura shuddered around her, the color of bile, throbbing with blood-black veins. Felix grabbed for the water pitcher beside the bed and fumbled for the clean handkerchief in his pocket. In that moment, it was a bloody miraculous thing, he never had clean handkerchiefs. He poured the water over it and started dabbing at her face.

"Those Obliviot Healers had her on some sort of medication. She kept taking it and taking it, and now . . ." His words collapsed as Bianca began to seize like a leaf in a strong wind.

He and Alder held her down as best as they could to keep her from falling from the bed or hurting herself. Felix whispered soft, soothing promises that she would be all right even as his heart hammered against his rib cage like a wild beast. When the episode subsided, Bianca lay unconscious. Alder met his gaze from where he slumped across the bed. "Now she's in withdrawal," he said, completing Felix's earlier thought.

"Do you know any healing magic?" Felix asked hopefully as he began to tuck the blankets more tightly around Bianca's fevered body.

"Some. I can do what I can, but to be frank, healing requires a deft touch, and my magic is more blunt than precise. Most of what I know are basics for the battlefield. What about you?"

"I can do my best to cleanse her aura, and I've picked up a few healing tricks. But most of what I know is in theory, not practice." Felix brushed a limp curl off Bianca's ashen face.

"Well, there is no better time to try. If you start on her aura, I'll go gather casting supplies." Bianca whimpered in her sleep, her lower lip quivering. "And I'll say a prayer to the Goddess. You should do the same, to whatever deities you hold with."

"I don't hold with any. They never seem to be listening when you need them most," Felix replied, but when he looked up, Alder was already gone.

Felix pushed away the lurking ghosts of dread that tried to creep in and haunt him as he took Bianca's slack hand in his. This wasn't the first time he'd been left alone in the dark holding someone's hand as they lay in their sickbed. But this time, Felix resolved, this time would be different.

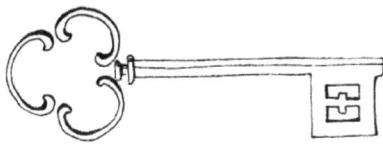

Chapter 32

SOMEONE HAD CARVED HER out. They stole away all her insides like an undertaker. Her bones were as hollow as a bird's and as fragile as glass.

Her eyelids fluttered like damp new butterfly wings in heavy, uncoordinated fits of movement.

The room came to her in fragments from behind sleep-blurred eyes. The air smelled sweet, not like the usual chemical perfume of the hospital, and the linens on the bed felt soft and loving rather than stiff and perfunctory.

Someone sat slumped in a chair by her bedside, snoring softly. It took her a moment to recognize him, Felix, the man who had been a cat. So not the hospital. Her memories began to topple like books from a bookshelf, one cascading into the other until they sat in her skull a jumbled mass of papers and binding, and she didn't know which to pick up and examine first.

Her head floated from the pillow, the movement startling the man next to her into wakefulness.

"Hey there," he whispered, his eyes wide, and his hands held up as though he were talking to a skittish animal. "You're awake. How are you feeling?"

The sound that came out of her was not the words she'd meant them to be but rather a terrible croaking.

"Right then, water first, talking after." Felix sprang from his chair and poured her a tall cup of water.

It shook when she tried to take it, so Felix pressed it to her lips. "Don't drink too quickly or you'll throw it all back up."

She did as he suggested, taking small sips until her throat no longer cracked. "What happened?" Her voice still sounded rough around the edges, but it was a vast improvement on croaking.

"Withdrawals from the medication you were on. You've been out a few days, but everything should start to feel better now that it's all out of your system. Provided you don't pick it back up again when we get back."

His last words had the ring of a question to them. Would she? She decided to shift the subject. "You sound awfully confident we'll be getting back. Does that mean you and Alder have a plan?"

Wisps of wariness spun in his eyes, but he didn't outright question her deflection. "We do. There is a festival of sorts the day after tomorrow. Loud music, dancing, food."

Bianca nodded, she remembered Alder mentioning it, and she could see where Felix was going with the plan too. "It's the perfect distraction, but what about my keys?"

Felix picked up the glass and handed it to her, a silent suggestion. "Alder thinks he knows where the old hag is keeping them. He'll sneak in and get them and meet us by the docks. He says they're usually deserted during the celebrations."

She tried to run her fingers through her hair and winced at all the snarls. "OK, but how do we get all the way back to the shrine and through the door before anyone notices we're gone?"

He leaned back in his chair, a smirk curling his lips. "We don't have to."

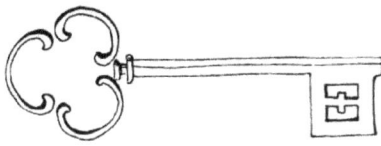

Chapter 33

BIANCA TRIED NOT TO notice the stares and whispers as she walked barefoot along the uneven cobblestone streets next to Alder and Felix. She caught snatches of words and conversations.

"Outsider . . . maybe it's possible . . ."

"Liar . . . Furies . . . Darkness . . ."

"Alder, son of Cedre . . . Such a shame . . ."

Clearly people here loved a scandalous bit of gossip just as much as people from home. She ducked her head and examined the stones in front of her feet rather intently as they walked. She'd begged Alder to let her go to the baths alone, but seeing as how she and Felix were technically prisoners, he hadn't allowed it.

The street they were on wended its way slowly past homes toward the deepest recesses of the cave. Natural light dwindled and was replaced by the pinkish crystalline glow of large glassy stalagmites spearing through the ground and walls. The air grew moist and heavy with tendrils of steam licking along the road, patches of emerald moss peeking through the spaces between the stones. The path ahead dead-ended at an archway, mosaicked around its edges with beautiful scrolling waves and tastefully nude bathing figures.

She passed under the arch and handed the two tokens that Alder had given to her to a bored-looking attendant who lounged at her desk slowly perusing a scroll. The attendant directed her to the left toward the woman's changing room with a flick of her wrist and the men to the right. Inside, carved stone cubbies with reed-woven baskets lined the walls from floor to ceiling. She pulled one out and withdrew a fluffy brown towel. She held the soft fabric to her face—she could almost picture the loth that gave its fur for the making of the towel and hear its haunting song.

She undressed quickly, tucked her things into the basket, and replaced it along the wall. Wrapped tightly in the towel, she followed the wafting steam down a hallway bored into the stone. She pushed aside a woven curtain and entered a large hollow. A hot spring poured along the back wall and ran into a series of milky pools. Stalagmites lit the room in a ghostly lavender hue. The steam hung in thick ribbons in the air, dancing around Bianca as she made her way to the pool at the back where water splashed in rivulets down the rocks. She dropped her towel and dipped a toe in the water. It was luscious. She slid the rest of the way in with a moan. As her muscles bled out tension, softening, she took a breath and dipped below the surface.

She broke back through the surface of the water, blinking droplets of water from her lashes and glided through the pool to the other side. A basket made of woven rushes perched on the edge stocked with bathing supplies. She pulled out a pumice stone for scrubbing and soap powder. Over breakfast, Alder went into excessive detail explaining how the soap was made from the roots of a plant found in the high mountains and how they had to trade with another village, a several-day journey, to obtain the pumice. She lathered from head to toe, weaving the lather through her matted tresses, carefully pulling each one free with a wince. The root soap smelled earthy and damp, much like Alder but without the smoky afternotes. She polished her skin raw, carefully skirting her scars, until it bloomed pink beneath her freckles, and for once, she didn't resent the black markings on her skin or take extra pains to scrub them away. Instead, she admired them with a glimmer of wonder and curiosity.

She swam back to the lip of the pool, leaning her head against it, letting her body float. She tried to empty her mind and let it drift, but it floated from thought to thought and bounced off of them like a leaf floating in a stream, bumping against rocks along its path. Had her parents ever visited Alatus? Had her mother ever bathed in these same pools? Being Travelers explained the business trips her father was always taking. He would leave mysteriously in the night and always arrived home just as mysteriously. She tried to catch him coming and going, and he always eluded her. When she was small, it felt like a secret game, now it was just a secret he had kept from her. One that weighed as heavy as a stone settling in her chest.

Two voices ricocheted down the corridor. Bianca's eyes snapped open, and dread soaked in, stiffening her muscles and pricking the hairs on the back of her neck. She sank into the water and peered over the edge of the pool. The two voices materialized in the steam as billowing shadows, they splashed into a wide pool a few over from hers. Bianca calculated the distance—if she was quick and with the steam for cover, she could maybe just make it out and back to the dressing room without being seen. She was loathe to let anyone see her in such a vulnerable state.

"I don't understand, Gaianna, you and Alder have been companions since childhood. You have always taken scout duty together, and sentry duty. Now this change of heart. Your father and I are concerned."

Bianca paused her escape attempt. Gaianna—that was the name of the woman who had stopped her and Alder the day before. The rude one. She sank back down and cocked her head to better hear the conversation, stuffing the inner voice, that chided her for eavesdropping and being no better than a gossip, deep down.

"Mother, by the Goddess I mean no disrespect, but could you please leave the subject alone?" Gaianna seethed. Bianca could almost hear her eyes roll.

"I don't care for that tone, Gai; I have let you stew long enough. Tonight is the Festival of the Goddess. Your father and I hoped that you and Alder would announce a betrothal this eve, and now there is this—this rift between you two. I believe we are owed an explanation."

"If you must know, we disagreed about the council's actions taken over his parents, nothing more. Now, will you let me bathe in peace, Mother?"

Gaianna's mother sighed heavily. "Goddess yes, Cedre and Dianthus have been gone quite a while. I don't understand, what is the matter with the way the council has handled things?"

"Mother, you do like to pry," growled Gaianna.

"Watch your tone. The Goddess will bestow no gifts upon those who hold disdain for their parents."

"All right, fine. Alder believes there is more to their prolonged travel, that is all, Mother. Prime elder caught him skulking around her office, seemingly looking for her lockbox. He claimed she is withholding evidence and accused Oleander of stealing vital Traveler documents from their father's house. After that incident, the prime elder tasked me with watching him and reporting his movements. He found out and has been infuriated with me ever since. So, it is as I told you days ago; we have irreconcilable differences and won't be getting betrothed."

"Well, that is a shame, dear, a real shame. I was hoping for a blossom-season wedding for you. Could you perhaps ask the brother, Oleander, to dance tonight? He would make a fine husband in Alder's stead; do you not think?"

"If you think so, Mother." Gaianna's words dripped with exasperation.

Bianca decided she'd heard more than enough. She slid quietly from the water along the rocks, keeping low. She grabbed her towel, and slinging it around herself, she dashed for the hall.

As she ducked behind the curtain, she heard Gaianna's mother cry out, "Is someone there?"

Bianca grabbed her clothes, hurriedly pulled the dress on, and dashed for the door as she did up her ties. She had a feeling Gaianna would be extremely displeased to find Bianca of all people eavesdropping on her conversation. She was halfway to the arched entry of the bathhouse when the heat of an accusatory gaze pulled her attention back. Gaianna stood, braced as if ready for a fight, wrapped in her towel, staring after her with her face pinched in anger.

"Ah good, you're done." Alder emerged with Felix a few strides behind, their hair damp, tunics clinging, Alder's brow knit together. "Is something the matter?"

Bianca looked over her shoulder again to find the changing room doorway empty save for swirling steam. She pasted a smile on her face as she turned back. "No, nothing, just lost in my own thoughts."

Alder nodded, satisfied, but Felix raised a brow and cocked his head questioningly, as though he could hear the white lie, and for all she knew, maybe he could.

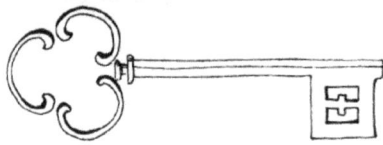

Chapter 34

F ELIX HAD TRAVELED BEFORE. Areth wasn't in fact his home Fragment, he'd spent a large part of his childhood in a Fragment called Earth before becoming Imogen's ward. He'd even traveled since with Imogen for meetings, but it still felt strange to be in a new place. The air tasted different; it felt different in his chest too, tight and thick in his lungs. Like something skulking in the shadows.

He paced along the scroll shelf, fingering and reading the tags that hung from the ends of the expansive collection. "Your father is a serious collector." He plucked at a label hanging off the end of a particularly ratty scroll and read, "*The Creation of the Doors and Void* by Arestta Flebbins, I didn't even know this text existed still."

Alder shuffled through texts, picking and choosing from piles, stuffing some scrolls into long waxed cylindrical tubes and then into a pack; others he discarded in piles strewn across the desk, chairs, and floors. He tossed a tube to Felix who caught it with catlike reflexes. "My father devoted his life to rediscovering the art of forming doors and maintaining them. I've read a bit on the subject myself; it's quite complex. Grab that one there on the shelf below, with the purple ribbon, it has to come too."

Felix tapped the first scroll into its tube gently and grabbed the next one, *Access the Void, an Architect's Guide*. He whistled. "Imogen is going to weep when she sees this one."

"That one can't be left for my grandmother and Oleander to find. He passed over it the first time, but once I'm gone, he will be back. That type of information is not something they need to have. I don't know what they're up to taking reports and keys, but I don't like it, and I don't want to leave any more fuel for their fire."

"You're doing the right thing. Coming with us," Felix reassured him quietly as he watched Alder look around the den with pain glancing off his gaze.

Alder cleared his throat, as if he could clear the vulnerability. "I swore oaths to protect my home, to protect my people. I know being what we are trumps those oaths, but I feel the breaking of them like a sickness in my gut."

Felix shook his head as he slipped the sheathed scroll into a rucksack with the others. "No, you're still keeping your oath. If Darkness is rising, everyone is in danger. You coming with us now, telling Imogen what you know, that, that could save them and so many more."

Alder looked around the room again, cinched the sack shut, and pulled the fire from the torches with a wave of his hand plunging the den into near darkness. The glow of the fire from down the hall dusted the edges of their silhouettes in a faint glow. Alder touched his sacred mark. "Goddess send you are right, Felix." He sighed weightily. "Come, we should ready ourselves for the festival."

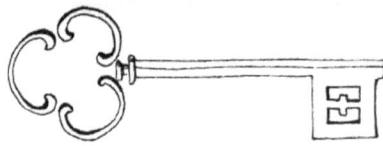

Chapter 35

DECORATIVE WOODEN BEADS CLACKED in Bianca's hair as she turned her head from side to side to examine her reflection in the mercury-glass mirror. Since she and Felix had refused to shave their heads for the festival, Alder had gone out to the market that afternoon and purchased a basket full of beads in varied shades of blue. Bianca was then subjected to well over an hour of hair tugging, braiding, and beading by a kindly neighbor woman whose daughter had long since been married off, until her scalp felt raw. She had to admit, if only silently to herself, that the effect was pleasing, if foreign. It was not how she'd ever expected to dress for a ball, or in this case festival, but from how Alder described it, Bianca couldn't tell whether there was much of a difference. Felix, however, scowled like a wet cat just pulled from a bath at the few beads and feathers put in his hair.

She smiled slightly to herself and slid a soft blue knee-length dress over her head. Birds with piercing beaks, wide wings, and gangly long legs were embroidered in flight across the fabric in a deeper shade of blue, interspersed with pale-blue clouds and turquoise posies. The garment belonged to Alder's mother, and with a bit of magic, it fit her as if it had been tailored for her curves. He'd even lengthened the sleeves for her, so they covered her scars after she'd blanched at their original length. She tugged the corset-like laces up the back until they cinched along her spine as snug as stitches.

The finishing touch was a set of blue stone bangles and a necklace—also Alder's mother's—that Alder was not willing to leave behind for his grandmother to steal once they departed. According to him, they were crafted with his mother's powers and thus carried drops of magic in them for later use if ever the wearer required. The multitiered necklace, laden with beads, stones, and even a miniature carving of the Goddess as the centerpiece, was heavy but it fit well. She did the final clasp behind her neck and ran her finger over the beads of the lowest tier, and shimmering white light rippled across the beads at her touch. She rubbed stars out of her eyes. Could she be seeing the magic Alder's mother had stored in her necklace?

The slam of the front door echoed down into the back bedroom. With a last glance to make sure she looked presentable enough, she went out to meet Alder and Felix.

"Is it done?" Felix asked Alder as she crossed into the front room, his back to her.

"It is, everything is in place." Alder froze as he noticed her presence. "Bianca, Goddess bless, you look stunning."

Felix turned, his eyes widening fractionally. "Yes." He swallowed as if he couldn't find the right words. "You clean up nicely."

Bianca flushed, he'd seen her at her worst, but he didn't have to remind her constantly. It made her insides squirm. "Yes, well, thank you. You both look quite nice as well." And she meant it. They both filled out blue linen shirts, if Alder a bit more so, tucked into neat belted black pants with navy square-cut coats over the top, twin in style to the green one Alder wore before. Though where Alder's showed his rank on the shoulder, Felix's was bare.

She looked for any hint of sorrow in Alder's eyes. Tonight, he should be getting engaged, and instead, he was about to become a fugitive. A strange, small part of her was pleased he wouldn't be marrying the cruel-faced woman, that he would be coming instead back to Areth with her and Felix. She didn't want to admit it, but he felt like an anchor, a kindred broken soul missing all the same pieces she was.

Bells sounded in the distance, reverberating through the town. "I take it that's our cue." Felix held an arm out gentlemanly to Bianca, and she took it.

Alder opened the door for them and then followed after. He offered Bianca his arm on her other side. She felt Felix tense slightly as she slid her arm into Alder's. He must be as anxious as she. But she was grateful to have them both there to steady her. There were so many things that could go wrong tonight that she could hardly breathe when she thought of them.

They joined a throng of people as they flowed down the street. Drums began to echo an adrenaline-fed heartbeat around the cavernous village, and everyone seemed to half dance, half run as they made their way toward them. The closer they came to the cave's center, the faster the crowd moved, and the harder they were pressed forward, like a river that rushed to a fall. The anticipation built around them, palpable in the air, as people let out whoops and cries.

The drumbeats rolled like thunder. A horn rang out low and loud. Bianca could barely keep on her feet as the crowd pressed them forward until they burst into the large circular opening that was the heart of the village. Everyone fanned out in a rush. Alder tugged Bianca and Felix along, a path already set in mind. She let herself be guided, her eyes spinning dizzily in every direction trying to see everything at once.

A large pyre built in the center of the circle in the shape of the Goddess sat waiting to be burned. All around, people spun fire, danced as a group of musicians played around the base of the pyre. Acrobats, scantily clad in nothing but blue feathers and paint, swung and tumbled from thick bands of silky blue material that hung from the stalactite roof of the cave. On either side of the circle, she could just make out tables so laden with food the legs bowed slightly. Erratically scattered throughout the festival were areas to sit on lavish blue rugs with plush reclining pillows. Alder towed them to one near the far end by one of the food tables, and they settled down.

A woman painted entirely blue, swathed in long gauzy strips of fabric that left little to the imagination, with large costume wings fixed to her back, swayed over to them. She knelt down to offer them drinks from a tray; her skin, dusted with mica powder, shimmered in the low sultry light emanating from the stalactites. Bianca took a cup with murmured thanks, and fire painted across her cheeks. She'd never seen so much naked flesh before tonight. While she did her best to avert her eyes, the men on either side of her seemed to have no qualms with the woman's flamboyant and elicit dress. Though she supposed for Alder, at least, this was a normal part of his culture, and Felix, well, she didn't really know anything about him, did she, other than the fact that he'd been perfectly kind while she was ill. They both had been, and for the moment that erased all their deceptions and near sinful glances at the women.

She raised the tankard of a bitter-smelling liquid to her lips and took a wincing sip. Alder chuckled at her grimace, then he leaned in close so she could hear him over the raucous music. "I wouldn't drink too much of that if I were you. It can be intoxicating. Tonight is a night to keep your wits about you."

The drums cascaded into a clamorous crescendo, then came to an abrupt halt, the last note reverberating around the cave in a split second of silence. There was a roaring cheer that followed. Alder pointed up toward the pyre. On a low dais not far in front of it's base, the council members all stood resplendent in feathered headdresses with yokes of beads around their necks. In the center of them all stood Alder's grandmother, her arms raised for silence. Oleander stood on her right with a smug curl to his lips.

"Goddess bless!" Ulrica cried, and another roar of approval erupted from the crowd below. She raised her hands once more for silence. "An age ago, this world, our home, was barren, and our ancestors fought like animals in a treacherous landscape. Then one miraculous day the Goddess hatched from the sacred shell. She saw us, and she pitied us. From her pity sprung tears that fell and moistened the ground. From that ground, she molded her vase and collected her tears. When her vase was full, she flew into the heavens and poured it over the desolate lands. She wept, and she poured until lush trees grew and water flowed. Then she wept with joy."

"In gratitude, our ancestors shore their animalistic hair and marked themselves in blue to symbolize her sacred tears and their devotion to her. An age ago on this day, the Goddess became our salvation!" More cheers drowned out her words, and she smiled benevolently down at her people.

For a third time, she raised her hands, and silence fell. "An age later, the Goddess still blesses us with her sacred waters, so as our ancestors did before us, let us rejoice. Forever may she *rain*!" She swept her arms up again, and a deafening surge of jubilation burst from the assembled. The drums resumed twice as loud, and everyone leaped to life like marionettes pulled from a shelf. They careened around one another and swiftly became a blur of color, paint smudged across an artist's canvas.

"They are coming," Alder hissed in Bianca's ear.

She followed his gaze. His grandmother and brother descended the dais and were sweeping toward them. The crowd parted deftly around her and the council, waters in the wake of a ship.

"Grandson." The prime elder nodded curtly as she came to a stop in front of them, her arm looped through Oleander's. The rest of the council fanned out around her, a wave breaking around a rock until they nearly surrounded the area where they sat. "I see you're keeping a close eye on our guests." The word guests may as well have been vermin.

She turned her head, and for a moment, her eyes bored into Bianca, who did her best to not look away despite the goose bumps that rippled down her spine. She felt sure the woman could wilt flowers with that stare. Oleander, on the other hand, she tried to outright ignore with his ostentatious leer.

"Of course, Prime Elder," Alder said stiffly with a slight bow of his head. "I am here to serve."

"How do you know they won't run away?" Oleander sucked a tooth, his voice pitched like a petulant child.

Alder gestured to the bangles along Bianca's wrist and a single cuff on Felix's. "They are bound by those just as much as if they were shackled. They can go no farther than I allow them to."

Oleander's face pinched. "Jewelry? You expect us to believe that pretty pieces of metal are keeping them here?"

Alder kept his face smooth as he stared down his brother. "No, but I expect you to believe that the magic in them is. I would show you the spell work more closely however . . ." Alder let the insinuation dangle there, Oleander's face visibly purpled.

Oleander growled, balling his fists. "You dare."

Ulrica held up her hand, and Oleander froze in his place. "Now, now, don't violate the sanctity of the holiday with fighting."

Bianca could have almost believed that she didn't like to see her grandsons fighting if it weren't for a wicked glint in her soulless eyes.

Ulrica drew herself up, like a bird preening its feathers. "Don't disappoint me, Alder." And then she was stalking off again, the council following like a staggered shadow.

"What I would like to know," Felix asked as the crowd swallowed the last council member, "is why that lot submit to an Inept like her. How has she kept her seat as prime elder so long when she can't even tell the bracelets are fakes."

Bianca hissed and swatted him. "Shush! You don't want someone to overhear you." Though she wondered the same thing herself.

Alder's eyes glanced around, scanning the crowd for prying ears. "Blackmail and coercion plain and simple." With one last glance over his shoulder, he turned to Bianca and Felix. "You two stay here, stick together. Eat, dance, act normal. I'll meet you at the farthest dock when the third moon sets over the mountains."

Bianca worried her lip between her teeth. "What do we do if the prime elder comes back?"

He shook his head. "She won't. She'll be too busy bestowing her benevolence on the people." He scowled before nodding to them both and slipping away into the crowd.

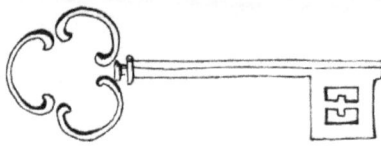

Chapter 36

ALDER KEPT TO THE shadows along the empty streets, wrapping himself in a small amount of magic to aid in stealth just to be safe. Physical adaptations were where his magic thrived. Spells for strength, speed, stealth, it was one of the reasons he'd risen through the guard ranks as quickly as he did. That, and a head for planning like his father.

He looked around for any stragglers not yet at the festivities before he ducked through his grandmother's front door and stiffened. There waiting in the quavering light of a single candle was Oleander. He lounged with his feet propped on their grandmother's desk and a crooked grin on his face, Bianca's keys knotted around his fingers. "So good of you to show up, Alder. Come for the bitch's keys, have you?"

Alder stood rooted to the floor, hands fisted at his sides, his eyes darting around the room looking for any sign of a trap, any sign that their grandmother knew he was here as well. She was the one he knew he truly needed to fear. "How did you know I was coming?"

"Because I know you, brother. I know when you're lying; I can see it in your eyes. It's the same look you used to get when you would tell Mother a tall tale when we were knee-high. She could never tell, but I could." He growled, head cocked to the side. "Or maybe she could tell and just didn't care."

Alder stepped forward, slowly, his fingers flexing to hover over where his knife was hidden beneath his feast-day clothes. Magic itched along his palms, pulsing, ready to be unleashed, but he gritted his teeth, subduing it. "Oleander . . ." His voice held both a warning and a promise.

Oleander slid his feet from the table and leaned forward. "You always thought you were better than me, didn't you? You and Mother and Father with your magic, always looking down on me." The keys chimed like warning bells as he pointed an accusatory finger at him.

"I don't know where that idea came from, brother, I've never looked down on you. I love you; we all love you." Alder tried to keep his voice calm as a rising sense of unease finger-walked up his spine. There was such venom and hate in his brother's words, a rot creeping into his soul eating away at it piece by piece.

For a moment so fleeting he thought it may have been a trick of the light, Alder thought he saw something akin to the last wavering flame of hope flit across Oleander's eyes. But then it was gone, replaced by a laugh, a hollow and broken sound filled with shards of disbelief and loathing. "If you loved me, you wouldn't be here for these." He shook the keys fisted in his hand as though they were all the damning evidence he needed.

"The two things have nothing to do with one another, brother. I can love you and still want to do the right thing. Don't you want to find our parents? Our sister?" he said through gritted teeth.

"They aren't worthy of my concern." Spittle flew from his face so contorted with rage that for a moment, he was unrecognizable as he stalked from behind the desk. "You want the keys, then come and take them from me."

Alder launched himself at his brother, suppressing his magic as it tried to flare habitually to life to speed his movements. It wouldn't be fair to his brother to use his gifts against him. His fist connected with Oleander's jaw with a sickening crack. Blood sprayed across his coat, but he was up a moment later, tackling Alder to their grandmother's finely woven rug.

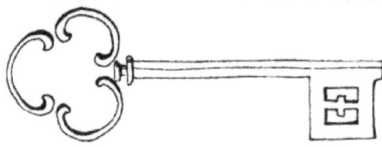

Chapter 37

FELIX GRABBED HER HAND, twirling her into the undulating crowd before she had the chance to get her feet under her. His arm snaked around her waist; his body pressed far too indecently close to hers. "Come now, Bianca," he whispered, his breath ghosting along the shell of her ear setting her nerves on end. "Everyone is watching, whether you think they are or not, and everyone expects you to act as though this night could be one of your last of freedom before the Circle comes to take us away. Dance with me. Dance like your life depends on it, because it does."

Her heart stuttered in her chest, she'd danced before, alone in her room to the threads of music from parties filtering under her door, to her mother's playing on the piano forte while her father spun her around the room. But the way these people flowed together; she'd never danced like this.

Sensing her skittishness, Felix placed his free hand on her hip guiding it along with the music. "Watch the way they move, feel the beat of the drums, and just let go."

She took a deep breath and she . . .

Just.

Let.

Go.

She let go of her worries, of her fears, her trepidations, her memories. She let the rhythm of the beats wash over her. Into her. She let it fill the empty spaces where all her grief and anxiety had been curled like venom under her skin slowly poisoning her.

She spun to face Felix, her chin tilted up to look him square in his peevishly glinting eyes. She flung one arm up around his neck, her fingers curling, the other pressed against his heart. She felt the pulse of it throb against her palm, its tempo as quick as her own. Feet stomping, she mimicked the gyrations and surging hip rolls of the women around her.

Sweat rolled down her back, heat flared in her belly, and time seemed to slow and stretch as she and Felix whooped, howled, swayed, and spun to the music.

Much to her amazement, she felt as though she'd grown wings in Felix's arms as he spun and dipped her. She'd never considered what it would be like to be this close to someone. She knew of romance; she'd read of it in books. But she'd not met many young men of her age that she found interesting in the slightest, so she'd never had the opportunity to imagine it for herself. But as Felix danced them into a dark corner reserved for lovers, she did. She could imagine the way her blood would sing if he pressed his lips to hers.

So lost was she in the fantasy that confusion struck when rather than leaning in closer, he pulled away, his fingers laced tightly in hers, and began to pull her, stumbling, down a shadowed alley.

Of course, it was all an act. And what a time to get swept up in a fantasy, when so much was on the line. Bianca chided herself as they slipped deftly into the night, their feet quick and silent along the cobbled stones.

Bianca only dared to look behind them once during their mad dash to the docks to see if anyone was following them. The buildings that stood on either side were haunting and dark. Bianca imagined the doors as screaming mouths calling to the council that their prisoners were escaping.

They pulled up just short of the docks. Felix peered around a corner and scanned the blackness for signs of life. Nothing moved. There wasn't a sound except that of the gentle lap of waves against fishing boats. He whistled a short tune, and they both held their breath in choreographed anxiety as they waited for a reply. It wasn't long before they heard the prearranged whistle sound back from the farthest dock. A figure stood from behind a cluster of barrels, and they darted across the open space to meet it.

Bianca could just make out Alder's face in the faint glow of the moon as it slid behind the mountain. His eye was beginning to swell, and blood leaked from the corner of his mouth, but he seemed otherwise intact. She suddenly became very aware that her hand was still locked in Felix's. She dropped it self-consciously, as though he could see the foolish romantic notions she'd let her mind wander to.

"Did you get it?" Her voice was barely audible, tense with anticipation.

Alder put a finger to his lips. He beamed, his teeth glinting against the dark like neat rows of polished pearls as he held it out to her. The shine of silver in his hand was unmistakable, her mother's keys.

She contained a loud sigh of relief, her heart ballooning with aching hope as she took the bracelet back from him and wound it securely to her wrist.

Felix and Alder pulled the packs out of their hiding spot, and Felix handed one to her. Bianca settled hers comfortably around her shoulders and tied the hip strap securely.

"What now?" Bianca mouthed.

Felix waved for them to follow him over to the cave wall, then he pressed a palm flat against the jagged black rock. The stains of his fingers flared liquid night. Bianca blinked against the flash. When her eyelashes fluttered open again, a soft glow in the shape of a keyhole called to her, the faint whispers of a song twined through the keyhole like thread through the eye of a needle.

She stepped forward, her arm outstretched, her fingers itching to turn the knob.

Light suddenly erupted around them. "The knife's edge, Alder, you have fallen off of it," a familiar voice whispered behind them.

Alder hissed, "Gaianna."

She raised a spear and pointed it at Alder's throat. "Betraying the council again, I see. Goddess, Alder, when will you learn?"

Alder didn't flinch, but he furrowed his brow. "No, Gaianna, when will *you* learn? The prime elder does not have my best interests or the interests of the people in her heart. She tells falsehoods, she is consumed with gaining power, she hides and steals and manipulates. She no longer walks with the Goddess, and she has no interest in finding my family. This is my opportunity to do just that. I beg of you, Gaianna. You and I were friends not so long ago. I beg of you one favor—let me go. I must find them."

A shout echoed down the alleyway, "He's escaped this way!"

"Oleander," Alder hissed through ground teeth, his hands fisted at his side. "It's now or never, Gai. Whose side are you on?"

Gaianna's jaw worked, teeth grinding, but Bianca saw her hand waver. She rolled her shoulders, once, twice, and then let the spear tip fall. "You are indebted to me for this," she scowled.

Alder bowed slightly. "On my honor."

Gaianna blew out the light, plunging them into darkness.

"Let's go." Felix growled in her ear. "Before the damn woman changes her mind and leads them straight to us."

Hurriedly, Bianca turned the knob and opened the door into the Void.

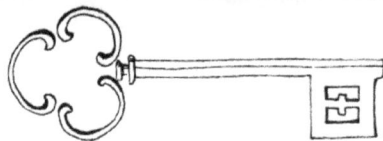

Chapter 38

THE TRIO TROMPED, STUMBLING into Imogen's dark kitchen.

A shrieking wail rent the air as jagged as broken bones dug from a grave. Putrid green light flared to life in the hearth and lamps scattered around the kitchen. A ghastly, ghoulish specter materialized from the kitchen sink, launching itself with an ear-splitting cry. It's hollowed-out eyes penetrated Bianca's soul, filling it with every fear she'd ever felt magnified by a dozen. It's wild tendrils of hair grew into ropes shooting across the space, threatening to trap, ensnare, and drag to the depths of the underworld.

All the blood drained from Bianca's face, and a raw, guttural scream flew from her mouth to match the ghosts as she darted back, tripping over Alder in her attempt to flee from the charging poltergeist.

Felix dove in front of her, his hands held up placatingly. "Maura!" he shouted. "Maura, it's just us!"

The ghost rippled. Its noncorporeal smoke-like form shifted from violent sickly green to a tender, translucent bruised blue. Its razor teeth and gaunt face were replaced with watery doe eyes and plump cheeks.

Bianca stared stunned into silence, gaping as the voluptuous spirit of an elderly woman in a serving cap and cook's apron flung herself onto Felix's shoulder with a sob. "Oh, Master Felix, ye be safe, oh thank the gods. I've been so worried for ye!"

Felix attempted to stroke the dead woman's back tenderly. "There, there, Maura, Bianca and I are back, and we've brought a friend. Where is Imogen?"

His attempts at soothing only seemed to redouble her hysterics. She started blubbering harder than ever. Bianca did her best not to gape openmouthed.

Alder stood next to her in respectful silence, seeming nearly as perplexed as her if the way he ran his hand over his shorn head was any indication.

"Maura, Maura, what's wrong? Where is Imogen?" Felix asked again in soothing tones.

Maura hiccupped, her blue-tinged hair floating around her face as she pulled away from Felix. "Oh, Master Felix, it was awful! They came in the night an' took 'em all!"

Felix's face went nearly as pale as Maura's. "Who came?"

Bianca's stomach fell into a pit, she knew. She knew before Maura even uttered a single word. Her finger's knotted into the blue skirt.

"The Furies, Master Felix. The Furies. Theys came in the night an' took them all, Imogen an' the others. They all came up to help Imogen find you and the missus there." She nodded toward where Bianca stood. "Ambushed them they did. How they made it through Mistress Imogen's wards, I'll never know."

"Dark magic," Alder piped up, his head cocked to the side. "I can smell it in the storm."

Sure enough, if she strained her ears, Bianca could hear the wind and the rain lashing against doors and windows and the unmistakable crackle of lightning along the atmosphere.

"Maura, please"—Felix gestured for her to take a seat at the table, taking the one opposite her— "tell us everything."

Bianca took a seat at the table as well, and all the lightness she'd felt from the night before crashed down around her.

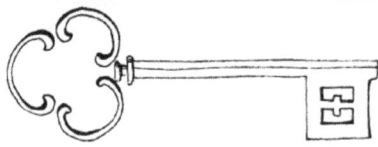

Chapter 39

FELIX WATCHED BIANCA STARE, eyes filled with frustration and tears, into the fire in the library hearth. Maura had fixed them a tea tray with flaky pastries, tiny cakes, crumbly cookies, and a soothing honeyed tea to bring up to the library with them. She'd haunted the kitchen for decades, feeding the home's inhabitants and seeing to all the day-to-day upkeep of the house with her magic. Though she was inexplicably tethered to the kitchen, she could manipulate every room in the house, lighting fires, drawing baths, making beds, growing rooms to accommodate extra guests. When Felix explained all of that to her, she'd simply shook her head, muttered about how that explained so much, and then poured herself a cup of tea that she had yet to touch.

Felix couldn't read the auras of the dead like he could the living, and right now, all the grief and dread he'd danced out of Bianca's at the festival was regrowing like a mold, covering her bright light. When days ago he'd shifted in front of her and she'd discovered the truth, he didn't think the sting of betrayal would ever leave her. Every time he caught a glimpse of the yellow smudges of it smeared across her auric field, it was a knife to his heart. Then as he sat by her bedside for days, cleansing addiction from her spirit, he prayed to all the gods he didn't believe in that if she would just open her eyes again, he could live with whatever hurt and wrath her aura unconsciously flung at him. He could take it all if she were alive. They didn't need to be friends like he originally hoped if only she would live.

Yellow streaks mottled through with black suppressed the opalescent swirls that were her essence, throbbing like a putrefied wound. His fingers itched to draw it out like poison from a bite, plucking helplessly at the stray thread on the wingback's frayed arm.

"Explain to me again why the house is different now?" Her voice sounded so small, so fractured like a chipped teacup.

He sighed, rubbing his fingers along the scar that hooked around his left eye. "Imogen placed it under an illusion, like a glamor, but for the whole house. She didn't want you to catch any hint of magic. Not at least until she knew for certain what had happened to your parents. She knew that they had kept you in the dark, and she hoped that she could find them before you discovered or had to know."

She opened her mouth to ask the question again, but he cut her off, replying before the words were out, "No, she didn't know why they hid it from you. But she did it to protect you."

She gave a derisive snort. "Protect me? Letting me think I'm insane doesn't feel very protective. All she did from the moment I arrived was to push me away, to lock me out."

"She didn't want—"

"I know, I know, she didn't want me to know," Bianca snapped, exhaustion leeching the venom from her words.

Felix sighed, flicking his gaze to Alder, who sat stoically watching the two of them argue over the rim of his cup as though it were a sporting match.

"I tried to let you know without actually telling you."

She shook her head, her lips pressed into a thin line, her hair spilling over her shoulder with the faint chatter of festival beads. "And what did you call this place again, this house?"

"A Reliquary," Alder answered. "I've always wanted to come and see this one; it's supposed to be one of the best. Mother and Father didn't like to stray too far from home, though."

"And it's a school?" He was relieved to see her finally take a sip of her tea, though she winced. It was likely cold by now.

"Think of it more like the Traveler version of the Academy. It's an institute for higher learning and a vault for all sorts of magical artifacts." Felix jumped back in before Alder could answer for him again. It wasn't that he resented him for being here and helping answer questions, but he felt as though it were his duty, a means with which to clean his conscience of all the filth that omitting the truth had built up on it. "Travelers tend to live quite a bit longer than Obliviots for whatever reason, so when they come of age, many Travelers choose to attend a Reliquary for a few years to learn more specialized magics and to study ancient texts. But it also functions as a haven for those seeking refuge. Even if you weren't related, Imogen would have been required by oath to take you in as her ward until your twenty-fifth name day."

Bianca mulled over his words, her lip pinched between her teeth. He could almost imagine he could hear her thoughts, see them fly across her aura like shooting stars.

"How long do our kind live?" she asked, but he knew what she really meant. How many years would she have with her parents if they could find them, or how many years would she have to live with the pain of their loss if they didn't?

"At least two centuries, sometimes more if you're the caretaker of a Reliquary like Imogen."

She pressed a hand to her stomach and set aside her teacup with a trembling hand. "Hundreds of years," she whispered, more to herself than to anyone else.

Alder stood from his chair, his long legs unfolding and carrying him to her side in a blink. He pressed his hand to her shoulder and gave it a gentle squeeze. "We will get them back. We will get them all back."

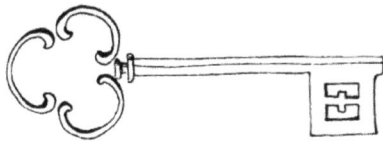

Chapter 40

THE SPECTERS SCREAMS ECHOING off the mine shaft walls were his lullaby. He didn't know how to sleep without them. They wailed, and they begged to be set free. Little did they know they were already dead. And here, that was as free as you could get.

They drifted at the edge of his pile of rags that he called a bed, whispering their regrets. But there was one face there he could never forget. She watched him with so much love in her eyes it burned. He wasn't sure if she was real, and most nights he hoped that she wasn't.

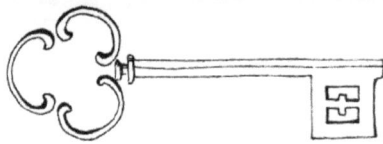

Chapter 41

THE BURNING SANDS STRETCHED out in either direction, and shimmering heat wafted across the barren orange landscape. Blisters peeled through her tender feet, and she began to run. The waste all around her rose into surging dunes. Something winked at her from the precipice. A dark silhouette.

She charged for it, her heart's efforts synchronous with her feet. Her breaths sawed against her lungs as she reached the zenith.

Before her stood an iron door. Rust marbled its knob-less surface. A keyhole stared at her like a single accusatory eye.

She reached for it, sure that if she touched it, a key would present itself, and she could see what lay behind. The idea filled her with equal parts anticipation and dread.

Thick vines sprang like vipers from the sand. Fat purple blooms burst into life along their length as they wrapped their thorny tendrils into her flesh. She tried to scream, but her bone-dry throat failed her, emitting nothing more than a rasp as the thorns grew, plunging themselves deeper into her skin. They drew from her, pulling her life's blood, drinking it in. As they drank, the flowers grew plumper and more luscious, their fragrance as putrid as a corpse, and Bianca withered. Her color leached from pale to gray, her skin shriveled, sloughing off speck by infinitesimal speck.

She tipped her head to the sky, and her last breaths seized as she beheld the swirling cyclonic mass of Furies descending upon her. The one nearest held its hand out to her as if it could claim her. Even in death, they could not let her be.

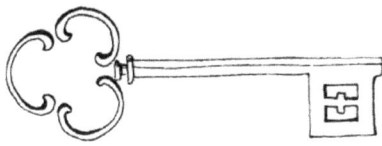

Chapter 42

"BIANCA." AN URGENT HAND on her shoulder shook her, gasping for breath into wakefulness. "You're okay. You were dreaming."

Alder and Felix's faces crowded her vision as she struggled, thrashing free of her bedclothes, soaked through with sweat.

Someone pressed a cool glass of water into her itching fingers, and she drank greedily, chest heaving. "How did you know?" She gasped between deep gulps.

Alder pointed to the rain-thrashed window where a group of flower petals were pressed between the glass clustered together. "The sprites came and found us," he said as though that should explain everything.

The room felt claustrophobic with both of their large frames filling the circular space, and Bianca felt suddenly shy being so exposed before them in nothing but her night shift. As if sensing her uncomfortableness, Felix passed her a knit blanket, one not soaked through, from the end of the bed. She took it gratefully, drawing it around her shoulders, and leaned over closer to the windowpane to inspect the clump of sprites.

Seemingly made of flat-pressed petals and leaves, twigs and brambles, the little creatures flitted along the glass, rather than in it as it appeared at first glance. "I know you," she whispered. "I thought I dreamt you." They tittered like a symphony of bees, their voices blending together.

"They said you glowed, and that you were screaming. They were worried." The springs of her bed groaned as Felix shifted to sit at its end. "What did you dream of?"

She suppressed a shudder. "It was nothing." She waved a hand dismissively. "Nothing to concern yourselves with. I have nightmares all the time."

Alder leaned against the windows along the wall, his arms crossed. He looked at her with concern-lit eyes under a furrowed brow. "If you were glowing, it means your magic was involved, so no, it's not nothing."

"He's right," Felix confirmed when she looked to him for a contradiction.

She squirmed inwardly. Sharing dreams with someone felt far too intimate; it was like being asked what you prayed to the gods for. Some things were simply meant to remain in one's soul and mind. But she did have to concede that she knew nothing about magic, and they did, so she told them of the sands and the door, the flowers and the Fury.

"A vision," Alder and Felix said at the same time, though the former said it with a tinge of derision where the later came out soaked in awe.

"A vision?" Bianca excitedly twirled an errant strand of thread around her finger. Could she really be doing magic without even knowing it? What of her other dreams?

"Yes, it's an incredibly unique magic. Diviners pop up once every few centuries or so. The magic is really powerful, but some people consider it to be, um, how do I put this . . ."

"Less than reliable at best," Alder offered.

Felix pointed at him, gesturing excitedly. "Yes, that! Less than reliable because emotions can get all muddied up in the translations of the visions, but when looked at from a purely logical standpoint, there is an abundance of evidence that they are incredibly accurate."

Alder snorted derisively, which made something wilt in Bianca's chest. Was this why her parents hid the truth from her? Was her magic little more than a joke?

"Scoff all you like, soldier, but I think what she's seeing could help us find Imogen, your parents, and all the others."

"Apologies, I didn't mean to insinuate otherwise. I just feel that perhaps this is a bit too convenient. How do we know this vision isn't a misdirection? Is it not possible for people to be sent visions?"

Felix thought for a minute, his paced steps becoming more deliberate. "Yes, yes, they can, but only if there is a strong enough connection between the two people. Which could mean . . ."

A riotous colorful hope blossomed in her chest more vibrant than a spring garden. "My parents are still alive."

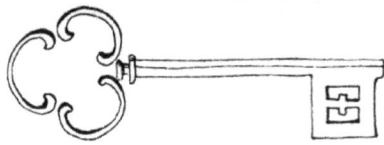

Chapter 43

BIANCA SPENT THE MORNING exploring Imogen's estate, the Reliquary. Truly exploring it for the first time with all the doors open to her and no illusions or other magics barring her way.

The main floor had sweeping arcades with baroque doors branching off into elaborate and sometimes fantastical classrooms. The ceiling in one looked as infinite as the night sky with a plush moss floor and toadstool tables. Another looked like a cartographer's dream with maps inlayed on the floor, hanging from the walls, and sprawled across the table. Each was as varied as the next, but they all held the same intoxicating aroma of crisp pages and long hours spent in thought.

The dining room, it turned out, was more of a dining hall that could grow and shrink at Maura's whims to suit the number of guests, teachers, or students in residence. Nothing looked dusty or peeling now. The gasoliers shined stardust silver with no spiders in sight.

By far the most notable difference, and Bianca's favorite, was in the library. The bookcases had had a growth spurt, the shelves reaching up toward the domed ceiling like saplings seeking the sun. A mezzanine that jutted regally from the back housed what Felix claimed were the most ancient and volatile texts the Reliquary possessed, accessible only with special dispensation from Imogen. But the best part was the orrery that speared down from the heart of the vaulted ceiling.

The representation of the Void dripped like an icicle from the ceiling, shimmering and twisting. Fragments protruded from it like irregular-shaped thorns on a rose, all uneven sizes and lengths. And around those spun suns and moons and stars. The whole thing was an endlessly pirouetting microcosm. The entirety of existence compressed into a magical clockwork marvel.

She stood gazing up at the orrery until the sky turned bruised shades, watching the firelight from the other end of the library and the reflection of lightning from the windows glimmer off all its twisting fractals.

"Your world just became a whole lot bigger, didn't it?" She glanced over her shoulder to find Felix half cast in shadow, a stack of books in his arms. She'd found that she resented his betrayal somewhat less now with the revelation that her parents lived. She'd spent the whole morning floating on a pink bubble of happiness as she reacquainted herself with her aunt's home.

Instead of answering his question directly she asked, "Do you know the names of them all? The Fragments, I mean."

He strode over to stand next to her, nearly close enough for their elbows to brush. He smelled like a hedonistic blend of pipe smoke and aged whiskey with the bittersweet undertones of dark chocolate. Strange that she should notice it now. He tilted his chin skyward to peer at the glittering cosmos, the apple of his throat bobbing before he spoke. "No, not all but some." He shifted his books to free a hand and pointed to a Fragment. "That one there is Oreyos; it's a Fragment made entirely of islands inhabited by the Naga folk, half man half serpents. They spend most of their time viciously warring with each other. Imogen has been forced to travel there dozens of times over the last century to help broker fragile peace contracts between their peoples."

Bianca found herself watching him instead of the orrery as he shifted his burden of books to the other arm so he could point to another Fragment. "And that one there is Ifris; it's home to the Drakar people. If you think the knowledge the Reliquary possesses is immense, you should see the Drakar libraries. They hoard knowledge like precious gems. Some of them come here to study or trade books. And that small twinkling one there with the four moons, that is home to the Seelie fae. They gifted Imogen a bottle of fae wine one year for solstice. I've never seen the teachers so drunk. Professor Ryhine, she teaches classes on crafting magical artifacts, normally she's as stiff as a board, but she had a single glass of the wine and got up on the table and started reciting lewd limericks." His smoky eyes turned almost iridescent as he laughed.

He turned to look at her, their eyes locking, and for a heartbeat, they were both smiling at each other, and Bianca felt as though someone poured molten chocolate all over her insides. Sweet and warm. But then the smile slipped from his face, and he took a step back, deliberately putting space between them. Bianca frowned, put a hand to her throat where all that sweet and warm had suddenly turned into a bitter cold lump, and took a step back of her own, completely unsure of what it was that she had done.

Felix cleared his throat, his attention turning to his books. "Yes, well, I've been gathering texts based on the things you saw in your vision. I have books on Fragments that have deserts, a compendium of doors and what they look like, a book on the creatures of Darkness, and I've been searching for a book on Death's Night Roses and their known uses, but I can't seem to find it. I'll have to look for it when I make a trip out to the greenhouse later."

"Death's Night Rose?" They both turned to head back toward the roaring fire in the hearth, lit by Maura the moment Bianca had walked into the library to keep the chill of the relentless storm away.

"Yes, it's also known as thieves' bane because it's usually planted around homes to deter thieves. It grows all over the Reliquary in the warmer seasons."

Bianca shuddered, remembering the effects of touching the roses from her vision. "Is that safe? To have such a lethal plant growing so close?"

"Oh yea, it's no big deal. Will's dad spelled it to leave the Reliquary's residents alone. Plus, it's well fed. I doubt even if someone did try to break in that it would drain them totally dry."

Bianca shuddered; she didn't want to ask what they fed the plant with. Or who.

The sherbet-cream glow of the fireplace washed over them as the shelves gave way to the plush sitting area where Bianca first found her parents' trunks. She'd asked Maura to poof them into her rooms for her that morning. She'd even donned another of her mother's dresses. This one was a delicate wisteria purple with eyelet lace ruffles along the hem, embroidered with violets, butterflies, and silvery crescent moons. The embroidery was done in such a way so the butterflies wings were raised off the skirt making it seem as though they were about to swarm and take flight off the stitched field of violets. Whenever she saw her mother wear it, she'd always found it magical. Now she wondered if it actually was.

They found Alder seated in one of the wingback chairs, a book propped in one hand and a cup of tea in the other. He had swapped out his native clothes for those of Arethian fashion, a neatly pressed cream shirt with a green cravat and matching waistcoat embellished with stitched tree limbs, gray trousers, and polished boots. He looked quite the picture sitting there, and Bianca told him as much.

"Well thank you. That is reassuring to hear. I feel quite out of place in them to be honest. And you, Bianca, that dress suits you. It brings out the green of your eyes if I do say so."

"Isn't anyone going to compliment my clothes?" Felix dramatically pouted as he flopped unceremoniously into a chair opposite Alder's, his legs kicked up over the arm.

Bianca's eyes flicked over his undone waistcoat, his disheveled hair, his wrinkled shirt, and his trousers with mud on the knees and frayed hems. "Apologies, Felix, your outfit is dashing. You look exactly like a bedraggled mouse that the cat dragged in."

He barked a laugh so deep and throaty that Bianca could feel it reverberate around her chest and make her heart stutter. Alder merely smirked and shook his head.

Felix clutched his heart. "Oh dear gods, Bianca, your cutting words wound me so!"

She rolled her eyes and spread her skirts to sit in the armchair next to Alder. "Can we be serious, please? What is it you think we'll be able to find in these books?"

"Well"—Felix shuffled through the books like playing cards—"if we can find a Fragment that contains all the elements of your vision, then we'll know where to find them."

"And how in the goddess's name are we to find them once we are in whatever Fragment it is that we find?" Alder leaned forward, elbows to knees, his chin resting on his balled fists.

Felix slumped into his chair farther and leaned his head back on the armrest. "One step at a time, Alder, let's not try to pay the troll's toll before he asks for it."

Alder frowned absently, fingering the fading goddess mark on his forehead. He sighed weightily. "All right, fine, we do it your way for now."

There was a loud crack, and a tray appeared on the low table in between all the chairs. A bottle of wine and some glasses, cheeses, sausages, nuts, fruits, and olives were arranged in a cornucopia of color.

Felix hopped, books swiftly discarded onto the floor, and eagerly snatched the bottle of wine. "Oh, Maura you sly old girl, Dead Cat wine, and a century old vintage at that. Fantastic!"

Bianca's lips curled. "Dead Cat wine?" she asked with a lyrical hint of laughter.

Felix winked and with a flourish of magic popped the cork and poured her a chalice full. "Ladies first." He bowed to her, offering the cup, which she accepted with a grin.

Bianca took a sip; the wine was purple, velvety, and honey sweet. It wrapped her instantly in a warm gauzy cocoon that was like a hot summer's day just before sunset with storm clouds on the horizon.

She popped a violet cherry into her mouth, already pitted and destemmed by Maura, its sultry flavor a delicious compliment to the wine.

"So what can I do to help?" Bianca asked as she rooted around on the tray for more tasty treats.

"Have you had any more visions?" Alder swilled his wine glass before taking a pursed-lipped sip.

Bianca shook her head. "I don't think so. Is there a way to, I don't know, induce them?"

"That should be a last resort." Felix pulled a small silver case from his breeches pocket. Inside, there was a row of bizarre-looking cigarettes tightly rolled in black paper.

"It shouldn't be an option ever," Alder clipped as he leaned over and took an offered cigarette.

Bianca declined one when Felix offered, thinking of the noxious fumes from Imogen's pipe. "Why not?"

"Because"—with a snap, blue flame danced at Alder's fingertips, and he quickly lit the black paper pressed between his lips—"that requires blood magic, which is an unpredictable abomination."

Felix puffed his cigarette to life, and lilac-colored wisps snaked from its end. "Don't be such a prude, Alder, blood magic is a natural next step to our existing magic. There isn't anything wrong with it."

Alder scoffed. "We'll have to agree to disagree on that point, Grayson."

Felix shrugged apathetically and took a long drag of the smoke that Bianca found she surprisingly didn't mind. It was reminiscent of cinnamon and cloves but somehow more alluring. "Well, give me something to read then, let me help with research," she suggested.

"All right"—Felix plucked a book from his stack— "try this one, it's an in-depth history of the Breaking. Look for anything on the creation and uses of Fury."

Bianca took the hefty leather-bound tome and cradled it gently in her lap, her finger tracing the gilt lettering on the front, *Beyond the Breaking* by Bartemus Starkey. "The creation of the Fury?"

"They were made, not born." Alder's lip curled in disgust. "Abhorrent beings spawned by the Darkness."

"If the Darkness is trapped, how is it spawning new minions then?" Unease spidered down her spine and began to spin webs along her ribs.

Felix tapped the side of his nose. "Ah, and that's the winning question. *If* we know precisely how they are made, then maybe we can decipher who, where, and how they are being made now."

Bianca squared her shoulders. "Right then, I guess I better get reading then."

The others picked up books of their own and did the same. The shuffle of pages and the pop of the fire serenaded them as they read.

Bianca cracked the cover and turned to the first chapter entitled "The Formation of the Circle, Who Were They, and What Were Their Real Motives."

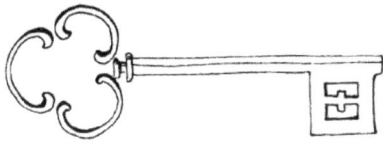

Chapter 44

THE PAGES IN FRONT of Felix blurred as the words written in a dead runic language danced across the page, indecipherable. It wasn't that he didn't have a head for languages, they were one of his special areas of study, and this one was normally not that challenging. But between the wine, the smoke, and the bewitching scent of the woman seated across from him, he couldn't seem to make the words make sense.

He swallowed hard, shoving down the coals of acrimony and disquiet burning in his throat. *She is not for you, she is not for you, she is not for you,* he chanted over and over to the beat of his thundering heart and the pounding of rain on the windows. As the last of his kind, he was doomed to a life of solitude. He could never take a mate outside of his species and doom her to a childless existence. It would be unfair of him to ask that of any female, and for a non-changeling to bear the offspring of a changeling was to sentence them to a gruesome death.

These were the facts he'd grown up with. And he was at peace with it. That wasn't to say he hadn't had the occasional casual dalliance or sordid tryst now and then because he had, so long as he and his partners both had taken a contraceptive tonic of course.

It had, of course, earned him a reputation, but he was fine with being the scholarly rake, taking women and knowledge in equal parts, using and discarding them. Respectfully of course.

But then she'd walked through the front doors of the Reliquary, and her aura sung to him, and he couldn't help but trail her, to watch her, to help her discover the truth. It was all for her own good, he'd told himself, he was just helping her because she'd lost all the same things he had, because she was pitiable. But he knew all along it was a lie.

As much as her looks of betrayal stabbed at him and chipped away at some aching part inside of him, the look she'd given him earlier, when their elbows had nearly kissed up against one another, that look. That look was worse. It was heated and tender and genial and all the things he couldn't let her feel for him. He had to keep her at arm's length just long enough for them to find Imogen, the teachers, and her family, so they could take the temptation of her away from here. Because despite his rakish reputation, he would not take a woman like Bianca to bed. Women like her were not for dalliances or trysts. Women like her were worthy of slow seduction and romantic notions. They were women worthy of carving your heart out for. Worth burning for.

Friends, he could keep his distance and still play at being friends.

As the day waxed on, the hour growing later and later with each swollen tick of the clock, he could see Bianca getting more uncomfortable. She rubbed her arms where he knew scars dashed down her skin under the layers of her sleeves. Her hand strayed over and over to her pocket, the ghost of addiction still clinging in the periphery of her aura, as she turned page after page until the movement brought a wince every time. And still she did not retire or complain.

He stilled as she looked up, sensing his gaze as surely as if he'd trailed his fingers down her neck. "What is it?" she asked, her voice tinted with the haze of long studious hours.

Felix shifted in his seat trying to appear nonchalant. "I was wondering if you might like to join me in the greenhouse? There are a few plants I think might interest you, and we can search for the book I mentioned earlier. Alder, care to join?"

The nymph shook his head, his eyes never leaving the page. "I think I may be on to something here, you two go ahead."

She smiled softly, and it was a ray of sunshine that cut through the clouds around his dark heart. She set her book down and stood. "That sounds wonderful."

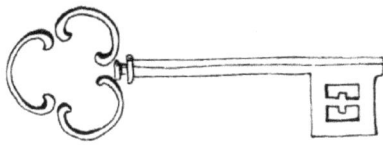

Chapter 45

"**Y**OU HAVE TO USE the paralytic before it wakes up!" Felix lunged past Bianca. She stepped out of the way as the pointed syringe in his hand swung by her head. It sank deep into the greenish bark of the dwarfed tree on the greenhouse table behind her. Its sinuous branches writhed and shrieked as the needle buried itself deep into the woody flesh of the trunk, then they went limp. Felix righted himself and wiped the sweat off his brow. "I give you the Gorgonian Willow," he said triumphantly.

"It's terrifying," she breathed, "and beautiful." She stepped closer, her heart thrumming, and raised a hand to stroke the sedated leafless branches of the tree. The green and gray bark appeared distinctly scaly, and at the tip of every branch hung a heavily lidded snake's head.

Felix grabbed one and squeezed its jaw open to show her its fangs. "This tree is dwarfed so its venom is less potent, but in a fully grown tree, the venom can turn you into stone. This one just gives you a bad case of stone dermatitis for a few weeks. It's still not fun and can give you some nasty scars if you scratch it too much."

"Why keep one then?" Bianca smoothed the sash of her gardening apron as she tentatively leaned in closer, careful not to jostle the branches or to get too close to Felix.

"Ahh!" Felix dug through the massive tangle of branches and pulled out one that was shedding. "Because the skin of the branches has powerful healing properties when turned into a poultice. It works on any skin ailment except, of course, for the skin condition its venom causes. It can even be used to grow new skin over cuts and burns." He looked at the sleeping tree fondly. "It's the only one in Areth as far as I know. Heck, it might be the only one outside of Gorgonia."

"Here." He passed her a blunt-hooked knife no longer than her palm. "Help me scrape the skin off of the ones that are shedding."

She took it, letting it rest delicately in her fingers as she pushed her way tenderly through the branches until she found one and, following his example, began to slough off its loose flesh. It was not unlike peeling a potato, a cold, venomous potato.

They worked without speaking for a time, with nothing but the symphonic storm raging around them casting the whole greenhouse in an eerie green glow reminiscent of an angry ocean tide.

Her arms began to shake, her scars stretching and burning from the repetitive motion. She paused her work, turning away, and discreetly tried to massage the pain from them, hoping Felix was too preoccupied to notice.

Felix cleared his throat behind her. She peered back at him over her shoulder. His waist-coat hung unbuttoned over a wrinkled gray shirt, his shirtsleeves rolled up haphazardly exposing magic stained arms and lithe fingers. "The poultice I mentioned will help with those too. If you would like me to make you a batch."

She felt his eyes rove over her arms and body, his gaze deep and penetrating as if he could see the innermost parts of her, as if he could see the way her withered and broken heart skipped a beat. He'd looked at her like that the night before too. Scarlet flames licked up her neck and face.

He stepped away. She chided herself; she was imagining things. Starved for affection in the wake of her grief and imagining things.

Then why do you not feel the same way when Alder looks at you? a despicable voice in the back of her innermost thoughts whispered. She silenced it swiftly, pasting a small gracious smile on her face. "That's very kind of you. I would be most grateful."

He nodded once before he ducked his head and began to gather their harvest into a woven rush basket, careful to tuck a waxed cloth over it to protect their bounty from the rain.

Bianca sucked in a lip, gnawing the corner of it as she drifted away from the worktable to examine some of the other flora thriving in the hothouse. There was a long row of beds planted with common herbs that she recognized, like chamomile and lavender. But then came beds of fantastical things she did not. There was a large saffron and vermillion shrub that Felix had called Flaming Dame. Next to it grew a thin-stalked plant that was labeled as Bungle-Weed with pearlescent pink-petaled buds protruding along its spindly branches. A trellis constructed against the far wall was covered in a black curled-leaf vine and with a label that read "Crimson Creeper" with a warning not to touch it, though it wasn't crimson, which left Bianca to wonder at the meaning of its name.

She circled back to where Felix had just finished tidying the worktable to find him dangling small frozen mouselike creatures in front of the snapping jaws of the wide-awake Gorgonian Willow. She took off her apron and hung it on a peg near the door. A vein of blue lightning silhouetted the Reliquary, gilding its windows silver. The resulting thunder left the windowpanes trembling. Bianca gasped, her hand jumping to her throat.

"When do you expect the storm to break?" Bianca called over her shoulder to Felix, her fingers pressed to the glass window as she watched the fog slink through the trees at the edges of the grounds. "I'd like to go see Will soon if I can."

"I don't think it will."

Bianca startled and spun around, surprised to find Felix so close she could reach out and touch him. "Why, why not?" Her throat constricted, her voice coming out breathier than she'd meant. Just imagining things, she was just imagining things.

He squinted out over the grounds. "Like Alder said, it isn't a natural storm. Great evil was done here when everyone was taken. It took a lot of incredibly dark magic to do it. It probably won't go away until everyone can be recovered and brought back, righting the balance. And even then, it might not work, I've never read about any magical repercussions of this magnitude before, though I imagine it had to have happened in the Darkness wars. It's just a matter of finding the right text on the subject. So I'm afraid your next tea-leaf reading will have to wait." His lips curled in a bemused smirk.

Bianca smiled. "I don't know that that's an experience I'd care to repeat anytime soon."

They laughed, and their gazes slammed into each other and for a stuttering heartbeat Felix's eyes burned opalescent. A beat later, the flame was extinguished, his eyes so cold and clouded that Bianca knew that once again her mind played tricks on her.

He tore his eyes from her. "I'll be right back. I need to go check the office for that herbology book."

He stalked off, leaving Bianca in stifling silence.

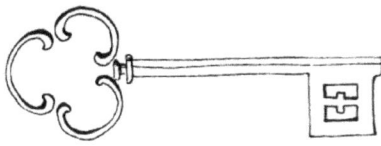

Chapter 46

THEY RAN FROM THE greenhouse across the open yard to the back servant's entrance through the driving rain and fog. She held up the hem of her sodden dress. Felix ran a half stride ahead of her, the basket laden with their harvest covered in an oiled cloth tucked in the crook of his elbow along with the book he'd been searching for.

They flung open the door and stomped the mud from their feet, hers bare, Felix's in boots. A shrill squeal of delight drew their attention as a bespectacled blur of frazzled red hair and a colorfully patched cloak flung itself across the kitchen and wrapped itself around her and Felix in an enthusiastic embrace.

"Will! What on Areth are you doing here? How did you make it here in the storm? Is everything all right?" Felix ran a worried hand over her soddened amber hair before running a worried eye over her as if assessing her for potential injuries.

A jealous hand gripped Bianca's heart at the tenderness between them, but she quickly forced it away. So what if there was something between them?

Will batted his shoulder playfully. "Stop fussing, you mother hen, it's just a bit of water, and I've had enough of that from Maura." She turned to Bianca and wrapped her in an extra hug, one that Bianca discovered she was all too happy to return, unlike their last encounter. Will pulled back and peered at her, much in the same worried manner that Felix had assessed her, her eyes made overlarge by her round spectacles. "You look well, Bianca, all things considered, far better than the last time I saw you. Though I do come bearing news that may unsettle you both. Come, Maura has sent tea up to the library where your friend waits. You'll want to be sitting when you hear it."

Felix's brow buckled. "I'll go change out of these wet clothes and meet you there." He nodded a quick goodbye, touching Will gently on the shoulder before ducking onto the servant's stairs.

Will smiled and looped her arm through Bianca's, steering them both to the stairs. "Did you want to change before we meet the gentlemen?"

Bianca shook her damp curls. "No, that's all right. I'm anxious to hear this news of yours."

Will's eyes darkened, her brow pinched. "Yes, well, it is quite unsettling. Let's talk about something more cheerful! Has Felix found the time to test you to see where your magical aptitudes lie?"

"No. No testing, though he does believe my peculiar dreams are visions."

"Ooo, how exciting," Will cooed, squeezing her arm as she did a giddy little skip at the top of the landing. "I've always loved the divination arts, obviously. Though my main aptitudes are in herbal and plant magic, so the only divination I'm any good at is the tea-leaf readings. I wish I had an exotic ability like Felix; his aura reading skills are quite rare."

Bianca's curiosity piqued, and her brow arched. "Really? I had no idea."

"Oh yes, there aren't many like him. Imogen had a bear of a time tracking down a tutor to train him."

"Is his magic related to his being a changeling?"

"Oh no, Travelers magic is different and unique across all beings. Though, it's said that your abilities and your mate's will complement one another, though, like two sides to the same coin, but that they will also bring out new and stronger magics when you combine them."

They reached the library doors, which Will opened with a flick of her fingers, her magic stained their tips a pretty rose gold.

Alder and Felix stood as they entered, both of them bowing slightly at the waist as though they were ladies entering a ball or guests arriving at an elegant dinner party. Felix's damp hair flopped over his forehead as he gave them both an indolent and appraising grin, and it shattered the illusion, though the idea of him dressed in tails looking at her that way made the corners of her mouth tilt up ever so slightly.

She took her usual chair by the fire next to Alder, and Will took the one by Felix. "So, Will"—Felix pulled a smoke from his pocket and lit it—"give us this dire news."

She sighed wistfully, her hands twisting in her bright-pink skirts. "Well, there's been an attack, in Thorne Ferry, on the inn. It would appear the Fury broke in and murdered your former governess, Bianca. I'm so, so sorry to be the one to tell you, I know you must have been close, and this is probably quite a shock."

Bianca didn't know what to say, pity and loathing knotted itself confoundingly around her heart. She didn't care for the woman, she hated her even, but to die at the hands of those beasts was an end she wouldn't wish on anyone, not even Perdita Rue. "But I don't understand. She didn't have any magic."

Alder pressed a steaming mug of tea into her hands, his blue eyes swimming with sympathy, before he turned back to Will. "Were there any other attacks?"

Will shook her head, her wild hair molten in the firelight disarrayed around her like the sun's corona. "The innkeeper was taken and a handful of other villagers who were dining at the inn at the time, all with full or partial Traveler heritage. Then, of course, Imogen and a few of the other professors were taken, but Faerlyn was left largely unharmed. My father and I gathered together the townsfolk right after the storm struck to strengthen the wards around the village and the Reliquary. Though there have been rumors of things stalking the edges of the wardings in the night, and the merfolk have been uneasy. Father said many of them have decided to swim down the coastline toward Briar Lark. We haven't had word from them since the bridges flooded, but it's a safe bet that they're also being affected by the magical stain of the storm."

"What does that mean?" Bianca's head reeled from all the dizzying information, and she was suddenly glad Will had suggested they be seated for the news. She took a long sip of tea, finding it full of steadying and soothing herbs. Gods bless Maura, it seemed she always knew what tea to fix.

Felix rested his elbows on his knees and shook his head, the smoke's glowing end dangling from between his fingertips. "It means we don't have a whole lot of time."

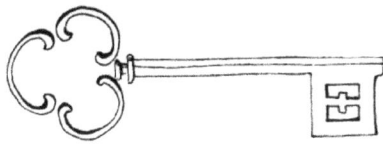

Chapter 47

ALDER LOOKED OVER THE rim of his tumbler full of smoky amber whiskey at Felix where he sprawled in his armchair, one leg cast over its arm. "You have a theory, don't you, Grayson?"

Felix sighed. He'd had that same faraway look ever since the women had taken their leave for the evening. Something stirred in that mind of his, and Alder wanted to know what it was he saw that he didn't. He wasn't fond of people solving puzzles before he did.

He sat up, plucking his wine bottle from the floor and swilling the scarlet liquid before taking a pull straight from the neck. "I've been hunted before. I know the signs." He gazed distantly into the crackling flames as though he could see his own past flickering in them before he looked up, meeting his gaze, his eyes steely. "I think the Fury are looking for her. I believe they scented her magic on the governess."

Alder blanched, his fingertips straying to the Goddess mark. "But Will, they didn't go after her?"

"I don't think she'd spent enough time with her. Bianca was there an hour, maybe less, whereas the governess and Imogen had been around her for days. Granted, Imogen wasn't in as close proximity, but they were still under the same roof."

He lit another of the black herbal cigarettes he habitually smoked and offered one to Alder, who took it. The effects of it were soothing, and he desperately needed that at the moment when his heart was pounding retreat against his ribs. Felix leaned back in the chair, his hand raking through his hair. "They must have tracked her here to the Reliquary. The wards were strong, but not as strong as they once were, and when they didn't find her, they took Imogen and the professors. But that still begs the question"—his eyes locked on Alder's once more as lightning struck outside accentuated by the tumultuous roll of thunder—"what is it about Bianca that they are so interested in? And why didn't they manage to take her before?"

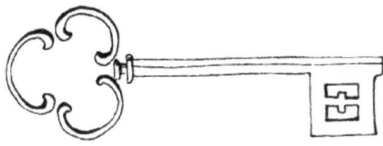

Chapter 48

THE LIGHTNING DANCED JUST outside the windows of her tower room. It crooked its fingers around the tower, tapping at the panes, inspecting her like a spider under a glass. She sat cozied up under the covers that smelled freshly laundered in her favorite night shift of ivory trimmed in lace and embroidered with dainty chamomile flowers and doves. She was pleasantly sleepy from a day of learning to use her magic and studying.

She pulled the pins from her hair, letting it tumble free, spilling over her shoulders and back as she pored over the book in her lap. When she'd climbed the ladder for bed at dark, a dish of candied violet shortbread cookies and a steaming cup of spiced plum cider with whipped cream waited for her on her bedside table courtesy of Maura.

That ghost is a gods-send, Bianca thought while she bit into buttery cookie after buttery cookie and chased each down with a sip of cider. How her magic had transcended even death was a mystery Bianca wanted to solve, but more pressing matters needed to be attended to first.

The Fury. She'd reached a chapter in *Beyond the Breaking* that detailed what Travelers knew of the creation of the Darkness creatures. The subject curdled her blood as she read.

"The Darkness, though not corporeal beings, are known to possess what we call the Instruments of Darkness. They are a sort of parasitic host, capable of containing the multiple consciousnesses and magics of the Darkness. The Darkness feeds on their emotions, namely their worries, fears, and grief. It is through their Instruments that they can wield their magic to its fullest potential, often creating hordes of unfathomably evil and bloodthirsty creatures whose taste for magic is unquenchable. The rituals that give birth to these monstrosities require large blood sacrifices; oftentimes whole villages were slain to acquire enough blood to make a small band of these creatures.

"The most vicious and intelligent of these beings were known as the Fury. They were not just mindless savages as many of the others born of the blood of Darkness. They could smell magic at great distances and could even wield in small parts magics of their own, making them formidable and terrifying adversaries. Even more concerning, toward the end of the Darkness War, there were several incidents of Fury being spawned by Instruments who were not actively possessed using what could only be stolen Traveler magic since it is a little-known fact that Instruments must be magicless beings. It is also important to note that Inept Travelers are also at risk of possession, though they cannot be used to the same degree. Those with full magic seem to be completely immune to possession, though the touch of Darkness can taint and twist a Traveler's natural abilities and turn their magic against them, effectively destroying them from the inside out."

Bianca stilled, breaths quickening as she reread the passage. Book in hand, she dashed down the ladder and to the library. She burst through the double doors.

Alder jumped to his feet, a small, curved knife drawn from gods knew where in one hand, and upset a precarious pile of books stacked by his feet, "Great goddess, Bianca, you startled me. What's wrong?" His brows stitched together as he resheathed his knife up his sleeve.

"An Instrument of Darkness." Bianca gasped for air. "The Fury must have been made by an Instrument. It's here in *Beyond the Breaking*. Starkey says an unpossessed Instrument can steal magic to spawn Fury."

Alder's umber cheeks turned pallid, and he sank back down in his chair. "Dear goddess"—he touched the mark on his forehead, turning the movement into an anxious sweep across his stubbed hair—"That's why they are being taken. Like fruits for a harvest."

Bianca shoved the errant locks of her hair behind her ears and took her usual chair next to his. "But how, how do you steal someone's magic?"

Alder's hands shook as he reached for his tea. He took a sip and winced. "Something stronger, please, Maura, and call Felix to the library please, would you?" Alder asked the empty air. A heartbeat later, a bottle of honey-colored liquid and three frosty chilled tumblers appeared on the table. He murmured his thanks to Maura and poured a stiff three fingers worth of liquor into each glass. He passed one to Bianca before throwing back his whole glass in one go and pouring himself another.

Bianca cupped her glass between quavering hands. Each moment Alder stalled; terror filled her lungs until each breath had to be dredged up from beneath its strangling depths. "Alder, please, just tell me."

The full weight of his bloodshot eyes bore into hers. "To steal someone's magic, to truly steal it and be able to wield it, you need to not only hold their magic, but also their life in your hands. The most logical and swiftest way to do that is to drain them of all their blood."

Numbly, Bianca pressed the rim of her glass to her lips. The amber liquid singed as it went down, but she barely felt it. The blood rushing in her ears suddenly sounded dreadfully like the ticking of hundreds of thousands of clocks. Each one maddeningly ticking down the seconds until her parents' end, or until theirs. She wasn't sure which.

When she finally looked up from her drained glass, she saw Felix standing by the mantel, one hand bracing himself, keeping himself standing as he took the news from Alder. On his face he wore a mask of pain written in words of torment that contorted his features. She knew she wore the same one.

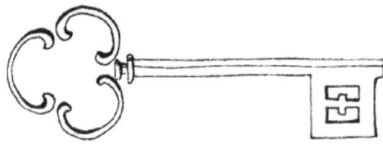

Chapter 49

T HEY DRESSED FOR MOURNING whether intentionally or not. Alder had magically
altered his clothes to the deep navy hue traditional for funerals in Alatus. Bianca
wore a black gown that Felix loathed himself for thinking looked stunning on her. Her
hair fell in loose waves reminiscent of a widow's veil.

He had even donned his best. Though his gray velvet waistcoat was rumpled, it was
buttoned with all matching buttons over a black linen shirt. He couldn't find a cravat,
though. He ran his hands through his hair in a last-minute attempt to tame the tangled
locks before surrendering.

The three of them assembled in front of the door where they had summoned it in the
downstairs sitting room. It felt a more suitable place, more formal than the library. The
song plucked at his heartstrings more firmly with it present, though he could always hear
its siren song trying to lure him in, calling him for help.

But today they weren't here to answer. They were here to add their song to the
cacophony. To try and call someone, anyone, for help.

"I don't know what I'm supposed to do." Bianca's voice hitched as she looked at the
door and Alder standing reverently next to it.

Felix looked down at her and attempted a smile, but it felt lopsided and wholly wrong.
"Don't worry, give me your hand and I'll help guide your magic."

She nodded and held it out to him, just like that, so blindly trusting. He would have
to talk to her about that one of these days. With a stuttering heart, he took her and drew

her to the door. He pressed her palm flat to the wood and lay his atop hers, their fingers intertwined. Alder's hand joined theirs only a hair's breadth away.

Felix drew his magic into his fingers, the pins-and-needles sensation a familiar relief. Bianca's magic flared on instinct, answering the call of his. He tugged it along gently, pulling it bit by bit, coaxing it to take the same shape as his. On the periphery of his awareness, he noted Alder's blue-tinged magic flowing into the same pattern as theirs.

The magic did its work. From them it pulled the song loose from their throats. It dredged up every clinging fibrous feeling of anguish, spinning it and weaving it into a tapestry of song. It was a despondent dirge embellished with their grief and misery. When it had gouged out every last pocket of feeling from them, it sent their song keening into the Void to fit seamlessly with the lamentations of the other Fragments.

Bianca's body sagged into his. He wrapped an arm around her waist. Every place her body touched his prickled with awareness as he helped her to the settee so she could regain her composure.

He grimaced as he stepped back, still feeling her, her aura enmeshed with his from their conjoined magics. With a few discreet flicks of his wrists, he plucked the coils of her aura off his and set them back where they belonged. But rather than his aura returning to normal, it looked as though it had been wounded, stabbed through with holes where the pieces of her had been. His heart felt the same.

He looked over at Alder who slumped, shoulders wracked in silent sobs, against the door. His fingers were laced behind his neck, locking his head to his knees, hiding from the world.

"When will we know if it worked? If someone will answer?" Bianca's voice rang hollow.

Alder lifted his head, his azure eyes rimmed with quicksilver tears. "We won't. They won't. Didn't you hear them? Our cry for help is but one among thousands. No one is listening."

Something unnamable gripped Felix's heart in its fist, squeezing, digging in its claws, refusing to let go. "We are. We are listening."

Part Two

The Darkness could see shadows of movement on the other side. It could hear the floundering of hearts as they released their magic. Each fading beat reverberated in the hollow around it, music to its ears.

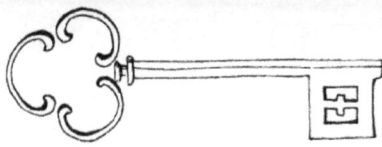

Chapter 50

THE DOOR WAS CARVED of windswept sandstone, inlaid with what should have been a mosaic mural had so many pieces not been chipped and missing.

Bianca suppressed a shiver as the ever-present glow of the Void trembled around them, plunging them into split heartbeats of darkness at a time. The air also now held a hint of decay, like the smell of a coming autumn but much less pleasant. "What's wrong with the Void?" Her voice quavered. "It's different than it was the last time we were here."

Alder shook his head, his brow buckled and his hands braced on either wall as though he suspected the stairs were about to drop out from under him at any given moment. "I don't know, but I don't like it. This was a terrible idea."

Felix grinned lopsidedly. "Come on, what's not to like? Behind this door is a desert Fragment, and the song has been sung behind it. We both get to help others and investigate a desert for hidden signs of Fury or an Instrument of Darkness."

Alder hissed through his teeth. "And if we find either, we are woefully underprepared."

"You look like you have enough knives on you to outfit a whole army. How is that unprepared?" Felix quirked his brow. "I will concede, though, that the Void is feeling a bit, what's the word?"

"Creepy beyond belief?" Bianca supplied.

He tapped his nose twice and winked. "Not the words I would have used, but yes, that description is quite adequate. Shall we then?" He stepped aside to make room for Bianca.

She trailed a finger along the keyhole, and the sound of the keys tittered against her wrist like gossiping sprites. She dashed away the tears in her eyes, wrung out of her from the piercing notes of the song as it swelled around them. As she lay her itching palm on the crumbling stone, the song swooped lower, a symphonic whisper of secret pain that Bianca felt as an echo of her own.

A key at her wrist grew, its bow the shape of wings in flight spanning the width of her hand. Her fingers began to glow around the stem of the key, her magic warming to life beneath her skin. As she pressed the head of the key into the keyhole, stars erupted along the back of her hand, shooting across her skin to drift among the chaos of other runes that swirled there. A tendril of air whooshed from the keyhole, caressing Bianca's cheek as the tumblers clicked. It whispered indecipherable nothings against the shell of her ear that sounded like sonnets of death.

She stumbled back, barely righting herself before her foot caught the lip of the landing. Alder's hand jumped out to steady her. Her eyes flung wide and wild. Felix reached for the door, his fingers curled around the latch.

"Wait," Bianca gasped, her hand outstretched. She just barely managed to pinch the fabric of his sleeve between her fingers. "I think Alder might be right; maybe this is a bad idea."

Felix's lip twitched into a half smile. "Come on now, Hastings, it's too late for that." And he flung the door open wide.

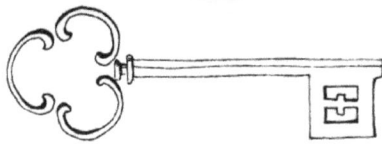

Chapter 51

BIANCA CROSSED THE THRESHOLD into the shadowy chamber beyond. It reeked of myrrh and soured wine.

"Can you see . . .?" The cold bite of steel nipped at her jugular, slicing off her words, stilling her breaths. She wanted to call out to Alder behind her to warn him and to Felix ahead, but fear tangled her thoughts. An unfamiliar calloused hand wrapped around her mouth, pulling her close, pressing her into a firm, broad body.

Alder entered, shutting the door behind him, muttering under his breath.

In a flash, light flared, blinding her with an ivory glow, searing her pupils. She swore against the palm clamped over her mouth, blinking back tears.

"What's this we've caught here? Little rats sneaking into the sanctum?" A cool female voice with a hissing lisp echoed around the chamber. "The question is what kind of rats are you? The normal varmints looking for loot, or do you belong to my stepfather?"

The light dissipated, breaking up and drifting toward amber lamps hanging on gilded chains where it settled, bringing out the little details of the room built of crumbling gray stone with chipped mosaics inlaid in the floors. But her eyes wouldn't take in the details; instead, they stuck on the bead of blood welling over silver steel, trailing down the apple of Felix's throat and the talon-tipped fingers that held it there.

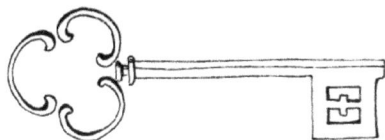

Chapter 52

ANGELIC WINGS HUNG FROM her back like billowing white clouds threaded with silver and gold. Her coppery skin seemed to glow from within, swathed in a jeweled dress that fit her as snuggly as a lover's caress and refracted the light that glowed from the lamps like shards of a shattered sun.

Elaborately plaited braids crowned her head, studded with gem-tipped pins, leaving the rest of her copper locks to tumble effortlessly over her shoulders in ethereal waves.

Alder sucked in a breath that sounded as sharp as glass as he dropped his knife and fell to his knees, prostrating himself before the woman's feet. "Goddess." Awe knit the breathless syllables together.

"Come off it, Alder." Bianca didn't have to look at Felix to hear the eye roll in his voice, somehow still snarky with a knife to his throat. "She's not your Goddess, she's a sphynx. Look at her claws."

Bianca's eyes landed once again on the hand that clutched a wickedly curved knife. Long onyx claws that looked uncomfortably like a Fury's protruded from the tips of her fingers where nails ought to be. Bianca's scars throbbed just looking at them. But past that her fingers were stained, nebulous, with magic.

"*She* would still like to know what the three of you are doing here?" The sphynx quirked an eyebrow impatiently, her hand on the knife unwavering.

Alder scrambled inelegantly to his feet, his embarrassment painted across his face. "I, we, well, what I mean to say is . . ."

"Oh, for god's sake, man, pull yourself together." Felix choked, half laughing at the larger typically unruffleable man. He flashed a charismatic grin at whomever held the knife to her throat, the corner of his mouth stitched up in an arrogant twist and gave a slight nod of his head. "We are Travelers, here in reply to the song."

"You? You three are all the Circle deigns to send the noble Fragment of Gypette in its hour of need?" She snarled, lips peeling back over an impressive set of chiseled canines, but she withdrew her blade from Felix's neck, nodding for Bianca's captor to do the same.

Bianca sucked in a relieved breath and darted away from the hulking man who'd held her over to where Alder stood. Her captor was a full head taller than either Alder or Felix, with the top of his onyx hair tied in a high knot at the back of his head, leaving the rest shaved exposing a burn   that marred the left side of his jaw and neck. His skin was coppery like his female counterpart, though much richer, and his hands were flecked not with magic but scars. He caught her staring, and for a breath-catching moment, they locked eyes. His left was a molten gold; his right was a blue so pale it was nearly white. He was handsome in a dangerous way that made her throat dry.

She quickly averted her gaze and clasped her hands in front of her skirts, turning her attention back to the sphynx woman, her ire flaring at the implication that they were not sufficient enough aid. She squared her shoulders, her chin tipped in defiance. "We have not been sent by the Circle, but we are the ones who were listening. We are the ones who came."

Those burnished, bronze-flecked eyes roved over Bianca's face, searching for something, the truth perhaps. The lines around her mouth softened. "You have lost as well."

It was not a question, but Bianca answered it anyway. "We have. Our loved ones, and many more, were taken."

Her eyes flashed like molten fire. "By Fury."

Bianca felt Alder go ridged next to her. "They were here as well?"

Thunder cracked outside as if in answer.

"Come with me." She beckoned for them to follow, she demanded rather than answered Alder directly, her claws retracting. "We should be safe for now. It should be a few days before my stepfather, Ocidynus, finds me, you will be able to rest safely here."

"Who—" The female silenced Bianca's question with a finger pressed to her lips.

"There must be silence in the halls of the Order." The sphynx pushed aside a sheer curtain and strode down a shadowed cloister constructed of crumbling gray stone and white marble colonnades without looking back to see if they followed.

Moonlight sliced through the rain in the courtyard, which Bianca could see in silver slivers between the etched columns reflecting off a quicksilver oasis pond. The night air was heavy with the cloying scent of plants blooming, stirred by the chilled night air. Chanting ghosted along the damp walk in a thick guttural language that her ear could not decipher.

Felix kept in step with her, their shoulders a whispered breath away from touching, the farthest apart the narrow walk would allow. Alder drifted in the sphynx's wake, his hand repetitively drifting to his goddess mark and then back to his side. They passed a cluster of hooded and robed figures tucked in an alcove seemingly at prayer.

The path branched off onto a wider causeway running along the far side of the cloister. Midway down, floor-to-ceiling wooden doors stood open like gods beckoning worshipers at the main entrance to a vaulted-ceiling room of worship. Bianca's footsteps faltered, slowing so she could get a better look into the room. Past a nave full of prostrated robed figures, an altar loomed, its sole purpose seeming to be to display a book in an ornamented glass case. A robed acolyte stood at its base intoning words of a musical quality as if by rote, scarred hands uplifted to heavens.

The scene was transfixing. After a moment, she tore her gaze from it reluctantly and hitched her skirts, quickening her step to catch the others as they rounded another corner.

She caught up with them just as they crossed the threshold into a residential quadrant. More care for comforts had been taken here with tapestries hung at regular intervals and an extravagant courtyard garden off the portico.

The sphynx swept through an arched doorway into a magnificently mural-lined sitting room lit with hanging glass oil lamps and richly carpeted in plush bohemian rugs.

The female gracefully sat in a curved wooden armchair by a hearth on the far side of the room. Herbs thrown into the fire enriched the air with an intoxicating aroma.

"You may be seated." The sphynx swept her arm out, going through the movements of graciously offering, though it was said in such a way that brokered no argument. She was a woman used to getting her way.

She, Felix, and Alder took seats on stiff-backed settees set to either side so there was no mistaking that they were the audience, and though her chair was but made of wood, it was a throne.

She cleared her throat, somehow managing to make it seem a royal gesture. "I am called Princess Xandrina Astarte Narsissa, and I am the rightful heir to the throne of Gypette."

She paused, as if allowing for dramatic reactions, before tapping the arm of her chair with a razored claw. "What may I call you all?"

Bianca found her voice first. "I'm Bianca, Bianca Hastings."

Felix, from his seat next to her, spoke next, leaning forward casually with his elbows propped on his knees. "I'm Felix Grayson, of Areth."

On the settee across the rug from hers, Alder bowed at the waist, his finger finding his goddess mark. "I am Alder, son of Cedre, Highness, from the Fragment Alatus. Goddess's blessings be upon you."

Xandrina's eyes settled on each of them in turn. "How curious," she murmured as if half to herself, "that a changeling, a human, and a wood nymph should end up here in Gypette, summoned by my song."

Felix shrugged casually as if to say life was often funny that way, an indolent grin spreading slowly across his face. "And what about you?" he asked, his words rolling off his tongue like honey, and Bianca began to wonder with a spark of irrational envy if he was trying to flirt. Though having never been flirted with, it was difficult to tell. "What is a princess doing in a monastery at the end of the desert?"

The princess propped her elbow on the arm of her chair and cradled her chin in her hand, a coy smile dancing on her lips as she turned her attention to Felix. "Well, changeling, I hope you are comfortable. It is quite a long story."

"You have my undivided attention, Princess."

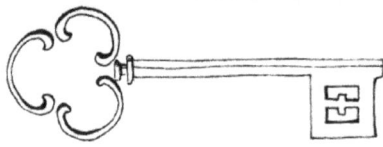

Chapter 53

BIANCA SHIFTED UNCOMFORTABLY IN her seat as she watched Felix give the princess his rapt and undivided attention. She too was curious, but the way he looked at her, his eyes swollen with inquisitiveness, crumbled bits of her heart to dust, the echo of them falling ringing in her ears.

Alder, too, seemed transfixed by Xandrina. He'd inched his way down his settee so he sat close enough to her that he could reach out and touch her, his hands white-knuckled on the armrest as though he physically restrained himself from doing just that.

Xandrina leaned back in her chair, settling her hands in her lap, seeming almost to preen under their regard.

"The first thing you must know is that the royal line is conceived with magic in order to keep our bloodlines pure. The queen can take no lovers until she's delivered a magically gifted heir. A Traveler has always held the throne of Gypette, for it was once prophesied that should one without Traveler magic sit on the throne, it would bring ruination to the Fragment."

"What happens if an Inept child is born?" Alder asked.

Xandrina's eyes snapped to him, indignation written all over her face. "That could never happen; our magic is pure and our spells for conception wholly without fault. They were a gift handed down to us by the Fates themselves." The inflection she placed on Fates left Bianca inclined to believe they were akin to the gods.

"Now as I was saying." The branded man who'd held her captive sauntered into the sitting room with a tray of drinks in silver chalices, condensation dripping down their sides. He offered first to the princess, their eyes locked, his fingers signed deftly at his side in a silent swift conversation to which the princess nodded in reply ever so slightly, but only Bianca seemed to take note of the exchange. "Nineteen years after my birth, I underwent the Ordeal, a sacred rite of passage meant to gauge my abilities and prove my worthiness. I, of course, passed and was anointed the heir apparent. As was tradition, my anointment was celebrated by the Feast of Fifty Days, during which games and contests were held. One such contest was a gladiatorial tournament, the winner of which would be awarded a select place among my mother's royal guards."

Bianca was offered a cup last; she took it from the man with murmured thanks. He smiled at her softly in a way she thought might have been apologetic, before he slipped away with silent grace.

"Ocidynus is a Valkry," Xandrina was saying when Bianca turned her attention back to her story, "a people conquered by my grandmother. They were a small coastal kingdom, and my grandmother wanted a seaport. They refused to negotiate, and things turned violent. Most of the orphaned children were taken and given work in the mines. A nasty way to treat them if you ask me, but you can see why his awarded position as my mother's guard was such a scandal."

Bianca paled, her fingers tightening on the stem of the silver chalice. She was no stranger to historical accounts of wars and attempted genocide, the people of the Drowned Marshes for one had a sordid and terrible past. But to witness it so close at hand, only two generations removed and not centuries, was another experience entirely.

"My mother's most trusted advisors cautioned her against it, but my mother, well, she never openly admitted it, but I don't think she approved of her mother's actions. I think she hoped that allowing him to keep his victory and claim his place in her royal guard was her way of trying to begin again." She took a long drink from her cup, and Bianca took the opportunity to do the same, savoring the tangy, chilled spiced wine.

"I cannot speak to how what happened next occurred. Most of it happened behind closed doors. We went on Progress, to introduce me to the kingdom as heir. We visited noble houses, the mines, and the like. Somewhere along the way, my mother became quite taken with the Valkry. By the time we'd reached the lands of the conquered kingdom, they decided to wed, and they did so with haste."

Alder frowned as he leaned back, crossing one leg across the other. "And was it legal? The wedding?"

Xandrina sighed, tapping her claws on her cup. "Yes, I'm afraid it was quite legal, done with all the proper representatives and officials. She even named him her king." She shook her head, her hair falling across her shoulders. "No Queen of Gypette has ever named a king. A consort, yes, a king, never. The news reached the capital before we did. They were gathered at the palace gates on the verge of rioting when my mother tried to announce their nuptials. It broke her heart. You see, the people believed Ocidynus had hoodwinked my mother; it is what we all believed. It broke her heart, and she took to her bed, refusing visitors, even me, all but giving her crown to the king."

"So you came here? To get away?" Felix pushed the hair out his eyes, his gray eyes still fixed on the smooth plains of the princess's high cheekbones.

"Patience, changeling." She purred. "A fortnight passed, and there was an attack on the palace. The king by all appearances led the assault at the head of a horde of the legendary Fury. Abrax and I managed to fight our way to my mother, but we were too late, the beasts were dragging her off. We tried to get her back, and well, let's just say Abrax is the only reason I am alive today."

"The Valkry King announced our deaths to the people the next day and took the throne officially for himself. Though he knows I am not dead. He hunts me even now." Her words were hot with fury and tears, and for a moment, her regal, flirtatious demeanor slipped, and Bianca saw nothing but another sad, scared woman who missed her mother. "And that is how I ended up in a monastery at the end of the desert."

Felix frowned from where he lounged with his chin propped on the arm of the settee. "There is something we're missing. As far as I can tell, this fits with everything else that's been happening, but I just can't quite see how."

"Perhaps this Ocidynus is an Instrument of Darkness?" Alder suggested.

"Could be," Felix conceded, turning to Xandrina. "Does he have any magic or Traveler blood?"

Xandrina shook her head. "I know little of him. I never saw him do magic, but that doesn't mean he didn't have it and conceal it. Tell me, though, what is this Instrument you speak of?"

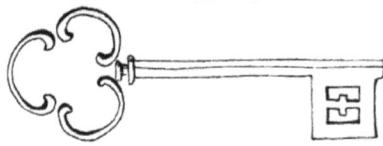

Chapter 54

FELIX LAID BIANCA DOWN in the canopy bed hung with gossamer curtains. She'd succumbed to exhaustion and the effects of too much wine not long before the pale-pink light began to dust the sky beneath the storm clouds. It had taken hours, but they laid themselves bare before the princess, giving her nearly every detail they knew.

He was right; she had a shrewd mind. She asked all the pertinent questions, digging until no detail was left overturned before declaring she needed sleep to mull it all over.

Felix draped a thin linen blanket across Bianca. She wouldn't need much more than that with the early morning heat already rolling in in waves despite the steady rain through the open windows that led out into the courtyard. For a moment, he let himself imagine what it would be like to curl up next to her, to feel her heartbeat against him again. But he shook the thought away. She was not for him.

He slipped silently out of the guest room and into the courtyard, feeling far too restless to go to his own generously provided quarters.

The courtyard garden was extravagant. If he had to guess at first glance, it was designed to look like a miniature version of the oasis in which the monastery was built, with a pond at the center stocked with silver-bellied glimmer fish with their jewel-toned backs and long pincers, and a variety of fruit trees and low-lying shrubs surrounding it. Rain trailed down the columns encircling the garden, feeding clinging mosses and puddling along the pathways.

Felix paced through the plants, identifying the ones he knew by name and taking careful mental notes of the ones he did not.

"Are you going to pace the day away, changeling, like a wombellow in it's wallow?"

He looked up to find Xandrina, her full lips and feline eyes smiling at him from between two columns. Her royal attire was gone, replaced with an admittedly alluring amethyst slip that hugged her curves and narrow waist in a very generous way.

His throat bobbed, but he threw on his best devil-may-care grin. "I might for lack of better entertainment."

"Sleep eludes you as well?" She raised her brow in a way that suggested she could either jump his bones or peel the meat from them, and that she would enjoy either.

He nodded. "Too many loose thoughts dangling."

"Come play stones with me." She flashed her wicked canines at him and crooked a finger.

With a shrug, he followed her to her room.

It was as he expected—lavishly decorated, with vibrantly colored silks and tapestries hung on the walls. A stones board lay set on the table as though she'd known he would accept.

She sat on the couch, and with nowhere else to sit, he did the same. She leaned forward, plucking a white stone from her side of the game board and putting it into play. She leaned back, looking at him expectantly. "Your move, changeling."

They played in silence for a few more turns before he broke the silence. "So, tell me, Princess, the book in the sanctum, what makes it so special?"

She stood and crossed the room, hips swaying seductively, to grab a bottle of wine and a pair of glasses. She curled up on the couch, filled the glasses for them both, and handed one to him. "That is no mere book. That tome is the most highly guarded artifact in all of

Traveler history. It contains spells and stories from the time of and before the Breaking, some so archaic and primeval that no one knows from whence they came. It was brought to Gypette by my ancestor, the Immaculate Inana Ishtar, to be protected and hidden. She feared what would happen should the book fall into the wrong hands."

Felix's brows crawled up his forehead in surprise, his cup frozen halfway to his parted lips. "The Inana Ishtar? The founding Circle member?"

Xandrina nodded, moving one of her pieces into a vulnerable position. "The very same."

"I thought she died in the Darkness wars?" He leaned down to take the stone with his.

"She feigned death to escape her forced marriage, taking the *Tome* with her. She then came to be with her people, to lead them."

"Her forced marriage?" Felix asked, leaning back and pulling his smoke case from his pocket. He drew one out and lit it. "Were not all of the original Circle members mates?"

Xandrina laughed, but it was as dry and mirthless as the typically arid sands outside the monastery. "That's what they would have you believe, yes. It's true that mates' magic multiply when they are together, but Prayllus saw the depth of Inana's magic and bound her by force. He used siphoning spells to leech her abilities."

Felix gawked. "That is heretical." Damn him, he was starting to sound like the nymph.

Xandrina sneered and leaned forward, plucking the smoke from between his lips and pressing it between her own, taking a long drag. "History is written by the victors, changeling. Do you really think the mighty and wise Prayllus would admit he needed the stolen magics of a female in order to bind the original Circle and break the world?"

"No, no, I don't suppose he would." He snatched the dangling cigarette from between her fingers as she leaned down and took not one but five of his pieces and victory.

Her grin was pure feline. "I believe that's game, changeling, care to try again?"

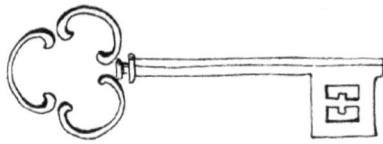

Chapter 55

*F*INGERS BRUSHED HER FACE, *threading through her hair. Stroking and soothing. The warm hum of an absent-minded tune wrapped her in a golden glow.*

"My star, wake up, my star." Her mother's voice pulled at the strings of her consciousness, dragging her from sleep.

She rubbed the cobwebs from her eyes, leaning into her mother's touch. "I don't want to wake, Mama. I miss you too much."

Claws dug into her scalp, ripping and tearing. "I said wake."

Bianca reared back, trying to wriggle loose from the hands clutched on either side of her head. A scream sawed its way from her throat as she beheld not her mother but the Beldam.

"What do you see?" Its jaws unhinged.

"What do you see?" Its neck snapped with a crack as deafening and final as a coffin nail.

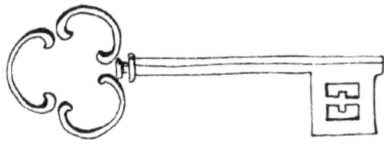

Chapter 56

Bianca braided her hair, still slightly damp from a quick bath, into a plait, the kind her mother used to do for her when she was small, as she stepped out of her room onto the colonnade. She bent down to brush the beaded rain off the petals of a vining trumpet flower as black as funeral garb when she heard a door close behind her.

"You look lovely," Alder said by way of greeting as he strode over to her from the threshold of his room adjacent to hers.

She did a little twirl, allowing the iridescent pink material to tulip around her. The neckline plunged, as did the back. There were no sleeves leaving the full length of her scars exposed. But the skirt petaled in a waterfall of tiers off her hips down to the floor, and it made her feel bold, despite its immodesty.

"Thank you, and you, you look comfortable." He was dressed in a simple light tunic and loose pants with sandals. He didn't appear to be armed, though Bianca knew better by now than to assume that was true.

"I am. I must admit I feel good about being here. I think it was the right choice. Though please don't tell Felix I said so, or goddess knows I'll never hear the end of it."

Bianca smothered a smile. "I won't, I swear it."

He chivalrously offered his arm, and she took it, allowing him to steer her through the garden. "Your change of heart wouldn't have anything to do with a certain beautiful princess, would it?" Bianca teased, the corner of her lips tipping up into a small smile.

Alder stumbled a half step, coughing to cover his fuchsia-stained cheeks. "I, well, I mean, she's a potential ally."

"That isn't how you look at me, and we're allies, are we not?"

Bianca enjoyed watching him squirm for an answer before she drew him up short, a few paces from the entrance to the princess's chambers where Abrax stood guard.

"I'm curious, Alder, and please don't take offense to this—erm—delicate question, but you are a nymph, and she is a sphynx. Could you, say, hypothetically, intermarry?" She admittedly knew little of what went on in a marital bed or what lovers shared between them. She'd only ever overheard snippets of gossip from other women her age, but she knew enough that asking made her skin heat crimson.

Alder's brow stitched together as it so often did when in thought. "Well, yes, it doesn't happen nearly as often as it did before the Breaking, the opportunities for inter Fragmental meetings are limited to the Reliquary, official trips through the Void. And there are, well, to put it as you say, delicately, there are more salacious black markets where people intermingle. Though not all beings can, eh, intermarry." Alder cleared his throat, refusing to look her directly in the eye. "Changelings, for instance, cannot."

"Ah." Bianca tried to keep the brittle peeling edges of her feelings from cutting into her voice. "Well, that is interesting information. I'm not entirely sure why it's relevant to me." She laughed, but it sounded too pitched and bitter.

Alder opened his mouth to say something else, but Bianca turned away horrified by the unmasked pity in his eyes and by how unveiled and indiscreet she must have been in order for Alder to so baldly make note of her interests.

She swept through the columns, past Abrax, her face as pink as her skirts, with a murmured greeting that he returned with a stoic nod. She stopped so abruptly when she entered that she was surprised she didn't feel the stones under her feet crack with the force of it.

In her chest she felt her heart flutter and die as surely as if it had been wrapped in thieves' bane vines.

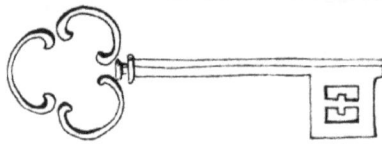

Chapter 57

FELIX WATCHED THE LOVELY pink flush to Bianca's cheeks slide right off her face as soon as she walked into Xandrina's sitting room. He wanted to jump up and assure her that this wasn't what it looked like. Yes, he had a glass of wine in one hand and the waist of the princess in the other, but he'd been a perfect gentleman. Well, mostly perfect, the princess was on his lap after all. And she did have her claws inside the undone top buttons of his shirt. But other than that, he was being a perfect gentleman. Besides it was all just pretend, a cat and mouse game for information. Though admittedly he wasn't too sure who was the cat and who was the mouse.

At least Xandrina had changed into something with more fabric. Though her new dress was still exceptionally sultry with a long slit exposing the length of her smooth coppery leg.

"Oh good, you're both finally here." Xandrina purred as Alder came to an abrupt halt next to Bianca. He looked like he wanted to commit murder, but Felix couldn't fathom why.

Xandrina slithered off his lap, her feathers brushing along his cheeks as she did, and prowled toward the balcony doors. "Come now, we have much to discuss." She crooked a finger, and none of them dared not follow.

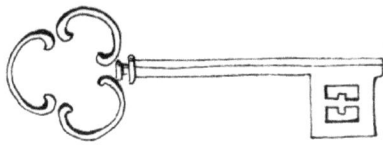

Chapter 58

AN ELABORATELY SET TABLE sat under a wide canopy on the princess's balcony, which sat on the edge of a seemingly bottomless gorge that Xandrina named as Fates Downfall. While curious, Alder didn't ask the origin of the name. He was too preoccupied grinding his teeth like knives on a whetstone.

Jealousy was a viscous poison in his blood as he took his seat, spine ridged, at the elegantly set table. Felix's scent was all over Xandrina's apartments. He knew he had no claim on her, and yet his hackles rose.

It was obvious that nothing had truly crossed a line between the two of them. To him anyhow. Bianca, on the other hand, looked like a crumpled flower. The pair of them sat too stiffly; there was a jagged edge to their flirtations. What he couldn't figure out was why. He had seen all the stolen glances, the wistful looks, and unspoken words that hung between the changeling and Bianca. So what was he playing at with the princess? Did he want information? Did he seek to put Bianca off? If that was the case, fine, he'd been toying with her long enough.

"I trust you both slept well?" Xandrina passed him a bowl of bacon-wrapped dates stuffed with some sort of cheese. The accidental brush of her fingers against his did unfortunate things to his heart.

"Yes indeed, thank you for allowing us to impose upon you." He forced a starched smile onto his face.

"And you, Princess, how did you sleep?" Bianca asked acerbically, stabbing at scrambled eggs on her plate.

Xandrina either didn't pick up on her tone or didn't care. She flippantly waved a hand as she poured herself chilled juice. "Bah, sleep, I had much more important things to do." She winked at Felix.

Something stabbed into Alder's palm. He looked down and realized the fork in his fist was split in two thanks to his magically enhanced strength.

Get a grip, get a grip, it's a game they're playing, He thought as he took deep piercing breaths, squared his shoulders, and tried to discreetly slip the broken utensil into his pocket.

He focused on his food and the wind howling through the gorge like the spirits of the damned. If he couldn't hear Felix and Xandrina speak, he wouldn't feel the need to vault over the table and pummel the smirk right off Felix's face. That would likely upset everyone, though, so he forced himself to tune out the conversation and recite weapons facts.

The dirk strapped to his calf was forged with Calthanian metals, the strongest metals mineable in all the Fragments. Found only under the Mountains of Cathar in the farthest reaches of Alatus. He'd been training with it since he was seven. The palm-sized push dagger in his boot was the first knife he'd made himself. The handle was made from the spine bone of a loth, and the blade was imbued with spells for stealth.

His name loudly spoken sliced through his thoughts. Everyone at the table looked at him expectantly. "Goddess forgive me"—he touched his fading mark—"I didn't hear your question."

"Have you also heard the tales of the Lost?" Xandrina asked him, her lips pressed into an annoyingly pretty pout.

"The children's fable, yes? The one meant to teach children to always double-check their spells? Of course, I've heard of it, every Traveler child has."

"Not me," Bianca fussed, half to herself.

He couldn't fathom how the conversation had turned toward children's stories, and he said as much.

Felix leaned back in his chair, throwing one arm casually over the back while the other held a sloshing wine cup that spattered the cuff of his shirt with plum-colored globules. "I don't think it's just a story."

Alder scoffed. "I don't see how your gullibility is relevant."

Felix leaned in, pressing his will upon the table. "Think about it, we've scoured every text for every desert dimension that fits the criteria of Bianca's vision, and none of them fit. The Lost could be it."

"But what about Ocidynus?"

Xandrina hissed as he uttered her stepfather's name.

"He could be an Instrument. Xandrina saw him leading a Fury horde. We're in a desert. How does this Fragment not fit the criteria?"

Felix's eyes crinkled with bald self-satisfied smugness. "Deaths. Night. Rose."

"What of it?" Alder growled; his impatience loomed like a reaper ready to seek vengeance.

"They won't grow here. Under any circumstance," Xandrina chimed in, her lips curled over her deliciously vicious fangs in triumph.

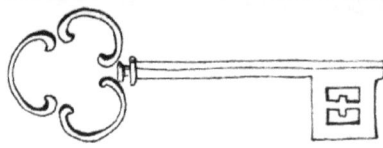

Chapter 59

"C OULD SOMEONE PLEASE ELABORATE?" Bianca asked. She ran her hands over her tiered skirts, smoothing them, but Felix knew she still unconsciously sought the comfort of that little amber bottle. He was very nearly jealous of the hold it had on her. Though he had no right to be, especially not with what he'd just done to her.

What he couldn't figure out was why Alder was in such a foul mood. He'd done his fair share of pissing the man off, but he usually did it on purpose. This time he'd done nothing, and yet the man's normally peacefully blue aura was black and sparking like a thunderhead, and it was all aimed in his direction.

He was going to need more wine. "The Lost is a tale as old as the Breaking. It claims that when the world was fragmented and the walls went up, pieces slipped through the cracks. The Circle was too busy trying to contain the Darkness. They didn't notice whole sections of Fragments falling away to gather like dust at the bottom of the Void."

"It's illogical. Why would the Circle not build a door and go check, if for no other reason than to stop the claims?" Alder spat, viciously assaulting the food on his plate with his knife.

"The same reason any ruler refuses to admit to a mistake." Xandrina glowered over the rim of her cup. "It would make them look weak."

"Preposterous." Alder's word landed as roughly as if he'd intended it to be a blow.

Xandrina's eyes narrowed, the atmosphere sucked in around her crackling. She seemed to grow exponentially, her aura pushing out, pressing into Alder's, her will bending his.

Felix swallowed a thick knot of intimidated awe. There was the ruler underneath the provocative conceited persona she affected to get her way. There was the fire and vim he knew she had.

Alder's pupils swelled, his teeth gritted, his aura pushed back. It throbbed, threaded with determination, and gods damned, Felix suddenly understood as embers flew where their auras met. The man was infatuated with the princess. He was a blind fool to not have seen it before.

"Fine," Alder ground out, his eyes locked with Xandrina's, "say the Lost is real. What in the goddess damned name does it matter? We don't know anything about it; there is nothing to readership, no basis for a plan."

"Ah"—the princess dragged her claws along the rim of her glass, making it sing—"that, dear nymph, is where you are dead wrong."

A bell toll sliced through the steady percussion of rain. The air around them snapped taut, and Xandrina stiffened, her eyes narrowing. She stood so quickly her chair was thrown back, crashing against the wet stones. Without explanation, she took off in a run, her skirts whirling behind her.

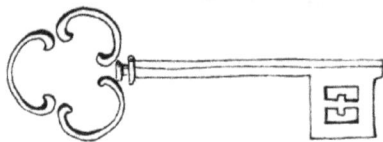

Chapter 60

O
N THE PARAPET, XANDRINA watched through the rain as a black swarm amassed on the horizon. Streaks of scarlet sky showed in brief flashes between thunderheads.

Shouts keened off the sturdy outer walls. Feet scrambled to get to armor and weapons, but Xandrina couldn't take her eyes off the death that flew at her on swift wings.

The damned creatures could fly. That was new. The beat of their membranous wings may well have been the sound of war drums growing closer. Through the spyglass, she saw at the head, leading the charge against her, was Ocidynus. He'd found her already. She whirled around, fear clawing its way up her throat. She hated the way it made her voice waver as she shouted "Abrax!" over the chaotic din and the heads of the wide-eyed Travelers next to her. She should have never let him out of her sight; she should have never wasted precious moments flirting and feigning interest in the changeling no matter what information he had.

Abrax's hand slipped into hers, giving her a silent reassuring squeeze that gripped her heart. She spun to face him. He was already dressed in armor, and he had hers, and her sword, thoughtfully in tow.

"*I am here, Merjaii,*" he signed. "*I will always be here at your back.*" The words were a knife in her heart, an echo of the ones he'd vowed to her weeks before. She could still hear his voice, calling her Merjaii—meaning beloved of my soul in Valkry—before her stepfather cut out his tongue and tore off his wings.

She shook her head, tears streaming unbidden down her cheeks as she pressed a hand to his stern face. "No, not this time, my love. Please, I'm begging you, flee with the Travelers, then I can die happy knowing you will live on."

He pressed a kiss to her forehead, and then to her lips with the burning passion of all the moments they would never have behind it. One hand dove into her hair, knotting it around his fingers like the threads of his love knotted around her heart; the other traced the line of her jaw before swooping over her shoulder and down her back to press her against the hard length of his body.

Abrax drew back as the sound of wings drew closer, and when she gazed up into his beautifully mismatched eyes, they were rimmed with tears as he signed, "*Never, Merjaii. I'm with you until the end.*"

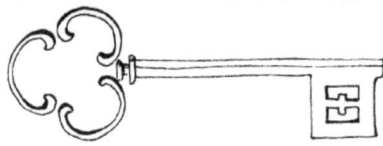

Chapter 61

B IANCA TRIED NOT TO openly stare at Xandrina and Abrax's embrace but seeing them together pulled away the haze of her own muddled emotions and she understood with a sharp clarity that whatever the princess had been doing with Felix meant nothing. There was something pure and tragically beautiful in the moment so raw it rendered their titles useless, stripping them down to two souls, two breaking and bleeding hearts.

Xandrina spun around, her bronze eyes ablaze, and pointed to Felix. "Changeling, the book we spoke of, you must get it. It could make the difference in this war. It will help you find the Lost Fragment."

"Is one book really so powerful?" Alder quipped, an anxious eye on the encroaching swarm and a hand on his dagger.

The princess laughed mirthlessly as she took her sword from Abrax and pulled it from its sheath. "All books are powerful, this one just more so."

Abrax helped her to slip a brown leather breastplate over her crimson dress, doing up the buckles with deft fingers. "Now go, before they get here, we'll do our best to fend them off."

"Come with us, there is no need for you to stay, to sacrifice yourself," Bianca pleaded.

Xandrina shook her head, her hand finding Abrax's, their fingers entwined as they turned to face the oncoming horde. "My mother, her name is Safiya." She looked over her shoulder at Bianca through hooded, sorrowful eyes. "When you find her, please let her know I tried."

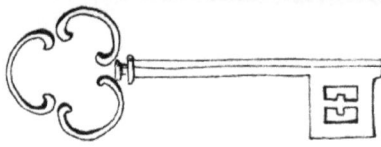

Chapter 62

X ANDRINA COULD SMELL THE fetid breath of death rolling off the approaching beasts, like grave dirt cast on the wind.

She whispered a prayer to the Fates of life and death, begging them to spare Abrax, before raising her sword and screaming in defiance as the Fury descended.

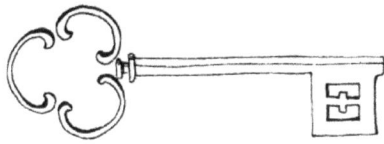

Chapter 63

S OMEWHERE BEHIND HER FELIX swore, "Fuck, go, we need to get to the book now."

Alder grabbed Bianca's hand, yanking her along the colonnade in a run. A horn sounded from somewhere deep in the monastery. They barreled through the doors of the vacant sanctum and headed straight for the glass-encased pedestal. From half a pace behind him, Felix wasted no time. He flung a ball of pure light at the glass shroud, shattering it into fine crystalline snow.

The echoes of metal clashing on metal echoed around the chamber in a sickening parody of the chanting of the monks that knelt there the night before as the fighting moved closer.

Bianca let go of Alder's hand and rushed the pedestal, grabbing the book.

Xandrina and Abrax burst through the entry behind them, slamming the doors shut. Abrax jammed them with a knife.

Xandrina spun to face them, her hair pulled free from her braids was a coppery halo around her head, and ichor ran down her chin as though she'd ripped out a Fury's throat with her teeth. She was bleeding from a wound along her shoulder, and venom lanced through her eyes. She was the picture of an avenging goddess.

Alder took a half a step toward her when she began to swear, "What in the damned Fates names are you still doing here? Get out, get out now while you still can!"

The harbingers of death beat against the doors. No longer were they skulking in the night, they were coming, claiming. Bianca fumbled with the weight of the book.

Fury hammered at the wood, splintering it like bones, ready to suck the magic and marrow out of them. "Any time now would be great." Felix hissed, darting forward and grabbing the book from her, half dragging her to where he'd conjured a door.

The sanctuary door screamed as it shattered, splinters sent flying like arrows across the room. Bianca turned to stone. It was worse, so much worse, than she'd imagined.

The undulating mass of creatures writhed their way in through the doorway, crawling like angry spiders across the walls and floor toward Xandrina and Abrax who stood unflinchingly in the center on the room awaiting the oncoming swarm.

On either side of her, Alder and Felix flung knives and magic at Fury in every direction. Alder's spells did the most damage, unbinding Fury's like ragdolls picked apart at the seams.

Bianca's fingers began to itch, to glow. Unsure of what her magic would do if she allowed it to unleash itself, she raised her palms. Brilliant pure, white light exploded from them. It clashed with the creatures of Darkness, peeling flesh from bone, unmaking them in a near perfect reflection of Alder's abilities though with much less finesse.

Bianca sagged to her knees, and the light of her magic flickered. There were too many of them.

A breath of brisk summery air tickled the back of her neck. Hands wrapped around her, dragging her backward into the Void.

Bianca heard a battle cry rip from the princess's throat and watched as she charged, Abrax at her side, her red hair streaming like a flag behind her, into the melee.

It swallowed her whole.

The door slammed shut.

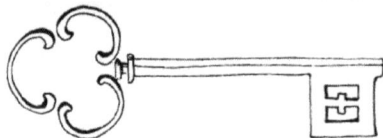

Chapter 64

"**W**E HAVE TO GO back. Open the door, we have to go back!" Bianca railed against Felix's chest, landing blow after blow.

Someone shouted her name and swore, but Bianca didn't hear them. "We can't just leave them there." Her voice spiraled endlessly into the Void.

Alder had his head pressed to the sandstone door, his finger tracing symbols into its wind-worn surface. Bianca didn't have to ask what they were, she knew in her gut he was sealing the door.

"Gods damn you, let me go, we can't let them die like that!" She thrashed against the arms that tried to sooth her. "Listen to me, damn you!"

Alder spun to face her, his cerulean eyes two chips of hard ice, and grabbed her by the chin. "No, you listen, and you listen well, Bianca Hastings. We cannot go back for them. They chose this sacrifice; we can't go back and let it be in vain."

He let her go, his hand fell limply at his side, ichor dripped from his fingers, and he limped down the stairs.

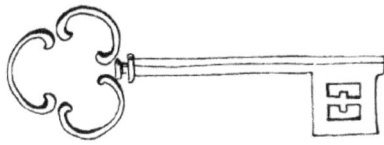

Chapter 65

"**O**PEN THE GODS DAMN thing already." Bianca's legs gave out. The library's chair half a step away slid itself underneath her just in time. "Let's see if it's worth the price paid for it." She massaged her temples, her hair tumbling down around her shoulders.

Alder slumped in silence in the chair next to hers, his eyes as blue and as distant as the sky, absently tapping where his Goddess mark once was, now completely worn from his skin.

Felix set the tome down on the table between them all. It was nearly two hands thick with a nondescript leather cover. There was nothing about it to indicate it was full of magics from antiquity worth hundreds of lives.

He hooked a finger in between the pages, and the whole room collectively held its breath as he flipped it open.

Next to her, Alder started to laugh as dryly as the rasp of a match, tears streaming down his cheeks.

"Blank," Felix muttered, one hand fisted in his hair, the other flipping from one page to the next, "they're all bloody gods blank."

Bianca stood on trembling legs and drifted like a wraith from the room.

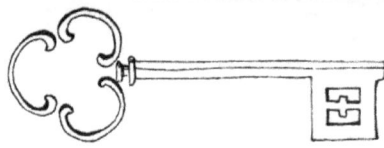

Chapter 66

LIGHTNING CAVORTED ACROSS THE sky in a merry waltz to the beat of the thunder, teasing the rain into a torrential frenzy.

The beautiful windows of the tower felt suddenly like the glass of a specimen jar, oppressive and confining. Ribbons cinched around her ribs, drawing them closer and closer together until each breath felt as though it may crack them. She tore at her clothes, ripping at laces. Buttons popped off and scurried under her bed for cover.

Her heart tick, tick, ticked, away the seconds. Its incessant persistence pounding through her skull, reminding her she was undeservedly still alive when so many, oh so many, were not. Why did they leave her here alone to wither without them?

The room shrank under the eye of the storm that felt more like the angry gaze of the gods than the violent stain of dark magics. Her breaths heaved, never quite filling, never quite satiating. She choked on the dusty air, thrashed her way across the room, and flung herself into the frigid rain.

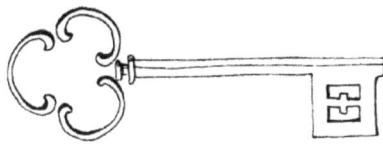

Chapter 67

FELIX KNEW THERE WAS something to the book he was missing, a fail-safe of some sort put in by Inana Ishtar perhaps. But his mind kept pulling him toward sleep, a half-lowered anchor refusing to let his thoughts sail.

The soothing warmth and crackling lullaby of the hearth's flames pulled him under, drowning him in rest.

The hairs on the back of his arms stood on end, stirring him awake, moments after his eyelids fluttered closed. Only the most persistent of embers in the fire remained.

Something dark and malevolent leaked through the room from the crack under the double doors. Feelings so thick with resignation and anguish it made bile rise in his throat. He knew those feelings; he'd circled that particular drain a time or two before.

He hauled himself to his feet and ran from the library so fast he was almost surprised when he found himself at the bottom of her ladder, self-loathing pooled at its base. Felix fought with every rung he climbed, wading against its current.

Gasping for air he crawled out of the hatch and spun wildly, trying to find her.

Her shift clung like a translucent membrane over her skin as if she's just been born en caul and not about to end it all. Lightning's ether clung to the air, teasing her hair into a tempest. The sight of her sent his heart cascading over the edge, as if by beating faster it could lend hers the strength to keep going.

Her fingers were a lead weight against the icy teeth of the wrought-metal railing, the only thing anchoring her to the world.

"Come back over the railing, Bianca." Felix's voice ghosted along the wind, steady and yet tenuous. "You don't have to do this. You can be more than what they did to you. More than what they took."

A strange, mangled sort of laugh spewed its way out of her, twisting until it sounded more like a sob. "You know nothing of this agony, Felix, or you would never ask that of me."

His hand slid against her hip, his fingers knotted into the sodden fabric of her shift. He leaned in close, breathing his words into the curve of her neck. "Ask me why I'm a ward, Bianca."

She looked over her shoulder at him, her curls plastered to her freckled cheeks, her eyes cast down to the drop below as if part of her still considered it, but then she opened her mouth, and the question tumbled out, barely a whisper. "Why?" She swallowed hard. "Why are you Imogen's ward?"

Felix wrapped his arms around her and hauled her back over the railing. His chest pressed to her back so closely that he could feel the thrum of her heart as it beat an erratic tune to match the rhythm of hers. In a moment of weakness, he pressed his nose into her raven-blue hair and inhaled the lavender and saccharine scent of sorrow that was her.

His breath battered his lungs as they sagged in relief. He squeezed her more tightly, backing toward the open door behind them. "Because everyone I knew and loved is dead, murdered for what they are."

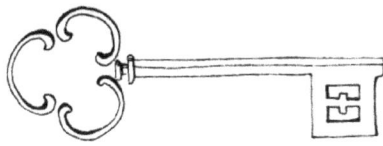

Chapter 68

FELIX WRAPPED HER IN a down-filled quilt, keeping a hand on some part of her at all times, even as she slid, teeth chattering, out of her sodden shift into another, then swiftly under the blanket's cover.

With a quickly muttered word to Maura, hot spiced wine appeared on the table as well as a steaming cup of bone broth. A fire sprang to life in the small stove as he perched on Bianca's bed and pulled her into his lap. Her head tucked perfectly in the hollow of his shoulder.

His hand paced tenderly across her back. He let small wisps of magic leak from his fingertips to warm her, guiding them to curl under the edges of the quilt to settle across her skin like velvety ribbons of sunlight.

He felt the whimper that slipped from her lips settle across his heart like a jockey on a horse. It egged it on until its beats thundered across his rib cage in a stampede. He took a deep shuddering breath. "Are you ready for a tragic tale of woe?" He breathed against her damp hair.

She nodded, inadvertently nuzzling his neck as she did. He tried not to let his arms stiffen against her as he began. "Long, long ago, before the Breaking, Changelings were divided into nomadic tribes. They wandered the land looking for a place to call home. You see, in those days, Changelings were at best mistrusted, outcasts for our ability to shift our appearances."

Felix pressed the mug of bone broth into Bianca's fingers and helped her guide it to her lips. "Then Darkness fell. Changelings fought alongside the Travelers, whether they had

Traveler magic or not. But that made no difference to some who saw war as a convenient excuse to take the lives of those they deemed undesirable. When the world was shattered to end the war, and the walls went up, only two tribes remained. Those who were left chose to take a single form and keep it, hiding their identities, giving them a fresh start. But they still lived with the fear of being hunted."

Bianca shuddered against him. "That's horrible." Her words chattered into one another.

He pressed his cheek to the crown of her head, breathing her in. "My family lived in a Fragment called Earth. They lived there for many generations until rumors of Changelings being tracked down by a sect that called themselves the Huntsmen once again reached them. The tribe broke up, scattering across Fragments. My ancestors remained, hidden in the foothills of the mountains. The period that followed is known to some as the age of the Clandestine War, or the war that never was. Year after passing year, our number dwindled. Word would come to my family from others through spelled mirrors that could be used to communicate across Fragments."

He had never told anyone this story before, the whole history of Changelings, let alone the next part. It felt strangely freeing, like untying a weight from around his heart that he hadn't known was there but had carried with him every day of his life. "We lived on a farm. My mother grew sunflowers so tall they towered over fully grown men. I don't remember much from that time, but I do remember the flowers." When he closed his eyes at night, he could sometimes see them still swaying above him. He didn't know if Bianca had ever seen a sunflower, they weren't native to Areth, but in that moment, an image of her beaming at a bouquet of the brilliant blooms with a smile creasing the corners of her eyes danced through his mind, and he realized he would give anything to make that imagining come true.

"From what I understand, they only ever went into town in the wagon once a month to buy supplies, leaving me home with my grandparents. But that was enough. Someone who suspected what we were saw. They came the night of the full moon. I woke to a loud explosion and a scream that tore my life in two." From that moment on, all his memories were divided by the tragedy. There were the hazy happy memories of childhood that came before and the stark and jagged memories of what came after. "I remember my mother pulled me out of bed and told me I had to be quiet, more quiet than I had ever been. She smiled, but I remember thinking it looked wrong, like it didn't quite sit right on her face. She told me it was a game. I could smell the blood in the air. Magic flashed outside the window. I hadn't seen magic used like that before. I thought it was the stars falling. That is, until I saw the blood. My mother tried to cover my eyes as we slipped past the front door. It was blown off its hinges; my grandmother lay sprawled over the threshold. She had always had such a fire in her eyes, and I didn't understand why it was gone, why she didn't get up and come to me and brush the hair off my forehead like she always did."

"What happened after that"—he drew a rattling breath, pulling Bianca closer—"it was my fault. I called out to her. When she didn't stir, I started to cry. The sound drew the Huntsmen. We made a mad dash for the barn; my mother fought her way to get us there. I don't know what happened to my grandfather and father, but there were bodies on the ground that I imagine were theirs. My mother barely managed to get us here to the Reliquary, to Imogen, before she collapsed. That's when we discovered the Huntsmen used poisoned weapons. It took weeks, but she succumbed to her wounds."

Bianca tilted her chin and looked up at him through hooded, tear-rimmed eyes. "It wasn't your fault, Felix," she said softly, her breath a whisper along his jaw. Then after a beat, she said, "How do you live with it? All the loss?"

He cleared his throat, his skin suddenly felt too tight against his muscles, the press of her in his lap too heated. He didn't dare look down into her eyes for fear of what he might do. The line of propriety and friendship was far too blurred for direct eye contact. "Yes, well, I suppose when you lose people, there comes a point when you have to decide whether you're going to follow them or whether you're going to live for them. Me, I decided I was going to live, and make no mistake, Bianca, it was the most gods damn difficult thing I've ever decided to do. I still have to decide to do it every day."

She nodded against him, and then they sat in silence, the only sound the storm against the windows. Her breaths grew even and shallow against him. He didn't want to break the spell, to let her go, because like this, if he closed his eyes, he could pretend she hadn't just thought to kill herself, he could forget he was the last of his kind, and he could forget there were no good reasons for them to be together and a mountain of reasons why they shouldn't be. Like this, he could close his eyes, and he could hope, which was the most terrifying thing of all.

When she was soundly asleep, he gently laid her down, tucked her under yet another blanket, and set to work on her aura. He pulled ropes of thick black hatred and loathing from it that sucked on her energy like leeches and banished them from the room. The layers of grief were more difficult to pull, but he managed to cast away some of it, so some of her natural radiance returned before he grew too weary and nearly collapsed in the chair by her wood stove where he sat watching her sleep until nearly sunrise.

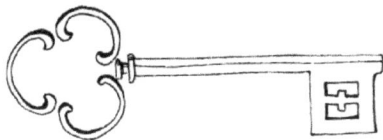

Chapter 69

FELIX SLAMMED THE DOOR shut, leaving the Void behind him. Maura floated over, a glass of wine in hand. She gave it to him with a pat on the cheek that felt like the kiss of cool autumnal wind. "Ye poor dear. Find out anythin' new?"

He sat on the kitchen bench, throwing the full weight of his exasperation down. "No, it was the same as every other Fragment I've checked in on in the past few days. Travelers missing, the stain of dark magic is everywhere, storms are flooding people out of their homes. I offered to bring some of them back here, but they all wanted to stay."

"Aye, I should think so, they'll all be waitin' for their loved ones to come back." Maura bustled at the stove, stirring pots, checking cakes in the oven, and dishing him a bowl of a hearty looking stew with a side of still-steaming crusty bread.

Felix murmured his thanks and nodded, taking a deep draw of the wine in his cup. "They are, but that doesn't mean I have to like it. The Fury mostly took the oldest or the strongest." Traveler magic aged in the blood like a fine wine growing in strength and intricacy over the decades. "But what happens when that won't satiate them? They'll be back for the younger ones like us, and we're scattered like lost lambs for the choosing."

She shook her head, the wisps of her translucent hair floating around her as she made a tea tray disappear with a crack to another part of the house. "Ye did explain?"

Felix snorted derisively before picking up his spoon to dive into his bowl. "You'd be amazed how many of them don't want to believe it."

He took a bite of the stew; it was the perfect blend of sweet and savory with chunks of meat and squash. He didn't think Maura could cook anything that tasted bad.

She sat down across the table from him—well, as much as a ghost could sit anyhow—and patted his hand. "At least ye tried, dear, and that's more than most can say. Anythin' that happens now is not on ye conscience."

He sighed. "No matter what, they're all on my conscience, Maura."

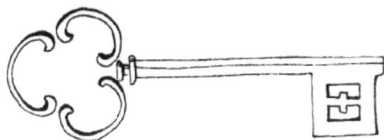

Chapter 70

GUILT AND GRIEF STILL gnawed at her like mice on a corpse when she rose a day later. But she still chose life, she still chose to cling to the frayed and withering threads of hope, and it was, as promised, the hardest decision she made every moment.

The night prior she wrapped herself in the shroud of the storm in her tower room, buried under blankets, subdued with a potent blend of sleep tonics and wine. She fought to dream something true, to see her parents, to peer into existence and pinpoint their heartbeats. Nothing came to her but twisted nightmares of ticking clocks and tortured souls.

Morning light tried unsuccessfully to bore through the writhing mass of dark clouds. Bianca's mouth was full of sour cobwebs and her head full of stones as she rose. She reluctantly dressed, each lace of her stays excruciating and tedious to tie.

She decided to forgo a trip to the kitchens and headed instead to the library. Though, as always, Maura must have known, a plate of shortbread sat waiting on a tea tray next to the *Tome of the Travelers*. She took both to the rug by the hearth. The whole of the house was cast in oppressive hues, the color and light leached by the brutalizing tempest that never waned. The fire's light was the only way to color the world again.

The tome weighed heavily on her lap and on her heart. It had cost so much, and yet its pages remained blank, withholding its secrets. Bianca nibbled her cookie and took a sip of tea and set to work, determined to make the book reveal to her what she needed.

Bianca pressed her fingers into the page, silently pleading with it to give her something relevant, something useful. The page absorbed the light as it leaked from her fingers. It spiraled like water around a drain until it coalesced into words. Fortunately, they were ones she could read; unfortunately, the recipe was for a salve to remove blemishes.

She scowled. "They're freckles not blemishes." She swore it laughed at her, its pages fluttering with mirth.

"Any luck?" Bianca looked over her shoulder at Alder as he approached. His eyes were hard as they fell on the book. He held his shoulders straighter each day, and his words grew more clipped and cold. And Bianca wondered if he, too, dreamt of clocks, ticking away the moments left in their loved ones' lives or in their own.

"No," she sighed, turning to a blank page. "Just a blemish salve."

Alder snorted derisively. "It's an ancient text you would think would have encountered freckles at least once before."

Bianca's lips twitched in what could have been a smile if she let it. She let the magic unspool across a new page, nothing.

She groaned through gritted teeth and flipped the page again and hissed. She jerked her hand back as blood beaded at her fingertip where the edge of a page bit into her flesh. "Damn book."

The blood welled, her magic swirling within it like a constellation in the heavens. It swelled, rolled off the pad of her finger, and dropped. Time seemed to expand as that crimson ruby fell toward the paper, suspended momentarily between flesh and page.

It collided with the aged parchment in a brief but blinding flash of light, a falling star colliding with the ground.

Bianca blinked spots from her eyes. "Great goddess, what have you done?" Alder groaned.

"What are you—" She stopped when she looked down at the page, bloodred words twisted across the page. She read the title aloud, "Astral Sight Serum, a potent decoction used to induce a powerful, divine vision state. Alder, this, this could be it, this could be what we need to find our families. But damn, what language are the instructions in? I don't recognize it."

Alder made a sign against evil on his forehead, muttering under his breath about goddess cured blood magic before he leaned over to get a closer look. "I'm not sure, but it looks like it could be old Changeling. It's a dead language, or it will be once, well, once Felix is gone."

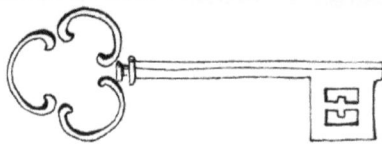

Chapter 71

THE CHARCOAL FELT LIKE an extension of his hand as he let it glide across the sketchbook's parchment. He didn't sketch anything in particular, his mind wandered and the charcoal just sort of followed. When he at long last paused to look down, he found an abstract composition of feathers, keys, flowers, musical notes, and an eye kissed in the corner by a star staring back at him filled with a brokenhearted accusation.

He clenched the paper in his fists, balled it up, and threw it in the corner with the other fifty or more wads of paper that had his soul sketched across them.

A brisk and precise knock echoed through his room. What could Alder want at this ungodly early hour? He swore as he peered at the timepiece on his mantle, the whole night gone up in a puff of smoke. He snubbed out the rolled herbs on the table next to his bed before hollering, "You can come in."

He resisted the urge to pull the blankets up over his naked torso when Bianca strode in after the overtall nymph. Damn him for bringing her here, into his space without warning. He'd been trying to keep his distance since the other night, and now the whole room would reek of her for weeks, which was both an arousing and a damning thought.

Her pupils swelled at the sight of his bare skin and then quickly flicked away, but that brief look branded his skin. He casually reached for a shirt, trying to appear nonchalant and unhurried. "So to what do I owe this pleasure?"

"We need your help translating a passage from the *Tome*. I believe it's old Changeling," Alder said, gesturing to the hearty book cradled to Bianca's chest. "She inadvertently triggered a translation with blood magic."

Felix could hear the disgust that dripped from Alder's words when he said blood magic. What a damn prude, it wasn't outlawed or anything, just somewhat frowned upon under certain circumstances. Bianca clearly took note of the inflection in his words, too, and crimson crept up her neck and cheeks.

"All right, then." He held out his hands, gesturing for Bianca to pass over the book. "Let me see."

She crossed over to where he sat on his bed with timid steps. His stomach clenched as all the times he'd imagined her coming to him in his room flashed uncomfortably through his mind.

Her fingers barely brushed his as she passed over the book, and his aura immediately tried to reach out and twine with hers. He pulled it back in with an immense amount of effort and mental strength as she skittered back as though his brief grazing touch was a bite.

He shook his head to rid himself of thoughts of her, even as the stormy lavender scent of her suffocatingly filled his nostrils. He skimmed the lines of text once, twice, three times. Just to ensure he'd translated it right.

"This is perfect." He stroked his chin as plans began to run amok in his head. "It says there is a flower called the amethyst lunar lacewing. When a decoction is properly made and taken by a seer, they will be able to project their soul anywhere provided they are anchored by another person for brief periods of time."

Alder's brow buckled. "That sounds dangerous," he said at the same time Bianca said, "That sounds wonderful."

The two looked at each other, Bianca's arms crossing stubbornly and Alder with a blatant look of shock sculpted over his normally stoic expression.

"It sounds wonderfully dangerous, how's that for a compromise?" He grabbed a blank page and started quickly scrawling notes on preparation before the *Tome* decided to fade out the page. "Now, it's going to need several days to prepare once we get all the ingredients. The trickiest is going to be the flowers. It says we need a bouquet the size of the drinker's heart, whatever the damn Darkness that means."

"I could head out to the greenhouse and check the botany books out there for any mention of purple lacy flowers?" Bianca offered.

Alder scowled, which Felix ignored. "You could, or we could perform a summoning."

The nymph's scowl deepened, chiseling out grooves along his forehead. "You have no boundaries, do you?"

"I have boundaries, and this is well within them. The questions asked have to be worded very specifically, and with this translation, we have all the information we need." He picked up his smoke and lit it again with a snap of his fingers.

"They don't like to be called upon, Felix. We could end up dead, cursed, or worse, something slimy." Alder wrinkled his nose, and Bianca smothered a hint of a grin under long delicate fingers.

"Something slimy, nymph? Really?" Felix sniggered.

Bianca cleared her throat. "Dare I ask what a summoning is?" She dug her fingers into her forearms with her inky fingers in a way that he knew meant her scars were bothering her again, and he made a mental note to check on the Gorgonian poultice's fermentation, as it should be nearly ready by now.

"It's a ritual performed to conjure an Oracle," Felix replied, shifting the book off his lap and kicking his feet up onto his mattress to recline against the wall. "And before you ask, an Oracle is a dead seer. Well, not quite dead. They died in their Fragment, and their bodies were buried or burned, but their spirits decided to exist outside of everything, even the afterlife. They can see everything that has happened or will happen."

She canted her head to the side, one brow raised. "Like Maura?"

"No, Maura's a house spirit. She bound her soul in service to the Reliquary."

Bianca blinked as if to mull this over before asking the question he knew was inevitable. "Why haven't we summoned one before?"

"Because it is beyond goddess damned reckless." Alder growled. "You have to be unbelievably specific with your questions. Even asking about multiple people at a time could invoke its ire. One wrong word and the information they give you could be catastrophic."

"All right, Alder, what's your plan, then? Sit around on our backsides for another fortnight poring over obscure botany books while the Fury and the Instrument drain everyone we love of their blood and magic? And what do you propose we do when they come here again looking for anyone else they can juice for their purposes? Tell them to wait just a minute, we only have a few hundred more texts to comb through, and then we'll be right with them?"

Alder seethed, his hands fisted at his sides, his shoulders held rigidly, as color rose in his cheeks before he threw his hands into the air in exasperation. "Goddess bless it, have it your way, Grayson. I'll go to town, to Will's, for the damned herbs and meet you both later in the library."

He stalked out, leaving Bianca behind to turn a wary eye on him. "So just how catastrophic can speaking to an Oracle be?"

Felix gave her his most winning smile. "I wouldn't worry about it. Alder's just being paranoid. I know what I'm doing; you just have to trust me."

She crossed her arms, her narrowed gaze raked over his face, but then she tipped her chin in the barest of nods and left.

Well, how about that, she trusted him, and damn it if that didn't break his heart.

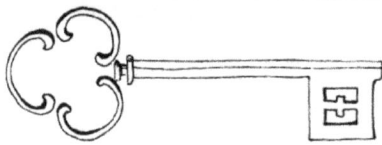

Chapter 72

WILL BUSTLED INTO THE library in riotously colorful skirts, her arms laden with supplies followed by a sullen-looking Alder, his arms overflowing with candles.

"Ooo, this is so exciting!" Will gushed. "I've always been curious about summonings. They're so mysterious and taboo."

"For a reason," Alder muttered half under his breath.

Will giggled and waggled her eyebrows over her shoulder at him. "I suppose we're about to find out, aren't we?"

Bianca could practically hear Alder's eyes roll as she hurried to help Will with her burden, resisting the urge to crane her neck to peer around Alder's broad shoulders for any sign of Felix.

"Do we really need all of this?" Bianca looked down at the hodgepodge of pale-purple crystals and dried herbs in her arms.

Will directed both her and Alder to set their armloads down on the hearth. "We do. The herbs and crystals help focus our intentions and will hopefully keep the Oracle contained, so if we make it mad, it won't be able to harm us."

"I feel so much better knowing we'll have tea herbs and rocks between us and the irritable unkillable being."

Bianca shot Alder a look. "If you don't want to help, then don't."

He at least had the good sense to look ashamed. He touched his forehead. "I apologize. This sort of thing makes me uncomfortable, but I'll do my part. I'll do anything if it means we can get our parents back."

"Glad to hear you're finally seeing it my way, son of Cedre." Felix swaggered his way over to them from between the stacks. "Does that mean if this fails you'll be willing to try some blood magic?"

Alder glowered. "Let's take it one asinine plan at a time, changeling."

Felix smirked. "Sounds good to me. Now"—he rubbed his hands together—"let's get this furniture moved."

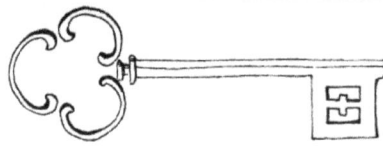

Chapter 73

F ELIX'S EYES WERE FIXED on the pages of the cracked leather book in one hand, a storm of concentration. His other fingers flicked and twirled, aglow with magic, as they guided a piece of chalk along the exposed floorboards. An elaborate rose of concentric circles blooming in its wake boarded in otherworldly symbols.

"The circle funnels and focuses our collective magics," Will explained as she placed her odds and ends and candles around the outer edge. "The symbols will help contain any foreign magics the Oracle tries to throw at us if we anger it, not that I think we'll anger it, but you never know with these things."

With a flick of her wrist, Will ignited the candles. The inner layer of their wax beaded plum purple as it dripped down the black skin of the outer layer.

Bianca clenched her hands behind her skirts to keep them from wringing together. She wasn't nervous about summoning the Oracle—she wasn't particularly nervous about any sort of magic, not having been raised to it like the rest of them. She had no predisposed notions about blood magic or summonings, but this moment felt like a precipice, and they were all about to jump.

The phantom touch of the future traced the length of her spine, whispering echoes of things to come in her ear in incoherent mutters and screams. If they did this summoning, there was no going back.

Felix snapped the book shut. "All set." He looked at each of them in turn, his eyes barely landing on her before glancing off again. "Everybody ready?"

Alder pushed off from where he leaned against the mantle, folding himself to sit at the edge of the circle. "Let's get this done."

Will piled her hair haphazardly atop her head, securing it with a long pin shaped to look like a sword with a flourish. "You do realize what a rarity this spell is, right? I mean, the last time it was performed was at least a century ago when Xavier Farrenzy tried to summon his dead wife. Isn't that just the most swoony and romantic thing you've ever heard?" She sighed breathily.

"How did it work out for him?" Bianca tucked her skirts under her knees as she settled in along the border of symbols between Felix and Alder.

"Oh well, that bit is less romantic. Apparently, he summoned her to ask if she could still do his laundry in Oracle form. So she put a nasty curse on him."

Bianca burst out laughing so hard she thought she might have broken her corset boning.

Will looked at her dreamy-eyed over her spectacles. "I suppose it is rather funny, isn't it?"

Alder shook his head at them both, muttering something about women and curses under his breath.

"Well, thank you, Will, for that reassuring story," Felix groused with a hint of a grin tugging at his lips. "Now if we could all focus, summon your magics, and focus them on the center of the circle."

Bianca wiped a tear of residual mirth from the corner of her eye and tried to focus on her magic. She began to tug at it, pulling up a continuous string of it and guiding it to her fingers until they itched. She pictured it pouring and pooling in the center until it became a reality, a glowing white thread. It twined its way to the middle and wove itself in with the wisps of Alder's blue magic, Felix's black, and Will's brilliant rose-gold.

"Now what?" Alder hissed from her right.

"Now we, uh, you know, call an Oracle." He cleared his throat. "Oh great Oracle from beyond, we summon you."

Bianca felt the collective anticipation glue their breaths to their ribs.

The four magics writhed together in the circle, dashing along the concentric lines like flicker bugs playing chase, but nothing happened.

"Perhaps if you made it more rhyme-y?" Will put in.

"Rhyme-y?" Felix asked, a note of incredulity edged in his words. "What, does rhyming make it stronger?"

Alder snorted back a laugh, but Will seemed not to notice. "Of course it does, maybe throw in some thees or thous, too, if you can to add more weight to it."

"OK, right, thees and thous." Felix cleared his throat and flexed his darkly glowing fingers before beginning again. "Oh great Oracle from beyond, we summon thee to aid us in our task for we have a question to ask."

The magics began to pulse along the lines, spiraling out and in faster and faster. A chilled wind swept down the chimney flue, extinguishing the fire until it was no more than the barest tongues of flame licking along the embers. The flames in the candles shot up into the air so high Bianca had to lean back to avoid losing an eyebrow.

Bianca slammed her eyes closed as a ball of light as brilliant as a dying star flared in the center of the circle painting the insides of her eyelids blue.

"Ah, infantile prophetess, what is it that you want that you couldn't see for yourself?" the voice crackled along the air like lightning, demanding in unspoken words that Bianca look at it. She flung her eyes wide, her gaze crashing into the spiraling cosmic gaze of the all-knowing entity that swirled in a noncorporeal smokelike form in the eye of the circle.

All else dropped from existence save for her and it as it shrouded her, taking her under its vaporous wings.

"Does this frighten you, little prophet, to look upon your potential future?"

Bianca shook her head, her blackish-blue curls brushing her cheeks that streamed with tears as it beheld the awesome infinite power before her. "No."

"And why not?"

Its question thundered with magic, wrenching the answer from her. "Because it means that I might have a future."

The oracle smiled, or at least she thought it did, then leaned in close, crooning in her ear, "The flowers you seek are here. The changeling will know the way, for they grow only on the graves of mothers whose lives were stolen in violence. Though beware, Prophetess, you may not like what you find."

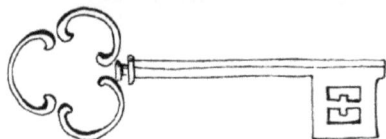

Chapter 74

S MOKY GRAY FOG SWIRLED around her ankles, sneaking chilled fingers up the cuffs of the high-waisted trousers she wore. Her mother had kept the scandalous piece of clothing for archeological digs. Bianca savored the freedom of movement as she slogged down the narrowing path through the woods that wound its way toward the foot of the mountain. Skirts warm enough for this type of weather would have been sodden and as heavy as her heart by now.

She kept her eyes on the barely visible tracks in the mud, avoiding looking at the dark and leering gaps in the trees. She couldn't let the fear of monsters in the dark turn her around now. Not today.

The mud squelched under her boots as she skidded to a stop, the dire wolf in the clearing sat watching her, its tail drumming the ground impatiently. Ten times as large as a normal wolf, he was an impressive site looming among the trees. She silently said a prayer to the gods that he wouldn't send her back.

"Good morning, Felix." She crossed the clearing, her eyes never leaving his. Even in this form, his scar curved around his left eye, the pain of his loss permanently etched on his face.

He lowered his head, his misty eyes burning into her with a question so clear she could almost hear it. *Why did you come?*

"I couldn't let you go alone." He pressed his wolffish forehead into hers. A silent thanks.

"How far is her grave from here?"

He huffed, shaking his head, and nudged her in the belly, pushing her back the way she came.

She glowered, crossing her arms across her chest, her chin tipped defiantly. "No. You don't have to do this alone."

The wolf Felix shook his head and huffed a sigh through his finger-long teeth that could rival those of a Fury for ferocity. But rather than persist in dissuading her, he bent his forelegs and gestured for her to climb on.

She'd ridden horses a plenty in the parks near her parents' home, but never in her wildest of dreams had she ever imagined riding a dire wolf.

His muscles quivered and contracted beneath her as she held on for dear life, her fingers fisted in the ruff of his neck, her body pressed close to the thick fur on his back. She felt each of his panted breaths.

As they ascended, the fog coalesced into billowing black waterlogged clouds. Blue lightning crashed through the trees like scared does startled by a hunter's prowling, raising the hair along her neck. Rain stung her face like bits of broken glass. Tendrils of her hair slipped the hold of her braid and whipped at her wind-lashed cheeks.

Felix bound over rocks, the pads of his feet moving deftly around obstacles. Occasionally, he'd stop to sniff for his heading on the rippling tides of the wind, then choose one fork in the trail or the other.

He picked their way across an eddying creek, the pebbles at its bottom covered in thick green and blue algae. She heard rather than saw the water race toward an edge, roaring as it tumbled over a precipice out of sight in the murk.

She began to shiver despite the warmth of Felix pressed against her. As they crested a narrow ridge line, the rain persistently found its way through every seam of her waxed canvas coat. Just ahead through the hunchbacked trees, she spotted a structure made of the same craggy stone that littered the forest and hillside.

The trees bowed out of the way as they entered a glen still in the grips of winter with snow blossoms pushing their little belled heads through the icy crust along the ground. The mausoleum at its center was etched with what she assumed was his mother's name above an open archway in old Changeling.

She slid from his back, the ice cracked like a broken looking glass under her feet, bringing her untold misfortune. "Would you like me to come in with you?"

Soundlessly, he shook his head and padded forward, his ears drooped through the archway. Bianca watched his great lumbering form, cast in the shadow of the stones, as he pawed at the ground, then lay down atop his mother's grave.

He tipped his head back and howled, a low keening, broken sound riddled with anguish and spiked with the bitter notes of love lost too soon. It echoed back along the wind and into the past where she hoped his mother could hear it. It was filled with last goodbyes and the dreams of a life not lived.

It pierced Bianca's heart, pinning it to her throat: it filled her eyes with crystalline sorrows, a reflection of the ones in his as he walked back out, a small bouquet of purple posies in his maw. He dropped them in her outstretched hand, then bent to press his great canine head into her shoulder, his huffing breaths hot against her neck.

She wrapped her arms around him, burying her face in his damp and matted fur, breathing him in. Even as a wolf, he still smelled of smoke and liquor. She could have stood like that with him for eternity, but he pulled away without meeting her gaze, as though he were ashamed, or perhaps he just didn't want comfort, not from her.

She tucked the delicate blooms into her pocket, taking care to make sure it was buttoned securely before she clambered her way back onto Felix's back.

The fur on his back had begun to freeze, and her fingers, grown numb from being out in the relentless gale, made it hard to keep her grip as Felix began the journey back down the mountain with long loping strides.

The rain redoubled its efforts, pelting down in blinding sheets, clinging to Bianca's eyelashes, turning the world into a hazy watercolor smudge. She raised a hand to clear the water. Just below them, fast approaching through the trees, she saw the stream that they'd crossed earlier had transformed, breaking its banks, into a seething river full of dark vigor and vim.

Felix's steps didn't slow on approach. She tried to lean forward, to shout in his ear that they should look for a safer crossing, when with a powerful surge of strength, he leaped without warning.

The wind stole her scream as she slipped from his back, plunging into the bloated stream. Its white-capped current grabbed at her boots and her hair, holding her more tightly the harder she struggled against it. It gripped her by the jaw and shoved a frigid hand into her lungs, robbing her of breath.

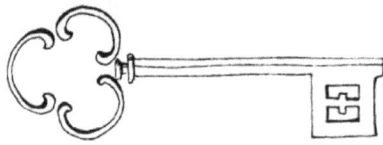

Chapter 75

FELIX CURSED ALL TEN of the gods as he ran up the front walk of the Reliquary for his stupidity. He could feel the hot, thick spill of her blood as it dripped down his naked torso. The tang of it coated his tongue.

He'd panicked when her head went under. He didn't think to shift before he bound into the river and grabbed her with his wolfish maw. They'd made it to shore just barely, and he'd easily pulled the water from her lungs, but the damage to her shoulder was catastrophic. Her scream when he'd revived her would haunt him until his dying day.

The blood-staunching spell he'd used was barely effective on wounds as deep as those that marred her shoulder. Her luminous aura flickered, his own curled around it, clinging to it, trying to tie it to his.

"Alder!" he screamed around pained breaths, casting his voice farther with his magic. "Alder!" He blasted the front double doors open with a flick of a finger, splintering the fine wood as easily as if it were made of eggshell.

The nymph ran out of the kitchens. "Great Goddess, what have you done?" Alder swore as he ran to scoop Bianca out of his weary arms.

His knees buckled and crashed under him. "She fell in," he gasped, his hands braced, keeping himself upright but just barely. "I didn't, I didn't mean to."

Alder growled, spinning swiftly on his heel with Bianca cradled in his arms, her head lolling against his chest. "You never bloody mean to."

Felix stumbled, his feet coated in a swampish slurry of mud and blood, as he tried to follow Alder to the healer's rooms. Tears singed his cheeks. He beat his fist into the floor with bone-cracking ferocity and shoved himself up and onto steady footing. Mud be damned. His footprints disappeared behind him, instantly dissipated with Maura's magic.

Alder had her carefully sprawled on a table, the tattered ribbons of her shirt cut away, leaving her exposed save for a thin sheet draped across her for modesty.

"What can I do?" Felix's voice cracked as he braced himself, white-knuckled, on the edge of the table.

"Don't you think you've done enough, Grayson?" Alder's voice didn't hold any fire or venom, it was pure frigid calm, which made it sting all the worse.

"She wanted to come. I tried to send her away." Felix reached to brush a dripping tendril of hair off her cheek, but Alder smacked his hand back.

"You're no good for her."

Felix's face twisted into a grimace, but he couldn't argue, not when she lay there so damaged by his own hand. "Don't you think I know that."

The nymph didn't meet his ferocity head-on. He instead kept his head bent in consternation as his icy-blue magic sutured Bianca's wounds layer by layer, knitting the flesh neatly back together. "Then you should try harder. She's been mooning over you, and you've been a damned fool to let her. She deserves better than life with a changeling."

Felix's canines lengthened, and the hairs on his nape prickled as a growl erupted from his throat. "Enough. You're crossing a fucking line."

Alder snorted derisively. "That's hilarious coming from you."

A thready whimper slipped from Bianca's lips, silencing them both. "Felix?"

His name so undeservedly on her lips felt like a curse and a prayer. He leaned in close. "I'm here, Bianca. I'm here."

Her eyes fluttered open, the green of them piercing his soul. "Felix, the flowers." She tried to lift her arm, gasping in pain as she tried to move the still tender and healing muscles.

He scrambled for the battered ruin of her coat cast in a heap at her feet. His probing fingers turned up nothing but empty pockets. "They're gone." His words sounded featherlight to his ears but hit as hard as iron. "The flowers are gone."

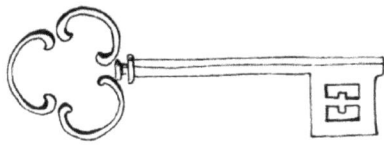

Chapter 76

THERE WERE THREADS OF tension snapping and sparking between Alder and Felix as they sat opposite one another in the library, so potent she could almost see them. She wasn't sure what set them off this time, but she couldn't quite bring herself to care, not when their carefully laid plan was shattering around them.

The warmth of the teacup in her hands pooled in her palms, seeping into her skin, and chased away the phantom tremors of chill still lurking along her bones. Even now by the fire wrapped in a wool shawl, she could feel them breathing down her neck, whispering promises of death.

"You're sure that you picked all of them?" she heard Alder ask Felix for the thousandth time through gritted teeth. His knuckles burned white where they clenched the arm of the chair.

Felix took a long drag off his rolled herbs, the violet smoke pluming. "What, don't trust the word of a changeling?" he bit back, his glassy eyes glaring.

A low noise somewhere between a laugh and a growl rumbled in Alder's chest. "No, I don't trust the word of an incautious, irreverent ass."

Felix flinched. Only just barely. If she'd blinked, she never would have seen it. His lips curled into a minacious smirk, his canines elongating just slightly so they kissed his lower lip in a way that made her insides flame in a curious way that she couldn't even begin to comprehend. "What are you going to do about it, nymph?"

Bianca sighed, stomping the heat down to embers as both men bolted from their chairs, chests puffed, just a pair of angry crows, and danced around one another to the tune of insults and thinly veiled threats. She swallowed her tea, letting it scald the back of her throat, letting it tease out the chill that lingered there, and peered at the dregs in the bottom of her cup.

The men's voices faded as her itching fingers spidered along the cup's rim. They had to find more flowers, somehow, but where? Her eyes slid out of focus as she thought until tiny shooting stars with silver tails danced across the edges of her vision at the bottom of the cup. They connected the leaves, much like they had before in the grocery, like lines traced between celestial bodies to form pictorial stories of the heavens. This time they formed a flower, the very one she was looking for, and a clock with hands spinning backward as if calling her to harken back to a moment forgotten. But what moment?

She closed her eyes and held the image of the flower in her mind, backlit by the flickering of firelight against her eyelids. Where in her past did she miss something that could help? She needed a lifeline, a sign. Unconsciously, she felt her magic unspool and wrap around her thoughts, dredging them up and throwing them past her in a warped, gray, rain-soaked haze. Remembrance after remembrance slipped by, each as useless as the last, the garbled melody of voices already spoken echoed phantasmic through her until her magic picked out the right ones. They drifted by as intangible as smoke illuminated by starlight, just bright enough for her to catch.

She bolted to her feet, the clatter of the cup hitting the floor, and the suddenness of her movements ceased the men's bickering as swiftly as a hangman's rope. "A black market." The words spun across her lips tasting of fate, and she blinked up at the men's startle and confused faces. "Alder, when we were in Gypette, you mentioned there are illicit markets. We can find the flowers we need there."

Alder gaped. "I, I, well yes, I did mention the market, but it wasn't so we could go to one."

Felix took a step closer, and the smell of him rushed into her personal space, feeding the embers of that inexplicable flame. "Are you sure? How do you know?"

She shook her head, choosing to answer them both at once rather than separately and indulge their petty fight; whatever it was truly about, it could wait. "Whether you meant for us to go or not, we are. I did a spell, a bit unintentionally, but it worked nonetheless, and it revealed the flowers are at one of these markets."

With a defeated sigh, Alder crossed his arms across his broad chest, his waistcoat and cravat all neatly and impeccably done up. "It's not markets, it's market. There is only one."

"The Masked Market." The corners of Felix's lips curled into a devious smirk, his eyes shimmering, lit up like silver fire, in a wicked toe-curling way as he ran his hand through his already-tousled hair. "I've always wanted to go."

If that statement didn't indicate what kind of trouble they were getting into, Bianca didn't know what did.

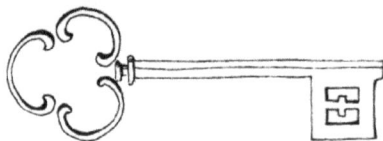

Chapter 77

THE CRUSHED-VELVET SKY, STUDDED with stars, swirled in hues of violent purple and blue. It clung to the ruinous spires of stones making the glittering heavenly orbs seem like pluckable gems, just a breath out of reach.

Mosaicked stones winked underfoot as patrons danced from stall to stall to the stilted and mesmeric melody that drifted from a lace-trimmed gazebo in the center of the Masked Market.

Excitement and awe bubbled up in Bianca like fizzy wine and blushed along her cheeks until she glowed beneath her silver-and-pearl domino mask. They stood at the entrance, little more than a fissure in the wall of the Void, soaking in the bizarre splendor of the small Fragment that made up the open-air market.

A small boy in a jester's belled hat and a fox mask trotted past them juggling vibrant fruit, and his reedy voice called out across the crowd that his were the juiciest and most delectable fruits. A fine-boned woman in the billed mask of a swan, with feathers pasted along her skin, sang from a perch in a rose-gold cage guarded by a hulking man in a silver helm and armor. Though what they sold was unclear, the sign in front of them loudly proclaimed in scarlet script their price was four hairs plucked off a virgin's head.

One part fete one part bazaar, everyone playing the part in full masquerade dress. "It's like walking into a dream." Bianca gasped, her hands fisted into the skirts of her off-the-shoulder midnight-plum-colored gown, ready to lift them to step over the threshold and join the throng.

"More like a goddess blessed nightmare." Alder grumbled, the corners of his mouth pulled down beneath his sharply cut black mask and matching suit that made him look like death incarnate, just as dangerous too.

Felix, in stark comparison, looked like a sybaritic prince with a doublet left half unlaced, a gilded crown perched askew on his head with a golden mask to match, frozen in a lurid grin. He ran a hand through his hair, leaving it simultaneously more tousled and dashing. "We should split up and meet back here in an hour's time."

He pulled three pocket watches from his coat and handed one each to both her and Alder. "These will sing when our time is up, signaling it's time to come back here whether we've found the flowers or not."

Bianca scowled as both men tucked their watches into pockets, precisely where they belonged. Her gown, despite its voluminous skirts and petticoats, sported not a single pocket.

"Here, let me." Felix held out his hand, taking the watch back. He stepped around her back. "Lift your hair, please." His breath brushed her bare shoulder, and for a brief moment, her breath hitched as she imagined him planting his lips there as she lifted her hair and bared her neck to him.

He wrapped the chain around her neck, the face of the watch settled between her breasts, and fastened it. Never once did his skin touch hers, and she found herself letting out a slight breath of disappointment as she let the curls of her hair tumble free.

She looked up to find Alder's eyes smoldering behind his mask, the branding heat of his gaze boring into Felix. "If you're quite finished, we have precious little time before the magic in this place begins to warp our minds, and we're trapped in this debauched circus."

Right, Bianca reminded herself, *don't be dazzled by the sights and the sounds, don't take food or drink from strangers, don't sing, and above all else, never give anyone your name.* They'd gone over the rules repetitively, but in the face of the extraordinary grandeur, that was the market. It was easy to forget, especially when it was spelled to entice and ensnare patrons into spending their lives away.

She swallowed the nerves that prickled in her throat, forcing them down until it no longer felt as though her corset were trying to strangle her, and then she took a step forward. As if it were an afterthought, she called over her shoulder, far more boldly than she felt, "I'll see you later, gentlemen."

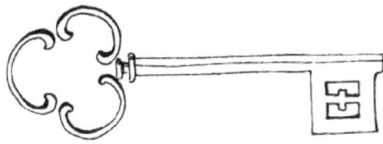

Chapter 78

DEBAUCHED CIRCUS, IT TURNED out, was an apt description. Though the farther from the entrance Bianca went, the more a sense of sinister wrongness wormed its way under her skin like maggots under the meat of a corpse. The gaudy gowns and suits of revelers became tattered and torn, skin sagged from bones, coiffed done-up hair unspooled around sunken, masked faces. The hypnotic cries of vendors pulled her attention to and fro, and the ever-present feeling of eyes roving across her exposed flesh made her wish she could peel it from her body.

A fog rolled through the jostling meandering people. It shimmered like stardust around their feet, the sickly-sweet smell of it making her eyelids feel heavy. It blunted her thoughts until she couldn't quite grasp what it was she was searching for. She drifted toward a stall, illuminated by the glowing bodies of creatures with fluttering wings trapped in corked jars. She floated closer, pulled by invisible strings of curiosity, and ran her finger across the blue glass, rousing the tiny figure inside. It stretched its arms and stood, its feminine figure no taller than the length of her middle finger, and pressed its dainty hands against the clear walls of her prison. The stains under the small female's eyes looked like the remnants of a night spent shedding tears, a haunting echo of her own morning reflection.

"Like what you see, miss?" The podgy peddler sidled up next to her, his fat greedy fingers fumbled to snatch the jar from its hook, jostling the creature inside violently. "She'd only cost you a handful of dreams. We could call it an even four if you like, that's a right bargain."

Bianca frowned at the man. There was something distasteful about his tone that she couldn't quite pin down. If only the smell weren't muddling up her thoughts, shifting them around like a pea under a shell in a game of chance. She shook her head, though it felt far stiffer and more leaden than she recalled it being.

She wanted to ask him where he'd found so many luminous creatures and why he had them imprisoned, but her tongue was a slug in her mouth refusing to cooperate. She gasped when something pulsed anxiously between her breasts, too slow to be her heart. She looked down to peer at the moony face of a watch and remembered. She fisted it in her hand, and her head instantly cleared. Bianca scowled down her nose at the man in front of her, his bushy caterpillar eyebrow scrunched as if he couldn't quite understand the sudden spark of clarity in her glass-green eyes.

"Well, are you going to hand over those dreams or what?"

"Pray tell, sir, how did you come to acquire such a collection of creatures? Surely, they didn't volunteer to be packaged up and sold."

With teeth bared, he growled. "Get out of here, girl. I won't have any high and mighty gawkers coming to my stall thinking they can judge me for how I make a living." His hands met her shoulders, and he shoved her away.

Bianca stumbled back into the milling people, the throng dragging her away before she could even register the shock. She floundered around for a brief moment, regaining her footing before she cast a scathing look over her shoulder at the stallkeeper with muttered curses on her lips. Someday when things were settled and her parents found, she would come back and find a way to free all those poor creatures even if it cost her every dream she ever had.

With the timepiece firmly in her grip and her wit sharpened, she thanked the gods for Felix's ingenuity in spelling them. The voices of the hawkers less hypnotic and unaffected by the intoxicating mist, she quickened her pace, eyes roving over the stalls and their wares.

Some booths sold the things you might expect to see at any market, food and fabrics, but then others sold things of a more peculiar variety. One stall she passed sold nothing but feathers, another unanswered wishes. A table just down from that sold vials of tears, each bottle carefully stoppered and labeled with a parchment tag in scratchy writing the occasion on which the tears were collected: first born child, death of a grandmother, skinned knee, a wedding.

She wondered what in the gods names you would need tears for, but she didn't dare tarry long enough to ask the craggy old hag who tended the collection.

Tucked into a far corner past the sultry red tent where women hawked their bodies for a price, a peculiar mask caught her eye. In the folds of a burgundy canopy with nothing visibly for sale sat a person behind a small table in an off-putting three-faced mask. One face looked left, the other right, with the eyes of the front face boring into her. The wearer raised a thick-knuckled hand and crooked a finger at her, demanding she come forward.

The ticks of the clock seemed to slow, and her blood rushed in her ears as she found herself compelled to go closer. As she approached, the person plucked a deck of cards from the table and began to shuffle.

Bianca stopped just shy of the patched canopy's edge, her heart skittering over her ribs. The mask reminded her of a story her father told her once about a three-faced god worshiped by the people who once inhabited the Drowned Marshes. One face saw the future, one the past, and one the present. But one face only told lies, one only told truths, and one only spoke in riddles, but it was impossible to tell which was which. Those who sought the gods help were often driven mad, unsure which advice they were given.

The person wearing the god's face ceased their shuffling, and their too-long spindly fingers fanned the cards out across the table. It trailed a long, rasping nail over the backs. They plucked one seemingly at random and held it out.

Bianca swallowed hard, she wanted to know what was on the face of the card even though she shouldn't, even though she knew the legends, even though she teetered on the edge of sanity as it was. But knowing the risks also somehow made it all the more enticing.

The pulse of dying minutes against her palm reminded her to ask, "Your price?" Though her free fingers fluttered at her side, desperate to fly free and grab the card that perhaps held her destiny etched on its face.

The voice that came from the mouth of the mask was neither male nor female. It was like the baying of wolves on a full-moon night, a stampede of deer through a mossy forest, the crash of the first waves against the first stones, it was the breaking of the world and the end of time. It was all that was and ever would be. "This, little one, is a gift. Though some may also call it a curse. It will cost you nothing, and it will cost you everything."

Bianca trembled, the voice echoing in her soul. Could the god of a long-dead people really be here in the back corner of an illegal market place, or was this person just a tremendously skilled play actor? There would be no knowing until it was too late, but what did she have to lose that had not already been taken?

She took a half step forward, the air around the maybe-god thickened like molasses on a winter morning. The gold foil-backed card was smooth under the pads of her fingers as she took its edge. She sucked in a breath, expecting, well, something. A spark, a weight, a knowing to settle upon her. But there was nothing. It felt like any other card, thick but light in her hand.

"Um, thank you," she murmured, and the masked person bowed their three-faced head in acknowledgment, then waved her away dismissively.

Bianca turned away, and curiosity ate at the edges of her thoughts like anxious darting fish, but before she could satiate the desire to flip the card and see what fate she was given, an aureate face frozen in a licentious smirk appeared out of nowhere. They gray eyes that danced within the hollows of the mask shimmered with excitement as Felix bent to whisper in her ear, "Hurry, come with me, I found the flowers, but there isn't much time."

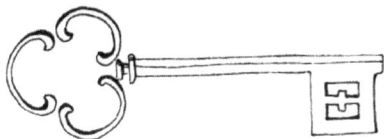

Chapter 79

THEY CROUCHED LIKE THIEVES behind a display labeled, "Cursed Jewelry, the perfect gift for the nemesis in your life." Though with the plan Felix proposed, they were quickly going to be more than like thieves.

"Alder wouldn't approve." Bianca hissed, eyes shifting to the stall across the way packed full to bursting under its striped awning with bunches of dried flora of all color, shape, and size. Bottles of powdered and dried roots and leaves hung from leather thongs along the edge of the roof like tassels on a rug.

She could practically hear his eyes roll in his head. "Why do you think I came to find you instead of him?"

The words settled into her like the warm glow of the morning sun, lifting the corners of her lips into a small smile. She forced her smile to smooth flat; being picked to be an accomplice to a crime should not make her this happy. "What exactly is the punishment for stealing from a vendor of the Masked Market?"

He tugged an ear thoughtfully. "Let's just say it's equal to the price of the item stolen ten times over."

"And the price of the powdered flowers?"

He shook his head. "You don't want to know."

"Fair enough." She hadn't asked, but she figured if he was suggesting stealing it that the price was not one they could afford. "So you create a diversion, I grab that jar there, and we run for it. Seems simple enough, but what do you have in mind for a distraction? It needs to be big enough to get the vendor's attention and give us enough time to get back to the Void."

His shoulder pressed against hers, she could have leaned away to give him more room, but she savored the heat of him against her bare skin, and they were trying to be discreet after all, too much movement might draw unwanted eyes. "That booth there, with the colorful boxes and cylinders, that's going to be our distraction."

Bianca's brow creased. "Okay, but how?"

His voice curled in her ear as he turned his face into the curve of her neck to whisper back. "Just wait and see. Run for our prize when the chaos starts. And, Bianca?"

"Yes?"

"Don't get caught with the flowers. If someone comes after you, toss them, slip them into someone's pocket, I don't care what you do, but get rid of them." And then he was gone before she could reply. His sudden absence was a chill wind that prickled along her skin and stole her breath.

She peered around the display, careful not to touch any of the cursed items, and a bead of cold sweat trailed down her spine. The jar hung on a cord among a bouquet of other powdered botanicals, but unlike the others, it had an iridescent quality, as though the drying and aging of the blossoms had concentrated its magical qualities. Her fingers itched, the spool of her magic spinning inside her, eager to get ahold of the flowers and increase its strength. She took a deep breath, settling it.

There was an ear-splitting crack and a scream followed by a stream of vibrant green light that exploded into a brilliant flower just over the heads of the market goers. There was a heartbeat, a fraction of a moment where time stilled to allow for the awe of all those assembled before pandemonium unleashed itself. Hundreds of the whizzing, banging, screeching, violent delights launched in every direction.

Her bare toes dug into the dirt as she bolted through the riotous chaos of terrified and confused patrons. Her vision tunneled as she hitched up her skirts to jump over a tipped-over wheelbarrow. She was nearly there.

She reached out her hand, and the concussion of a too-close incendiary blew the glass vile into her grasp and flung her sideways. The tether of the vial snapped as she tumbled toward the ground.

An unnatural burst of wind scooped her up before she could hit the ground, righting her. It smelled of liquor and chocolate. She whipped her head around, her gaze crashing into Felix as he ran for her, his hand outstretched, fingers aglow.

"Run!" He snatched her free hand, entangling his fingers with hers and pulled her along behind him, darting around disoriented people. Sulfuric smoke battled against the sickly spelled fog, and a rainbow of colors danced in every direction and flew through the crowd raining sparks.

Through the haze, Bianca saw the looming figure of Alder where he stood as rigid as a statue waiting for them by the fissured entry. Felix shouted for him to go, go, go! His words barely audible as all three of their watches began to sing a shrill and horrendously off-key tune. The three of them barreled into the Void, a cloud of smoke on their heels.

She and Felix collapsed on the stairs, breaths panted and ragged. Alder glared down at them both, his arms crossed. "I take it you two are somehow responsible for the madness and mayhem?"

Bianca's struggled breaths turned into an unstoppable fit of giggles as she pulled the mask from her face, and she held up the vial by its frayed cord. "Yes, well, at least we got this."

Alder's azure eyes flashed with an emotion she couldn't quite pin that seemed to be split somewhere between triumph and nerves.

Felix plucked the glass jar from between her fingers and held it up for closer inspection. "Let's go home and make some magic."

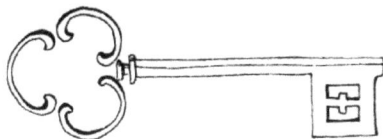

Chapter 80

"**M**AURA, YOU BRILLIANT GODDESS of a woman, I'd kiss you if you weren't dead," Felix declared as he hunched over the small cauldron in the kitchen. "I can't believe you started the decoction days ago."

"Well, dear, I do what I can." Bianca swore the ghost's cheeks tinted a deeper shade of blue as she waved Felix away from her work.

Alder leaned against the wall, one leg kicked back, his arms crossed. "So how much longer will it need once the amethyst lunar lacewing is added?"

Felix flung himself down at the table across from Bianca, with only their discarded masks between them, stopping her from reaching out and taking his hand again. "By tomorrow eve we should be able to administer it, if you're ready, Bianca, and still willing."

"Of course." She didn't even hesitate, there was no room for it.

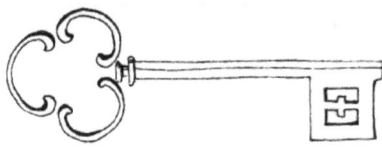

Chapter 81

B Y THE SHATTERED GLOW of the lightning, Bianca peeled her singed dress off her body, the silk now more reminiscent of eyelet lace than the smooth fabric it was at the beginning of the evening. She tugged loose her stays, breathing in her first full breath in hours, and switched her shift out for a lighter, more comfortable night one with lace ribbons trailing over her shoulders like the tails of comets.

She sat down on her bed, the springs groaning only slightly in protest, or perhaps in welcome, when a glitter of gold caught her eye. The card. How could she have forgotten she'd tucked it into her bodice?

She dove for the floor, her knees cracking against the wood. She picked it up, cradling it in her cupped palm. On its back, a gold leaf was stamped with the image of a bird trapped in brambles. Her breaths suddenly seemed to saw their way up her throat unevenly. What fate did the god of a dead people give her. She fingered the edge of the card, willing herself to flip it over, and then a firm knock at her trapdoor stilled her.

"Bianca"—Felix's voice slipped through the cracks—"are you awake?"

Bolting to her feet, she quickly tucked the card into a small jewelry chest on her dresser. She couldn't say why, but she had a squirming sick feeling in her gut that as typically carefree and rule-breaking as Felix was, he would be concerned about the card and its origins. "Yes, I am. You can come in," she called breathlessly as she pulled a shawl over her shoulders.

Felix lifted the hatch and ascended just enough to rest his elbows along the floor, his gray eyes reflecting the light of the storm, though he refused to meet her gaze. He slid two bottles across the planks toward her. "I brought these for you." His voice sounded uncharacteristically small in a way she didn't quite understand. It was almost as if he were nervous, which in turn filled her belly with the voracious wing beats of migrating moths lost in the dark, desperately seeking the light.

She crossed the meager space between them and crouched down and picked up the first, a stoppered bottle with a dropper top.

"That is a concoction of my own." He smiled at her crookedly, the ghosts of remembrances past drifted across his eyes. "I call it bliss. A few droppers full under the tongue will make the shadows in your eyes disappear and fill the ache in your chest, and unlike what those Obliviot healers gave you, it's nonaddictive. Just don't take too much or you'll end up a bit deliriously happy for a few days."

She could feel the pain behind her heart easing already, ever so slightly. She knew kindness could have that effect sometimes. An act done selflessly to help a friend could be as healing as any tonic. She tapped a finger on the lid of the other jar, wide mouthed and squat. "And this one?"

Felix ran a hand through his already bedraggled hair, his rumpled rolled-up sleeve falling all the way to his elbow, exposing the corded length of forearm covered in the sigils of all the magic he'd used of late. "It's the Gorgonian salve, for your scars. It finally finished fermenting. It's quite potent; they should fade to nothing in a day or two."

Their eyes locked, and something tore through her at the raw emotion burning in his eyes. It looked like fire and life and the first light of the morning. It emboldened her so much so that before she could stop herself, she leaned over and pressed a featherlight kiss against his cheek right below his scar. She retreated just as quickly as she'd advanced, scarlet creeping up her face, and she brushed a lock of hair behind her ear. "Thank you, Felix, I appreciate all you have done."

When she looked up, bold enough to finally meet his gaze once more, she found his eyes shuttered and locked, devoid of all emotion and darkened to near black. Her heart sank in a pond of instant regret, and she wished she could drown herself in it, too, for being so brazen and improper.

Felix cleared his throat, clearly uncomfortable. "Yes, well, my pleasure, Ms. Hastings. Good night." He descended in a blink, the hatch slamming in her face with such finality it sent her burrowing under the quilts of her bed to curl up in shame and hide from the brutality of it.

As sleep finally welled up to take her by the hand and walk her into the land of dreams, she licked her lips, and her last thought before leaving consciousness was that Felix tasted like he smelled, of chocolate, smoke, and whiskey.

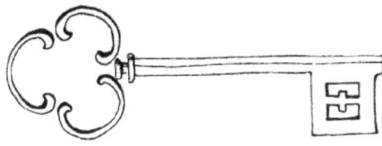

Chapter 82

THEY GATHERED AS ALWAYS in the library in front of the fire, the furniture already cleared and a cushion for her head already provided by the ever-thoughtful Maura.

Bianca dressed in one of her favorite dresses for the occasion. She figured if the whole thing went sideways, she wanted to at least look nice when she died. Her midnight-blue dress matched her hair, which she'd taken the extra time to sweep up into a knot with little star-studded pins to tuck it into place. Embroidered all along the edge of her bodice and her hemline were plum pansies being pollinated by busy beaded bees. The rest of the garment had swooping blue jays appliquéd in lace all aflutter. Her mother's keys wrapped safely along her wrist gave her the strength she needed to face the unknown.

Felix rolled his wrinkled and stained sleeves up and tossed aside his waistcoat in a heap on a nearby chair and busied himself with measuring out a chalice of thick amethyst decoction.

"Now you'll lie here"—he gestured to a plump and tasseled brocade pillow on the floor—"and I'll anchor you while the trance has a hold. I don't know how long it will affect you, but we'll be here for you the whole time." Felix's words were soft in a fair imitation of soothing, but there was a bitter edge to them, a distance after her impropriety the night before.

Her nails bit into her palms; she couldn't meet his eyes as she settled herself on the floor. "I was actually hoping to have Alder anchor me. Is that all right with you?" She looked up at the nymph where he leaned against the mantle in his freshly pressed waistcoat and silently willed all her discomfort and pleading into her eyes, begging that although he didn't approve, that he would help her. She couldn't stand the thought of Felix being forced to put his hands on her again, not after the previous night, and not like this, not when she'd spent the night dreaming of his hands on her in other ways she knew she could never have.

He touched his forehead, the Goddess mark long gone, giving her a curt nod of understanding. "I would be honored."

He knelt on the floor behind the pillow, removed his cuff links, tucked them into a pocket, and rolled up his sleeves in crisp, neat even movements. Felix frowned as though he'd lost some sort of competition, though Bianca wasn't sure what it was he thought he'd lost.

Bianca stretched out her legs, careful to smooth her skirts, and took the chalice from Felix. The aroma of the decoction was less than pleasant, not too dissimilar from the compost bins she'd encountered in the greenhouse. Felix crouched down next to her, his eyes level with hers, still painfully shuttered, though for a heartbeat, she thought she saw something in his hooded gaze. He opened his mouth as if to speak and then thought better of it and instead pulled a flask from his back pocket. "Cheers," he muttered, and tapped it against the rim of her cup. "Bottoms up."

He took a long draw, his throat bobbing as he slugged it down. Bianca sighed and followed suit, though she immediately wished it was whiskey in her cup. The decoction was as odious and thick as a warm slug, its flavor bittersweet like the frayed bits of a last hope.

It congealed sharply, and her throat constricted. She began to cough and choke on it, her breaths battering their way around it as it crept far too slowly into her stomach.

"Easy, easy now." Alder's long calloused fingers curled around her shoulders, lowering her down until her head rested comfortably on the cushion. They felt wrong, oh so wrong, on her skin as his magic slipped along her skin. "Don't fight it."

She wheezed, her hands finding and clawing at her throat. Someone tugged them gently away as a purple mist clouded her eyes, and she was pulled, like a clam pried from its shell, out of her body and thrown into the cosmos.

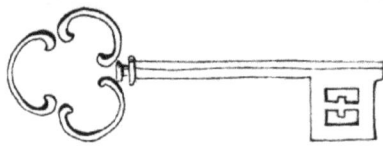

Chapter 83

"THE KEY TO MAGIC is intention, as you know." Felix's voice echoed through her through the dark empty space in which her soul walked. "It is no different with this potion. Your intent will guide what you see. Focus on the Instrument, focus on how the Fury are getting into our Fragments. There you will find our answers."

She closed her mind's eye to the vast emptiness and pulled her intentions to the forefront of her being, choosing first the Instrument. Who were they?

A kaleidoscope of color cycloned around her like a blur of leaves in a windstorm until the spinning slowed and an image teetered on its edge like a coin before coalescing into a coherent image. She stood in front of a cabin surrounded by a wood of hunchbacked trees, their graying leafless branches hung with lichen like the beards of wizened old men.

The cabin creaked open, and a young man with pure blond hair, that shone around his head like a halo, and pointed ears stepped out. He was followed by a waifish woman, who judging from their resemblance, had to be his mother. They were speaking to one another, but Bianca couldn't understand their words. To her ear, they may as well have been speaking through water.

She watched the mother give her son a gift, a silver pendant made of swooping intersecting circles on a length of black leather cord. His eyes lit up golden in the midday sun. Bianca didn't understand what in the gods' names this had to do with the Instrument. Surely, neither one of these people were destined to be the vessel of the Darkness.

The image splintered, fragmented like shards of broken glass, and she plucked at them with her mind, desperately trying to see, to understand.

The pieces reordered themselves around the same mother and son, only this scene was a nightmare. They both screamed as the dirt beneath them suddenly bucked and rolled. Together they fell, skinned knees bled, and a cut opened on the woman's cheek as her face collided with jagged rock. Trees in the distance cracked. The man yanked his mother to her feet, and they ran on. The woman struggled to breathe through her tears and fear, but his face was set and determined.

Fissures rent open along the path, and spires of pure crystal stone jutted toward the sky, like great fingers tearing through the peel of an orange. A crevice opened right under the young man's feet. With a violent jerk, he fell. Still clinging to his hand, his mother slammed into the ground, her fumbling fingers barely grasping his. And then he was gone, and his mother's hand was left suspended in the open air empty. A wave of stone crashed, obliterating the vision.

Her inner eye blinked, and she was staring the man in the face as he sobbed, curled along the sandy bank of a river. Gashes along his body bled blue, soaking into the moist ground beneath him.

A flutter of lashes and the man stood with a young woman whose teeth gleamed like needle points. She was an exotic and terrifying beauty. She traced her fingers along the concentric circles of the man's pendant. His fair brow buckled under a fringe of hair grown long; he tucked the necklace beneath his tunic out of sight. The woman became enraged. She threw herself at his chest, clawing at his shirt front. He struck her, throwing her back as her long nails raked across his skin, and ran.

The images began to wink by so fast they dripped like fat beads of candle wax blurring into each other. The man alone in the desert, tears on his face. A building on fire. The man running, his shadow stretched long in the moonlight across the sands. A cavern against a cliff face. Tunneling, the man dug into the back of the cavern until his fingernails splintered and bled. He argued with something or someone Bianca couldn't see; filth coated his face like the paint of war.

A knife bloomed in someone's chest, planted there by the man. He used the blood in a ritual and creatures of Darkness were born. His eyes turned a sickening shade of amber, threaded through with black.

Bianca wanted to look away, she didn't want to see anymore, but she had to know, she had to discover how they were making it into other Fragments. She forced her will, pouring all her need into it until she stood on a step inside the Void. She spiraled down, down, down, soaring past doors so fast they looked like nothing more than playing cards tipped off of a table, fluttering down to the floor.

The farther she flew, the more prominent the sense of wrongness she'd always felt and dismissed became. The stench of rot among a bouquet of flowers. At the very bottom, a cacophony of screams echoed from a hole. A gaping wound in the wall.

Decay spread from it, rust twisted its fingers in the wrought design of the stairs, vines of putrefaction clawed their way across the walls, consuming a nearby door. She edged her consciousness closer, wondering what in the gods' names it was.

A whisper, carried on a foul breath, wrapped around her, slithering around her mind's eye, "The Bore," it hissed, the word echoing through the gash and around her head.

Her vision perched and vaulted past the festering edges and into the Bore. There was nothing but unending tangles of darkness slashed through with glimmers of crystal as she fell, and then abruptly, she stopped. She stared into the darkness, and after a sickening heartbeat, it stared back at her with amber eyes, and a voice ragged from disuse grated across the empty space between them. "There you are. We've been waiting."

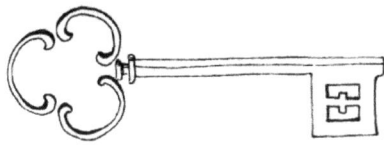

Chapter 84

THE INSTRUMENT LAUGHED AT the startled green eyes that peered down at him, from some great magical distance, in horror.

She was coming as was foretold. It was time to make ready.

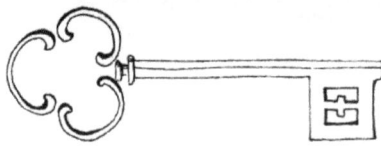

Chapter 85

Bianca clawed her way back into her empty husk, tearing through her subconscious and crashing back into herself. She thrashed against the hands locked onto her shoulders until they released her at last so she could roll over and spew the residual potion from her body.

Sweat dripped from her temples as she hacked up magic and blood and bile into a bowl held in Alder's dark hands. Soothing hands pressed cool cloths to her forehead and stroked the loose hairs away from her face.

Alder's stoic gaze met hers. "Did it work?" His voice sounded far too husky, and his eyes kept darting over her shoulder to the spot where he should have been.

But if he'd not been her tether, then those hands on her belonged to . . . she turned to meet Felix's gray eyes, his brow twisted with concern. "Are you all right?"

The corners of her lips pulled down, dragged by the invisible weight of all she had seen. "How long was I gone?" Her words felt like barbs in her throat, sticking and catching painfully.

"Here, drink this." Felix pressed a steaming mug into her hands that smelled of whiskey, lemon, and honey. "Maura sent it up a few moments before I felt you pulling to come back. You were screaming quite a bit."

She opened her mouth to ask why he was her tether instead of Alder, but he pushed the mug to her lips before the words could rasp past.

A small smile teased at the edges of his mouth, and a spark of knowing slashed through his eyes as though he could sense what she was thinking. "Your magic kept trying to throw off Alder. I had to step in and take over the spell work so we didn't lose you."

She nodded her understanding, remembering the way her magic had first reacted to Alder's touch, though she found it peculiar. With nothing but the dregs of her drink left, she tried to rise, but her legs felt boneless beneath her. Alder darted forward, and both he and Felix helped her to stand and guided her to a chair. With a flick of his fingers, Alder drew a footstool over and helped her to prop her feet upon it.

The flickering firelight cast purple shadows across half their faces and burnished the other half bronze. In that strange light, both men with their eyes shining reminded her of a painting she'd seen once at the Academy with her father recovered from some far-off place. "The Seeds of Grief and Torment" was its name, and she understood now that the loneliness and anxiety of the unknown was just the beginning seeds of grief bursting from its husk, and if left to grow alone without love or even kindness, it would sprout and bloom into something far darker. Something like the man who became the Instrument.

She felt the burning sting of tears collecting in the corner of her eyes. Swallowing the beginnings of a sob, she recounted to them what she'd seen, sparing them the more gruesome horror, partially for their benefit and partially for hers. She didn't want to have to relive them so soon. "It's called the Bore."

Alder's face was as ashen as the dead embers in the fireplace. "How? How is it even possible? Shouldn't the walls stop them from getting through to the Void?"

Bianca shook her head, the last of her hairpins giving way to the chaos of her mane tumbling down around her shoulders. "I got the sense that it went around them somehow. They found their way through like rats in a maze."

"The walls divide the realms and contain the Darkness, but nowhere is written that they completely encircle the Void." Felix pulled a smoke from his back pocket and lit it, leaning back on his heels. "It explains some of the missing Travelers as well."

"They needed keys to get into the other Fragments to take the ones they truly wanted with the strongest and most potent magics in their blood, so they ambushed the Travelers in the Void to take their keys." Alder took a smoke from Felix and went to the mantle where a decanter full of amber whiskey sat and poured them each a stiff glassful.

Felix accepted his with a nod before settling himself cross-legged at Bianca's feet so close that if he leaned back, his head would be resting on her knees, so close she could thread her fingers through his hair. "Any idea how many other Instruments are out there?"

Bianca traded her mug for a tumbler with murmured gratitude and took a long swill, allowing the burning liquid to sear away the flickering images left behind in her mind, a residue of what she'd seen. "Ocidynus for certain, but I'm not sure it matters. I believe the one I saw is the most powerful. I think whatever plans the Darkness has lain hinge on him and his success."

Felix and Alder both shuddered and took deep gulps from their glasses. Thunder cracked outside, and the rain lashed the windows with a redoubled ferocity as though sensing they spoke of dark matters.

Alder found his voice first, hissing to cool the liquor burn. "We must make a plan to leave straightaway and leave word for Will in the event that"—he took another sip as if to brace himself to get his next words out—"in the event that we don't return."

With a wince, Bianca threw back the rest of her drink. "I may have left out one minor detail."

"What's that?" Felix asked as he puffed lavender smoke rings into the air, belying just how anxious he really was underneath his mask of stony apathy.

"They know we're coming."

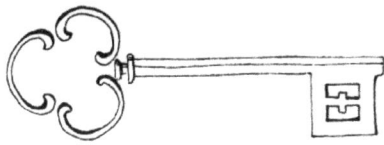

Chapter 86

*T*HE INSTRUMENT SHARPENED HIS *knife on a bloody whetstone. The scree, scree, scree of the blade sent sparks across her vision, alighting his sunken cheekbones and hollowed eyes in shattered flashes.*

She turned to run, only to find Fury at her back, their maws open to show off their uneven rows of teeth in a mockery of a grim smile.

"You escaped us once, you will not again," the Instrument's voice echoed behind her as rough as a cascade of bones.

The Fury reached for her, its talons painted with dried blood.

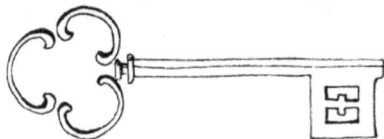

Chapter 87

BIANCA WOKE THRASHING AGAINST her bedsheets, her scars alight with fire. She sat panting and utterly alone in the rain-soaked darkness. The wind howled through the cracks in the windows.

She stumbled from the bed, her breaths short and ragged, her pain in her scars seared through to the bone. With stiff fingers, she fumbled along the dresser for the jar of Gorgonian Willow poultice. Her fingers contracted as lightning slashed through her arms, and the lid of the jar slipped, crashing to the floor and shattering. She dove her fingers into the thick ointment. With jerky movements and a bitten off scream, she managed to make her hand move.

The moment the poultice touched her savaged skin, it was like a warm breath had blown out the flame. Greedily, she dug in, scooping globs and massaging it into her scars from shoulder to wrist. A relieved sob slipped loose, and once free, it grew until they fell unbidden.

As she slathered on another layer, her scars began to glow the polished onyx of Felix's magic. It needled her skin in a not unpleasant sort of way, and she watched in awe as it shrank her scars until each luminous black line was no thicker than an embroidery thread.

With a flick of her fingers, she lit the gas lamp by her bed from where she sat puddled on the floor as the radiance leached from her forearms. She had to search now for the markings hidden among her freckles, which was a far cry from how they used to glare at her.

She'd dreamed of being rid of the angry pink marks since she left the hospital. Fantasized about them fading with time. She'd expected to feel relief or gratitude or even elation at their erasure, but instead, she felt untethered. As though she were losing yet another link to her parents, making their disappearance less real, less meaningful.

She climbed into her bed, pulling the quilt over her head like the scared little child she felt she was inside despite her age, but every time she closed her eyes, she saw him, the Instrument, looking at her with those empty eyes. Her lungs seized, refusing to inflate, and her fingers shook as his words to her screamed through her mind, ricocheting against the inside of her skull, growing louder and louder with each turn of phrase. "There you are. We've been waiting."

She flung herself from her bed, tears rolling thick and heavy down her cheeks, blurring her vision as she threw the hatch door open with a crack, echoed by the thunder. She ran as quickly as her feet could carry her down the halls, her bare footfalls muted against the carpeted floor. The eyes of the portraits seemed to follow her even in the dark, bruising her with their cast stones of judgment.

Her knuckles rapping against the door echoed as desperately as the knocks of a man buried alive against the roof of his casket. But at last Felix's door opened a crack, and smoke burnished with the golden glow of flickering lamp light spilled into the dark and dismal corridor.

Felix looked down at her, one arm leaning against the doorframe, his shirt half undone, his hair a mess, and his eyes rimmed with the haze of mild intoxication. He quirked a brow, his forehead creasing in concern. "Hastings? What are you doing here?"

Her voice felt as fragile and delicate as antique lace. "I know this is highly inappropriate, but the nightmares." She wrung her hands, twisting a ribbon from her shift. "May I stay with you? I, I don't want to be alone."

He stared down at her long enough that shame began to slither up her spine and worm its way around her heart, but then he did the unexpected and stood aside, opening the door just enough for her to slip past him.

Her eyes fell to his bed the moment she stepped in, a large tangle and sprawl of pillows and bedclothes. Fortunately, it was big enough and her fear consuming enough that she barely batted an eye at the impropriety of the situation.

Their eyes locked as the door clicked and Felix spun around, the corner of his mouth hitched in a slight smirk. "I hope you don't snore, Hastings."

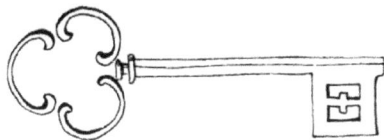

Chapter 88

HIS HAND CLENCHED AND relaxed, his fingers ached as he watched her sleep. They screamed to be let loose to run through her hair. To brush away that errant tear that leaked from the corner of her eye even as she slept. Every moment was a battle of wills against his instincts to draw her in closer, to smooth the ragged and torn edges of her grief in a way that no one had been able to for him.

He needed to do something with them, now, before they took on a mind of their own. In the flickering of the lamplight, he rolled over. He fumbled for charcoal and one of his many sketchbooks by his bed. He sat with his spine pressed rigidly against the headboard and began to draw her in a series of swooping curves and lines. He started with the way her hand curled near her face, resting on his pillow. Each finger long and delicate, the splotches of magic seamlessly giving way to her generous freckles.

Oh, her freckles. How many afternoons in the library had he spent watching her over the lip of his book, the words blurring out of focus as the smell of being near her drove him to distraction, and imagined kissing every single one of those delicious freckles.

He drew the spill of her hair across the bed like an oceanic wave breaking on the shore. He drew the star by her eye, the flutter of her lashes against her cheeks. Her lips he saved for last, giving them the time and attention they deserved until he had a complete portrait. A frozen moment that he could keep forever, even when he couldn't keep her. He could never ask her to make that kind of sacrifice.

Gray watery morning light spilled in from the slit in his heavy drapes and cut across the floor in an abrupt reminder that they were running out of time. In a few short hours, they would wake and discuss their plans, and then whatever came next was in the gods hands.

Too bad he wasn't sure he believed in them, prayer could come in handy in a situation like this.

He set his sketchbook aside, dimmed the lamp, and curled up on his side facing Bianca. She'd shifted slightly while he was lost in thought, her hand stretched out as if to bridge the gap between them. He reached out until their fingertips were only separated by a whisper's breath, not daring to take her hand in his, not fully. Then he let his lids fall heavy, and he let her gentle breathing lull him to sleep at last.

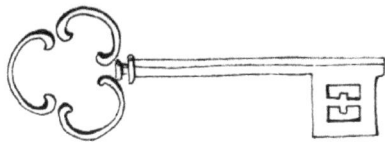

Chapter 89

ALDER SAT STIFFLY ON the parlor couch. He'd tossed and turned all night, unable to settle his mind. He'd taken a walk to sooth his raging mind. He'd seen from the shadows Bianca entering Felix's room in the wee hours of the night. He wanted to rage at the changeling for leading her on still even after what happened by the river, but he couldn't bring himself to, not when they were about to risk their lives. Who was he to deny them a little bit of comfort? When they got back, if they got back, he would have to set them straight. He'd grown to love Bianca, as if she were a sister, and he didn't want to see her heartbroken, not after all she'd been through, after all they'd been through together, and this path the two of them were on would inevitably lead there.

He had to admit there was a small part of him that was jealous too. To have someone to hold in times like these. Images of the winged princess kept coming to him unbidden in the night. The way her copper curls teased along her bare shoulders, the way her eyes caught the sunlight. He had no right to think of her in such a way, not when she was alive, and certainly not now, but there was no telling that to the dark and lonely hours before the dawn.

"So, what do you have to say, nymph? Any grand ideas on how to get us out of there alive?" Felix raised a brow in a silent mocking challenge from where he leaned ankles crossed against the arched doorway into the parlor.

Alder crossed his arms defensively. "As a matter of fact, I do." He'd wrestled with the idea for some time, and though it was risky, it was the only plan he could come up with.

"Well, let's hear it then." With a snap of his fingers, Felix lit a rolled cigarette, its lavender smoke curling around his head.

He glanced at Bianca, seated on the opposite end of the couch from him, her emerald eyes shining beacons of hope so fragile they may as well have been made of thin blown glass. He leaned forward, resting his elbows on his knees. "We have to enter through this Bore. It doesn't seem there is any other choice. But I don't think it's a good idea to try and leave by it. We don't know who we will find and in what shape they'll be in. Dragging them back through the Bore would be as good as sentencing them to death. I propose we summon a door."

Felix laughed mirthlessly. "You want to summon a new door to the void? That's a dead form of magic."

Alder held up a scroll, and Felix froze, understanding dawning on his face. "You've been studying, you sly nymph."

"I have."

"If you don't mind me asking, what is that?" Bianca cut in.

He passed the delicately rolled scroll to her. "It's *Access the Void, an Architect's Guide*, one of the last remaining accounts on how the magic that connected Fragments to the Void worked. I've been studying it, and I believe I can construct us a way out of there."

Bianca unfurled the scroll a handspan and squinted at the spiraling language written in a nearly dead tongue. "What about after we get everyone through? I'm assuming you can seal the door like you did before, but the Bore will still be open. There will be nothing to stop the Instrument from coming after us."

He ran his hand over his head and tried to summon the confidence he wasn't sure he had. "We'll have everyone back at that point. Hopefully, they will all be strong enough, and together, we can collapse it. I know it's not a permanent solution, but goddess willing, it will buy us time."

"I'll be damned, son of Cedre, it's as good a plan as any." Felix smirked. "It will probably all go to shit, but it's a start."

Alder rolled his eyes and stood to go. He was beginning to think the goddess damned changeling didn't have the ability to be serious under any circumstance.

Bianca passed him back the scroll and folded her hands resolutely in her lap, her chin set and determined. A small smile played at the corner of her mouth. "All right, when do we leave?"

"Before nightfall, if neither of you have any objections, I don't see any sense in waiting."

He left on the heels of their murmured consent, whispering a prayer to the Goddess as he ascended the stairs.

They both trusted him. He just hoped he was worthy of it.

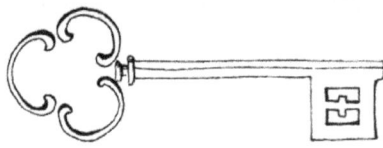

Chapter 90

LIGHTNING STRIKES SLASHED ACROSS their faces, the rain pattering gallows drumbeats against the windowpanes. Bianca felt strangely calm. Resolved. She stood to go, knowing the next few hours may be her only chance to prepare and sleep.

She paused in the archway and turned to look at Felix and was surprised to find him already gazing intently at her, his pupils blown wide. She opened her mouth to whisper good night, but he lunged, catching the words before they could fall from her lips. His mouth came crashing down on hers in a way that suddenly felt as inevitable as a wave breaking on shore. His fingers knotted in her hair, drawing her into him. His other arm wrapped around her waist as he spun her and pressed her into the wall. His knee braced her between her thighs, anchoring her as the kiss seared through her. It was every wish on every star come true all at once.

The kiss was reckless and claiming, breaking and remaking parts of her she hadn't known existed. His moan pressed into her mouth, burrowing its way through her and planting itself in her core where it sparked like fire spells.

She pressed her hand to his chest, his heart beating through his ribs against her palm. Tentatively, she slid it up, along his neck to cup his stubbled cheek. With timid fingertips, she traced the scar that she'd stared at more times than she cared to admit. His pain and his past permanently etched onto his tragically handsome face.

Felix pulled back, his breaths heaving against her, and groaned. He pressed his forehead to hers. "I'm sorry, Bianca, I'm so sorry. This isn't fair." A tear slid down his cheek. She dashed it away.

His eyes were a cyclone of anguish and hunger that she didn't quite understand. He leaned down to kiss her again, but this time the press of his lips was soft and slow, igniting a whole new fire that spread across her skin and burrowed deeply and painfully into her soul.

He pulled back. "I know that you aren't meant to be mine, but no moment beyond this one is promised, and I had to taste you just once." His voice was choked and rough under the burden of his words whispered against her lips.

"Felix," Bianca tried to plead, her voice tangled and wretched. A slithering of cold dread seeped in deep down, dousing the fire that was burning there. She knew what was coming because she knew him. She could feel him slipping away. This beautiful broken man who would do anything for her, and she for him, she felt him sliding infinitesimally farther between each ragged breath.

His tears came thicker, their foreheads still pressed together, they mingled with her own until it was impossible to tell whose tears were whose. "I can't let you go into the Bore tomorrow without telling you that for whatever it's worth, although I can never have you, that my aching heart will love you until my last breath."

She tried to lean up to kiss him, to show him that she didn't care, that she would be his no matter what came, but his fingers tightened on her hair, this time holding her back instead of holding her to him. This was, after all, a goodbye, a door closing in her face.

Then, just as abruptly as he'd swept her off her feet, he tossed her heart into a chasm and slipped away into the dark, leaving her crumpled on the floor. All her peace and resolve shattered.

Part Three

It could smell the world beyond. It could hear their cries. The Darkness gnashed its teeth, ready to sink them into the meat of the world, to bleed it dry for what they did to it.

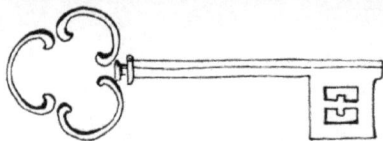

Chapter 91

Felix looked the same as ever standing on the steps of the Void, prepared to descend to the Bore, as if what happened between them mere hours before hadn't irrevocably changed him as it had her. It was carved across the shredded remains of her heart, and now he wouldn't even look at her, choosing instead to stare at the spot just over her head when addressing her. "If your visions are correct—"

"They're correct." Bianca snipped off the end of his sentence. She wanted him to look at her. They could die, and he wouldn't even look at her.

He shifted, not uncomfortably, just down a step to make more room for Alder. "Right, so your visions say the Bore is at the bottom of the Void. I don't know how far down that is from here, so we should take it easy on the way, conserve our energy, and also, Maura packed sandwiches." He held up a rucksack with a small smile hooking the corner of his mouth.

"Goddess bless, this isn't a picnic," Alder grumbled behind her. She looked over her shoulder at him. He was dressed once again in the green coat and brown breeches of his home with a veritable arsenal of daggers strapped onto his person and his quarterstaff on his back. He looked like a man ready for war.

"Here, Bianca, I brought this one for you." Alder held out a knife with an exquisitely carved antler handle. "I know we haven't had time to train with it, but it's better to have it just in case."

Bianca's heart constricted. "Thank you, Alder, that's very kind of you." She took the nearly forearm-length blade from him, and he helped her to hook its sheath on the belt of her mother's trousers opposite a leather hip pouch left to her by Will filled with vibrantly colored vials and poultices for healing various ailments.

She'd once again opted for freedom of movement over propriety. She even asked Maura to take in the flowy legs a bit to make them more formfitting and less likely to snag or trip her up. Over that, she'd simply worn a cream blouse with a dark brocade corset over top. She'd managed to slip her lock picks in along the boning channels, and with great pains, she tamed her hair, knotting it into a fishtail plait, just like her mother used to when she was small.

"Well, let's get this over with then." Felix turned away from them and began the descent.

Alder gestured for her to go ahead of him. The sounds of their boots and the clinking of her keys echoed in an off-kilter melody parallel to the summoning song that whispered from every door.

The taint from the Bore felt more potent, though perhaps it was just that she knew it was there that the musk of a days old corpse seemed barely masked. The light too seemed to grow weaker as though it were afraid to show its face, afraid of what it would see.

Alder paused as they passed the door to Alatus. Felix didn't seem to notice, charging on ahead, presumably in his own thoughts, but Bianca took a moment to wait with him as he brushed his fingers along the carvings of the moons over the peaks.

"You'll see it again," she whispered as she pressed a hand to his arm. "You'll see them again too."

He looked down at her, his azure eyes haunted by grief and lack of sleep. "Goddess send it is so," he murmured, touching his forehead. He patted her hand, and they continued on, catching up with Felix who'd never even noticed their absence, or if he did, he chose not to comment.

They spiraled down, down, down. The song grew fragmented like an out-of-tune music box. Thick fissures that wept blackness vined through the cracks in the cobbled stone walls.

Dread crept over her like an early frost crawling over spring blooms, shriveling the pale-pink petals of her hope. It cracked open her bones and sucked happiness from her marrow. It sniggered in her ear. How could she have ever thought that light would triumph over the Darkness? After all, didn't night persistently conquer day?

Leaden despair filled her chest, pressing on her lungs, and her knees buckled beneath her. She folded in on herself, caving under the sheer enormity of it. It was a wonder she didn't just cease breathing.

Quicksilver eyes clashed into hers, sensuous lips twisted as though trying to speak to her, but all she could hear was the reverberation of the corrupted song stuffed like cotton into her ears. Frantic fingers twitched, pulling invisible marionette strings around her, until the veil was lifted. She blinked up at Felix, worry creasing his face. "There you are," he whispered. His gaze flicked to her lips, the lower one sucked between her teeth, and for a heartbeat, she thought he might kiss her again, but a thrashing behind them drew his attention, and he sprang past her to where Alder lay twitching on the stair.

With deft fingers, he began pulling and plucking at the space around Alder. "The corruption from the Bore is attacking your auras," Felix cast the explanation over his shoulder.

"Why isn't it affecting you?" She pushed hair off her brow, which was matted with cold sweat.

He glanced back at her. "Who says it isn't?"

She saw it then, the tenseness of his shoulders, the gritted teeth. "What can I do to help?"

"Not a thing, unless you suddenly have the ability to see auras and the things affecting them."

Bianca squinted, she thought maybe she saw the occasional wisp of something smoke like in Felix's hands as he plucked and pulled and a hint of deep green around Alder, but if she tried to look right at it, it vanished, just her tired eyes playing tricks on her. "I can't. I'm sorry."

Alder grunted; color returned to his too-pale face. Felix gave him a hand, helping him to sit. "What in the goddess's name was that."

"Just a taste of what's to come I'd imagine." Felix sighed, pulled a pair of smokes from his trouser pocket, he lit both, and handed one to Alder who took it, inhaling deeply.

"Goddess damn." He growled as he stood. "It's like there wasn't a single spec of hope left in all of creation."

"I think it's trying to scare us off. We're getting close."

"How can you tell?" Bianca asked.

Felix gestured with the lit end of his smoke. "Look at the doors."

She craned her head to peer at the next door down. There was something off about it. It was the palest shade of gray, as though it were made of ash rather than wood. She reached her arm out, stretching her fingers nearer but not touching. The words pestilence and plague fluttered through her thoughts.

"What"—Bianca swallowed hard, afraid to hear the answer— "what's wrong with it?"

"It's dead," Alder rasped, his voice riddled with disbelief. "I didn't think that was possible."

"It seems we will have to suspend our definitions of impossible and possible for the time being." Felix stood and pulled a handful of loose stones from his pocket, passed one to Alder, and stepped down, then one to Bianca. "Obsidian infused with my magic, to aid in aura protection."

The nymph flushed angrily. "These would have been nice to have earlier," he ground out.

"Yes, well, you have them now." Felix smiled, but it didn't reach his eyes. He turned without further comment and continued on.

The festering dark consumed the last of the light farther down, eating at the stones on the wall like a ravenous blight. They each conjured a small ball of flames—flickering globes of silver, pearl, and sapphire, that only illuminated small pools in front of them, barely able to beat back the black.

"Fuck," Felix swore as they rounded the last step.

The Bore was a wound stabbed through the fabric of existence, fetid and putrefying, weeping its wretched bile into the Void. It was darker than her darkest dream and more terrifying to behold than the face of death.

"Dear gods help us," Bianca whispered, the sound muffled by the miasmic fog seeping from cracks in the ruined stone.

"Your gods aren't here now." Felix growled, and then he charged headlong into the Bore, leaving Bianca and Alder no choice but to follow.

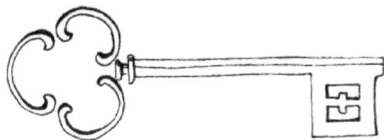

Chapter 92

THE BORE FELT LIKE falling. She was neither up nor down. Her stomach lurched into her throat; her hair floated up around her as if she was drowning in a black ocean. Time suspended, memories and dreams drifting past her in little onyx glass bubbles glowing and dimming like flicker bugs on an endless loop. She saw the iron door, the Thieve's Bane Vines, her mother braiding her hair, the Beldam, her father smiling at her over the pages of a well-loved book, the hall of ticking clocks. Worst of all, she saw flashes of the Instrument's life, of his mother, his pain, the blood that he spilt. They floated by until she no longer knew what memories were hers, which were real, and which were visions or dreams.

She tried to move, to fight for direction, but the atmosphere in the Bore was as thick as choked-on sobs, as thick as blood on the hands of the Instrument.

And then just as suddenly as she entered, she was clawing her way out through burning sands like the first being birthed from the fertile ground of the gods. Gagging and spluttering, blinking confused into the too-bright world.

She rubbed grit from her eyes and looked around. The pale sand stretched on until it met a dusky rouge sky. Three partial suns drifted over a distant plateau creeping slowly toward their zenith. Behind them, their fiery cosmic entrails unfurled in spiraling rose-gold ribbons.

Strange bulbous spiny plants littered the dune between her and the remnants of a town. In the distance, serrated sawtooth ridges blackened the horizon over which skulked a nefarious thunderhead; even at a distance, it felt unnatural. It could only be the stain of dark magic. One thing she did not see, or more accurately two things, were Alder and Felix. She spun in place, her boots slipping in the stardust sand.

A whimper was all that slipped from her lips as she realized she couldn't shout for them and risk being heard by listening ears with ill intent.

She knew she should stay put; that was, after all, one of the first things she'd been taught about expeditions. It was in the Academy's *Explorers Guide to Safety*, a tome she'd read more often than her book of fairy stories growing up until its spine was held together with nothing but ratty thread and hope. What she also knew was that she was vulnerable. On the wide expanse of glittering sand, anything could spot her, not just her friends, and that thought shoved icy needles of fear in between her vertebrae. So she moved, slowly at first, down the steep incline, and then faster as the sand slipped and tumbled, pulling at her feet trying to make her lose her balance.

At the base of the hill, the white sand bled into hard-packed scarlet ground, cracked like dehydrated lips, abused and worn by the scorching trio of suns. She went sprawling as the sand unceremoniously deposited her, her palms skinned against the unforgiving soil. She bit back a cry, eyes darting around to make sure nothing saw or heard her.

Bianca stumbled to her feet and darted for the looming buildings squatting behind a haze of heat. Her boots stirred a wake of dust kicked up with every step. She slowed, lengthening her stride to try to diminish the evidence of her passage. She drew up short, crouched, and moved at a crawling pace as she met the edge of the peculiar town.

The flat-fronted buildings sagged as crooked and dilapidated as rotten teeth. A bone-drying breeze whistled through the narrowly spaced wooden structures, sending herds of dried brambles scurrying about. She held her breath and waited, heart hammering away the seconds like a ticking clock reminding her that she was nearly out of time.

There, something just a few buildings down, the hem of a skirt whisked around a doorjamb. Every logical part of her screamed not to investigate, but her heart, her heart whispered that maybe, just maybe, it was her mother.

Her feet started moving before she could talk them out of it. She darted over the parched runnels raked through the space between buildings, wide enough to have been considered a road had there been any sign of anything to ride or drive down it. Panting, she slammed into the doorframe of the building and slipped inside. She blinked spots from her eyes as they adjusted to the abrupt darkness.

"Mother?" Her voice rasped like a match dragged along the striker. "Mother?" The skeleton of some sort of ale house or tavern lay cadaverous around her; its fractured remnants littered the floor.

A scurrying clatter of bottles behind the bar stilled her heart. Cold sweat trickled down her spine as she slowly swept one toe across the roughly hewn floorboards followed by the other. She inched closer to the rounded end of the counter, arms outstretched to defend herself against whatever was on the other side.

The pinched face that looked up at her had too-large eyes that seemed recessed into its starved sockets. It cowered like a cornered animal trying to decide whether to fight or flee, but it was human, or humanlike. One of its pointed ears had a bite taken out at the top, and its fingers that twitched and curled at its chest were cracked and blistered. Its too-pale, almost-swamplike skin was seared by the sun.

Bianca lowered her hands and squatted down to eye level with it—with her, she realized as she took in its tattered dress and decidedly feminine albeit emaciated figure. The woman in front of her cocked her head to the side, stringy ropes of dreaded hair sliding off her shoulder.

"Hello." Bianca wet her lips. "Can you help me? I'm looking for my friends."

The woman's black eyes narrowed on her. Something about the intensity of her gaze made the hairs on the back of her neck stand at attention, teasing the edges of her memory. "You're one of them," the woman's voice hissed through needle-sharp teeth. "One of them with your sparkly magics. He's lookin' for you, funny, isn't it? You, here lookin' for him, and all the while he's been sending them out there lookin' for you. Knows you coming too. I'd wager, planned it in his wee little head with his voices, always talking to his voices, doesn't talk to me anymore. No, he doesn't have need for old Kes-Sei, won't put her out of her misery neither."

The blood drained in a dizzying rush from Bianca's face as recollection slammed into her. This was the woman, the one from a sliver of the visions who'd been with the Instrument. She'd wanted his pendant, but clearly there had been something more unseen between them. She'd been beautiful in the visions, but now she was a shell, a mad shell of whatever she once was. "Kes-Sei, that's your name, right? Can you help me, help me find him? I need to find the ones he took."

Kes-Sei drummed her fractured nails against her skull, muttering to herself. Bianca inched closer. "I can get you out of here, Kes-Sei, but I need your help."

Her head snapped back, her black-eyed gaze suddenly sharp and filled to the brim with a raw ferocity that crashed into Bianca's. Her jaw worked side to side, the sharp points of her teeth grinding into one another. "He wants the sparkly magic. I used to be sparkly, not like you, pretty thing, but now I'm hungry, always hungry, and who's to say he'll know if I have a taste."

She lunged at Bianca, her teeth gnashing. Bianca threw up her hands, her fingers starting to glow, but Kes-Sei's hands wrapped around her throat as they both tumbled back. Her head cracked against the floorboards; a plume of dust erupted beneath them. Ears ringing from the impact, Bianca thrashed, trying to buck the fiendish woman off her to gouge her eyes, anything to stop the horrible crushing feeling against her windpipe.

Her fingers sparked, her magic struggling to unspool as stars and darkness flickered on the edges of her vision. She couldn't focus on the sensation of it long enough to make it do anything. Her heart threatened to burst her eardrums with its incessant pounding. She managed to get a leg up and knee Kes-Sei in the side, which dislodged her only slightly, but it was enough for Bianca to take a sucking breath, pulling enough oxygen into her lungs to direct her magic.

A blast of white light struck Kes-Sei in the face and sent her careening back into the edge of the bar. Bianca scrambled to her feet, spat blood on the floor, and sent a boot-shod foot right into the woman's jaw. "Bitch," she seethed as her boot connected with the side of her head. A sickly crack echoed around the dust-muffled room, and Kes-Sei shriveled up into an unconscious heap on the floor.

Bianca doubled over, her hands braced on her knees, her breaths heaving. The floorboards behind her creaked, and she whirled, the magical tongues of flame licking against her palm ready to be flung at whatever came at her next.

Alder and Felix gaped at her, both with a lethal combination of magic and daggers twined in their hands.

"Damn"—Felix's face split into a devilish grin—"that might be one of the most attractive things I've ever seen, you vicious woman."

Bianca lowered her hands and brushed blood-spattered locks off her forehead to hide the crimson blush that stained her cheeks stoking to life, the residual embers still burning hopelessly in her core from their kiss. *The one he effectively took back*, she had to remind herself, he had no right to be flirtatious now.

Alder elbowed Felix in the ribs and cleared his throat. "I'm glad we found you so quickly; this place is crawling with remnants." He put his various knives back into their sheaths. "Though I see you managed quite well on your own."

"Remnants?" Bianca asked. "Is that what her kind are?"

Felix crossed the room and nudged the unconscious woman with the toe of his boot. "No, she's some kind of siren, see the faint ruffle of gills there on her neck?" He pointed to the spot just below her jawline where three slits with rippled edges were barely visible.

"Remnants is what we've decided to call the people here. We've encountered two vampier, a wraith, and we've seen sign of a wyvern. We think they've been here since the Breaking, like your Instrument. Frozen outside of time and existence." Alder rubbed the spot on his forehead where his brows creased. "We should kill her or tie her up and get out of this goddess forsaken ruin."

"In a hurry to go die, Alder?" Felix cast over his shoulder sarcastically.

Bianca rolled her eyes, turning to reprimand him for being cruel, when the faint glimmer of something on the floor caught her attention. She stepped over Kes-Sei's limp body and pushed through the dust moats curtained through the air.

She picked at it with her fingernail, trying to pry whatever it was loose while the men bickered behind her, drawing no more of her attention than one would pay to birds singing in the early hours of the morning in the place between waking and sleeping. Whatever it was wasn't coming loose, so she pulled the knife Alder had gifted to her from its sheath and wedged it between the splintered wood and the shining object. The boards released it with a groan of protest.

It was the pendant gifted to the Instrument by his mother. Bianca turned it over in her hand; the length of leather cord was still attached to it but just barely. She ran her fingers along its silver looping design, and something about it made her magic hum in her blood.

A hand on her shoulder drew her gaze, Felix. "What's that?" He bent down, the heat of his words curled against the shell of her ear and sent shivers skittering down her spine.

She stood up, turning toward him. "It's the necklace the Instrument was gifted by his mother."

Alder leaned across the bar to get a better look. "Odd to find it in such a place."

She shook her head. "I don't know that it is. Kes-Sei," she glanced down to make certain the siren was still out of it, "She wanted it. He might have traded it to her. She kept muttering things about him. I think she helped him in some way."

"I shudder to think how," Felix murmured, as he leaned in to run a finger across the metallic knot in her palm, the whisper of his touch ghosting along her skin.

She clamped her fingers around the pendant and drew it away, tucking it into the front of her bodice as she took a half step away from him. "Yes, well, we should probably get going, right?"

Alder rapped his knuckles against the bar. "Right, those mountains are at least half a day's walk depending on how bad that storm over them is."

A scream rent the air in two, splitting it between the moment of relative calm before and the moment of heart-throbbing anxiety after. The ground trembled beneath them. Alder crept on deft feet to the threshold and peered out.

His blanched face turned back to them, and his hands motioned frantically as he mouthed the words, "Go go go," punctuated by panicky hand signals.

Felix and Bianca moved without question. Felix grabbed her by her hand, pulling her toward the back of the room through the only other visible doorway just as the sound of splintering wood exploded behind them.

"Run!" Alder screamed over a deafening roar and a sickening hiss. "Don't look back!"

They skidded out the back door, leaping over the carcasses of old crates, and hit the packed dirt, feet pounding toward the open desert.

Bianca's lungs caught fire, her breaths sawing in and out of her with a dull blade as the blistering heat from the sun turned its gaze toward them. The ground around them quaked, even the pebbles scrambled away from whatever pursued them. Sweat stung her eyes, and her muscles screamed as she looked ahead to where Alder led them, his long legs pulling him farther faster, toward the lip of a cliff, the chasm below it leading gods knew where. They were about to be trapped between a crevice and a monster.

Her fingers itched, and white sparks cracked and popped along their length, her magic seething to be free, ready to defend. She ripped her hand free, sick of running, sick of always feeling trapped, and spun to face the damned creature head-on, magic blazing.

A snake, as tall as an ancient tree, its maw open, tongue scenting the air darting between sword-long fangs, pursued them. Its ridged scaled body writhed across the ground with deadly grace, coming right for them with murderous intent in its slitted red eyes.

Bianca planted her feet and raised her hands, unspooling every bit of her magic she could, pulling it up into her palms. She'd be damned if she kept running. Something hard crashed into her, wrapped around her, and then she was gazing up not at the beast but at the cloudless magenta sky as she plummeted off the cliff.

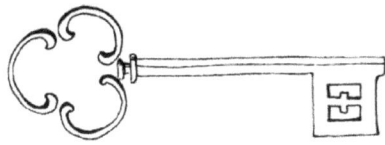

Chapter 93

FOR THE SECOND TIME, Felix dragged Bianca on to the bank of a river—he was really going to have to stop getting into situations like this with her. At least this time she was conscious.

Alder spluttered next to him, spitting water. He shucked off his heavy green coat, tossing it vehemently on the ground. "A fucking basilisk, a goddess damned basilisk. I didn't think those existed. They're supposed to be children's stories."

"Yes, well, so is this entire place," Felix pulled his knapsack off and started rummaging through it. "So, much like we have to suspend our definition of impossible, I think it would be wise to also assume that all the stories are real. Damn it, the sandwiches are soggy."

Bianca glared at him furiously in a way he shouldn't find attractive. "The sandwiches, Felix? Really? Why did you stop me? We could have killed it; now it's slinking off gods knows where."

"Ah yes, well, those shiny red scales aren't just to make it look pretty, they reflect magic, so whatever big bad spell you were about to throw at it was about to ricochet right off of it and hit all of us."

Alder flopped onto his back on the ground, his skin smearing with the red chalky dust. "They also don't like water, won't cross it if they can help it."

A delicious pink tinge crept up her cheeks, highlighting her freckles. "Oh, well, thanks for chucking me off a cliff then."

"Any time." He smirked.

"Now, we just keep going along the river, and we can arrive at the mountains safe and sound, ready to face the next thing trying to kill us." Alder groaned.

"Is that complaining I hear, soldier?" Felix nudged him with the toe of his boot.

He cracked an eyelid revealing a bloodshot blue eye. "No, just a fact. Trying to make sure you don't forget since you seem to be making a joke out of everything."

"Someone has to keep things light. Ah, found it." He pulled his silver flask from the bottom of the pack, pulled the stopper, and held it out to Alder. "Here take a drink and then we'll go."

The man sat up and sighed, but he didn't protest. He took the flask and raised it in a salute. "To fighting impossible battles," he said, before he took a drink and passed it on to Bianca.

She held it in her long delicate fingers, the same ones he could still feel the phantom touch of ghosting over his face, and murmured, "To the ones we love and those we've left behind."

Bianca passed it back to him, careful not to let their fingers touch unnecessarily. He sighed wistfully. "To the Instrument, may his wait for us beyond the Veil be a long one."

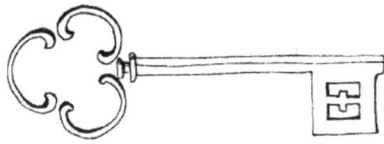

Chapter 94

BIANCA'S FEET COULDN'T SEEM to stay steady as they picked their way along the carved-out bank of the river. Her boots pinched, and the alcohol made her thoughts slightly distorted around the edges, just barely dulling the erratic hum of nerves that threatened to burst from her body.

"What's that ahead?" Alder held up a hand, drawing them all up short as he pointed at something in the distance.

A black shape hid itself behind a wavering haze of heat mixed with the first shimmering drops of rain blown across the barren land by the magical storm pinned to the mountain range.

Felix peered around the burlier man, shoved his hair back off his forehead, and shifted his eyes. The pupils enlarged, and the smoky gray of his irises intensified, with flecks of gold and amber threading through. "It's a skiff."

Alder's eyes lit up. "Goddess bless, that's perfect. We could be at the mountains in no time."

"Hold on a moment." Felix put a hand on Alder's tattooed shoulder. "There is a hooded figure sitting on it, almost like it's waiting."

Bianca worried her lower lip, afraid she knew the answer. "Waiting for what?"

He shrugged, the muscles along his back rippling visibly through his still wet shirt. "Us presumably since it appears to be looking our way."

Bianca's insides hollowed out. "Is there anyone that didn't know we were coming?"

"May as well see what it wants." Alder growled low in his throat and began stalking along the river's edge again without looking back to see if she and Felix would follow.

"Now who's impulsive?" Felix grumbled as he started after him.

"I heard that, Grayson," Alder called back over his shoulder. "Magic at the ready just in case."

Bianca hardly had to think before her magic flooded to her fingertips, the now familiar pins and needles along her skin. She lifted them to catch the thickening rain drops, they sizzled against the pads of her fingers, evaporating as they hit flesh until she had a spiraling cloud of mist in her palm.

All around them, the crimson ground had the same effect as the heat of her magic, turning engorged drops of precipitation into billowing clouds of vapor that eddied around their knees and billowed over their heads until it was so thick they could barely see in either direction. They shielded their eyes from the downpour, though it did little good.

"Where did it go?" Bianca barely caught the threads of Felix's shouted words. Alder's were muffled entirely by the thickening cloud that swaddled them.

"I am here." A voice like the creak of a coffin's hinge cracked through the fog like lightning. It pulled them toward it, their feet turning without thought in its direction. "Come make a deal with me, it's been so long since I've made a good deal."

It sat as still and unruffled in the rain as a garden statue. The space beneath its cowl seemed depthless and eternal, its robes an umber so rich it leached all color and pooled around its feet.

Reflexively Alder threw a knife at it, the silver tip of it slicing end over end through the sheets of rain. The thing simply reached a corpselike white hand that plucked it from the air as though it were nothing more dangerous than a passing butterfly.

'Well, that's a neat trick," Felix muttered through his teeth. He edged closer to her, angling his body slightly between her and the thing sitting on the upturned belly of the boat.

"You do not need to defend yourself against me. I seek to do you no harm, Alder son of Cedre, nor you, Felix, last of the Changelings, or you, Bianca Hastings" It sniffed the air. "Ah, I haven't encountered one of your kind in at least a lifetime, maybe more."

She cocked her head to the side, and her soggy braid slipped from her shoulder, but before she could get the words out to ask what he meant, he waved a thick-knuckled bony hand to dismiss her. "But that is neither here nor there. You are here for a vessel to grant you safe passage to the mountains, but it will come at a cost."

Bianca hugged her arms to her chest, his words rankled like a sliver worming its way to her heart, though she couldn't quite determine why, and it was right, now was not the time for extraneous questions. "What is your cost, then?"

"You are seeking those whom you have loved and lost, those he has taken. I require but one memory of them. It's been so long since I've tasted anything as delectable as a remembrance."

Felix's face drained of color, his hair matted to his forehead in the persistent rain, and he took a step back. "What the fuck are you that you eat memories?"

It grinned, or at least Bianca imagined it did in the depths of its hood. She could envision a cruel slash of a mouth curling at its edges, peeling back against crooked and rotted teeth. "I am the Noctus."

"Dear goddess." Alder sucked in a jagged-edged breath.

The Noctus turned its head toward the nymph. "I came before your gods"—its voice scraped across her ears—"and I will be here long after."

The hairs on the back of her neck stood at attention, wary of the being before them. What in the blessed afterlife came before the gods? "Why are you helping us?"

It chuckled, or at least that's what she assumed the rasping noise it made was meant to be. "Who says I am?"

Alder half turned his head, keeping one wary eye on the Noctus, not that he could harm it if it decided to do anything nefarious, and one eye on her and Felix. "I don't see how we have another choice, this storm is more potent than the one in Areth. We'll waste precious time fighting to get through it."

Time they didn't have, the unsaid words hung thicker than the fog between them. She jerked her chin in agreement, and Felix did the same.

Alder stepped forward, his fists clenched at his sides. "All right, Noctus, let's get this over with."

It held out a hand, its fingers upturned and jagged like the legs of a deceased spider. "Give me your hand, this will hurt for but a moment."

He barely had his arm raised when the Noctus lashed out as quick as any fiber and latched onto his nails, sinking into the tender flesh of Alder's wrist. There was a peculiar glow that surged around both beings, green around the nymph like the forests of his homeland and as black and empty as death around the Noctus. Through their connection, a small green thread was drawn from Alder, it twined around the Noctus's fingers and then dissipated beneath his skin, and as it did, the depth of the black around it grew somehow more luscious and vibrant. Alder cried out through ground teeth, sweat beaded on his brow, and when the Noctus released him finally, faintly luminous raven-colored crescent marks were etched onto his wrist.

The same ritual was repeated with Felix, though his glow was more like a wicked storm threaded with lightning, so smoky it almost bled into the mist around them. His corded shoulders went rigid, and his knees nearly buckled beneath him as he cried out. Bianca wanted to reach for him, to help him stand, but as if he sensed her intent, he threw an arm back, motioning her to stay where she was. When the Noctus dropped his hand, he was panting and pale. "You're a fucking monster is what you are." He moved to stand by Alder, his gray eyes glancing over at her, filled with pity-laced worry, as he rubbed at the marks of the Noctus as if he could wipe them away.

Bianca squared her shoulders and stepped forward, her hand outstretched, determined to look upon this being without fear, though her fingers betrayed the sentiment by quivering.

Its nails bit into her skin, but she felt them like fangs upon her soul. Pure light wrapped itself around her, and in it floated a memory she'd been unaware of:

She played on the richly carpeted floor of the parlor by the fire with her dolls, their faces painted to look like hers and her mother's and her father's. Her parents watched her from a ways off, their voices pitched in hopes that she wouldn't hear them, but she was good at hearing things from great distances. It was a new trick she'd learned, one she hadn't told them about yet, one she kept just for herself. They'd been excited about her new tricks at first, but now they made her mother's forehead wrinkle and her father frown.

Her mother paced, her silk underskirts rustling with each step. She had a smile painted on her lips, but her words and her green eyes didn't reflect the happy face she showed her daughter. Her piled golden curls bounced atop her head as she shook it at her husband. "What are we to do, Eli?" She worried her lip between her teeth. "No one can know, if they find out . . ."

Her father was colored like her, with hair so black it was almost blue, but he had warm purple eyes so full of love that she was always drawn into them. Though now they were full of something else she couldn't quite name, an emotion that was beyond her understanding. They were brimming with it beneath sternly buckled brows. "Beatrice, please." He grabbed her mother's hand, drawing her to him and folding her into his lap. "We will think of something. We could ask Imogen if she . . ."

"No, absolutely not." Her mother's hand fluttered at her throat like an anxious little bird.

"She's family, dear, we can trust her." He nuzzled his head against her mother's neck in an affectionate gesture she'd seen him do every day for her whole life, but it didn't make her mother's smile real.

"We can't trust anyone with this."

The images slipped away like water down a drain, the brightness around her ebbed, and she was left blinking her rain-kissed lashes at the empty space where the Noctus had been with a tender wrist and an even more tender heart. Whatever it pulled from her was important somehow, a piece to a puzzle she would never be able to finish.

"Are you all right?" Alder and Felix both looked her over. The concern that filled their eyes pulled at the edges of the gap left in her mind where the memory the Noctus ripped from her used to reside. It felt like a hole in an otherwise beautiful tapestry that you wished you could ignore but your eyes were forever drawn to the flaw.

"I'm not sure." The words to describe her feelings felt as intangible as mist. She toed the hull of the boat. "But it doesn't matter, does it? We have things to do."

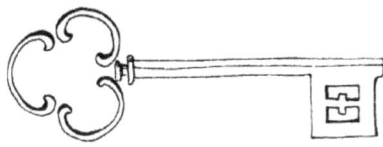

Chapter 95

WITH THEIR MAGIC, ALDER and Felix set the ores of the boat to rowing at a clipped pace, the bow of the boat skimmed over the white-capped currents of the river as it raged against them for having the audacity to try to go upstream.

The mist dissipated to sinuous ribbons along the shore, though the rain remained relentless. They were soaked through, their clothes sticking to them like second membranous skins. The saw-toothed mountains grew daunting, almost seeming to bend over them to peer closer at who dared to come near.

A solitary rickety dock jutted out into the river like a broken accusatory finger. "There," Bianca called out, her teeth clattering against one another.

"I see it." Alder took control of the oars and guided them as gently as he could on choppy waves to moor the boat on the dock. He hopped out gracefully, knotting the rope with magic. Felix slipped behind Bianca, his hands wrapped around her waist, branding her even through all her sodden layers as he helped hoist her up onto the dock.

The waterlogged boards protested, squelching underfoot as they tread swiftly to land, the planks giving slightly underfoot. The whole of the Lost Fragment seemed to take a sharp intake of breath and hold it as they made it safely to land, as if leaning in waiting with bated breath. Bianca swore she felt it, like eyes upon her back, breath panting down her neck, a whisper on the wind chanting a sickening yet eerily familiar nursery rhyme in her ear,

"Little bitty Mary-Beth
Tripped and fell to her death.

In a well she fell so deep,
Now she lies in eternal sleep.
Careful now,
Creep softly, dear,
While we whisper in your ear.
Listen close and you will see,
We can tell you how to cheat,
Cheat the death that waits for you,
We will tell you what to do . . ."

Bianca stumbled as the words tumbled chaotically through her mind. Dear gods, were they about to die? Was it the voice an ill omen sent from the god of death to warn her? Was her mind slipping? Her foot snagged on a rock. Felix wrapped a hand around her arm, yanking her upright, catching her at the last moment as the toes of her boots scrambled for purchase on the slick ground. He dashed his hair off his forehead. "Are you all right?"

Ahead of them, Alder paused, his gaze piercing and questioning through the rain. She pinched her lip between her teeth. "I . . . I . . . don't you hear that?"

She dug her hand into his forearm as she turned, her braid whipping back and forth, eyes wild as she searched for the taunting voice. Felix placed both hands on either side of her face with startling tenderness. He brushed a stray hair from her forehead, and his finger rubbed against her star. "Hear what?"

He leaned in close when she didn't answer, his voice low, pressed to her ear. "It's OK to be afraid." Then he pulled back expectantly.

Her breath rattled against her lungs as she gazed up into his pristinely gray eyes, the same muted shade as the sky. Something settled over her, a knowing in the depth of her soul that in his eyes she would always find comfort, and suddenly none of it mattered—the voice, her worries, none of it. She was overcome by the sudden urge to tell him, to tell him that no matter what, she would choose him, for this, this right here mattered more than anything else. But now was not the time. The clock in the back of her mind was ticking the seconds fast enough that they could be mistaken for gallows drumbeats. She could wait because they would survive this, and she would tell him the first moment they stepped back into the Void. She shook her head and stepped back out of his grasp. "I'm fine. It was just the wind playing tricks on me. Let's go."

She nodded to Alder who tipped his chin in answer after running a silently assessing eye over her, before he started off down an obvious worn path at a slight jog. The crimson ground gave way to loose black scree with serrated edges like shattered glass. It swelled beneath their feet, rising, bringing them closer to the mine. A sense of familiarity tickled the back of her mind, like waking to find you were in a dream that you'd had once before. Only Bianca knew this dream was a nightmare. On every stone she saw the blood that the Instrument had spilled, either his or another's, to carve his mine, to forge this path.

Time tightened, drawn taut like a harp string. It hummed around them in tune with the magic in her blood, with the ticking in her mind, until it was a deafening cacophony urging her on faster, farther. Her eyes skimmed the immediate way ahead, plotting her next steps so as to dance around any obstacles.

She crashed into Alder's ridged spine. "What the . . ."

He grabbed her, yanking her behind a boulder. He pointed through the billowing curtains of rain, and her heart stuttered at the sight. "Fuck."

Ahead of them, a deadly tangle of vines prickled to life, a writhing sea more lethal than a mass of venomous serpents. Death's Night Rose covered the path between them and a gash in the mountain wall ahead. Its blooms unfurled in the rain; their petals shaded like fresh purple bruises. Their thorns stirred, reaching for the spot they hid, sensing the blood of those who did not belong.

A shriek echoed from the cleft in the onyx mountain wall, so shrill it reverberated down her bones. She knew the sound well, for it haunted not only her dreams, but also her waking hours. The Fury.

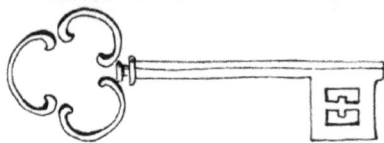

Chapter 96

THE VINES RECOILED, CHURNING the mist, as the beasts marched two abreast from the mine adit. The puddles along the ground quaked in fear as their clawed feet smashed into the scorched and muddied ground. Bianca felt each step echo in her heart as the largest one in the lead tilted its pointed chin to scent the air with its slitted nostrils.

Rain dripped off her eyelashes and rolled like cold fear down her cheeks as she prayed to all the gods that they didn't smell them. She bit down on her lip, nearly drawing blood, as Felix leaned in, startling her, his voice pitched so low she wasn't sure she heard him right. "As soon as they pass, we make a run for it into the adit."

Her eyes bulged. It was insanity. There were so many things wrong with that plan that surely Alder would object. The Fury could turn and see them, the vines could grab them, or both. But even as she thought it, she saw Alder from the corner of her eye agree.

The Fury bared its stained teeth and spoke in a voice like a rasping death rattle to the others behind it in a garbled tongue that she didn't understand. It rolled its neck, cracking the sharp vertebrae with a sickening crunch, then spread its ghastly wings and took flight. The rest of the hoard followed closely behind.

The moment the last one took off into the air, Alder launched himself over the rock they hid behind and sprinted toward the cleft in the wall. She and Felix dashed around the side, their pathway quickly narrowing as the Thieve's Bane slithered back over it. She thanked the gods for pants as she dodged and leaped over the wriggling mass, nearly stumbling over a partially dismembered skeleton, one of the plant's victims.

Her breaths sawed through her lungs, her muscles in her legs wept in protest, quivering, but they were nearly there. Alder made it, swallowed first by the shadowy dark of the mine, then Felix. She was mere steps away, but the vines were beginning to crawl over the threshold, trying to cut her off. Her feet slipped in the muck as their thorns stretched, their needle-sharp tips elongating, ready to rip into her flesh. Without thinking, she launched herself over them blindly into the mine.

Her pant leg snagged on a thorn; the sound of fabric ripping and the feel of icy air on her skin stilled her heart. Did it cut her? Two pairs of hands reached out and caught her, pulling her away from the ravenous rose. They dragged her back away from the entrance as the spines speared forth, growing from needles to swords, piercing the air, reaching hungrily for the intruders that slipped past it. They clustered, fighting for a way through the doorway, claiming and growing until they blotted out the sliver of light from the outside, plunging them into inky darkness.

Light flared around Felix's hands. "Are you hurt? Did it cut you? Are you bleeding?" He bent down, probing the hole in her pant leg with his glowing fingers, feeling for a wound.

His magic caressed her skin, singing to her own, sending a wave of goose bumps up her leg and piercing her heart. "It's fine. You're fine. You're safe." He breathed a deep sigh of relief that echoed her own and one from Alder as well from where he hovered over Felix's shoulder.

A manic giggle slipped from her lips that she stifled with a bitten fist. "Yes, safe and sound in a den of monsters, how comforting."

"Speaking of"—Alder stood, a globe of azure light balled in his palm—"where are they? Those that left can't have been the only ones."

Felix peered around her down the shaft of the mine. "Well, even if they weren't, we need to move, and there is only one way to go."

Bianca spun to face the waiting dark, and much like the Bore, it breathed, the walls seeming to have a life of their own. "Into the belly of the beast."

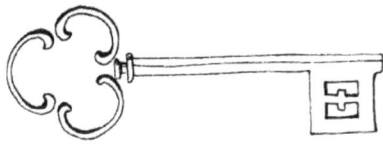

Chapter 97

T HEY CREPT ALONG THE outer wall, Alder in the lead, followed by Bianca, then Felix in the rear, each with one hand on the wall, their fingers trailing along the coal-black stones to keep their heading. The air around them hung thick with dust, anticipation, and the nauseating scent of fear, though Bianca could no longer tell if the latter seeped solely from her pores or if the whole place reeked of it, the rock suffused with it for decades.

Bianca lost her sense of how deep they were as the tunnel narrowed, the walls pitted as though carved in bites and desperate handfuls. Memories of her visions sluiced through her mind, images of the Instrument wracked with grief and plagued by voices clawing at the walls with bloody nubs. He was her, and she was him, and their grief bled together in her heart. Silent tears cut paths through the grime streaked on her cheeks. She brushed them away with itching fingertips, burying the feelings in the deepest recesses of her mind, behind a thick wall. Now was not the time to feel empathy for a monster.

Shimmering flecks caught the glow of their magics, redoubling it and winking it back at them across the ceiling and walls of the shaft. The deeper they went, the more chilled the air became until her breaths frosted in front of her face, and the thicker the sparkling bits became until they spindled along the cracks in the rock like glittering opalescent roots.

Slivered branches sprouted off the main tunnel. Alder scouted several only to find that they ended abruptly. With nowhere to go, no other path to follow, and no one in their way, it was beginning to feel increasingly like they were rabbits being coaxed into a trap. Bianca worried her lip, afraid to point it out and have her worst fears confirmed.

"What are they?" Alder whispered as they came to a juncture lit by a tangle of pulsing white veins that twined along the crags.

Felix inched closer, his brows furrowed. He pressed a finger to it, then hissed and pulled away. "Magic, it's raw magic."

"What in the goddess's name?" Alder touched the absent sigil on his forehead and backed away from the vein as far as the tunnel would allow. "Who is it from do you think?"

Felix touched it again, a shudder quaking across his shoulders. He drew his fingers back and licked them as though he could taste the distinct flavors of different magics. A sudden wave of curiosity swept through her. What flavor would her magic be if he tasted it? Fire branded her cheeks at the intimate notion, and she shoved the thought aside as he spat on the floor. "There are too many to differentiate."

The corners of Alder's mouth pulled down. "We better keep moving."

A tremor shook the mine shaft, small stones took the opportunity to slip from their places on the wall, and dust poured from cracks as they scrambled for footing. Bianca shielded her eyes from the raining debris, Alder shouted over the roar, his words muffled, but she could read his intentions in his wide eyes. They needed to move, and quickly, before there was a cave-in.

They ran through the main tunnel like drunken sailors stumbling home from a pub while on shore leave while side tunnels collapsed on either side, sending gasping plumes of wreckage spewing into their path.

Her shoulders pinched, her breath caught somewhere between them as they spilled out onto a narrow ledge, just in time for a cascade of boulders to seal off the shaft behind them. Felix leaned over, his hands on his knees, his breath coming in harsh gasps. Alder's hand laced behind his head as he stared in awe at the rubble that was the tunnel they'd barely escaped.

Bianca sat down hard, trying to smooth her breaths. "Good thing we didn't intend to go back the way we came."

"Whatever magic is in this place is unstable; we better get across before another tremor strikes." Alder pointed to a questionable rope bridge attached to the far edge of the precipice on which they stood. "I don't want to be on that if it strikes again." He offered Bianca a hand, which she graciously took, and hoisted her to her feet.

Felix righted himself, rubbed an arm across his face, smearing the dirt and the sweat, leaving it streaked across his face like the paint of war. "Let's get moving, then." This time he took the lead, stepping from splintered plank to splintered plank with deft catlike movements. The bridge barely swayed under his feet as he moved across it.

She'd never been fond of heights, but weeks of living in the tower with many an hour spent contemplating leaping from its balcony had mostly cured her of her wariness. The only thing she had to fear now was her own desperation. Her chest felt tight, as though she were hooked, and something had reeled her in. She wanted to believe it was the presence of her parents that tugged at her heartstrings, but a small and terrible voice that she ignored hissed that it might not be.

With her eyes glued to the outline of Felix's rigid shoulders through his linen shirt, she managed to make the crossing without looking down once. He met her gaze, his lips parted as though to say something, but then he thought better of it as Alder stepped up behind her. "Any idea which way to go?"

There was a warren of tunnels arrayed into the wall ahead of them, none appeared any different than the other, all led off into dismal darkness, threaded with the strange magical veins still pulsing as though they surged with the lifeblood of the mine.

Felix stood at the entry of each in turn, his outstretched hands aglow. He came to one on the far left, and though Bianca could see no discernible difference between this tunnel and any other, Felix clearly sensed something. He took off running, barely remembering to shout over his shoulder, "They're this way!"

The tunnel was scarcely wide enough for Bianca to squeeze through head-on. Alder and Felix had to sidle along with their shoulders cocked at an awkward angle through every wending curve, but they didn't let that slow them. The whole mine seemed to hold its breath.

"Stairs!" Felix warned, as the top of his head disappeared from view over Alder's shoulder.

Bianca wet her lips, her glowing palms slick as she began the descent down the stairs a half a beat behind Alder. Calling them stairs was akin to calling a Fury a cuddly creature. The flats were so narrow she had to scale them sideways, and the distance between them was at unnervingly irregular intervals, but she managed by pressing her hands into one side of the vertical shaft and her back into the other, making the descent little better than a controlled fall.

Always chivalrous, Alder reached up at the base of the stairs to hoist her down, his hands wrapped around her hips. Her eyes jumped around the small carved-out hollow where they were spat out, her eyes immediately landing on where Felix stood, but unlike normal, her gaze didn't stick on him. Instead, it slid past him to what he faced. The iron door.

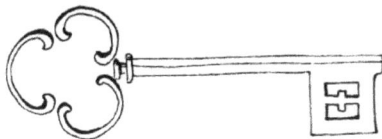

Chapter 98

THE DOOR STOOD AS though plucked from her dream, the lock on the latch hanging as heavy as the head of a condemned man. Rust flecked its hinges and crept across the flat plain of the door. Felix lunged for the lock, his hand luminescent as he shoved magic into it.

His scream ricocheted around the small cavern, spearing Bianca in the heart as he was thrown back by a wicked blast of muddied light. She darted over to where he landed, cradling an injured hand in his lap. "Fucking thing threw my spell back at me." He moaned through gritted teeth.

Bianca darted to his side and knelt. She gently cupped his hand in her own and unfurled his fingers to inspect the wound; the skin was an angry shade of blistering red. A keyhole shape was carved out of the center of his palm as if fileted, the skin around it cauterized by the rebounded magic. Blood, leaking through the cracks of his fingers, pooled in her hands. "Alder, we need to stop the bleeding." Her fingers itched to do the magic herself, but fear was a ferocious hindrance to intent when it came to doing magic correctly, and she was afraid. Afraid for him and afraid of what was behind the door; the acrid taste of it coated her throat.

Alder conjured a quavering blue light between his fingers, the stain of the magic seeping down his wrist, already forming minuscule runes as he flicked the magic into the space above Felix's wound. It twined around Felix's fingers and wrapped across his palm like a bandage, immediately staunching the flow of blood before soaking into him in a flash. In the space of a blink, the afflicted hand went from fresh injury to having the appearance of being days old. A sigh of relief slipped from his lips. "Thank you," he murmured, to which Alder just nodded, his eyes twin icicles fixed on the door.

"How do we open the goddess damned thing if we can't use magic?" He growled.

A small smile curled the corners of her lips. "We pick the lock."

Felix quirked an eyebrow at her, his eyes suddenly alight with curiosity. "Don't tell me you know how to pick locks?"

She stood, slipping her fingers into the top edge of her corset, fingering the lock picks one at a time from the boning channels, before turning on her heel to crouch before the door. "Of course, I do."

She heard Felix scramble to his feet. "That's not a proper skill for a young lady to have." His words almost seemed to curl with amusement.

She snorted a laugh. "Isn't it? I thought they taught it to all the noble ladies—embroidery, dance, piano forte, lock picking."

"You're full of surprises, aren't you, you devious little creature?" His words licked against her ear as he leaned in close to get a better look at what she was doing. "You'll have to teach me, Hastings."

"Of course." She felt the tumblers tripping into place as she moved the picks with just the right finesse. She could almost see them in her mind's eye, the way they were aligned. She'd always thought of her abilities with locks as a special brand of magic all her own, that is, before she knew she had actual magic. "Let's get out of here alive first."

All three of them let slip an audible sigh of relief as the click from the lock's release echoed against the stone walls. She pulled the shackle free from its loop and cast it to the floor, sending it skittering across the floor to land at Alder's feet. "Thank the Goddess," Alder breathed as he rushed forward to help Felix pry the door open.

The faces inside shied away from the light that they held aloft in their cupped palms. Whimpers and the soft cry of a babe echoed along the roughly cut tunnel that served as a prison cell.

"Felix?" A shadowed and hunched figure struggled to stand. It limped toward the light, its familiar voice filled with dust and disbelief. "Bianca? What, how, dear gods, how are you here?" Imogen's wan face bloomed out of the darkness.

Felix reached inside and scooped an arm under the old woman's shoulder, half dragging her, half supporting her out of the cell. Her hair hung limply across her creased forehead and hollowed-out cheeks. Her dress, nothing more than rags, slumped off her shoulder, her once plump frame now wrapped in skin that hung off her body like a too-loose coat. Her right foot looked twisted, as though it were badly healed, making her shuffled movements awkward and jerky. She reached an arm out, snaking it around Bianca's waist and pulling her into a weak-limbed hug. "I'm so sorry, Bianca dear, for everything."

Bianca's heart cracked as she patted her aunt's back awkwardly, feeling her rib bones beneath her dress. "There is no time for apologies now, though I'll gladly accept one once we make it back home."

Alder ducked his head, his voice pitched low as they braced themselves against the walls, riding the waves of another tremor. "This drift isn't stable enough to withstand opening a door, not if these quakes continue. We need to get everyone up to the ledge. I can try there."

Felix nodded. "Okay, let's move quickly then."

All along the cramped cell, people began to stand hesitantly and stagger out at Alder's rushed instruction. "Everyone, quickly up the stairs, we'll get you out of here." His firm and commanding tone didn't match the worry in his eyes as they raked over each face that passed through the door.

She did the same, craning around his muscled form, as Felix led Imogen away toward the stairs. She shifted, rocking on the balls of her feet, twining the end of her ratted braid around her fingers, waiting. For her parents, and for the mother of the fallen princess who bought them their lives with her blood.

A cry ripped through Alder, and he rushed forward to envelop a man a head taller than him, who was his near twin in image save for the overgrown and matted beard, with eyes sunken with hunger. Cedre cradled a small unconscious girl to his chest, her bare toes dangling over the crook of his arm.

Cedre leaned down and pressed his forehead to his son's. "Goddess blessings, my son, I never thought I would see you again."

Alder's hands twisted in the back of his father's torn coat, his eyes brimming with silver tears as he leaned down to kiss his sister, Iris, on the cheek. "Nor I. Where is Mother?"

His father's eyes went dark, and he choked on whatever words he'd been about to say. He faltered, but Alder held fast to him, "Come on, we have to go. I think I can get us out of here."

As they moved aside, Alder's eyes locked with hers, filled with something that looked too much like pity for her own comfort, and that's when it dawned on her that there was no one left in the cell. "Time to go, Bianca." He kept his voice level, but the hammering of her heart drowned it out.

That couldn't be right, Imogen was here, Cedre, and Iris, surely at least one of her parents was here also. She ran through the doorway. Alder's plea echoed down it, but she ignored it, her illuminated fingers trailing across the stones of the dank walls of the drift. It was long and barely tall enough for her to stand upright, but it was deep. On nimble feet, she quickly reached the end, but there was no one. An ugly feeling sank its claws into her soul. Gods be damned it was unfair to come so far and not find them.

The faint echo of her name from frantic lips reached her, barely a whisper down the corridor. They were waiting for her. She spun around, and her elbow bumped a jagged rock, snagging the fabric of her shift, ripping clean through it. She cursed, glaring down at the offending stone only to catch a glimpse of something soft and blue. She bent to grab it.

The silken scrap of forget-me-not fabric felt fridged in her fingers, as smooth as the marble of a mausoleum. It felt like death, though whose death she couldn't be sure. It was undoubtedly her mother's, for knotted inside the scrap of garment nestled a sapphire earring carved in the likeness of a flower. The whole miniature bundle reeked of heartbreak and death, feeling as unforgiving as a freshly dug grave. With a sickening pang, she was suddenly unsure that finding this was better than finding nothing at all. It was like finding an errant piece to a puzzle but not knowing to which it belonged or a signature on a note addressed to her but with the writing washed away. What did her mother mean by leaving this? Was it a goodbye or a breadcrumb on a larger path?

Felix's voice thundered down the cell. "Bianca, now, we have to go." His gray eyes flashed like falling stars in the peculiar half-light of his and her magic.

The first notes of wailing and screams followed on the heels of his shouts. Something was horribly wrong.

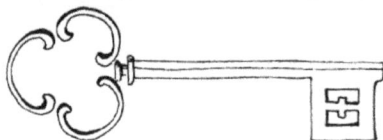

Chapter 99

FELIX RAN OUT OF the drift, Bianca in tow. Before them on the ledge, the wing beats of the Fury sounded like war drums. They swarmed across the bridge and out of the mouths of the other shafts like ants, crawling over one another with near mindless savagery, their claws ripping and tearing, their teeth sinking into any bit of flesh.

Magic blasted through the air, striking Fury and rebounding off stone. A Fury swooped, snatching a woman by her shoulder, its talons ripping clean through the meat of her shoulder. Blood sprayed thick and hot across his face. Without thinking, he shielded Bianca and raised his hands, magic blazing like torchlight in his upraised palms before he let it fly in the direction of the nearest beast.

His eyes darted around the fray, searching for Imogen and Alder. The former stood over a wounded woman, her white hair wild in the wind off the creature's wings, her magic burning through any that dared to come near. Alder and his father fought back-to-back, their magics a blur of sea green and blue, while his little sister clung to his pant leg, her eyes wide in terror, her mouth frozen in a scream. They were holding their own, but it could not last, they would be overrun in mere moments.

His heart stopped as he saw Bianca fling herself at a descending monster, her raised knife in one hand, her magic in the other. She buried the knife to the hilt in the thing's chest with a guttural cry before singing its face with a nasty spell that melted its skin off to the bone. She wrenched the blade free, ichor streaming from its tip in ribbons that unfurled themselves across her bodice. If they weren't in mortal peril, he might have found the whole display more than a little attractive.

Another wave of monsters surged over the lip of the ledge, and one tore straight for Bianca, bloody saliva leaking from its maw. Before he could shout a warning, it snatched her by her ankle and tossed her into the air like a cat toying with its prey. It raked its talons along her shoulder, and her cream-colored shirt turned crimson, her face leached of all color, as it flew off down a main shaft. He tried to keep his eyes on her, but the beating of black wings blotted out his view as claws snagged onto his pack, and the ground slipped out beneath him.

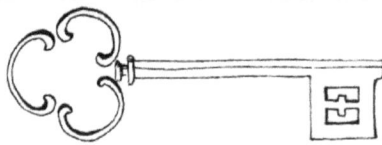

Chapter 100

SHE WAS DROWNING IN a sea of pain, lost in the sound of her heart in her ears. Felix held fast to her arm, keeping her afoot as she slumped into his warm chest. Her eyelids fluttered, fighting to stay open, to understand. She'd been plucked up and flown through a maze of tunnels before her consciousness had slipped. Now they were in a crowd, the Fury herding them like chattel into a large roughly hewn black cavern toward an ebony dais.

All across the ceiling, the veins of magic tangled like thick roots, twining between stalactites. The very air was alive with the humming of their pulse. It mimicked her own, quickening as they were shoved to their knees before the altar behind which the roots of magic converged into a blinding mass of ethereal light.

She blinked, shielding her eyes from the crystalline glow, and darted her eyes around the room looking for those she cared for most. Alder was huddled with his father and sister against the cavern wall. Their lips moved quickly, but she couldn't make out what they said. Imogen held up a young woman with an arm encircled around her shoulders, blood ran down her face, but she was alive and mostly whole. Her eyes sought Felix's, but his gaze was fixed on the nightmare scene that began to unfold in front of them.

The Fury leaned off the altar, and the people nearest began to thrash, trying to force their way back from the raking claws, their faces stricken. One of the beasts hooked a woman by her knotted-up emerald-hued hair, and she bucked, her arms flailing in every direction haphazardly as magic sparked from her fingertips to no avail.

The monster dragged her to the back of the dais and strung her up with gruesome shackles anchored to the wall, suspending her by her ankles so her body was pressed against the brilliant beating convergence of magic. Without ceremony, it ran a razor-sharp claw across her neck, silencing her screams.

A tall decidedly male figure emerged from the shadows of a spire, silhouetted in the light of the magic. He watched as the woman's blood poured over the glimmering surface, almost as if he stared beyond it.

Fear bit into her heart like a meaty apple as the shadowed figure moved closer to the edge of the dais. Knowing surged through her—the length of his stride, the stoop of his shoulders. The Instrument.

She leaned forward, drawn to him, almost as if their souls were inexplicably twined together by a dark thread. Felix's hand wrapped around her wrist, his breath panicked against the nape of her neck. "Fuck, I know what it is. Bianca, oh gods, I know what it is."

Her brow furrowed, she cocked her ear back over her shoulder to hear him better. "What is what?"

"It's the gods damned wall, he's going to let it out. The Darkness."

The walls of the cavern shivered, rippling as though it were merely a veil and beneath it something slumbered, something that was waking.

Panic burned between her breasts, searing her skin. Her hand fluttered to her chest and found a singed hole in her blouse. Her heart stuttered. It wasn't panic that caused the pain, it was the pendant aflame with some sort of magic. She dipped her fingers into her bodice, pulling the pendant out by its tattered leather cord.

It dangled from the center of its string; the tarnished silver reflected the light of the pulsating magic along the walls. A flash of memory, a sliver of vision sliced through her mind's eye—the young man and his mother, the last gift she gave him. It could be a lifeline, a salvation, a tether to his old life to pull him back from this brink of destruction. For what was the Instrument if not a heartbroken man whose soul had been ravaged by grief, much like her own. Though his had been left to fester where hers had been tended to by friendship and purpose.

But perhaps, gods willing, he could still be saved. She lunged forward ignoring Felix's frantic shouts, throwing herself between the bodies that separated her from the dais. She fumbled through the recollections of the Instrument's life for a name, for his name. Unbidden, one sprang from her lips. "Malum," her voice pitched over the cries and whimpers, "Malum, you don't have to do this."

Cold, dead eyes clashed into hers, glinting like the point of a knife. His lips curled in a harsh approximation of a smile as he swooped, his movements like a striking snake, and plucked her up. He drew her close, pressing his lank, near-skeletal body against hers. His tongue darted out along his lips. "You came."

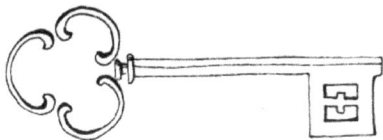

Chapter 101

MALUM HAD HARDLY DARED to believe this day would come. They would soon be free, and she was there as they had promised. He pulled her in close, his bony cheek pressed to hers as he twirled her around in an exaggerated waltz, dancing to the music that thrummed through his veins.

She tried to speak, to show him something, but he was beyond caring about petty things like the trinket she held or the tears that dripped across her tender features. Why was she not rejoicing? Surely, surely she could hear them too.

"Can you hear them? Can you hear them singing? Singing. Screaming. Scratching. Clawing. Bleeding to be free." He could feel the magic coursing through her veins, pushing and pulling. He knew how it would feel to have it slip hot over his fingers as his knife bit into her sweet, tender flesh. He licked up the long column of her throat and groaned.

She was so beautiful, so delicate, like a painted glass doll. He wanted to watch her shatter. Would she turn into glittering faery dust? Would she stay soft and pretty, or would she break into jagged stabbing edges? He trailed a jagged nail across the fragile skin under her jaw, and she cried so beautifully as her blood beaded along his fingertips. He shivered rapturously and flicked the crimson droplets at the throbbing wall where they exploded like starlight.

A tremor ran through the blackened cavern floor, reverberating up his spine. He felt the wall behind him cleave in two. He turned to meet his destiny, absently casting the exquisite creature with sad eyes to the ground as he did. They would play with her later. The Darkness needed her for after; she would be the thing to tip the scales in their favor.

The black mass of smoke was a nest of writhing snakes, full of their faces contorted in expressions of triumph as they twisted into a cyclonic mass. The Darkness, at long last, was free.

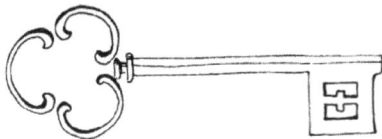

Chapter 102

BIANCA WATCHED, STRICKEN, AS Malum's body rose into the air, pulled by invisible marionette strings. The essence of Darkness poured from the cleaved wall and into him through a cracked open jaw, bulging eyes, and flared nostrils. She wanted to look away, but her eyes were stitched to the horrible image of his arms flung wide, his spine arched unnaturally, and his legs dangling like a rag doll as the Darkness claimed him.

The bold veins in his too-pale milky skin began to change from blue to black. Black lightning sparked along his limp fingers. The stain of magic, the color of pooled blood, shaded first his fingertips, then his hands, until it spilled up his forearms.

The last of the Darkness wormed its way beneath his flesh, black maggots using his body as their host. The intensity of the lightning along his hands magnified until it was rolling off his seemingly unconscious form in waves, striking the walls and beings at random. The Fury fled in a flurry of wings and gnashing of teeth into the cleft torn into the wall and into the mine as stone hailed down.

An arm wrapped around her waist, dragging her back off the dais—Felix, she could tell from the way his body felt pressed into her back. "Alder and Cedre managed a door, but just barely," he shouted into her ear over the screams of the Travelers and the fleeing monsters, a symphony of death and terror. "We have to go now before they can't hold it any longer."

He set her on her feet but kept an arm around her waist as they dashed toward the far side of the cavern where the mass of prisoners pushed and shoved one another through a white-edged shimmering rip in the stone twin to the one behind them and yet opposite in every way. Beyond it she could sense the Void, and though tainted with the Darkness magic, it was nothing compared to the utter despair and destruction that emanated from the wound Malum had made to let the Darkness free.

Over the bobbing heads of scrambling Travelers, she spotted Imogen by the makeshift door, firmly yet hurriedly trying to keep order among those who clawed their way to freedom. Her eyes grazed the diminishing crowd until they landed on Alder's broad frame, his father sagged against him, little Iris clung to his leg, her eyes squeezed shut.

Bianca crouched, untangling the trembling child from her older brother's leg. She soothed a hand over her curling black hair and whispered close to her ear so she could hear over the crash of stones, "My name is Bianca. I'm going to make sure you get somewhere safe, all right? Alder and your father will be right behind you."

The little girl nodded, still refusing to open her eyes, but she released Alder's pant leg and twined her arms around Bianca's neck. Bianca stood and passed Iris to Felix.

Alder reached out, snagging her hand. His eyes beneath his creased brow were peculiarly drained of pigment, now as pale as a robin's egg. "Take care of her, Bianca." His words were strained, a breathy imitation of his usual timbre.

She searched his face, her eyes flicking to where his father lolled near unconscious on his shoulder. "You're coming?" Small pebbles cascaded from fissures in the ceiling, pouring out like water from a well pump, pelting them, biting into their skin like flies on a carcass.

A taut smile tugged at the corners of his cracking lips. "Of course, just go on ahead. I'll be right behind."

Felix shouted her name from the fractured doorway right as a bolt of lightning struck between her and Alder. The explosion of magic between them sounded like the clash of two warring gods before consciousness bled from her, leaving her in silent, starless darkness.

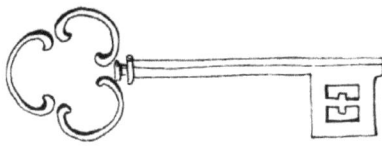

Chapter 103

FELIX DRAGGED BIANCA'S LIMP body over the threshold and into the Void a hairs breadth before the fissure snapped shut.

He cupped her bloody face in his hands, his thumb stroking the star under her eye, smearing the mud and the blood. The steady albeit battered shimmer of her aura reassured him that he hadn't been too late, that life still resided in her. Imogen sat a step above him cradling the child against her bosom, rocking her gently and soothing a hand over her head. Both of their auras were in shreds, but they too were going to survive.

He slipped Bianca gently from his lap and stood, pressing a palm to the wall where only moments ago the roughly hewn doorway stood. He couldn't leave that stubborn bastard behind. He had to get him and his father out, even if it was just their bones. He threw all his magic into it, screaming all his anguish and frustration into it, but nothing happened. The wall didn't so much as crack. "What the fuck." He bashed his fist into it, as if the force of the hit could somehow propel the magic through the stones, but all it left him with was bloody knuckles.

"Felix, that's enough." Imogen's voice was full of weary patience. "You cannot force the door back open."

"Then I'll go back through the damned Bore before you have it closed. I'll find another way out," he shouted, his hands tearing through his blood-and-grime matted hair.

Instantly, he regretted the harshness of his words as they landed, making the poor weeping child in Imogen's arms flinch. Imogen's shoulders sagged, her hand pressed over Iris's ear to muffle her words. "They're gone, Felix. The magic they used would have drained them of their life-force; surely you saw that in their auras. And if they somehow managed to survive that, the Darkness has them, and their deaths will hopefully be swift, which will be a mercy. The only thing left in that gods forsaken land is the dead, and the dead can keep it. So, unless you wish to join them beyond the Veil, I suggest you pick up my niece and we head home."

He hung his head. Yet again he'd failed, failed to keep those closest to him safe. Would there never be a time when someone near and dear to him didn't suffer? As he hoisted Bianca into his arms, he made a vow, not on absent or nonexistent gods, but on her life, that he would never again let her in, let her near enough to be failed by him again. She deserved better.

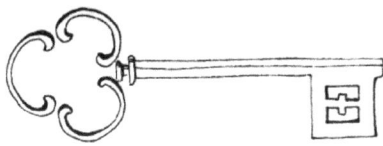

Chapter 104

Bianca blinked gossamer threads of sunlight from where they clung to her eyelashes. The first thing she noticed were the pressed floral faces of the sprites peering down at her through the panes of glass. The second thing she noticed was the tap-tap-tapping of a heeled shoe on the weathered floorboards, not with impatience but to keep tune for a hummed melody. She rolled over, her body aching, though not nearly as much as she expected it to, to find a steaming cup of tea and a heaping plate of shortbread cookies with sugared violets pressed into a thick layer of glaze, and despite everything that had happened, a warmth spilled over her heart, coating it like a candied apple. She was home. It may not be the home she'd been raised in, but it was a home nonetheless.

"I'm glad to see you're awake, dearie." Imogen sat on a low stool by her bed, bundled in a shawl, sipping tea and gazing over her half-moon spectacles at Bianca with a piercingly green stare that was so reminiscent of her mother's she wondered how she'd not noticed it before. "I believe I owe you a great apology."

Bianca sat up, bolstering her pillows at her back before reaching for the cup of tea, lavender with a nice bite of ginger, a hint of rose, a healthy dose of honey, and a splash of whiskey. Maura, that sweet dead woman, always knew the exact right thing to send up. "I, too, owe you an apology. I left, Felix and I, we left, and the Reliquary was attacked."

Imogen waved her words away. "My dear, the attack on the Reliquary was not your fault; in fact, I'm glad you and Felix weren't here, gods only know what would have happened if you had been. Hiding the truth from you, however, was an egregious lapse in judgment. I thought at the time I was doing what was best. I did suspect, after all, that your parents had separated from this life for the most part and had raised you apart, but after what happened to them, I never should have left you ignorant of the potential dangers of who we are. It is a mistake I hope to remedy by offering you a place here at the Reliquary as a student so you may master your skills. Wilhelmina tells me you are a quite adept seer, a trait that runs in the family."

Bianca was stunned. "You want me to learn, to study here at the Reliquary?"

"If you're interested, either that or you could wait and see what happens. The future is uncertain, after all, even with the ability to see into it."

But Bianca was already shaking her head. "No, no, I want the place. I can't just sit idle while I know what's out there, what could be coming. I want to learn. I want to help, whatever comes."

Imogen nodded curtly, set her teacup down on the end table, and stood, the drape of her dress showing the damage of her time away. "Good, I expected no less from Beatrice's daughter. I just ask one thing."

Bianca picked absently at the fraying edge of the quilt, sensing that this would perhaps be a request she wouldn't like. "All right . . ."

"I ask that you keep your mother's keys put away while you study here. I don't want them being flaunted about."

"You don't trust the other students?" Anxiety crept along the tender freshly healed bits of flesh along her back as though they sensed the threat of potential Darkness.

Imogen sighed the weighty sigh of a woman with the mantle of responsibility upon her shoulders. "I trust no one, Bianca, save a few, and I'd advise you to do the same."

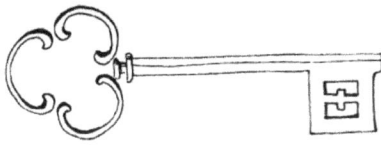

Chapter 105

S HE SAW HIM FIRST leaning against the bookcase in the library near the orrery. He looked just as she remembered, which seemed a funny notion considering it had been only hours since they parted, but she'd strangely thought that what they'd been through would show on his face. Though after a moment's consideration, she thought perhaps it did. From the way he held his shoulders, the grip of his hand on the book he read, he looked weary.

She padded softly on bare feet over to where he stood. Her heart was broken with loss, but at the same time, it was full, held together with the feelings she had for the beautiful and equally broken man before her. It emboldened her.

His eyebrows flicked up curiously as he saw her coming at last and set his book down. Before he could protest, and before she could second-guess herself, she wrapped her arms around him and pressed her face into his firm chest, breathing deep that deliciously hedonistic smell that was the essence of him. He stiffened beneath her touch, but his arms didn't come up to embrace her in return as she'd hoped.

Bianca tilted her head up to meet his gray gaze, but he refused to look at her. She just needed him to see, to make him understand, to fillet her heart and lay it bare before him. "I know you said this could never be, but, Felix, life is too short. Between us, we've lost too many people to see it as anything but, and I don't see the point in pretending we feel nothing, in pretending I feel nothing."

He pushed her arms off him, stepping away. "Bianca, please stop. There is no need; there has been a misunderstanding."

Her heart began to sink in the murky waters of confusion and doubt. The words he said made sense individually, but strung together, they painted a picture she couldn't see. "I don't understand."

"You were depressed, Bianca. I could see it looming on the edges of your aura like a threatening storm. You had a death wish, and I simply wanted to give you a reason to live, for Imogen's sake. I didn't mean it. I didn't mean any of it."

Bianca hugged her arms to her chest as though it could keep her heart from shattering in her rib cage and impaling her on its broken pieces. "I don't believe you."

Felix ran a hand through his tousled hair and shook his head. "Of course, you don't, you're a naive little maiden barely off your mother's apron strings and out in society."

"But you said you loved me." She could hear the tremble of her lip in her words and hated herself just a little bit for it.

His smirk no longer looked endearing; instead, it twisted his face, contorting it into an ugly pitiless mask. "What can I say? I'm good at seducing women, it's what I do. Now if you'd simply like to have a ride, you could come warm my bed for a night or two. I certainly wouldn't mind getting between those pretty little legs of yours . . ."

The crack of her palm as it struck his face echoed along the library shelves, effectively slicing off whatever vulgar notions he'd been about to say. "Gods damn you, Felix Grayson."

He had the audacity to laugh, the tips of his fingers tracing the line of her palm print already blooming along his jaw. "They already have."

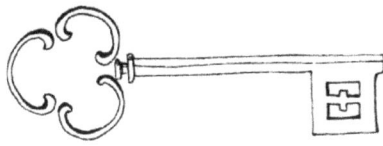

Chapter 106

Bianca clung to the edges of the celebration like a shadow on a wall. The bottle of velvety mulberry wine blunted the sharp edges of the knife in her heart. Children chased flicker bugs across the wide lawn, Iris among them, and played games. A mischievous little redhead covered in freckles kept turning himself into a pumpkin, much to the amusement of the others who danced around him as he shifted back and forth chanting nursery rhymes.

A banquet table sat off to the side of the festivities. Maura had outdone herself. Up and down the table cake stands sagged and platters overflowed with roasted meats and vegetables. There was even a peculiar chocolate fountain for dipping fruits and sweet breads. But she couldn't bring herself to partake.

No matter where she looked in the crowd, her eyes kept gravitating back to Felix. He danced with every eligible woman up from the town, twirling them, their pretty skirts blooming like upturned tulips as he twirled them. He whispered in their ears, making them giggle and blush.

At some point, Imogen made a toast, and everyone raised a glass to the fallen. Bianca tipped her bottle back, finding it empty. She cast it aside and stumbled her way back to her tower alone and unnoticed.

She didn't bother to light the lamp, and Maura, who must have sensed her dark mood, didn't either as she shed her black dress. In the moonlight, the scars on her back glowed silver. They didn't hurt as her old ones had since the wounds were healed with magical means. She looked at the jar of Gorgonian salve on her dresser, remnants of the original jar salvaged from the floor, plucked it up, and shoved it deep into the drawer. She wouldn't be removing these ones. She wanted to remember.

Next to the jar sat her jewelry box, and peeking out from between the seam was a shimmering corner of gold, the card. She plucked it from the box and held it up in a ribbon of moonlight. Her finger traced the embossed bird in the brambles on its back. The words of the maybe-god whispered across her memory. *"This, little one, is a gift. Though some may also call it a curse. It will cost you nothing, and it will cost you everything."*

Gift, or curse, maybe what was on the other side would hold an answer or a clue, something that could help her. She flipped the card before she could talk herself out of it, potential costs be damned. Staring up at her was a woman nearly identical to her in every way, down to the star-shaped freckle by her right eye. The woman waved, her fingers glowing with magic, and little floating orbs of light drifted into the frame. The woman plucked them like low-hanging fruit, her magic soaking them in until she burned brightly, glowing like a rainbow of refracted light from a prism. She was beautiful, but then she started to change. Smoke filtered in past the edges of the image, twining around her like snakes breaking and molding her. Her body and face contorted as she shifted from one thing into another, each more horrible than the last, until she was all sallow skin stretched over a too-thin frame. Spikes grew from her vertebrae, and her eyes dilated hollow and dark until nothing remained but a horrifying monster. A gilded ribbon flitted in like a bird, twisting itself into a golden scrawl that read, "The Menuras."

She dropped the card, her head reeling nauseatingly. She gripped the edge of her dresser for support as she fought not to lose her stomach contents all over the floorboards. When the moment passed, she stumbled over to her bed, her hand white knuckling the frame.

The cup of tea on her bedside table was strong and laced with sleep-inducing herbs. She threw it back in long gulps before peering into the bottom of the cup to read the leaves. Her magic sketched images that promised death, heartbreak, and catastrophe. She sighed, setting the cup down a little too hard against the saucer with a loud *chink*, collapsed onto her bed, and curled up under her blanket.

Her last thoughts, embittered by wine and disappointment, before her head hit her pillow were that she was grateful for Felix's words. His deception had set her free. The love she'd thought she had was a distraction from her true purpose. She could learn what she needed to here at the Reliquary about her magic, she could help in the coming war, and she would find her parents. She would bring them home, even if she had to become a monster to do so.

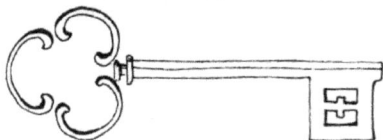

Chapter 107

THE CANDLE FLAMES DANCED above the prime elder's desk, casting back the growing dark. She was shuffling through scrolls and missives from the villagers when a knock came at the door.

"Enter," she crowed.

The girl Gaianna strode in. She was a sensible young woman with a stern but pretty face; she would make a good match for Oleander if she could get him to see sense. He kept arguing that he didn't want Alder's castoffs or some such nonsense. She knelt before Ulrica's table, a scroll extended in her hand. "There is a man here to see you, Elder. He claims it is a matter of urgency."

Ulrica's brow rose, her curiosity and ire peaked. Who would have the audacity to seek an audience at this late hour? "Well then, send this stranger in, let's see what's so urgent it couldn't wait for the council session tomorrow."

Oleander swaggered into the room just as Gaianna left. "Who was that, Grandmother?" He tossed a crisp pear into the air, caught it, and took a loud bite. Juice dripped down his chin, spattering vulgar droplets across his unbuttoned green coat. Ulrica's lip curled in distaste.

"Make yourself presentable, grandson. We have company."

He rolled his eyes but quickly did up his buttons, set the pear aside on the scroll shelf, and dutifully came to stand behind her, his left hand resting on the back of her chair. She reached up to pat it affectionately; he was, after all, her favorite, her protégé who she knew was destined to make their family great.

The figure swept into the room like the fall of night, his black cloak billowing behind it almost as if it were made of shadows. He stood looming in the center of the room, imposing and unbending, and though a sick film of dread coated the back of her throat at the sight of him, her indignation at its refusal to bend a knee overwhelmed her better sense. "Who are you that you think you can come in here without showing me the proper respect?"

A hiss slithered from under the cowl of the man's cloak, but he did not answer. Oleander shifted uneasily on his feet; she could almost hear his grip tighten on the back of her chair.

"Well?" she demanded, though there was a slight tremor to her words that she hadn't intended as the hollow gaze from under the hood made sweat bead on the nape of her neck. "Who are you?"

The man threw back his hood. A strangled scream slipped from the prime elder's lips, and Oleander stumbled back, landing on his backside with a loud crash, taking stacks of scrolls with him.

"We are the Darkness." The voices it spoke with were as ageless as the wind in the trees and as harsh as the winter snows. Its coal-dark eyes were set in the sunken skeletal face of a man with pointed ears and long lank hair that skimmed his broad shoulders. The Darkness was nebulous beneath his skin, marking him for what he was, The Instrument.

Ulrica stood so quickly her chair clattered backward, landing on its side next to a scrambling Oleander. She hurried around to the front of her desk and threw herself prostrate onto the ground at the feet of the Darkness. "Forgive me, Master, I did not know."

Oleander crawled to her side, keeping his head low, sniveling apologies of his own.

"We have come to hold up our end of the bargain struck. You gave us the most powerful Travelers from your Fragment, and we give you the magic you desire in return."

"Thank you, oh thank you." Ulrica's tears streamed down her weathered cheeks.

"Stand, boy." The Instrument of Darkness curled his bloodred fingers, and magic flared to life in them, reeling Oleander to his feet and then higher as though gripped by the throat until his toes barely touched the floor.

Oleander choked and spluttered, his mouth gaping like a dying fish. Ulrica sobbed, clawing at his feet, begging incoherently.

The Instrument fisted Oleander's jacket and drew him closer, he opened his maw, and a tendril of Darkness writhed serpentine into its new host. His feet kicked against the ground as his body convulsed. Oleander's veins turned black as onyx, and his twitching fingers began to glow like a moonless night.

He slumped to the floor, crumpled and slack-jawed, unconscious. Ulrica backed away, her hands held aloft in a pitiable attempt to fend him off, but the Instrument just leaned down toward her, his teeth, filed into points, glinting in the candlelight like polished silver, and laughed. "You should be careful what you wish for when making a deal with the Darkness."

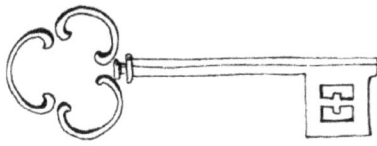

Chapter 108

AFTER WEEKS OF RAIN, Maximilian was looking forward to the walk to the Reliquary. He hadn't been bold enough to leave his cottage near the docks during the seemingly endless squall. Prior to that, Imogen's orders for everyone who couldn't keep their magic discreet to lay low since there would be a stranger in town had kept him cooped up. He looked normal enough, unlike some of his selkie or merfolk neighbors, but he lived in constant fear of slipping into one of his episodes. At the best of times, it made him uncomfortable, but for it to happen in front of a stranger would be mortifying.

But gods be blessed he'd been episode free for weeks, and he desperately wanted to have an excuse to talk to Will. He missed the way she smiled at him whenever he went into the shop. She was the only one who didn't treat him differently, and that was saying quite a lot considering he'd died in her shop twice now. Once was a musket ball to the head and the other a rather messy drowning. Both times he'd come to with her hovering like a benevolent goddess over him with rosy cheeks, wild hair, and a hot cup of tea. She didn't vomit or ogle him like a carnival sideshow.

It wasn't easy being what he was, even on an isle like Thorne where all the inhabitants either had magical proclivities, Traveler magic, or were beings that didn't naturally belong in Areth, those seeking sanctuary. He was a Grimm, possibly the last, and contrary to popular lore surrounding his kind, he didn't actually kill people or help ferry their souls into the veil. He absorbed them, taking the death from them so that they could live. He had very little control over it. He didn't even get to choose whose death he took, since there were no others of his kind to teach him. Death would just sneak up on him and tear him from his body when he least expected it. He could go months without dying, or he could die multiple times in a single day. There was no rhyme or reason to it. He'd lived for only twenty summers, but he'd died thousands of times.

The lights of the Reliquary loomed over the treetops as he trudged along the main road through the woods. Hope fluttered like the wings of songbirds next to his heart. He would see her soon, perhaps he would even be able to muster the courage to ask her to dance. But as he stumbled on his next step, the hope in his chest died. He could feel his life slipping slowly through his fingers like grains of sand. It was a magical death. He'd experienced one like it before, some poor soul burning themselves out with a spell beyond their capabilities. He just hoped it had been a worthwhile one. He held up his hand in front of his face and watched the skin wither from sun-beaten-brown to gray, his veins became more pronounced, his breaths more labored. His lungs felt as brittle as an autumn leaf under the boot. And just as he was beginning to feel like the agony would never end, he was no longer a leaf underfoot but a berry, his bones snapped, and his viscera mashed into a pulp. Not just a magical death then, but a rockslide or a building collapse, his least favorite.

"Poor bastard," he muttered with his last breaths, though he was uncertain whether he meant himself or the person whose death he was taking. Maybe he meant both.

To Be Continued in book two.

M.A. BROWN IS A stay-at-homeschooling mom living in Colorado with her husband and four kids. She loves to write fantasy with a healthy dose of romance, dreamy worlds, and a whole lot of magic. When she's not creating, she enjoys hiking, camping, and gardening with her family.

Follow her @writer.m.a.brown or find her on her website www.mabrownauthor.com.

@WRITER.M.A.BROWN

T HIS BOOK WAS NEARLY seven years in the making. There were so many times when I wasn't sure I would ever hold it in my hands, including an entire year where I decided not to even look at it.

There are so many people I am grateful for but, first and foremost, thank you to my husband, without you this dream would have never become a reality. You are my everything, always.

To my mother, thank you for buying me fantasy novels when we were supposed to be buying back to school clothes. Without my obsession with reading, I don't think I would have ever considered writing my own book.

Thank you to Heather for reading and rereading and rereading this book even in its very messy early stages, I don't think I would have had the courage to let anyone else read it if you hadn't read it a million times first.

To my absolutely amazing and talented cover artist, Magdalene, thank you for being so supportive and for bringing the chaos of my brain to life for everyone to see.

My editors, you took this tangled mess of a story and made it worth reading, thank you.

Thank you to the Midnight Tide Publishing family for welcoming me, you are all so wonderful and I am so grateful for each and every one of you.

Thank you to every Indie author who answered my questions without hesitation, your help was invaluable to me. And an extra special thanks to my street team, beta readers and arc readers, your feedback and support means the world to me.

And last but never least thank you God for gifting me with the words that fill these pages.

More Books You'll Love

I F YOU ENJOYED THE Songs That Beckon, please consider leaving a review! Then check out more books from Midnight Tide Publishing!

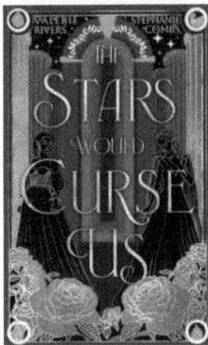

The Iris were sent to us from the stars, but their rule is controlling and oppressive. Every season, we send our brothers and sisters to the marriage drafts . . . but the selected never return.

Aella

My world falls apart when my best friend and I are drafted to compete for the hand of Esterra's most eligible bachelor, the devastatingly handsome Iris prince. As an elemental fae, it should be the greatest honor, but the competition is filled with violence. I question my true purpose as we fight to survive in games rigged against us.

Arianwen

Life should be simple—go on my rite and return to marry a man I've never met—but when a handsome stranger falls from the sky, everything is turned upside down. Secrets and lies unravel, leading me to question everything as I find myself pulled into a rebellion. My heart longs for a better world, but am I willing to forsake duty in pursuit of it?

We both face choices: Love or duty?
Loyalty or adventure?
Fight or surrender?
Is fate truly written in the stars, or have they abandoned us?

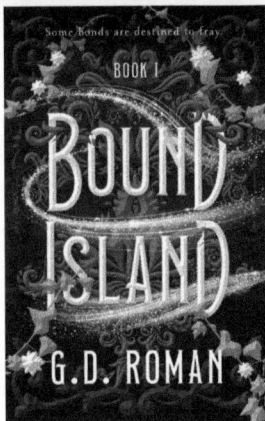

Until the Knots of Avalon break.

Brye, Lenna, and Tara have lived their entire lives on an island surrounded by mists and protected by magical bonds. Nothing could be more perfect. Until one night, when magic begins to fray at the seams, and their lives change forever.

The Healer - Brye's healing abilities are her pride, making her the best match of the season. If only someone were interesting enough for her. Until she catches the eye of Prince Gareth, the least interesting one of all.

The Mist Maiden - Lenna has lived her life in the shadow of her sisters. Until Beltane, when her magic explodes. Now, she has been chosen to be a Mist Maiden, protector of Avalon. A role she was never destined to play.

The Warrior - Tara knows that she is meant to be more than being someone's mate. A warrior through and through, Tara strives for the extraordinary. No matter the cost. Even if that means she might have to sacrifice her growing feelings for Aiden.

As Avalon slowly becomes an island lost in the mists, will the sisters strengthen their bonds and save their home, or will they break apart forever?

9 798988 333135